Guillermo Cabrera Infante

Map Drawn by a Spy

Translated from the Spanish by Mark Fried

archipelago books

English translation copyright © Mark Fried, 2017

First Archipelago Books edition, 2017

Library of Congress Cataloging-in-Publication Data
Cabrera Infante, G. (Guillermo), 1929-2005. | Fried, Mark, translator.
Map drawn by a spy / by Guillermo Cabrera Infante ; translated by Mark Fried.
Mapa dibujado por un espâia. English
LCCN 2017025451 | ISBN 9780914671787 (paperback)
LCC PQ7389.C233 M3713 2017 | DDC 863/.64--dc23
LC record available at https://lccn.loc.gov/2017025451

Archipelago Books
232 Third Street, #A111
Brooklyn, NY 11215
www.archipelagobooks.org

Distributed to the trade by Penguin Random House
www.penguinrandomhouse.com

Archipelago Books gratefully acknowledges the generous support from
Lannan Foundation, the National Endowment for the Arts,
the New York City Department of Cultural Affairs,
and the New York State Council on the Arts, a state agency.

PRINTED IN THE UNITED STATES OF AMERICA

Map Drawn by a Spy

You were really not one of them but a spy in their country.

Ernest Hemingway ("The Snows of Kilimanjaro")

I have here a map made a few days before the attack on the island's capital. As you can appreciate, the map is rather crude, but it fulfills its purpose very well… You can see how the map distorts the characteristics of the city and its surroundings. It is believed this map was drawn by an English spy.

Guillermo Cabrera Infante (*View of Dawn in the Tropics*)

Although an old, consistent exile, the editor of the following pages revisits now and again the city of which he exults to be a native.

Robert Louis Stevenson (*The Master of Ballantrae*)

The reader will perceive how awkward it would appear to speak of myself in the third person.

Pat F. Garrett (*The Authentic Life of Billy the Kid*)

You may well ask why I write. And yet my reasons are quite many. For it is not unusual in human beings who have witnessed the sack of a city or the falling to pieces of a people, to desire to set down what they have witnessed for the benefit of unknown heirs or of generations infinitely remote; or, if you please, just to get the sight out of their heads.

Ford Madox Ford (*The Good Soldier*)

Here again, we must be careful not to exaggerate: many of us loved the bourgeois tranquility, the antiquated charm that came over this battered capital in the moonlight; but even our pleasure was tinged with bitterness: what could be more bitter than walking its streets, around its church, its city hall, and tasting the same melancholic joy as when visiting the Colosseum or the Parthenon under the moon. Everything was in ruins: houses uninhabited…, shuttered, hotels and cinemas requisitioned, marked off by white barriers we stumbled upon suddenly, bars and stores closed for the duration of the war, their proprietors deported, killed, or disappeared, pedestals without statues, gardens cut in two by quarrels or disfigured by gun emplacements made of reinforced concrete, and all those big dusty signs on top of the buildings, electric billboards that shone no more.

Jean-Paul Sartre ("The Republic of Silence")

Prologue

SOME ANIMALS SEEM to have been created by divine Providence or nature or fate for the sole purpose of one day embodying a metaphor, geological eons or an eternity later. The way a number of Hebrew poets hiding behind Biblical anonymity used the snake, for example, or the dove, deformed and transformed them into creatures of myth. Other animals, like the sloth or the jackal, have come to personify even in their names moral attitudes of which, needless to say, they are blameless. Similarly, some men exist as little more than metaphor, like the figure representing historical evil in modern times, the Man in the Iron Mask, who first launched the saga of the unknown political prisoner and now embodies that legend. Other men bespeak more prescience than presence and manage to predate by years the historical moment when they become indispensable as metaphor.

A century earlier his name would have meant something else in Cuba. The Aldamas did not simply belong to the Creole aristocracy: they were its essence, *la crème de la crème*; in other words, they gave meaning to the notion of aristocracy in Cuba. One of the Aldamas, Miguel, had a palace made to measure as if he had ordered it from a tailor, built with untold amounts of quarried stone, marbles, and precious woods. The mansion, located at the top of one of Havana's loveliest lanes, was once a central attraction and, although the lane later became a commercial street and is now an ugly thoroughfare, it stands there still, converted into a colonial museum, its ancient multicolored

< II >

frontage scraped down to the naked stone and then concealed under the soot of the twentieth century, so blackened it looks more like a lithographic reproduction than the three-dimensional original. The towering columns of the sumptuous neoclassical portico – a façade is a mirror of the owner's soul – reveal that its proprietor imported not only his political ideas but his lifestyle from a France dubbed Revolutionary. But in his heart of hearts Miguel Aldama aspired to be precisely the opposite of a Frenchman, that is, an Englishman concealed behind a private door.

Inside his palace was an inaugural jewel: the first flush toilet in America. This Aldama was a patrician noble, a protector of the arts and letters who opened the gates of his palace every Friday to a literary salon. He was also a noble patriot whose all-too-frank political opinions attracted the attention of Spanish authorities and finally earned him exile. Like the entire Creole aristocracy, the Aldamas were slave owners. Their sugar refineries, their sugarcane and tobacco plantations, plus their mansions, haciendas, and persons, were attended to by thousands of slaves imported from Africa. Following the custom of the period, the Aldamas' slaves were also named Aldama. Thanks to the ironies of history or biology, the white aristocratic Aldamas disappeared within a century of their apogee and today that illustrious name of yesteryear is held only by the descendants of their black slaves. Pablo, alias Agustín, Aldama lives still and is of course the grandson or great-grandson of slaves, although it is possible that some blood from the original Aldamas may run through his veins, since he is more dark mulatto than black.

I know little of Agustín Aldama's private life, among other reasons because he spoke rarely and never of that. Truth be told, his could not have been a very blessed life, though he did treasure a photograph of his niece as if she were a daughter (or perhaps she was his daughter, since one of the

< 12 >

things I discovered by studying Aldama is that a quiet man can be a quiet liar). When he did speak, Aldama talked about his public life, especially his revolutionary credentials. The loquacious passion that seized this taciturn man when enumerating his civic virtues made these credentials seem suspect, yet it is a fact that he had once been, as they say, a man of action, and he wore proudly the scars that bore witness to that time. In the forties he had been a member of one or several "action groups," as they were known in Cuba, and judging by his various silences and evasions, he must have changed sides often. Not that he would have been a traitor, rather, as the Argentine put it, "a man of successive and conflicting loyalties."

In the UIR – these groups were always shielded by acronyms – Aldama met or said he met Fidel Castro, at that time no more than an amateur thug. The actions undertaken by the Unión Insurreccional Revolucionaria discouraged any temptation to turn its initials into a verb – *huir*, to flee – composed as it was of men whose courage had been tested far too often. In particular, its members shared with their deranged leader, Emilio Tro, a taste for the darkest humor. They gave each other risible nicknames – a man lame from a war wound was known as Prettyleg, another whose mouth had been shattered by a gunshot became Bulletlip, twin assassins were known as the Dead Ringers, one of their leaders, J. Jesús Jinjauma, had a deputy named Lazarus of Bethany and whenever he liquidated someone in an act of vengeance he hung from his victim's neck a sign that invariably read: "Justice takes time, but it comes." On the audacious occasion I am about to describe they managed to unite black humor, a braggart's valor, adroit timing, certain literary inclinations, and the name Castro.

It happened that another of the action groups, the ARG, captained by another Jesus, Jesús G. Cartas, better known as the Stranger, a pseudonym

< 13 >

that paid homage to his foreign looks, had perfected a technique borrowed from Chicago's gangster days. When the intent was to settle accounts with a rival gang, they used two cars instead of one. The first would drive by the target to spray the entrance to the marked house with lead – the newspapers in those days were fond of gardening terms. Once over their alarm, the angry thugs would run into the street to see if anyone was wounded and sometimes to shoot a few useless bullets at the fleeing car. Then the treacherous second vehicle would come over the horizon at their backs and open fire on the mercilessly exposed group. That was how the ARG attacked the home of Jesús Jinjauma's mother while the UIR was meeting inside. Despite the risks, the UIR resolved to respond by risking an assault that evoked the technique's origins, while adding a twist of its own.

The retaliation took place in the "Chicago" of Hollywood: in front of a family movie house, affectionately known as Cinecito, owned by Manolo Castro, who was National Director of Sports, a former student leader, and a member of the MSR, an ARG ally. He was chatting with a business friend in the lobby of the theater when out of nowhere a vehicle raced past and shot up the front of the building. Castro and his friend, taking refuge behind the box office, were not wounded. A short while later, seeing that the second and lethal car did not appear, they stepped into the street. That was when two hit men standing on the opposite sidewalk opened fire. The businessman was seriously wounded but survived, while Manolo Castro died on the spot under his glowing marquee.

The ARG, the MSR, and a lone prosecutor accused the other Castro, Fidel, who was not related, of being the fatal shooter; his guilt was not proven at the time, just as his innocence is not proven today. But Emilio Tro in his grave (the UIR leader had died a short while before, a death ironically filmed by the local news, having like Manolo Castro been unarmed while treacher-

< 14 >

ously attacked by the allied forces of the MSR and the ARG at the tail end of a pitched battle with machine guns, rifles, and tanks on the streets of Marianao), Tro must have smiled a last merciless smile in gangster heaven: it was in the best tradition of the UIR that there be two Castros on the battlefield. Most comical of all was the fact that Castro had killed Castro.

The UIR was where, I repeat, Aldama said he met Fidel Castro. It could be. What is certainly true is that Aldama retained an indelible mark from those days: he had taken a bullet in the head that passed through his eye. So he was a one-eyed man. What's more, he suffered from terrible neuralgia headaches on the side of his face where the bullet had either entered or exited. I learned this later on. At first I did not even notice he had only the one eye: perpetual dark glasses concealed the absence, as well as the eye in attendance.

The day I met him he had just arrived at the embassy in Brussels. He went straight to bed to recover from the journey and then strolled into the office in the middle of the afternoon. I had never seen a Cuban so tall. He barely fit through the door: a six-foot-six giant with overlong arms and legs and gigantic hands that were bony claws, and he was extremely thin. He spoke in a deep, gravelly voice and whenever he did so, which was not often, he said little. His dark glasses, jutting jaw, and kinky hair clipped close to his head all accentuated his cadaverous skull. Over all, I had the impression his inscrutability was entirely deliberate: Aldama was now a security officer, employed by the Ministry of Foreign Relations. At least that is what he took pleasure in appearing to be. But that was at the end.

At first he claimed to have been sent by a well-meaning vice minister in order to find an amicable resolution to differences between the ambassador, Gustavo Arcos, and his first secretary, Juan José Díaz del Real. Rumors had reached the vice minister, Arnold Rodríguez, that the two of them, after

< 15 >

arriving at the embassy the best of friends (the ambassador had requested the first secretary as a personal favor), now wanted each other's heads, and some feared the situation might degenerate into bloodshed. Díaz del Real had already killed an exiled Cuban in Santo Domingo, in the days when it was known as Ciudad Trujillo and he was ambassador in the Dominican Republic. The murder nearly cost him his life and the Cuban Embassy was set aflame. For his part, Ambassador Arcos had been involved in the assault on the Moncada Barracks in 1953 and, although he was a gentle man, he was capable of turning violent. The two always carried hefty pistols. Aldama was supposedly a friend of both – indeed, when he arrived he seemed to be closer to the ambassador than to Díaz del Real, but that was when he arrived.

Soon he changed sides, or better put, he took the side of the first secretary against Gustavo Arcos. In the beginning he did so obliquely, by making comments when he and I were alone in the diplomatic offices; later on, he did so continually because, not only were we always alone, but Pipo Carbonell (the third secretary and the only other Cuban official) had made common cause with Arcos, breaking with his patron, the first secretary, who had asked Arcos to bring him to Belgium in the first place. Amid this crossfire of ever-shifting loyalties and disloyalties, I was trying to hang on to my post as cultural attaché by cleverly remaining independent of both sides. At first I managed thanks to my knowledge of French, since at a certain point (when Arcos was off in a Czech sanatorium seeking treatment for the incurable wound he suffered in the attack on the Moncada) I was the only one in the embassy who spoke the language. But my position was precarious and soon became compromised due to an intrigue woven by Carbonell, which made Arcos suspicious of me, until the ambassador realized he had too many enemies in the embassy as it was, and that my work was essential for his survival. By then, Aldama was practically not speaking to Arcos, but he would not forget the confidences

< 16 >

the ambassador had shared with him, one after another (as anyone would with someone he considered a friend), many of them of a serious political nature, including disclosures that bordered on the scandalous regarding the nefarious personality of Fidel Castro. All this Aldama (and also Díaz del Real on his own) stored up for future use against Arcos.

Aldama lived on the top floor of the embassy in a small room he had essentially turned into a lair, which he could reach directly by elevator from the garage. Once, after he had disappeared for days and was apparently ill, I went there to see him. I found him lying on a bed so enormous it made his long prostrate body look minuscule; he was suffering from one of his frequent attacks of facial neuralgia. The maid, a friendly, uneducated, good-hearted woman from Galicia, had heard him moan one night and got up to ask him if something was hurting him, and he answered that no one was hurting him. She told me this the following day, which was why I climbed up to his lair. With the only window hermetically sealed and the room in darkness, the odor in it was indescribable. It was the only time I saw him without his dark glasses and his lifeless eye looked elongated and dead like glass, perhaps it was glass. With the other he watched every one of my nervous movements about the room. I confess I felt afraid, though I know not of what or of whom. Perhaps I was recalling the bloody past that had produced this Cyclops, perhaps I had an intimation the role this apparent invalid would play in the future. I do know that I left the room understanding enough to feel a certain pity – yet I did not feel sorry for him in the least.

With time, the situation in the embassy became untenable. There was a moment when Díaz del Real, in answer to a summons from Gustavo Arcos, took his gun out of his desk drawer and went upstairs, shouting as he waved the weapon:

"I'm going to kill that sonofabitch right now!"

< 17 >

I remember I sat frozen at my desk, waiting to hear the shots. Too long a time went by and Díaz del Real reappeared. He took his pistol from his belt, unloaded it, and put it back in the drawer – all without a word. He never mentioned the incident again nor did he ever offer an explanation as to why he held back. His silence was what gave me the distinct impression that his murderous intentions had been real; pulling out the gun had been much more than simple bravado.

The intolerable situation dissipated somewhat when Díaz del Real was transferred to Finland as chargé d'affaires at the beginning of the summer of 1964. A short while later relations between Gustavo Arcos and I could not have been better. For his part, Aldama displayed no enmity toward me. He inherited the office formerly used by Díaz del Real, although, unlike the first secretary, he spent all day doing nothing. That summer was a busy one. My mother had been with me in Belgium since the beginning of the winter and was preparing to return to Cuba via Madrid, where my brother worked as commercial attaché. I had an operation on my throat. I remember that my final attack of tonsillitis was hurried along or provoked by an outing with Aldama, who was determined to visit a Belgian bar astonishingly named New York – I say astonishingly because it was run by a Moroccan beauty. That night I vomited whatever I had consumed (in the street Aldama had already thrown up a mix of wine and chunks of food) and I had a fever of 105 degrees. The next day the doctor recommended emergency surgery, and two weeks later, tonsil-free, I was saying bon voyage to my mother and my daughters, whom I did not expect to see again until I was back in Cuba. Then a postoperative euphoria made me realize I could see them in Madrid. Thus I set off on a voyage in my old (beloved, not aged) Fiat 600 from Brussels to Málaga, by way of Madrid, where I picked up my mother and daughters and took them, along with my wife, on a trip through the south of Spain.

< 18 >

Upon my return two weeks later, I discovered that Arcos was planning to travel to Cuba for his vacation (it was already the middle of August). No one would be sent from Havana to replace him, so according to the diplomatic hierarchy I was to become chargé d'affaires on an interim basis. It was then that Aldama's attitude toward me began to change, although I failed to notice at first. Not long before we went to Spain he had bought an 8mm movie camera and shot an entire roll of film of my mother. After the trip we still chatted in the basement where the diplomatic offices were, and he still referred to "up there" (the first floor, where the ambassador had his office, and the second floor, where both of his chosen enemies, the ambassador and the third secretary, had their residences) as the place the bad guys lived. I, on the other hand, belonged to "down here." But soon barbed references to my good relations with the ambassador began to crop up, and the man he had called "my brother Gustavo" a few months earlier was now never called anything but Arcos. For a time each of his infrequent comments was loaded, until at length he fell back into his usual reticence, although he continued coming to the basement daily to sit and stare at blank papers with his single eye.

Arcos went off to Cuba and Pipo Carbonell's wife went with him, leaving Pipo (the third secretary) to stay on in the embassy a bit longer. I moved up to the first floor to work as chargé d'affaires and I moved into the second floor residence with my wife; Pipo Carbonell lived on the same floor at the other end of the house. Aldama continued residing in his cave on the top floor. At this point his attitude toward me became even more tight-lipped, if such a thing were possible, and he was rarely seen around the embassy. He would get up late and we would all have lunch together in near silence, not only because he said nothing, but because Pipo Carbonell was afraid to speak in his presence. At those happy meals Aldama sat with his back to us, facing

< 19 >

a sideboard where he could observe, reflected in its glass doors, everything that happened at the dining room table. A few times I caught a sidelong glimpse of his ubiquitous eye shining with a unique luster behind his dark glasses. On occasion he smiled to himself. But never a word. His presence at those lunches was so oppressive that Pipo Carbonell nicknamed him the Tonton Macoute. Soon, in light of his favorite pastimes, I took to calling him Jambon, first cousin of James Bond.

If Aldama had come, as he said at the beginning, to pour diplomatic oil on troubled Cuban waters in Belgium, then with the departure of Díaz del Real for Finland his assignment was over. Now his second target was out of the embassy as well. At this point he began to go about the city on mysterious missions. Although poorly equipped (he spoke neither French nor English, much less Flemish, and there was no Cuban community in Belgium), he would sometimes be gone for two days at a time. It is true that once, some time earlier, he had been contacted by a Cuban exile, a man with a limp since his nickname was Gimp Kaysés or some such, I recall seeing Aldama leave the embassy that day as dusk fell and Díaz del Real, then still in his post, asked if he was armed. The question, though posed nearly in code, was clear enough for me to understand, and I caught his terse response: "No, comrade, no need," followed by the transformation of his hands into fists. I never knew the result of his supposed interview, but apparently nothing came of it: Aldama continued at the embassy and no lame man appeared to beef up the rather scrawny ranks of exiles willing to make the return trip to Cuba.

However, now his missions seemed of a different order and he acted ever more mysteriously, barely speaking to anyone. His silence was interrupted flamboyantly one day when his car caught fire. Aldama had brought with

< 20 >

him (a manner of speaking, for he came by air and the car arrived by sea) an aged Buick, black and enormous, which must have been at least ten years old. Since he had no parking space in the ambassador's garage, he parked it in the street. When the weather turned cold, the Buick, evidently accustomed to the warmth of Cuba, refused to start and spent much of the winter covered in snow, a gloomy, nearly sinister embodiment of an oxymoron (an immobile automobile), antediluvian, gangsterish, and permanently useless. There it remained until spring when apparently whatever ailed it got repaired. He asked me – and I agreed – to find room for the car in the garage, and there he whiled away the hours when he was not elsewhere. From the garage one day several stentorian shouts for help reached our ears; all of us – Pipo, my wife, and I – tore down the stairs to find the automobile in flames and Aldama paralyzed by fear. It was Pipo who went at the car and practically with his bare hands put out the fire, which had begun, appropriately enough, in the starter. In fiddling with the mechanism Aldama had managed to set it ablaze. Once he left us – which he did immediately after Pipo extinguished the fire – we laughed like crazy, not so much at the misfortune he had brought on himself, but at the sight of his panicked face. The car, now permanently unfit for battle, lived on abandoned in the garage. Better that way. No longer would it make the dreadful impression it had when perpetually parked by the curb, astonishing our well-heeled neighbors and delighting the local boys who used it as a handhold when skating down the street.

In the embassy there was a young Belgian replacement secretary with a homely face, but tall and plump, and with enough heft in her thighs and behind and bosom to appeal to a Cuban. She was looking for a suitor. She tried me first and of course had no luck; even if I had not been married, I never would have laid a finger on her, less out of diplomatic prudery than

< 21 >

for reasons of aesthetics: I detested her fishlike mouth, and for me women's mouths are crucial. She then sought out Pipo and had even less success. Finally, it seems Aldama had his turn; all we know for sure is that we saw them holding hands in a park some time after the girl had left her job at the embassy. None of this would matter in the least except that, after Aldama's departure, a Belgian woman with a voice not at all young would call the embassy to curse those who had obliged her Agustín to go back to Cuba. Evidently, women liked our spy Jambon, who thus lived up to the reputation of his English cousin.

Aldama, who did no work at the embassy, who never worked at all, since he had no skills or knowledge of anything, put an end to his strange outings in order to concentrate on the embassy itself. One day he murmured that he had linked up with the commercial attaché (who belonged to a separate ministry, with offices in another part of Brussels, and did not live at the embassy) to "make things crystal clear here." "Here" evidently referred to the embassy – or could he have meant all Belgium? On another occasion, after my wife undertook a thorough cleaning of the messy embassy kitchen, where she was planning to cook, he hissed: "Could it be true? The counterrevolutionaries do more for Cuba than the revolutionaries?" I let that comment lie, like many others, because I believed his days were numbered. Gustavo Arcos had promised me when I agreed to take charge of the embassy that Aldama would be returned to Cuba in a few days. Those few days, it must be said, became weeks, then months, and later an eternity. Now Aldama's attention focused on Arcos's personal affairs. He was interested, above all, in getting his hands on the ambassador's bank statement, God knows with what purpose, perhaps to send it to Cuba, although Arcos had done nothing more criminal than place his personal savings in the bank. As always, Aldama was as effective as

< 22 >

he was discreet. "The honorable ambassador is wrapped in flames," he said one day when he sat down at the table for lunch, and he said no more. But this was sufficient. I called the bank and told them to send no more statements of the ambassador's account until he returned. At the same time my wife took it upon herself to get up before the first mail delivery, which arrived at eight AM. Aldama always got up late, but once or twice my wife saw him roaming about the house, maybe waiting for the mail, maybe in search of something else. But what? What else was there in the embassy that might jeopardize Arcos in Cuba? What to do to free ourselves from Aldama?

In December I had to leave the embassy on two occasions. On the 24th my wife and I went to Rouen, in France, close to where Carlos Franqui was living temporarily. We spent two days there, worried all the while about what might happen between Aldama and Pipo, then returned on the 26th. Nothing had occurred, fortunately. On the 28th I left for Barcelona to receive the Joan Petit Biblioteca Breve Prize, awarded by Seix Barral for my first novel. I spent only two days in Barcelona by myself, and during that time I could not stop fretting about what Aldama might do to my wife. Upon my return, I learned that Aldama and the commercial attaché (whose name is not even worth mentioning) had spent the entire time prowling about the house and had made a mysterious call to Madrid, apparently to the Cuban Embassy. As before, Aldama deployed his technique of secretive indiscretion or indiscreet secrecy. The real objective of his actions was to instill fear – but realistically what sort of fear could this pitiful apprentice secret agent possibly inspire? What mysteries could he reveal? What conspiracies could he uncover? In the embassy, as in our lives, everything was on view, transparent: I was nothing more than a functionary trying to fulfill my duty, while my wife and Pipo Carbonell, as long as he remained at the embassy, simply helped me in that

< 23 >

effort. The point was not to fear that useless beanpole but to get rid of him. And yet his endeavors to sow panic had their effect.

His method consisted of wandering about the building at the strangest hours. Sometimes we heard him in the hallways at three in the morning. Other times he disappeared and reappeared when least expected. It was not unusual to see him walk into the embassy after a long absence as if he had left only moments before. At first he would murmur some excuse that made his expeditions out to be important missions, but later on he did not even bother justifying his bizarre behavior. On one occasion he appeared in my office to ask me to change an American fifty-dollar bill into Belgian currency. How that bill came into his possession is still a mystery wrapped in shadows, but I believe his purpose – he could have changed it in any bank or exchange house – was to spark my curiosity and set me to wondering where he got hold of it. (Something vague in his attitude induced me to conclude the money had been obtained from American agents, but the intimation was so fuzzy I could never swear that was his intent.) Given how things were, I called Gustavo Arcos several times in Havana asking him to free me of Aldama's ominous presence, but without success. I always took advantage of Aldama's absences to communicate with Arcos. Once the call I had requested came in at the very moment Aldama returned. It was worthy of a noir film, me waiting in the basement for the call, while listening to Aldama's footsteps above me in the first floor offices. In the end I managed to pick up the telephone at the first ring and speak with Arcos in Havana without Aldama suspecting a thing.

Luis Ricardo Alonso, the Cuban ambassador in London, came for a visit with his wife. Since he was an old friend, I explained what was going on with Aldama, and indeed in the short time he spent at the embassy Luis Ricardo

< 24 >

had the opportunity to observe it with his own eyes. Juan Arcocha, the press attaché in Paris, also came to visit, and together he and Alonso worked out how they might liberate me from Aldama: Arcocha would speak to his ambassador in Paris and Alonso would communicate with someone high up in the ministry, presumably the minister himself. At a meeting I attended of heads of mission in Western Europe, it seems Alonso and Carrillo (the ambassador in Paris) made the case to Vice Minister Arnold Rodríguez. During one of the sessions Alonso, speaking to me across the table, said, "We've freed you from your nightmare." Then, on a separate trip I made to Paris to meet Rodríguez again, the vice minister told me explicitly, "Tell Aldama he has to return right away to Havana." Then he added, "Tell him carefully so he doesn't seek asylum on us." It was the first time I heard anyone mention such a possibility, but that warning linked the mysterious outings, the fifty-dollar bill, and his impenetrable activities to a possible defection.

As soon as I returned to Brussels, I had the secretary call Aldama in. I had noticed that my trips to Madrid and Paris, which were routinely communicated to him, made him slightly but visibly nervous, despite his habitual inscrutability. Now, when he entered my office, I swear I thought I saw him tremble, a quiver made more perceptible by his gigantic stature. Fearing some unforeseen reaction to the news of his transfer to Havana under circumstances that were not entirely favorable, I had left open the drawer in which Gustavo Arcos kept his pocket pistol. It sounds like cheap melodrama, but I was prepared to use the weapon if Aldama made the slightest threatening gesture – which in him would not have been as strange as it might seem. But he accepted the news calmly, with no suggestion of violence. He only asked that he be given more time "to ship his car from Antwerp and wind up his business in Brussels." Of course that was a delaying tactic. To dissuade him

< 25 >

I told him what Arnold Rodríguez had added, that suspicions he might seek asylum came from high up in the ministry. That revelation seemed to blind his only good eye and he became difficult. No longer addressing me in the familiar *tú*, he said, "Well, *compañero*" – and it was comical to hear him use that formal address – "I would ask you to send a cable to the ministry communicating my request to depart not now but in two weeks' time."

He had the right to make the request and I sent the cable. When the response came in the affirmative, he grew cocky and said, "Well, it seems the ministry knows what's what." That was one of the last times we spoke, and in his tone and stance there was a clear declaration of war. It was evident he had set out to destroy me and to achieve that end he would not only enlist the assistance of his brother (a high-ranking security officer), but also draw on his long-standing clout in the organisms of state security. That statement was the first stone he threw, the first shot across the bow; now he would not rest until he had accomplished the task. He may have had lousy aim, but he could count on assistance from his patrons, something that in my euphoria at the triumph of good over evil I gleefully discounted. However, the immediate future (and certainly what came after) would teach me that good's triumph over evil is but momentary, and that my sense of security at that moment was no more than a veiled form of hubris.

< 26 >

Map Drawn by a Spy

******* ******* USUALLY SAT NEXT TO THE DRIVER out of some shallow democratic sentiment. But that afternoon, on the first of June 1965, Jacqueline Lewy, the secretary, had asked him to drop her near her house and he decided to sit in the back with her. That saved his life.

The Mercedes climbed the steep hill up Rue Roberts-Jones to the rotary at Winston Churchill Avenue, traveled a distance under the shade of plane trees, then turned down a side street and dropped Jacqueline off not far from her home. She thanked him, said goodnight in French, and he remained in the backseat. The car returned to the main road and headed toward the Embassy of Chad.

He might have been thinking ahead to the reception when the car stopped for a moment at a red light, then moved on, and he looked up. A truck was crossing the road diagonally, but the Mercedes kept going. He yelled at the driver to stop, but the man drove on as if he did not see the truck. Then he screamed at him to speed up to get across ahead of it, but the car continued apace. He felt the blow, heard the loud crash and the sound of breaking glass. He was thrown forward against the front seat, but was uninjured. The two vehicles occupied the middle of the intersection, truck wedged into car, the passenger side of the car crumpled in. During the fleeting moment when he saw the truck advancing and knew a crash was inevitable, all he could think about were the times he had sensed this very thing would happen sooner or later. The driver, José, was not really a driver, rather the husband of the cook,

< 29 >

both of them recommended by the García Lorca Communist Club as "trust-worthy people." From the first day it was obvious that José knew nothing about driving, but the embassy needed a chauffeur and perhaps given time he would learn, despite being none too bright. Clearly he had not and now he had crashed on the way to a reception. He got out of the car and, ignoring the stares of onlookers, examined the damage: the right front was a mess and now that the truck was backing up he could see a part of the car's motor had been thrust into the passenger seat and the damage was irreparable. That was when he understood that had he been riding as usual he would be seriously injured if not dead; as it was, neither he nor the driver was hurt. Because he wanted to calm down before arriving at the reception, he refused to look at the driver, and just told him to wait. He crossed the street to a corner café, asked for the telephone and someone said, "At the back." He called the embassy and spoke to his wife, Miriam Gómez. No, he was not injured and now all he needed was Jacqueline's telephone number to ask her to get in touch with a garage. Having done that, he left the café to tell José to stay put until the tow truck arrived. Then he flagged down a passing taxi and gave the address of the Chadean Embassy. When he arrived at the reception, he realized his hands were trembling, though not perceptibly.

His first move after greeting the ambassador and his wife, who were standing by the door in their national dress, was to grab a glass of whisky from a tray held by a sleepwalking waiter. Then he went to a corner occupied by several diplomats from Arabic countries whom he often ran in to, avoiding with a wave of the hand the group of representatives from socialist countries, which he eventually would have to join. He downed another whisky and felt better, then made a joke or two in English with the Iraqi ambassador and let time pass. He was still thinking about the accident.

< 30 >

It was nearly nine o'clock at night when he returned to the embassy. Telling Miriam the details of the accident and José's stupidity, he was still feeling happily light-headed. No, he did not want to eat anything; he had had his fill of hors d'oeuvres at the reception. What he wanted was to lie down. Half an hour later he was in bed reading. He kept reading long after his wife fell asleep, knowing full well a night of insomnia lay ahead. At four o'clock the telephone rang. He had felt no premonition, but the sound of the ring in the diplomatic offices below sent a shock through him. He ran barefoot down the stairs and picked up the receiver. It was a long-distance call. From Cuba. After the hello, and moments before the caller identified himself, he realized it was Carlos Franqui.

"Listen, Zoila's sick. She's really sick. You'd better get yourself ready to come."

"Wait. Sick with what?"

"They don't know, but it's serious. Take the first plane you can."

"I can't just leave. I'm alone in the embassy. I'll have to ask the ministry for permission."

"Take the first plane and you can straighten the rest out here."

He went back upstairs to get dressed. The clock on his bedside table said four thirty. He told Miriam Gómez about the call and she decided to get up. They went into the kitchen to have breakfast as usual, but he could not eat a thing, he just drank black coffee. He asked Miriam to help him notify the embassy staff and then he sat down intending to write last-minute reports as he waited for dawn, but first he called the minister of foreign relations. In Havana it would have been at least midnight. He asked for the long-distance number and, after a pause that seemed interminable, managed to reach Minister Raúl Roa and tell him who was calling.

< 31 >

"What's up, *chico*?"

"Mister Minister, Carlos Franqui called. My mother is very ill and he tells me I should return to Havana."

"So do it, *chico*."

"Thank you, Minister, but what should I do about things here? You know I'm alone in the embassy."

"There's nobody who can take your place?"

"Nobody. Here in Brussels there's only the representative of the Ministry of Foreign Trade and the guy knows nothing about embassies. But there is the consul in Antwerp, Guillot…"

"Leave Guillot in charge then."

"But he has no diplomatic status."

"*Chico*, don't worry about that nonsense now. Leave Guillot in charge."

"Very good, thank you so much."

"You're welcome. See you later."

It seemed to him that Minister Roa had been asleep when he called, though his response seemed alert enough. As soon as it was light, he would call Guillot at the consulate in Antwerp and also Jacqueline. He proceeded to write reports until nearly seven, at which point he made the call to Jacqueline, explaining what had happened and asking her to come in as soon as she could since she needed to get his plane tickets. She arrived not long after and set about typing the nonconfidential reports, while he continued writing and copying in the hope that the effort would lessen the anguish in his chest.

Jacqueline called the airlines. The only routes to Havana were via Madrid or Prague. The Madrid plane would not leave for two days, while the Cubana flight from Prague left the following day and would get him to Havana on Friday. There was a problem, though: there was no direct flight to Prague that day; however, he could fly from Brussels to Amsterdam and from Amsterdam to Prague. Having decided that was best, he then asked for a call to be put through to his brother in Madrid.

Sabá Cabrera was even more startled to get an early call, and before he could explain his brother said he had had a premonition that something terrible was about to happen. He told Sabá about the call from Havana and his decision to travel to Cuba as soon as possible, then he hung up and continued writing reports.

Jacqueline told him the plane to Schiphol would leave at nine AM and the one from Holland to Czechoslovakia at noon. He decided to finish the reports and then get ready to go. But first he called the consul in Antwerp and explained the situation. Guillot, always affable, said he would move to the embassy in Brussels immediately and take care of everything. Now he felt calmer. Letting the trade envoy get involved in diplomatic affairs, something the man had attempted on a number of occasions, had worried him, but he decided to let go of all the internecine struggles and just get ready to leave. By eight AM he was in a taxi on his way to the airport. The only luggage he carried was an attaché case with a shirt and a pair of casual slacks, since he did not plan to be in Havana any longer than necessary.

In the airport, standing in line to enter the passenger area, he saw a familiar face trying vainly to exit the entrance door. He seemed like an apparition, but was in fact Jaime Sarusky, accompanied by Suardíaz, a pair like no other. He managed to get in finally and they spoke briefly, since he was running late. Sarusky asked for money to get to Paris, and he told him to talk

< 33 >

to Miriam Gómez at the embassy. Sarusky had already called the embassy, which was how he learned that he was on his way to the airport. A strange encounter. They said an unfriendly goodbye.

In Holland, Schiphol seemed less the name of the Amsterdam airport than one of the rings of hell, the word itself an omen of something evil. He had a three-hour layover and while waiting he heard them announce something like his name. It seemed he had a telephone call. He went to the booth and heard Miriam's voice. Before she said so, he knew his mother had died. He wandered about the waiting room, unable to sit, his eyes nearly blinded by tears, until they called for the flight to Prague. The entire time he clutched his attaché case in one hand and in the other a package containing a round of cheese and a box of crackers he had bought for his grandmother. At last, he was in the air flying toward Prague, in other words flying to Cuba by the most indirect route possible.

A car from the embassy was waiting for him, since Jacqueline had called ahead. They took him to the International Hotel. Later in the afternoon he went to the embassy, where the chargé d'affaires showed him around and he was surprised at how attractive everything looked. That was the work of the previous ambassador, who had been recalled to Havana and removed from his post, the chargé d'affaires explained, and in an apparent reference to that ambassador's private life, he added: "Those people always have good taste." He neither agreed or disagreed, just listened, though he was tempted to ask what sort of people the man meant.

In the early evening at the hotel he received a long-distance call from Havana. It was his ex-wife phoning to give him the news of his mother's death. In a choked voice he said he already knew and told her he would arrive the next day on the Cubana flight. He slept poorly that night, plagued once

< 34 >

again by a recurring dream that he was at the airport in Cuba trying to leave and discovered he had no passport, or that during his visit he had forgotten to go to the ministry and now he could not depart. He awoke very early and went out to walk the neighborhood. He had always detested Prague and now it looked more lugubrious than ever, despite the early summer and the lovely pruned shrubbery around the hotel.

He arrived at the airport long before the plane took off at eleven. During the flight he could not sleep as he normally did, so he entertained himself watching the passengers and trying to guess who they were and what they did for work. He wondered which ones were the security agents placed on every flight. Finally, his thoughts turned inward and back to the curse of the birds. When he was a child, he used to hunt birds in an empty lot not far from home, as well as in the country, really anywhere. Being enthusiastic but inept, his reach always exceeded his grasp, and though he possessed excellent bows and arrows he killed very few birds. One day, accompanying his grandmother to a farm, he stayed outside to hunt and saw a *totí* blackbird flying toward a dense growth of cacti. He realized the nest had to be there, went closer, and saw that it contained several baby birds. He began to shoot arrows at the little birds, heedless of the cries of the mother flapping inconsolably around the nest. He killed all the baby birds or thought he had. The fact is that once his hunting frenzy was spent he felt horribly guilty and hid behind the house until his grandmother finished her visit. They returned to town and he still felt terrible. A few days later his newborn sister died from an umbilical infection and he believed her death was punishment for his massacre of the birds. From that day on, he gave up hunting. Then recently, in the yard of the embassy, a magpie had made her nest. He went to have a look and Jacqueline warned him not to move it, since the magpie would

< 35 >

abandon her young. But he wanted to see the baby birds, so he bent the bush down and tugged the nest to one side. A few days later, the maid reported that all the young had died, abandoned. He felt truly guilty about it and for days awaited a punishment to fit the crime.

Down below, he spied countless palm trees sprouting from the red earth and knew they were flying over Cuba. The plane continued its descent and soon they were circling Rancho Boyeros. They landed. He changed his glasses for dark ones, then left the plane. He saw a group of people waiting for him. Coming toward him first of all, his hand held out silently, was Lisandro Otero. They shook hands. Soon other faces, other people surrounded him, and someone took his passport and the attaché case, which later mysteriously reappeared in his hand. Marta Calvo, his ex-wife, came over to give him a kiss. Also her sister Sara Calvo. Then he was aware of Carlos Franqui and Harold Gramatges taking him aside. Suddenly he was outside the airport terminal and getting into a car that Harold was driving. Carlos Franqui was riding in front and at his side sat Marta and Sara. Franqui asked about Sabá and he said he was in Madrid ready to come.

"Better he shouldn't come," Franqui said.

"Why?"

"Well, we're entering a period of persecution and dogmatism. He'd be better off staying in Spain."

"But you know what he's like," said Harold. "If he doesn't come, he'll feel guilty, he likes to have his hand in everything. If he doesn't… you can imagine."

Harold let the phrase hang in the air, as he often did. He said he did not understand how any persecutions might affect Sabá, and then he fell silent and looked out the window at the sunny expanse, the sky bleached white,

< 36 >

the express road lined every so often by palm trees. The car continued along Rancho Boyeros and entered Havana by way of Avenue of the Presidents, passing in front of his parents' building; he could make out the deserted balcony and the shuttered windows. They drove on toward the sea and he realized what funeral home they were taking him to: the Rivero, by the shore. The car turned right onto Calzada, passing directly in front of the Ministry of Foreign Relations. Finally, they were at the funeral home.

He climbed the stairs and in the vestibule a sign surprised him:

CHAPEL C
ZOILA INFANTE

Seeing her name in black and white, the reality of his mother's death hit home. Another flight of steps took him to Chapel C and soon he was in the anteroom, which was filled with friends and acquaintances. He saw his father, smaller, shrunken, astonishingly aged, emerging from the sweltering chapel and walking toward him.

"Come, so you can see her, the poor woman."

"No, no."

"Come, you must. She's laid out in there."

"No, no. I don't want to, I don't want to see her."

His father was pulling on his arm and he practically had to cling to the door frame to keep from being dragged into the chapel. The situation was tragicomic, his father insisting he see his mother's body while he was determined not to see her like that, dead in the casket; he wanted to remember her as she was alive. His father gave in at last, and he went to sit with his former wife and her sister, on a sofa against the wall.

"How did it happen?" he asked Marta Calvo.

< 37 >

"Nothing to tell you. She had an earache she barely complained about, and when old Guillermo took her to the hospital it was too late."

"Did it really happen like that?"

"Well…," said Sara Calvo, and she stopped.

"Well…," his ex-wife picked up, "no one thought it was anything serious. You don't die from an earache."

"I guess you do."

"Well, the point is she'd been in the hospital since the morning, and when I got off work I decided to go see her, thinking it was nothing important, and I found her alone in her room with nobody there to help her. She was unconscious and I got scared and went out to call Carlos Franqui and Alberto Mora to see if they could do something for poor Zoila and that was when the doctor first came."

"They thought it was blood poisoning," Sara said.

"Yes," Marta agreed, "at first they thought that, but then they realized it was more serious and they called in a brain specialist, but it seems it was too late."

"In any case, they did not do all they should have," said Sara.

"Later that night I went back to the hospital," Marta said, "and it was almost dawn when she started making strange noises that seemed to come from her chest, and I got very frightened and called a nurse, and I guess she was already in a coma because in a little while – I had barely gone downstairs – they came to tell us she was dead. I didn't understand a thing."

One person and then several more came by to say hello to him, offering their condolences, hurried and inane as always. He barely recognized Norma Martínez, she was so much older and needed glasses now. Then several other

< 38 >

people came over, among them an elderly woman he did not recognize. She turned out to be a neighbor of his mother's who kept repeating, "A saint, a true saint."

He felt somehow less tired yet more fatigued, and the smell of marigolds and the murmur of the wake gave him a stabbing sensation of the absurd: it could not be that his mother was lying there next door, dead. It was a lie. None of it was true. He was not here. To shake himself awake, he decided to speak with his former wife.

"I'm taking the children with me."

"Well," Marta said, "we'll have to see about that."

"What do you mean, we'll have to see?"

"Just that," said Sara, "the girls are better off with their mother."

"But they've never been with their mother!"

It was true. Until now the girls had been raised by their grandmother, his dead mother. One of them had lived for two and a half years with him in Belgium, but the other had been with her grandmother since birth.

"Well," said Marta, "now they should be…"

"But don't you realize they would be better off in Belgium with me, than here?"

"Yes, I know," Marta said, "but they should be with their mother now."

"Their real mother," said Sara.

"Yes," said Marta, "with their real mother!"

He felt his anger rising and he spoke too loudly. "But that's stupid. Clinging to such narrow-minded ideas."

"It's not narrow-minded. It's the truth. I'm their mother."

"And I'm their father…"

< 39 >

At that moment Harold Gramatges came over, diplomatic as always, and said softly, "*Please*, let's not discuss this now. Isn't there a better place to do it?"

He knew Harold was right and he fell silent. Marta began to rock on the sofa, staring straight ahead, her small, deep-set eyes focused on a point on the wall with a determination he knew all too well. Sara tried to speak, but Harold turned his back on her and walked to his chair on the other side of the room. He himself sat in silence, then said, "I'm going to go find some coffee."

On the wide staircase that led from the vestibule to the street he ran into Carlos Franqui speaking with Gustavo Arcos, who reached out his hand, offering his condolences, then said to Carlos, "Ah, Franqui, you're always on about something." And Arcos turned back to him, "Franqui here tells me he just saw Aldama prowling around me."

"That's a fact," Franqui said. "He was dressed as a chauffeur and driving a cab, and he went around the block twice. The first time I saw him I didn't pay much attention, although I was pretty sure it was him, but the second time I got a good look."

"Well," said Arcos, "even if it is him, what could he do to us?"

"Do?" said Franqui. "He couldn't do anything, but it is very strange. Very unusual…"

"Let's go have a drink," he suggested, and they went down the street to a bar, where there was neither coffee nor beer, only clear Coca-Cola. They drank clear Coca-Cola, then returned to the wake and saw Martha Frayde and Beba Sifontes in the lobby. The two of them gave him their condolences, then Martha pulled him close and put her mouth to his ear.

"Your mother died from lack of medical attention," she whispered, and

< 40 >

said no more. He nodded, too pained to respond. "That is the simple truth," she added, letting go of his arm.

Together they went up to the wake, where they ran into Olga Andreu, who brought her face close to his, embracing him without a word. He noticed she was tensing her mouth in a half smile that made her thin lips even thinner. They remained standing in the middle of the room, talking trivialities, as always happens at wakes. He kept quiet, feeling out of place in Cuba, in Havana, in the Rivero Funeral Home, among his friends, at his mother's wake. In the midst of it all he noticed an old white-haired man with pale, lusterless eyes coming toward him and he recognized Eloy Santos, nearly out of breath from the climb up the stairs, who said, "I didn't know. They came to the house to tell me there was news, but they didn't say who it was. Right now, on the stairs, I saw the name. They didn't tell me a thing, nothing except I should go to the Rivero Funeral Home and I got myself over here. But I swear they told me nothing..." And he continued to excuse himself as if he had committed a crime, as if he were guilty of putting the name Zoila Infante on that terrifying notice board. Other people came close to offer their condolences, among them Raulito Roa, who said, "I feel for you, but I can only stay a moment."

"Thank you. That's all right. My father is over there."

"I'll go say hello."

"Thank you."

"No reason to, *mi viejo*."

Then he turned and saw Norma Martínez again, and again he was surprised to see her looking so old. She was still sitting on the sofa, her long legs crossed and her hands in her lap, and she looked tired. He could not help imagining her without her clothes.

< 41 >

Suddenly there was a bustle in the room next door and he knew it was time for the funeral. That very phrase sounded distant and alien, as if it were time for someone else's funeral and not his mother's. Then there was general movement all over the wake and he felt himself being hauled, first by his father, then by someone he did not recognize, down the stairs and along the sidewalk, around the corner and into a big black car, and soon he was sitting between the driver and a fat blond woman who was crying and grabbing at his hands. He had no idea who she was. Probably a neighbor. The weeper clung to him and as the car pulled out she rested one of her huge breasts on his arm and wailed about his loss, and now with one of her fat hands she was stroking his thigh, crying and at the same time trying to console him, hugging him in his grief, and he felt as far from his grief as he did from her caresses, and told himself this was the last thing he needed.

The cortege climbed Avenue of the Presidents and for a moment he feared it would pass by his parents' building and the girls would see it. But the hearse turned down 23rd Street and he saw no one he knew. Now they were taking 23rd all the way and at a funereal pace.

In the first car his father was riding in the backseat between two people he could not make out. Meanwhile he was being pressed ever closer by the blond weeper, who was now stroking his thigh even higher up, too high. He told himself this was unbelievable, this stupid girl was going to give him an erection, and he refused to believe this was really happening at his mother's funeral. It was so trivial and extraordinary, like in a dream. The blonde continued crying and telling him he had to be brave, to face – yes, face, using that very word – he had to face everything bravely, and her hand continued caressing him from his knee up to nearly the top of the thigh.

They crossed Paseo Street and the blonde – who was not blond, it was

< 42 >

obviously a dye job – continued stroking him. Now she was squeezing his arm and repeating his name several times, while still working his thigh with her other hand. Finally, the hearse turned down 12th toward the cemetery, and for an instant he was glad they had arrived. Then he remembered he was at his mother's funeral and felt guilty about that moment of relief.

The two lead vehicles followed the hearse through the main gate of the cemetery and they all stopped at the esplanade next to the entrance. There everyone got out to walk the rest of the way to the tomb. As he set off, he sensed vaguely that he was being photographed.

The cortege reached an open vault. He had said he did not want a grave-side farewell, and now he was afraid someone would start speaking. Fortunately, no one did. The casket was lowered into the tomb and a large slab was placed across the hole. It was over. Harold Gramatge took his father by one arm and him by the other, and turned them toward the mourners, who came one by one and shook their hands.

Harold drove him and his father home, and came up with them to the apartment. When he walked in, he saw his grandmother seated by the window, staring into space.

"Oh, my poor son!" she said. "What we have lost! It should have been me, my poor son, not her, since I'm no good for anything."

He went over and put a hand on his grandmother's bony shoulder. Marta Calvo was also there, and Hildelisa, the cook, maid, and live-in companion, whom he only knew from the bubbly letters she sent his mother when she was in Belgium. There were other people in the room, but he barely recognized anyone. He went out to the balcony, sat on a chair, and gazed at the park. He saw a splendid June afternoon; he saw boys and girls playing amid the bushes that lined the avenue, and caregivers or mothers sitting on the benches;

< 43 >

he saw the eternally beautiful park, and the first tears began to flow. He sobbed unconsolably. Marta came to his side and touched his shoulder. She too was crying.

"She's dead," he got out between sobs, "and everything is just the same: the park is the same, the same people are playing and sitting. Everything is the same, except she's dead."

His ex-wife cried, so did his grandmother. Harold Gramatges said something consoling, but he did not hear it. Suddenly he felt calmer. He asked for his daughters.

"The girls are downstairs," said his grandmother. "When we heard Zoila had gone on to a better life we had Dulce take them, the neighbor on the first floor."

He looked around and saw that the living room was practically empty. Only Marta remained, plus Hildelisa, while Harold and the others were gone. He saw his father walking toward him from the rooms at the back, drying his eyes with a handkerchief. Some time must have passed, but he had not been aware of it.

"I don't want the girls to know anything," he said. "Not now. When they ask for their grandmother, tell them she is still in the hospital."

"Why do that?" his father asked.

"That's how I want it, that way the blow won't hit so hard when they find out, it won't be so sudden."

"All right, son," his grandmother said, "we'll do it the way you say. Hildelisa?" she called toward the kitchen.

Hildelisa appeared. Now he noticed she was wearing a pink dress and that she was attractive in a Cuban way: fat, with mischievous eyes now red from crying. While his grandmother told her he did not want the girls to

< 44 >

know until he decided to tell them, he thought about how funny her letters were. She nodded her head and wrung her hands in her apron.

"Who was that woman who sat next to me?" he asked his father.

"Ah, that one. That's Rosalba Liendo, a girl who lives on the other block. She loves – loved, your mother a lot. Why?"

"Nothing. She's a bit exaggerated, that's all. She acted like a hired mourner."

"Oh, no. She's just a poor girl. Very kind and very good."

He looked out at the park, then turned toward the balcony next door.

"What about Héctor? He wasn't at the funeral or the wake."

"Imagine that," his grandmother said.

"He was at the hospital last night and the night before. He must be working now."

"Ah," he said, nodding, "I was surprised not to see him."

"But his wife was there for sure," his grandmother said.

"Yes," his father said, "she was there."

"I didn't see her," he said.

"Of course you did," his father said. "I saw when she went over to you."

"There were so many people," he said.

He gazed at his grandmother curled up on her footstool by the window, and did not remember her looking so gaunt. He studied her hands, and then her feet in the slippers her daughter, his mother, Zoila, had brought her from Belgium. He saw how misshapen her hands were from arthritis and he thought about the old woman's capacity for suffering.

"Roa, the minister," his father said suddenly, "sent a wreath."

"Oh, good," he said. He was looking at the park again, now with eyes that were more relaxed although his thoughts remained unchanged: she is

< 45 >

dead, but life goes on. "Guillermo," he turned toward his father, "why don't you go get the girls, I'd like to see them."

"Let me go," said Hildelisa, and out she went.

His uncle Niño and Niño's wife, Fina, came in. They were late returning from the cemetery because Niño had not felt well. They sat, some in the living room and some on the balcony. Hildelisa came back with the girls.

"Papi! Papi!" the two of them cried at the same time. Ana, eleven years old, and Carola, seven, kissed their father.

"Where's Grandma?" Carola asked. "Is she still in the hospital?"

He looked at his grandmother and saw she was about to burst into tears.

"Yes, she's still in the hospital."

"So when is she coming home?"

"We don't know."

He looked at the television set and on top of it sat his attaché case and the box with the gift from Holland. He did not know how they made it there.

"Hildelisa, get the girls ready, I'm going to take them out for a bit."

"You're going to take them out?" his grandmother asked reproachfully.

"Yes."

"They shouldn't go out on a day like today," his father said.

"And what does that matter?" he said, trying to make it sound as little as possible like "leave the dead in the grave and let the living misbehave."

"No, no matter at all," his grandmother said.

"But I don't think they should," said his father.

"We do, we do, we want to go," said Anita, "don't we, Carolita?"

"Yes, where are we going?"

"To Coney Island, Papi," Anita said.

"All right, let's go get you dressed," Hildelisa said, and she took them to their room.

< 46 >

"How are you planning to get there?" Fina asked.

"On the bus. What else?"

"No, don't do that, the buses are awful."

"They never come," his uncle said, "and when they do they're packed tight."

"If you like," said Fina, "we can take you. Otherwise you'll get home very late."

"I just want to spend a little time there with them, so they can have fun."

"When are you going to eat?" his grandmother asked.

"When we get back," he answered. "I'm not at all hungry."

"But you can't have eaten anything the whole blessed day," said his grandmother.

"Yes, I ate on the plane," he lied.

A silence descended that fortunately did not last long because the girls returned dressed in their Sunday clothes. He got up from his rocker on the balcony and they departed.

They took the Malecón toward Marianao. The afternoon was coming to a close in a glorious sunset that stained everything amber, pink, and red: even the sea was pink. They traveled on in silence. There was a peacefulness in the car that did him good.

They went through the tunnel and then through the gardens of Miramar. It was beginning to get dark, but even so he marveled at the beauty of the tropical foliage: palms, arecas, ficus, bougainvilleas, and royal poincianas in bloom. No one said a word until they reached the amusement park; when the girls started bouncing up and down they were so excited. At the gate, when he had to pay, he realized he had no Cuban money, only a few thousand Belgian francs and a few Czech bills. He told his uncle, who said not to worry and he paid for the tickets. They all went in.

< 47 >

The girls, as always, wanted to go on all the rides at once and eat cotton candy at the same time. They bought cotton candy first, then went over to the carousel, which Carolita wanted to ride, but Anita wanted the roller coaster. They could do that after. While Anita and Carolita were on a children's version of the roll-o-plane, the weight of the day hit him. He chatted with Fina while Uncle Niño listened in silence. He chose to talk about nothing that mattered. Darkness descended quickly and a light breeze began to blow. He was astonished to have not felt hot all day, even though he had never changed out of his Belgian summer suit.

Getting into the car, Carolita froze suddenly. "What's wrong, Papi?"

"Me? Nothing, why?"

"I was watching you," and it was true, she had been staring at him while she rode the roll-o-plane, "and you looked so sad."

His aunt and uncle looked at him and then at the girl.

"It's nothing, I'm just tired, once I get some sleep I'll get over it."

They returned to Havana, or better put to Vedado.

They sat at the dining room table. Hildelisa brought out a plate of yellow rice with potatoes mixed in.

"I'm sorry. Rice and potatoes is all there is."

"We've got to adjust, my son," his grandmother said from the living room.

"I didn't say anything, Mamá."

"You haven't said anything, but I know you're used to eating well."

"What about the girls?"

"They already ate," said Hildelisa, "downstairs at Dulce's house."

He sat down to eat and confirmed what he had already suspected, that he could not swallow. He did his best to eat the rice and potatoes, but they just made a chewy mess in his mouth.

< 48 >

Carlos Franqui and his wife, Margot, and the neighbors Héctor Pedreira and his wife, Teresa, came over that night and they talked until late. After they left he felt the emptiness of the apartment bereft of his mother, and he sat up for a while longer on the balcony. When he turned in, he found both of his daughters asleep in the big bed that had been his mother and father's. He undressed in silence and lay down between them, putting his arms around each child. He left the door open.

EARLY THE NEXT MORNING he went to the ministry and met with the vice minister, Arnold Rodríguez, who offered his condolences. Arnold's office was near the main entrance to the ministry, which was in the former Gómez-Mena palace. Arnold was a follower of Che Guevara, and when Che heaped scorn on bureaucrats in a speech not long before, Arnold took the diatribe literally and gave up his desk. Now he worked sitting on a sofa, and the folders and papers that ought to have at least been on a table were spread out on the floor or piled up in corners. Since they had seen each other at the beginning of the year in Madrid at a meeting of Western European heads of mission, as well as later on in Paris, there was little they had to speak about, so they just exchanged comments of no consequence. Then he went to the office of Minister Roa, who received him behind his desk. He sat on a sofa to the left and Roa came over to sit beside him. Roa offered his condolences and told him he had not been able to go to the funeral due to all the work, but that he had sent his son. He said he knew that and thanked him.

"Well, to get to the point, we're very satisfied with your work in Brussels and we're thinking of sending you back as chargé d'affaires."

"Oh, thank you very much."

"When do you think you could go back?" the minister asked while he shined his left shoe on the cuff of his right pant leg.

< 49 >

"In a week at most."

"That's good, seems right. Now there's something I want to ask you about. It's only a rumor, but is it true that this man Arcos is a drinker, has he taken to the bottle?"

Roa spoke, as always, too quickly, stumbling over his words, and for a moment he did not understand. But right away he knew the source: for sure one of Aldama's reports.

"No, Minister. Not that I know of. I have never seen him drunk. He drinks wine with his meals and things like that, but I have never seen him even tipsy."

"So, no," Roa said. "I thought it was just a rumor, no matter."

But he felt mortified. He had the distinct impression that Roa wanted the rumor to be true. Roa's family on his wife's side, the Kourís, harbored a long-standing grudge against Arcos. They blamed him for the decision of her brother, then commercial attaché in Brussels, to seek asylum in the early days of the Revolution. The family believed that Arcos's systematic persecution had driven Kourí to seek refuge in the United States. Since he knew Arcos well enough to be certain he would be incapable of doing anything systematic, he doubted the story held any truth. Roa, of course, never wanted Arcos to be an ambassador, but he had had to swallow it, not only because of Arcos's revolutionary past from the days of the assault on the Moncada Barracks, but also due to the friendship between Arcos and Raúl Castro. For the past few months rumor had it that Arcos would not return to Brussels and instead would be put in charge of the Cuban Embassy in Italy. At least that is what Arcos had once confided when he called him from Brussels, and what's more he had promised to take him along as cultural attaché in Rome.

"Well, Minister," he said, "I won't take any more of your time. I'll be back next week to get my instructions."

< 50 >

"Yes, yes, of course," Roa murmured, and they said goodbye. Back in Arnold's workspace the vice minister told him he ought to go see Rogelio Montenegro, head of the Europe VI office (Western Europe), to share impressions. He agreed to do so on Monday, since now he was too tired, and he left.

He walked to his parents' building, which was at the other end of the same avenue. Despite the midday heat, the sun allowing for no shade, he enjoyed being under that deep white sky. He took off his jacket and carried it over one shoulder and he loosened his tie. On Avenue of the Presidents he took the sidewalk under the trees, rather than the sun-drenched gardens in the median. When he reached 17th Street he felt tempted to go on to the Writers Union one block east, but decided to go straight home. Though he was not hungry, it was lunchtime.

He arrived sweaty and took the elevator to the third floor. In it, a beautiful blond woman who was going higher up said hello to him. He returned her greeting but did not have the foggiest idea who she might be. Once home he asked about her and from his description they said it was Leonora Soler, who lived on the fifth floor.

Lunch was a bit of white beans, rice, and a few potatoes. He barely ate a thing. It was not so much lack of appetite as how unappealing the meal was.

After eating, his daughter Ana wanted a heavenly custard from El Carmelo and they walked the half a block to the restaurant. The sweet cost a peso and he thought a dollar was a lot to ask for a dessert in a revolutionary country. While his daughter nibbled he ordered coffee, but the waiter said coffee was only for customers having a meal. They returned home where there was also no coffee, since it was not yet their turn for the ration. "What about the *café con leche* we had this morning?" he asked. It wasn't *café con leche*. It was ersatz coffee made with burnt sugar and milk

< 51 >

from the ration for his younger daughter, who was not yet seven. He felt a retrospective repugnance.

He sat on the balcony. The people walking by on the sidewalk across the street and in the gardens in the median seemed strange. He asked Hildelisa if she knew where his binoculars were – she did – and focusing them he observed people walking with a steady but tired stride, arms hanging down flaccidly, under a cloud of lethargy, everyone seemingly overwhelmed by a profound sadness. It could have been the three-o'clock sun, but there had always been sun in Cuba and these were all sorts of people. Elderly, middle-aged, and young all walked that way. Then he realized what they looked like: the zombies from Santa Mira in *Invasion of the Body Snatchers*!

He went to his room to have a nap. Before falling asleep he had a vision of his mother in Kraainem, Belgium, climbing the staircase from the living room to the bedrooms on the second floor of the house. He wondered why an apparition so precise and at the same time disturbing came to him. It was like a ghost.

He got up about five PM and went to the bathroom. Not knowing why, he opened the medicine chest and saw his mother's false teeth, forgotten there. Despondent before that pitiable object, he called Hildelisa so she would throw it away.

At six his uncle Pepe Castro arrived from Oriente, having made the trip because of the news, traveling the thousand kilometers however he could. With his head shaved Pepe Castro looked even taller and thinner than usual. He was wearing sandals. Pepe ensconced himself in the kitchen, behind the closed door, with his sister Ángela, the grandmother that everyone in the house, children, grandchildren, and great-grandchildren alike, called Mamá. When he came out he was speaking loudly, as he always did. "A heroine,"

< 52 >

he said, "a true heroine!" He was talking about his niece Zoila, the dead woman, the woman disappeared *forever*, because Pepe Castro, who had been a materialist vegetarian for innumerable years, did not believe in the great beyond or spirits or eternal life. "A heroine," he repeated, "that's what she was: a true heroine, really!"

Pepe came over to where he was seated on the balcony, but did not sit down (Pepe rarely sat) and looking at the sky, he pursed his lips and poked at his cheeks with his tongue, as was his habit whenever he was thinking. He looked his uncle over and it felt good to see this man he had loved with special affection ever since childhood. He peered at his sandals and recognized them. Pepe followed his glance and said, "They're yours. Zoila gave them to me when you left and they've been great. They're fabulous." He was glad his old Swiss sandals were of use to his uncle Pepe.

A little while later, Niño and Fina arrived to see how old Ángela was, and Pepe began to repeat what he had said before about Zoila, that she was a heroine, but soon he disappeared into his sister's room behind the kitchen. Niño and Fina had also come to invite him and the girls – who he learned were playing in the apartment below – to their beach house the next day. Fina offered to pick them up. He agreed, mostly so the girls could go with him to the beach, since that might be their only opportunity.

In the evening Carlos Franqui came over with his wife, Margot, and then Héctor Pedreira and his wife, Teresa, turned up. Once the girls were asleep he tried to find out how his mother died.

"Martha Frayde told me," he said to Franqui, "that Zoila died from lack of medical attention."

Franqui began to shake his head, as he did when he was upset.

"Martha Frayde told a lie," he said. "Zoila had all the attention she

< 53 >

should have had. Alberto Mora and I took care of that. There was nothing to be done."

"What happened," Héctor said, lowering his voice so that his father, who was reading in his room, would not hear, "is old Guillermo did not take her to the hospital right away. By the time he did, it was too late."

"But it wasn't only Martha Frayde. Marta Calvo said she spent a long time with Zoila in the hospital, and when she got there at four in the afternoon they hadn't even examined her. That was when she called you, Carlos, and Alberto."

"Listen, they took good care of her, even Ramírez Corría, the best brain specialist we have, came to examine her. But it was too late."

"I don't get it," he said. "How can someone die from an earache?"

"It was more than an earache," Héctor said. "It was an infection in her middle ear; that can be very dangerous."

"Wasn't Zoila always taking aspirins?" Carlos asked, although the question was a rhetorical one, "That masked the symptoms."

"Precisely," said Héctor. "What's more, she felt the pain but didn't think it was anything more than her usual headache."

"I don't know who to believe," he said.

"Believe whoever you want," Franqui said, "but we're telling you the truth."

"Nowhere in the world," he said, "do people die from ear infections."

"It was God's will, my son," he heard his grandmother say from her room behind the kitchen. She had been listening, as she did to every conversation.

"Well," Franqui said, "I think it's time for us to be going."

"Yes," said Margot, "it's getting late."

They said goodbye and left, while Héctor Pedreira and his wife stayed on. Héctor took advantage to change the subject to his favorite topic: the

< 54 >

movies. They talked until late. Then they left and he went to bed, stretching out again between his daughters.

The following day the girls woke him early, thrilled to be going to the beach. At about nine, Fina arrived in her car. He said he had promised to visit Carmela, his wife, Miriam's, mother. Fina offered to take him, and from there they could go on to Tarará Beach.

Carmela served him coffee she had obtained on the black market. He accepted with pleasure; coffee was not something to live without. The girls were impatient and Fina stayed in the car to signal that the visit would be brief. Then the telephone rang. Strangely, it was for him, a long-distance call from Brussels. His wife was on the line.

"How are you, love of my life?" Miriam Gómez asked.

"Fine, how about you?"

"I miss you. When are you coming back?"

"Next weekend, Saturday or Sunday, I think."

"You'll bring the girls, right?"

"Of course."

"Hang on, there's someone here who wants to talk to you."

The familiar voice on the other end of the line was in Europe, but the speaker enunciated so pedantically it sounded as if he were right there in Havana.

"Guillermo, this is Heberto."

It was Padilla, who said hello and offered his condolences in a different way.

"I am calling," Padilla said, "because Miriam let me read your novel and I think it is marvelous. I think it is the best that has ever been written in Cuba."

"Thank you."

< 55 >

"No, no need to thank me. If I did not think that was true, I would not say it. We talked about it a lot when you won that prize, but now I think you have got to publish it right away."

"Seix Barral is doing it."

"No, I mean in Havana."

"Oh, I'm not so sure. I've got an exclusive contract with Seix Barral."

"That is the least of it. I will speak with Carlos and he will give you permission for sure. It is ver-y im-por-tant this book be pub-lished in Cu-ba."

"Okay, we'll talk about it."

"Fine. Here is Miriam. Ciao."

"See you later."

"My love? Hurry up and come back, I'm so lonely without you."

"Yes, next week for sure."

"Okay, see you later. Here's a kiss. Let me talk to Mamá."

"A kiss from me too. Carmela, Miriam wants to speak to you."

Carmela smiled her usual guileless smile and dried her hands on her apron before taking the telephone. When she hung up, he said goodbye to Carmela and he and the girls went down to the street.

It was a luminous morning, the ten-o'clock sun shining as if it were noon. As they zipped along at a good clip, the streets bereft of cars looked familiar yet alien. He was riding up front and the girls were chatting in the back. For the first time since arriving, he felt good, and the moment he realized it he felt guilty. While the car passed the cemetery, he looked the other way. Now the thought of his mother's death pained him, intensely, as much as it did at night. He turned to Fina and asked about her work as a gym teacher. Once they were through the tunnel and out of Havana, the tropical vegetation crowding the road again held his attention. The entrance to the Guanabo highway, which used to be like a garden alongside the sea, was unkempt;

< 56 >

weeds had overwhelmed the careful geometric design. The entire stretch from behind La Cabaña Fortress to the beginning of the Guanabo highway now resembled an immense vacant lot. What a shame, he thought. So what if that venerable flower garden was built by Batista, something should be done to bring back its former splendor.

Farther down the Guanabo highway, in front of the drive-in, they turned left into Tarará, which had been a private beach, and it looked as beautiful as before. Groups of scholarship students were doing marching exercises on the streets nearby. At the last house, nearly at the edge of the sea, the car came to a stop.

Niño came out to greet them. The girls, thrilled to be at the beach, were first out of the car. He got out and went to say hello to Venancia, Fina's mother and Niño's mother-in-law, whom he had known for years. She seemed the same, except a bit hard of hearing.

While the girls changed in one room, he went into the other and put on an old pair of swimming trunks he had found at home and the sport shirt he had brought from Belgium. On the porch he sat on a metal swing painted white to wait for the girls. Anita came out followed by Fina in her suit and the three of them headed for the beach. The street was boiling under the sun, and they had to walk to the sand on tiptoe. He and Fina found some shade under a few palm trees and Anita ran into the water.

In a little while Niño, dressed in an old pair of shorts and a shirt just as old, sat down beside them to smoke.

"Where's Carolita?" he asked.

"She's coming," Niño said.

They chatted about inconsequential things, how calm the sea was and how blue the sky, how white the sand that stretched to the horizon on their left and as far as some distant palms on their right. He thought about his

< 57 >

wife, Miriam, and he wanted her tall perfect body to be there, walking along the edge of the sea.

"What's up with Carolita, why isn't she coming?" he asked again.

"She'll be here in a minute," Fina said.

This excessive worry about his daughters was something new in him, but the feeling was so strong he got up and walked over to the street to see if Carolita was indeed coming. The street was deserted, but then Carolita appeared, racing toward him as if on hot coals. Following her were two or three dogs. When she reached him, Carolita was flushed and at the same time furious:

"Those damned dogs!"

"What did they do to you?"

"Nothing, they followed me."

He laughed, watching her catch her breath and still seeing the way she looked running angrily down the street. The dogs never came as far as the beach. The two of them walked over to join Niño and Fina.

"Fina," he asked, "what happened to that boxer the Príos had?"

He was referring to a magnificent dog owned and then abandoned by former president Carlos Prío. The dog used to wander the streets of Tarará and other beaches as if searching for something he had lost. He had last seen him maybe three years ago and in his memory the dog looked like a pathetic ghost.

"Oh, that one," Fina said. "He got hit by a car about two years ago."

"Too bad."

"Yes, too bad."

"Was he pretty, Papi?" Carolita asked.

"Yes, an enormous beast."

< 58 >

"But he was really a fine dog, the poor fellow," said Fina, finishing his sentence.

"The same thing happened to the other Ready," Carolita said.

"Do you remember that?" he asked.

"Yes," Carolita said, "perfectly."

"This girl has a great memory," said Fina.

"Does she ever!" said Niño.

"Well," he said to Carolita, "let's take a swim."

"I'm afraid, Papi."

"What are you afraid of?" Niño asked.

"The sea, what else?"

"Don't be silly, girl," said Fina.

"Let's go," he said, "come with me."

"No, I'm afraid."

"We'll just go to the edge."

"Really?"

"Really."

She pondered a moment.

"Okay, but only that far."

"Fine. Give me your hand."

At the water's edge she let go of his hand and backed off with each wave.

"Come, sit here," he said, sitting where the water touched the shore.

"No, I'm fine here."

"Come on, don't be silly."

"No, I said no."

Anita came toward them, in the water up to her waist.

"Why is that little girl so afraid of the water?"

< 59 >

"Because I am," said Carolita.

"But you'll get over that on your own, won't you, Carolita?"

"I'm not going in the water."

"Just come and get your feet wet at least."

Carolita seemed to think it over.

"Okay, but just my feet," and she walked to where he was sitting.

"Sit here."

"You aren't going to push me in, are you?"

"I promise I will not push you in."

"Okay, fine."

Carolita sat down next to him. From the water Anita called to him, "Papi, look how I go under."

That phrase would echo around his brain like a prophetic ritornello over the next few days, as would the image of his daughter plunging her head into the water once or twice.

After lunch – rice and white beans, barely edible, but apparently now the national dish – he sat on the porch to chat with Niño and Fina while the girls had a nap. But at three o'clock Anita came out saying she had an earache. He looked in her ear, could not see any inflammation, and asked Fina for an aspirin. They did not have any. "They're hard to find," Fina admitted. There was no oil to warm up and put in her ear either. He said to his daughter, "Lie down for a bit and it'll go away." She obeyed him, but it did not go away. A little while later she was back on the porch, crying. He told her they would be going soon, and picked her up and caressed her cheek so the pain would pass. Suddenly it began to rain. First a few fat clouds hid the sun, which he was thankful for, then came a spattering of immense drops as loud as hail. Now a tropical rainstorm sent tons of water pounding down on everything.

< 60 >

After half an hour the rain had not let up, but they decided to return to Havana in any case because the pain in Anita's ear had grown worse. They ran to the car and drove up the street, plowing through the streams coursing down either side of the road toward the sea. On the highway all the water in the world seemed to be falling on the old car, whose windshield wipers did not work. Inside, Anita was crying from the earache and Niño, driving, kept giving her looks of concern. Both men were thinking the same thing: an earache had killed Zoila and, although in her case infectious meningitis had been ruled out, God knows what this sudden earache was about. He recalled Anita's words, "Papi, look how I go under," and he saw her plunge her head in the water. He told himself no, it could not be, such a tragedy cannot happen twice. At least, he trusted it would not.

The car crept blindly forward; in the rain you could not see a thing. Niño opened the driver's window and stuck his head out, but so much water poured in it was not worth it. He decided to stick close to the righthand edge, but when they reached the Guanabo highway there was the risk of running off the embankment. Fortunately, only a few cars were left in Cuba.

The rain stopped when they reached Havana. They drove through Vedado and beyond their building to the Marfán Foundation, the girls' clinic, which they found right away. Anita was still wailing. After a few minutes in the waiting room, the doctor on duty appeared – he was very young. They told him what was going on and what they feared, without explaining in front of the girls that their grandmother had died of something similar. The doctor showed them into an examining room with the girl still howling. He brought out an otoscope and lit up the inside of her ear; her wails grew louder. Soon the doctor looked up and said, "It's nothing. Just an external otitis. With the drops I'll give you and a few aspirins – have you got any? – tomorrow she'll

< 61 >

be as good as new." They said they had no aspirins and he promised to give them some as well.

When they got home, Anita was still moaning, but less than before. He decided to call the girls' mother. The rest of the family, including Niño and Fina, gathered in the living room while Hildelisa put Anita to bed. He wondered out loud if they should call another doctor, a specialist. "Only a few are left," he was told. Someone suggested looking in the telephone book. "Useless," he said. "It's at least six years old." Fina decided to call a doctor friend of hers. The friend gave her a name and she phoned him. No, the doctor was not in, he would be back later that night.

In a little while, the girls' mother and her husband arrived and he brought them up to date on what he believed and what he feared. Marta went to the bedroom to see Anita and found her awake listening to a story Hildelisa was reading out loud. Despite the aspirin and her capacity to withstand pain, she was still moaning.

"What time is that doctor getting home?" he asked.

"They said later," Fina said.

"But how much later? When?" Niño asked.

"Later. At ten or eleven, I suppose."

"We'd better stay so we can take her, Fina," Niño said.

"Sure, that's fine," said Fina.

His grandmother came over to him.

"Would you like something to eat, my son?"

"No, thank you, Mamá."

"But you have to eat something."

"I'm not hungry."

"You need some nourishment."

< 62 >

"I know. But I don't feel like it."

His grandmother went off to her little room behind the kitchen.

Time passed, but not the tension.

"Why don't you try calling again?" he said to Fina.

"Okay. It's only ten, but I'll see."

The doctor had not arrived and Anita was again moaning from the pain.

"We'd better give her another aspirin," Fina suggested.

"Don't give her aspirins," the grandmother said from her room. "Remember what happened to Zoila."

"Right," he said. "Don't give her any more aspirins. Let's wait until the doctor sees her."

Meanwhile, he and Marta agreed that Anita would stay with him at the apartment in Retiro Médico – his old apartment, now rented to Marta and her husband – which was not far away, and Marta and her husband would sleep at his parents' apartment. In case the otitis was contagious, they did not want Carolita to catch it.

Close to eleven o'clock Fina got hold of the doctor. They could see him at his office in his home that very night. All but Marta and her husband went along. The doctor was not in a good mood and his surliness left no doubt he was a counterrevolutionary. But he examined the girl right away and said, "It's an otitis media."

The same diagnosis made of his mother, although too late. He and Niño looked at each other and he thought his uncle was about to faint.

"The doctor at the Marfán Foundation said it was an otitis externa," he said.

"Well, tell that doctor to go back to school."

"Is it dangerous, doctor?" Fina asked.

< 63 >

"All internal infections are dangerous," the doctor said in the same cutting way. "We'll have to perforate her eardrum."

The doctor began to prepare his instruments, among them a long hypodermic needle. For Anita, laying eyes on that and screaming happened simultaneously. The doctor tried to calm her using the same bedside manner he inflicted on adults.

"Come on, come on, this isn't going to hurt at all. It's just an injection to put your eardrum to sleep."

He and his uncle took Anita by the arms to steady her.

"Don't move, Ana," he said, "and you'll see it won't hurt."

The doctor had to proceed with Anita wailing and staring at the needle in terror. The doctor worked ably and managed to inject her quickly. Then he pulled out another hypodermic, its needle just as long, and with a sure jab perforated her eardrum.

"Now we have to take out the pus," he said, and he picked up a siphon, which he used to clean out her ear just as quickly and efficiently.

"Well, my girl," he said, using his first friendly word, "It's over."

"Thank you, doctor," Fina said.

"No reason to," said the doctor.

"How much do we owe you?" he asked.

"That'll be twenty pesos," the doctor said.

He paid him, and they all thanked him. The doctor said she should take penicillin and he wrote out a prescription. They left 19th Street, where the doctor lived, and went to his old apartment at Retiro Médico at 23rd and N, where Sara and her husband, Luis Agüero, were waiting, along with Marta and her husband. They put Anita to bed, then Marta and her husband left

< 64 >

along with Sara, while Luis stayed to keep him company. They talked about nothing consequential, letting the hours pass, and every so often he would go to the bedroom to check on Anita. She was always sleeping deeply.

"What books have you read lately?" he asked Luis, making conversation now in the early morning.

"*Buddenbrooks*," Luis said, "by Thomas Mann. It's the story of a German family in the last century."

"I know it. Not as good as *The Magic Mountain* but it is a good book."

"I was really impressed by the character of the child who dies at the end."

"The one with the rotting mouth?"

"Yes, that one. Thomas's sister was also a great character, though right now I can't remember her name."

"Tony," he said.

"Right, Tony. It's great how Mann," and Luis could not hold back a long yawn, "depicts his useless life and her rebellion against his uselessness."

Luis Agüero yawned again, he was falling asleep. But he did not tell him to go home, because he was afraid of being left alone. All night he had been thinking that his mother was claiming her favorite granddaughter from the great beyond, and if he was going to stop her he had to stay awake. The thought filled his mind at every pause in the conversation. Finally, Luis himself said he had to go; it being Monday he had to get up early. He did not dare ask him to stay until dawn, though he wanted it more than anything in the world. When the door closed behind Luis, he felt immensely alone and went to check on Anita: still sleeping. Silently he closed the bedroom door and returned to the living room. He moved his chair so that it blocked the corridor to the bedrooms, since he suspected his mother would come in

< 65 >

through the closed front door, and he had to keep her from getting by. He made himself as comfortable as he could and when it began to get light he was able to sleep a bit.

He awoke and saw it was morning. He went to the bedroom. The girl was still sleeping and showed no signs of fever. The only indication of illness was the bit of cotton batting in her ear. He returned to the living room and went over to the balcony window to a view he had contemplated so many times while living in this apartment. The sea, streaked blue and purple, was nearly green near the asphalt ribbon of the boardwalk twenty-three floors below. The Spanish pseudocastle of the Hotel Nacional dominated the skyline and behind it, nearly directly beneath the rising sun, the authentic castles of El Morro and La Cabaña marked the outer limits of Havana on the other side of the bay.

He sat back down, feeling spent. Then he reached for the telephone and called home to let them know Anita was all right.

MARTA CALVO RETURNED at about eight o'clock. She had found a doctor to give Anita the penicillin, which she had managed to buy They waited for the doctor, who turned out to be a tall, friendly man and, as he revealed in conversation, a committed supporter of the Revolution, who praised what it had accomplished for child health and who discounted as lies the gastroenteritis epidemic everyone in the city was talking about. Anita took the shot in good spirits and the doctor promised to return in the afternoon to give her the other. He did not charge a thing.

He told Marta to take Anita home after the second shot and he went there to sleep. Strange noises inside the apartment woke him at about four in the afternoon. It was his brother, Sabá, arriving from Madrid. As usual,

< 66 >

they said little to each other. He related the details of Zoila's illness, avoiding any reference to the funeral and to death itself. Sabá wanted to know more – just as he had when he first arrived – about what caused his mother's sudden departure from the world of the living. Soon Sabá departed to see his wife and children, who still lived on the corner of 23rd and 26th.

He wanted to take a bath, but there was no water. Maybe it would come on later, much later. So he sat on the balcony and watched people walk by. Once or twice he used the binoculars to get a better look at a pretty girl in the distance.

At five o'clock Anita was back. She needed only one more injection, which the doctor would give her the following day. She looked bright-eyed and full of life. He sat her on his knee thinking that maybe he had rescued her from death. Marta Calvo left and he invented a wild story for his two daughters, making it up as he went along.

At six his father came home from work and closed himself into a bedroom, apparently to read, but perhaps to cry. He asked his grandmother about Uncle Pepe and learned that he had returned to Oriente. He wished he could have spent more time with his favorite relative. Even though the man was obviously crazy, he was strangely lucid in applying his ethos of absolute vegetarianism to daily life.

At seven everyone ate, except for Sabá, who had not yet returned. It was the same bland food, but miraculously containing meat. Maybe Hildelisa, whose culinary skills were no match for her letter writing and joke making, had bought some on the black market, or maybe it was the small monthly quota. He ate little and took no pleasure in it.

He loved Havana at night. Despite having seen from the Retiro Médico tower that all the illuminated billboards were gone, he heard the soft tropical

< 67 >

summer night calling to him to at least take a stroll on the streets of Vedado. But he did not feel like going out. In a little while, Oscar Hurtado phoned to see if he would be home that night. He told him to come over.

Oscar Hurtado of the enormous body and careful enunciation liked to talk about all sorts of things that always led to the same topic, the great beyond of our days: outer space and extraterrestrial visitors. On the balcony that night, however, real day-to-day problems took precedence over flying saucers and Martians. The state had taken over Studio Theater, a company that was revolutionary even before the Revolution, all of whose members were Communist-leaning fans of Bertolt Brecht. The takeover occurred for strictly moral reasons, or at least that was the claim put forth by officials: like every other theater group in the world, Studio Theater was full of homosexuals. The director, Vicente Revuelta, got turfed out and a functionary from the Cultural Council was named to replace him. He thought this was a bad sign, but Oscar was upbeat.

"These jerks," Oscar said, "were the worst ones attacking *Lunes* at the meetings in the library."

Lunes de Revolución was the arts magazine he ran during the first three years of the Revolution, which was shut down after the staff protested the suppression of a short film made by his brother, Sabá. The closure was preceded by three meetings at the National Library attended not only by every government official in the realm of culture, but also by the heads of the government: Fidel Castro, President Dorticós, Carlos Rafael Rodríguez, etc. There, and at a previous meeting at Casa de las Américas, the people from Studio Theater had railed against the movie and then against *Lunes*.

"Now those little faggots are quaking in their boots," Oscar said, "but boy, were they ever dancing for joy when they ganged up on us. So, fuck them."

< 68 >

Oscar had no idea what was behind the recent persecutions, although he did know that Antón Arrufat had been fired as editor of *Casa de las Américas* magazine for publishing a poem by Pepe Triana that had homosexual allusions. Arrufat also got blamed for the invitation that brought Allen Ginsberg to Cuba after the poet loudly and repeatedly proclaimed his gay militancy and scandalized the leaders of the Revolution by crowing in public that he wanted to go to bed with Che Guevara!

"Those people thought they had God by the whiskers," Oscar said, "and now they're being harassed even more than we were."

He thought these persecutions were bad news, but he said nothing and just listened.

"I'm writing a poem," Oscar said in the same breath, "which I plan to dedicate to Zoila. You know, this is the end of an era."

It touched him to hear his friend say that the death of his mother was the end of an era: Zoila and Hurtado had been good friends for years; Oscar used to visit them at the apartment on 27th Street. Though he sometimes liked to make fun of this big timid man, he felt real affection for him. After Hurtado left, he stayed put on the balcony, reflecting that for him at least Zoila's death was indeed the end of an era. His grandmother's voice coming from her little room pulled him out of his reverie:

"My son, when do you plan to go to bed?"

The following morning he and Anita went with Franqui to the children's hospital to see a friend of Franqui's, Dr. Pérez Farfante. Despite having walked by it often when he lived on 27th Street, and even though his bus stop was right in front, he had never been inside. In the waiting room he was shocked by the many signs of poverty, almost misery: children sitting on the floor and poorly dressed mothers waiting in the corners. It looked like a scene out of India, and they decided to wait for the doctor at the entrance,

< 69 >

where they could gaze at the lovely trees along F Street. Right then Humberto Arenal, who had been a tireless collaborator at *Lunes* and the director of *Lunes*'s television programs, came by. He was thinner than ever and his poorly shaven beard cast a shadow that made him look even more diminished. Humberto told him he was very sorry about his mother's death, and that he had not attended the wake or the funeral because he had been ill. Arenal had long suffered from diverticulitis, which sometimes had him one step from the grave. Today was one of his bad days, but when he was well he was fun to talk to. The two of them shared an intense interest in women, a tie that bound them. But now neither of them was in the mood to tell that sort of story.

When Dr. Pérez Farfante came in, he looked at Anita quickly and said she was cured, but that she should stay out of the water. He told him he was taking her to Europe and she would not be going to the beach for a long time. Then he asked the doctor, as a way of payment, if he wanted anything from Brussels.

"Yes, a pair of loafers."

Later on, he went to Minrex, which was the new revolutionary jargon for the Ministry of Foreign Relations, and dropped in on Arnold Rodríguez, who was on his sofa dealing with several urgent matters in a file held precariously in his hands. Once again he thought it would be a lot more comfortable and effective to work at a desk or even a table. He left Arnold fighting bureaucratism and went to Political Desk VI, Western Europe, to speak with the director, Rogelio Montenegro. They exchanged pleasantries before turning to the Belgian situation.

"I can see you're working like crazy," Montenegro told him. "Sometimes your reports make us burst out laughing. You've filed a record number."

< 70 >

"Yes," he said, "I've been working hard."

It was true. In less than six months he had brought the embassy up to date. Now he wanted to find out something that Rogelio Montenegro would know.

"What happened with the report about the Russian Embassy and the new Belgian school?"

He was referring to a diplomatic incident in which the Cuban Embassy had to mediate between the Soviet Embassy and the Belgian Ministry of Education. The Cuban Embassy was directly across from the Soviet Consulate, at the end of Roberts-Jones Street, behind the new and sumptuous Soviet Embassy. To one side of the walled Soviet compound lay a vacant lot. Belgian officials planned to build a school there, since there was a real need in the neighborhood. The Soviets, for security reasons only they understood, were opposed; they protested to the Belgian Foreign Ministry and repeatedly asked the Cuban Embassy to join them. First, lower functionaries like the cultural attaché asked them to write the Belgian Foreign Ministry, then higher-ups in the Soviet Embassy insisted they do so. Even the ambassador himself got in on the act. The Russians went so ridiculously far as to send him a model letter to use as a guide. But instead of the model letter, the Russian official mistakenly sent over a copy of the response they had received from the Belgian minister of foreign relations, which politely put the Russians in their place.

He did not want to take a stance for or against the school, though he could see the Belgians were right, and he sent a long report to Political Desk VI asking for instructions. To make things clear, he included a piece of an Uccle map where he had marked out the properties occupied by each embassy and the empty lot where the school would be built. But Political Desk VI never

< 71 >

responded, despite a second report repeating the request for instructions. Now Montenegro explained why.

"Well, you know how it is," he began, with that evasion so typical of Cubans, "we received your report and we sent it to the vice minister, who sent it on to the minister hoping for a decision. But the minister didn't decide anything, he just sent your report on to the cabinet. Your report should be sitting on the president's desk by now…"

Montenegro let that last sentence hang and he understood that the report or a summary of it would be given to Fidel Castro for a decision. He was astonished by the bureaucracy. His tiny report had gone all the way to the hands of the prime minister for a decision that he himself could have taken ipso facto! He could now appreciate the desk Che Guevara envisaged in his speech as interpreted by Arnold Rodríguez.

"Don't worry, before the end of the month you'll get an answer in Brussels," Montenegro said. "When are you going?"

"Next Sunday."

"There are a few things we wanted to discuss with you, but right now that won't be possible. I'd better send it all to you in the diplomatic pouch."

"Is it important?"

"No, just procedural questions."

"Well, I could come back tomorrow if you like."

"No, we're in the middle of a reorganization of the political desks. After the Madrid meeting they took up, or rather once again took up, how to deal with Political Desk VI. The embassies are going to be restructured, but that won't affect yours for the time being, I think. Have you spoken with the minister?"

"Yes, on Saturday."

< 72 >

"And did he give you your instructions?"

"I think so."

"What do you mean, you think so?"

"Well, Roa…"

"The minister," Montenegro said, correcting him.

"Minister Roa told me I would be put in charge of the mission and we talked a bit about problems in the embassy. That was all."

"Everything's fine, then."

"Well, I'm going to get going. I'll let you get back to work."

He went to the passport and travel department to see if they knew he was planning to leave on the weekend.

"Well, *compañero*," the lead employee said, "we have not received any instructions. If, as you say, you are gong back as the head of mission in Belgium, you'll need a new passport. Although in reality, if your passport isn't expired the day you go… When did you say you were going?"

"I plan to leave on Sunday."

"This Sunday?"

"Yes, this Sunday."

"Well then, we'd better get your ticket."

"There will be more than one."

"How's that?"

"My two daughters are going with me."

"How old are they?" she asked, taking up a pen.

"Eleven and seven."

"Okay, you'd better give the information to that *compañera* over there," she said, pointing to another employee in the same office. He did what she asked and gave the ages and names of his two daughters.

< 73 >

"And, *compañero*," the lead employee called over, "don't you want a card to buy in the Diplomercado?"

That was the name of the legendary store set up for foreigners and nationals employed in the foreign service, where rumor had it you could buy all the things lacking in nearly every home.

"No, thanks. If I'm leaving on Sunday, I don't think it's worth the trouble."

"Fine, *compañero*. Leave everything to us."

He went home to face the lunch. Eating a steady diet of such lousy goop made him think of the Diplomercado – and long for the future.

He had a siesta and then sat on the balcony, binoculars in hand, to watch the women walking by. For the first time since leaving Belgium, he thought about sex and suddenly he missed his wife. He was enormously anxious for Sunday to come. He surprised himself by thinking of his trip back to Brussels as a return: the return ought to have been this trip to Cuba. The dog Ready came to lie at his feet, pulling him out of these meditations; he scratched his head and neck. The animal thanked him for the caresses by stretching out on the floor. He noticed a young woman on the sidewalk across the street and went back to his binoculars.

In a little while Anita and Carolita, who had been playing with their friends on the floor below, came in. Both of them hugged him, Anita more demonstratively affectionate than Carolita, who was always reserved and timid.

"Papi," Carolita said, and she stopped.

"What, my dear?"

After a long pause, she spoke again:

"When is Grandma coming home?"

< 74 >

"Yes," Anita said, "we want to see her. Can't we go to the hospital if she can't come home?"

"No, your grandmother can't leave the hospital yet and we can't go see her because she's in the ward for infectious disease."

He was pleased he had prepared an answer ahead of time.

"So when is she going to come?" Carolita asked again.

"One of these days," he lied, and it pained him to pretend his mother was still alive. He decided to change the subject.

"Where shall we go today?" he asked them.

"Are we going out?" Anita asked.

"Yes, if you like."

"Yes, yes. Let's go to the woods."

"Yes, yes, to the woods."

"Okay, we'll go to the woods but first go ask your uncle what he has planned and if he wants to go with us."

The two went running to the back of the apartment.

His brother would come along, but first he had to pick up his two sons so they could come too. They went to the home of his sister-in-law, Regla, at the corner of 23rd and 26th, to pick up the boys. Regla's two daughters joined them as well. From there they walked to the woods, crossing a bridge over the Almendares. When the first houses in Marianao came into view, the sun began its daily plunge and the sky turned from white to yellow to dark blue.

They went down the slope on the far side of the bridge and reached the first trees. It was obvious it would be dark before they got very far, but they went on anyway. Suddenly, Alina, one of Regla's daughters, felt ill, her belly hurt. They turned around and headed back, but before reaching the road Alina

< 75 >

felt another stomach cramp and defecated in her pants. It was embarrassing for the girl and for the adults, and Anita complicated things further by making fun of Alina. Sabá and he both scolded Anita, who kept on laughing. He had to smack her to get her to stop. They were all full of regret on the way home.

Back at the apartment, he got a call from Titón, Tomás Gutiérrez Alea, who invited him to lunch the following day.

That night Virgilio Piñera, Antón Arrufat, Pepe Triana, Jaime Soriano, Calvert Casey, and a young black man he did not know but who came with Soriano, all dropped by. Later on several said the unfamiliar man was an agent from G2, which Soriano refused to believe. He did not know what to believe. The strange visitor did not open his mouth, despite all the talk about what worried them most: the recent persecution of homosexuals. Antón Arrufat was the most outspoken.

"We're thinking," Arrufat said, "of holding a demonstration at the Palace with signs and everything."

"Who are we?" he asked.

"Vicente, the people from Studio Theater, and some others, all homosexuals."

Virgilio Piñera, as usual, made himself small in a corner of the sofa, smoked nervously, and said nothing. Calvert Casey tried to speak, but even before a small gathering of friends he stuttered and stumbled and managed only to say:

"I-I th-think th-that A-antón i-is r-r-r-right."

He disagreed.

"It seems to me," he said, "you people are wrong. You shouldn't have a public demonstration. They wouldn't let you anywhere near the Palace, you wouldn't even manage to leave Studio Theater or wherever it was you started.

< 76 >

It would be a demonstration against a government measure, in other words, a counterrevolutionary act. Besides which, people would think the government is right. Everyone here, revolutionaries and counterrevolutionaries alike, suffers from the same macho complex. They're against all homosexuals, no matter who."

Some time later his words would weigh on him, and that very night he did not know if he had spoken as a friend or as a diplomat. But Pepe Triana's response strengthened his argument, at least for the moment.

"But we are revolutionaries, or at least we're for the Revolution."

"That doesn't matter, Pepe," he said. "The only thing that matters to the Revolution is obedience, and a demonstration would be an act of disobedience."

"So what should we do?" Virgilio, smoking nervously, asked from his corner.

Ever since the days of *Lunes de Revolución*, they had all looked to him for direction, but now leadership from him was the last thing any of them needed. Nevertheless, he spoke up:

"I think the best thing would be to buckle down to work and stop having meetings at Studio Theater or anywhere else. This fever will pass, just as it did when they arrested you, Virgilio." He was referring to the day in 1961 when Virgilio Piñera was taken from his home in Guanabo to the local jail and then transferred to Castillo del Príncipe because he was a homosexual.

"Yes, it did pass," Virgilio said without raising his voice, "but the people who were in prison with me in Príncipe and didn't have connections are all still in jail."

"That's another reason why I'm right," he said. "You're more or less protected. And Haydée Santamaría won't let them imprison you, Antón."

< 77 >

"That was when I worked at Casa. Now I'm not so sure," Antón said. "I don't know what's going on with Haydée."

"And now Edith García Buchaca isn't around to get me out of Príncipe," Virgilio said.

"Well," he said, "another point in my favor. I think what you have to do is make yourselves as small as possible and let the wave pass."

He really could not say if he was giving his friends honest advice or if he was speaking for the stranger's ears. The stranger remained in his spot and said not a word.

He tried to give the conversation a humorous twist. "You, Pepe," he said, turning to Triana, "buy a couple of those cigars you used to smoke that made you look so macho. And you, Virgilio, stop smoking cigarettes and take up cigars."

He was reminding them of an occasion, again in 1961, while Virgilio was in prison. Pepe Triana turned up at his house at 23rd and N, mannishly smoking an expensive cigar, and he said to him:

"Your legs betray you," pointing to Pepe's legs in fifth position, just like a ballet dancer's.

Pepe laughed, but Virgilio was not in the mood for jokes.

"This is really serious. Listen, they went to visit René Sánchez."

"They went? Who went?" he asked.

"Social Turpitude," said Antón. "It's a new department in the Interior Ministry."

"Listen to this," Virgilio continued, "they had the gall to go to René Sánchez's house and suggest he get married so his problems would be over. You knew they arrested him not long ago?"

< 78 >

"Imagine Virgilio getting married at his age," said Antón in a jocular tone.

"Well," said Virgilio, taking up the joke, "as long as I get to be the bride."

Everyone laughed, even if there was something forced in the laughter.

"Seriously," Virgilio said, "in Soriano's case it's even worse."

"What happened to you, Jaime?"

Jaime Soriano was the only one of the visitors, except perhaps the stranger, who was not homosexual.

"Well," Jaime said, speaking slowly as always, "I went out to see someone in the wee hours." Jaime was always mysterious about his private life. "I went out late at night and got back near dawn. And, well, last week an agent from the Interior Ministry turned up at my house asking my mother about me. I wasn't home. It turns out the president of the Defense Committee on the block, who lives across from me, saw me come home late one night and decided to keep watch and realized I come home late every night. That agent from Social Turpitude, or wherever he's from, wanted my mother to explain why. He left, but he came back when I was there and I had to explain that I went out to see someone I didn't want the neighbors to know about. Then he asked, and this is the worst, why I changed my clothes so often!"

Everyone laughed heartily.

"That last bit came straight from the president of the Defense Committee."

"Imagine old Guillermo doing such things," he said. "I don't know if you know, but my father is the president of the Defense Committee on this block."

< 79 >

"You're taking this all very lightly," Virgilio said, "because you're going back to Belgium. But imagine us living under these conditions. I'm terrified!"

"Yes," he said, "it seems really serious, but I don't think you should be terrified. What is frightening is the idea of organizing a demonstration of homosexuals."

"It wouldn't be only homosexuals," Antón said.

"Well," he said, "of unorthodox people then, right? Going to the Palace to demonstrate against Dorticós. You'd be thrown in jail before you even got there," he glanced at the unknown visitor, "and rightly so. The Revolution cannot allow that sort of demonstration."

"W-well, so, so, so wha-what can we d-do?" Calvert Casey asked.

"I don't know," he said. "I think the best thing would be to try to keep your heads down and ask the Writers Union to intervene."

"The UNEAC?" Arrufat said. "The UNEAC people are more frightened than we are."

"Guillén could do something," he said.

"I don't think Guillén will do anything for anybody," Virgilio said. "Not even Bola de Nieve. In fact, they say Ramiro Valdés has sworn not to rest until Bola de Nieve and Luis Carbonell leave Cuba." Valdés was minister of the interior.

"That guy," Arrufat said. "His obsession with homosexuals is really weird."

"You said it," said Pepe Triana, "incredibly strange. He's the one directing the government campaign against us."

"What he's doing is making it seem like there are more of us than there are," Virgilio said, using the female form for "us" and stressing it.

< 80 >

He laughed along with Virgilio, but he was the only one who did. He looked at his watch and said to Soriano:

"Soriano, it's almost midnight. I think you'd better find your way home."

He said it only half seriously, but Soriano understood.

"I've been thinking of going for a while."

The rest took advantage to leave with Soriano; homosexuals now felt safer in the company of a heterosexual.

THE NEXT DAY AT about ten in the morning Ana Magdalena Paz telephoned. Ana Magdalena had been his student at the School of Journalism, where she stood out for her intelligence and her shyness. He was astonished she would call.

"It's Ana Magdalena, Ana Magdalena Paz," she said. "I want to tell you how sorry I am about your mother."

He thanked her. She continued speaking, stuttering a few times, hesitating, and finally saying, "I want to see you. You're going back to Brussels, right? I want to see you before you go."

He joked that she could not very well see him after he went and she got embarrassed. So he asked her when.

"Could it be today?"

He suggested that afternoon. She agreed. "Where in Havana could we meet up?"

He suggested Floridita, if the restaurant was still open. She never went to such places, but she thought it was. He would meet her there at four o'clock. After hanging up, he told himself Ana Magdalena must have changed a lot over the past three years.

< 81 >

Titón called to him from down below, probably not wanting to come up because of his old quarrel with Sabá. He looked older, fatter, balder, and he had brought along his wife, the two of them astride a motorcycle. They walked to a restaurant called La Palmera. Titón looked happy with his new wife, who was young and very pretty in pants and a loose blouse. Titón wore a short-sleeved shirt, and they both offered a contrast to his suit, collar, and tie.

He ordered rice in squid ink, avocado salad, and a beer. Titón and his wife ordered fried hake, rice, and avocado salad, which was the only salad they had.

"The Chinese vegetable growers aren't siding with Mao," was Titón's commentary on the absence of lettuce. It surprised him to hear such a mockingly critical comment from a person as orthodox as Titón used to be. But there was more to come. Titón talked the entire time. His wife just laughed, showing her lovely perfect teeth at every joke. She did not say so much as half a word.

Titón spoke in a low voice, but freely and frankly, without apparent concern for the waiters' comings and goings. He described the situation: the persecution of homosexuals, the Cultural Council's imposed orthodoxy, problems at the university. About the university he went on at some length and recounted his personal experience: he and two others from the Film Institute attended one of the trials the Student Federation was holding of supposed counterrevolutionaries on campus. At the "trial" there were two accused, a boy and a girl. The two were on a stage along with their accusers and the judge. The jury was the audience. The boy was charged with behaving strangely – and that could mean many things, from homosexual to "exclusivist," meaning that he wasn't very popular with his classmates. She was

< 82 >

accused of being "exquisite": she dressed too well and had excused herself too many times from the supposedly voluntary labor cutting sugarcane. The audience yelled throughout and even though the accusers demanded explanations, they would not let either of them speak. Finally the accusers announced that the two should be expelled from the university and called for a unanimous vote of the assembly. Immediately after the vote, a voice rose up from the back: "Somebody here didn't vote!" And a tall frightened boy who apparently had not raised his hand was hauled from his chair and pushed onto the stage. They decided to put him on trial too. Disgusted with it all, Titón and his two friends got up to leave. Then a cry rose up from the crowd: "Three counterrevolutionaries are trying to leave the assembly!" A group came at them, closing off their exit route and pushing them toward the stage. Titón and his two companions tried to say they were not students, but members of the Film Institute, mere spectators. At last, onstage, they were able to identify themselves to the president of the assembly, who screamed out to the audience: "*Compañeros*! They are from the ICAIC! These *compañeros* are from the Film Institute." The assembly calmed down and let them leave. As Titón was leaving, the "trial" of the student who had not voted was getting underway.

While he told the story, Titón did not touch his food. His wife ate. He did too, a reprieve from the miserable combination of the quota and Hildelisa's culinary arts.

"What do you make of that?" asked Titón.

"It's very bad," he said.

"That's how things are. When are you leaving?"

"Sunday."

"It's the best thing you could do. Stay away for a while."

< 83 >

He appreciated the advice and knew that Titón, an old Communist sympathizer and one of the star directors of the Film Institute, was not speaking idly, but was truly preoccupied by what was happening.

"And that isn't the worst," Titón said as they walked back to the apartment. "The top student in the school of architecture jumped off the roof of that building near your house, on the corner of G and 25th, after he was accused of being strange and was expelled."

There was a tinge of bitterness in Titón's voice.

"That's how things are," he said again, and he repeated it once more.

They arrived at the building and he said goodbye to Titón and his wife, who happily climbed aboard their motorcycle. He thanked them for the lunch, though he did not add "and for the conversation."

Ana Magdalena arrived on time, but did not want to go into Floridita. That pleased him and they decided to take a stroll through Old Havana. They walked down Obispo and it felt good to be on that beloved street, now emptied of cars and pedestrians. Hardly anyone was about, but his happiness dissipated as soon as he saw that the familiar stores were permanently shuttered or – to his utter astonishment – converted into housing, the old iron curtains pulled down permanently and the little cutout doors now entranceways to the living quarters behind.

They followed Obispo downhill and the poverty hit home. Everything was dust and cobwebs: a place long left inactive. Any store window still visible was empty. Their steps echoed on the sidewalk and for a moment it seemed to him he was in a movie, walking through a ghost town in the Wild West.

Ana Magdalena, as was her wont, barely said a thing and he wondered why she wanted to see him. Finally he asked her.

"Oh, no reason, I just wanted to see you. It's been so long…"

< 84 >

And she fell silent. He thanked her and she thought that was one of his jokes and her face grew serious. They continued downhill, leaving behind the shells of La Moderna Poesía, the Internacional bookstore, Lex publishing house, the Swan bookstore with its Proustian echo, all of them had disappeared.

"This is nice, isn't it?" Ana Magdalena said. He said yes, it was pleasant to walk in Old Havana, but he did not confess he was on the animated streets of his memory, full of people, the bookstores packed with enticing reads.

They reached a corner. As often happened to him, he did not know which, Aguacate and Obispo, or Obispo and Compostela, but here a building had collapsed and the sight gave him a shock. They found other ruins and his momentary astonishment gave way to a feeling of finality, of something coming to a close. He was sorry he had come. It was all Ana Magdalena's idea, and to make things worse he found her less attractive, her youthful allure buried under early wrinkles and her adolescent shyness transformed into a way of life.

They came to City Hall, a building whose beauty seemed to him to compensate for the demolition of Santo Domingo convent nearby and then of the Ambos Mundos café to make way for a strange building that was to be a helicopter terminal, but never saw a single helicopter. This boondoggle of the Batista era was now a warren of bureaucratic offices. They went through Plaza de Armas and across from Segundo Cabo Palace they decided, in silence, to turn up Presidente Zayas Street, which everyone called by its old name, O'Reilly, strangely Irish, like a few other streets in Havana.

Uphill on O'Reilly the impoverishment of Old Havana was more scandalous than on Obispo, perhaps because it had seen fewer repairs. They walked by the former Martí bookstore and the Casa Belga, another bookstore

< 85 >

transformed into a weird housing project. Farther along they ran into Teixidor, who had been an art critic, whose views fell somewhere on the spectrum between localist and anarchist. He had last seen him before leaving for Belgium, when the man was selling a very well preserved edition of *Ulysses*, which he had bought for five devalued pesos, or better put, five pesos emptied of their real value by the Revolution.

Teixidor looked at him with his same old ironic and crafty smile, and observed Ana Magdalena with a mixture of curiosity and latent lust. They shook hands and exchanged a few words. He realized instantly that Teixidor, previously so garrulous, was now opaque and gray. The man was in perfect harmony with his surroundings: Teixidor belonged to Old Havana; the man and the place belonged to each other. They said goodbye and continued on their way.

Back in Albear Park. He knew that small square so well from his teenage years, when he lived just three blocks away and had to come here to get water to carry home early in the morning, before the first students arrived at the Havana Institute, where he studied and across from which he lived in a miserable tenement with his family and their poverty. Hemingway described the square fairly well in passing, but the square belonged to him. He felt that this entire dilapidated corner of the city belonged to him: its aged trees, its statue of the man who built Havana's first aqueduct, its handful of pigeons, and above all its great pool of water in which beggars used to wash more than their faces. And he let Hemingway's ghost slip back into his beloved Floridita, now certainly in ruins. Horace came to mind and his immortal verse, and not for the first time.

Ana Magdalena Paz was leaving. It was late in the afternoon. He felt no sadness at her sudden flight, she always departed like that, rather he felt

< 86 >

disappointment at finding none of the silent beauty he used to see in her, a sort of rare passivity that, in her, was a form of action. He did not say see you later, he said goodbye, and he watched her walk to the corner to wait for the bus that would take years to come.

He crossed Central Park and headed toward San Rafael Street, which still conserved some of its old charm, and noticed a crowd at the bus stop and more people reading something on the trees. He went over and saw there were papers, scraps of paper, pinned to the trunks. Since the readers moved methodically from one tree to another, he joined them and read a notice handwritten by someone evidently not used to writing, who wanted to move to La Víbora and was offering to trade for an apartment in Havana. All of the notices – only one was written on a typewriter – were messages about exchanging homes, the only trade allowed by the government, but the ads gave that corner of the park an air of a Moroccan marketplace, such as he had never seen in Havana. People reading notices mixed with those waiting for the bus, each as poorly dressed as the next, looking nearly destitute. These actions – reading, busing, waiting – were performed in a conspicuous silence. As in the case of Teixidor, the transformation of hubbub into silence made a deep impression on him.

That night for the first time he dreamed about his mother and saw her as he would always see her, fully alive. She was running errands here and there, as if she had never died, and in his dream he behaved much better as a son than he ever had in real life.

The afternoon of the following day, after another lunch of white beans and rice during which he wondered where so many white beans came from, he and his brother, Sabá, went to see Consuelo Montoro, the mother of Adrián García Hernández. She now lived in a modest home at the edge of Miramar,

< 87 >

out where the neighborhood loses its name. Consuelo Montoro was a real character. Years before she had decided not to get out of bed and since then she lived her life between the sheets, served by a loyal maid who fulfilled her every request.

It was intensely hot when they arrived, yet Consuelo was under the covers as if the cold were insufferable. They talked about her only child, whom she had had fairly late in life, and how he was managing in Madrid. Although she loved Adrián dearly, she spoke about him with remarkable detachment, as if he were merely an acquaintance. She wrote him frequently, and more often than not the letters were signed Franz Liszt or George Sand. It seems Adrián's father had left behind a collection of rare and valuable letters, and Consuelo Montoro was sending them to her exiled son one by one, in the guise of personal letters. He could only imagine the surprise of the reader in the Interior Ministry when he opened a missive written on aged paper in faded ink and in a strange language. Adrián received quite a few of those letters from his mother, though one day, long before she died, they stopped arriving. He figured it more likely the Interior Ministry had caught on than that all the letters had been sent.

Now Conseulo Montoro wanted to send Adrián a painting, a Sorolla bought by his father in Spain, which must have been valuable. She wanted either Sabá or him to carry it to Adrián.

"But that's illegal," he said.

"Maybe in the eyes of some officious bureaucrat," said Consuelo, "but the painting belongs to Adrián, it's an inheritance from his father."

"I understand," he said, "but I'm certain the customs officials at the airport won't share your opinion."

"But you're a diplomat. No one will go through your bags."

< 88 >

"You never know," he said.

"So how can I get Adrián his painting? For sure he needs money."

Sabá looked at his brother. "Don't worry, Consuelo, I'll take it."

"No, I'll take it. I'm going back first."

"Okay, Eulalia," Consuelo said to the maid, "take it down."

The portrait, in Sorolla's post-Impressionist style though evidently a study, came off the wall and into his hands, precariously wrapped in a sheet of newspaper.

"Good thing it isn't very large," he said.

"It will fit in your suitcase easily," Consuelo said, as if she knew the dimensions of his suitcase.

They said goodbye and set off, carrying the painting, in search of a bus, while the sun set out of view beyond the beaches.

That night Rine Leal came to the house and later on Oscar Hurtado dropped by. They talked as they had many times at *Lunes*, about everything that was and would be, setting aside the persecution of homosexuals to concentrate on Oscar's favorite subject: other worlds inhabited by intelligent beings. Oscar had read everything there was to read in science fiction and widely in astronomy, and he had a prodigious memory for both the important things and every triviality about life in outer space. He was a fervent admirer of Ray Bradbury, in his opinion the best short story writer alive. Rine Leal, as always, was exclusively interested in theater, but he took part in the conversation about Martians as if it were another form of drama. They chatted until late and after they left, as was now his habit, he stayed a while longer on the balcony gazing at the street and the park in shadows.

In the kitchen he opened the refrigerator to get some water. His grandmother spoke from her room:

< 89 >

"My son, when are you going to bed?"

"Now, Mamá," he said, thinking she must never sleep.

The following day, Saturday, he went to the Foreign Ministry to pick up the passports, and dropped in to see Arnold, seated as ever on his sofa, going through papers.

"What's up?"

"Ah," raising his head from the documents, "what's happening? Come, come in."

"I've come to say goodbye to you and to Dr. Roa."

"Oh, good. But Roa isn't in. He's home resting. He had an accident. A car crash."

"I didn't know."

He did not know anything. He had not read the newspaper, the only one, the official and officialist *Granma*, whose name always made him laugh. Not that he would have known anything even if he had read the paper; rarely did it cover accidents, crimes, or robberies.

"*Muchacho*," Arnold said, "he nearly got killed."

"No."

"Yes indeed, and the driver was killed. Dr. Roa's pretty banged up, but nothing serious."

"Well, now what do I do?"

"Go to his house to say goodbye."

"I don't know where he lives."

Arnold gave him the address.

"So what are my final instructions?"

"The ones Dr. Roa gave you. When was that?"

"Last Saturday."

"Then the ones he gave you last Saturday. Don't worry about that."

< 90 >

"No, I won't worry."

"Did you speak with Montenegro?"

"Yes, some days ago."

They said goodbye, Arnold holding out his hand without rising from his sofa-desk.

From the corner a taxi took him right to Dr. Roa's door. He gave his name to a policeman at the gate, who went inside and returned a moment later.

"Dr. Roa is sleeping," he said. "Come back later, *compañero*."

He walked to Fifth Avenue. It was a beautiful morning, so he continued on to Franqui's house, which was not far, and found him playing in the yard with one of his sons. They shook hands and remained outside. Franqui had a pathological fear of hidden microphones and preferred to have his conversations out in the open. He told Franqui what had happened at the ministry and at Roa's house, and Franqui filled him in on Roa's accident. A truck crossing Fifth Avenue hit his car nearly head-on and people were killed

In the afternoon he went to see Gustavo Arcos to say goodbye. After talking idly for about an hour, he bid farewell to his mother, Doña Rosina, and at the door Gustavo said, "We'll see each other in Italy." Raúl Castro had promised to name him ambassador to Italy and now, due to the death of the current ambassador, the post was open. Arcos had said repeatedly he would take him along as cultural attaché. "No," he had corrected Gustavo, joking, "as cultural adviser."

He thought about going to the cemetery, but did not feel strong enough to face his mother's tomb.

That night there was a goodbye party at his parents' apartment. Nearly all his friends came, those who would accompany him to the airport and those

< 91 >

who would not. They talked late into the night and when he finally got into bed he lay wide awake until the dawn nearly surprised him.

In the morning he went to say goodbye to Carmela, who sent thousands of kisses to her daughter Miriam. The afternoon was spent packing his daughters' clothing and receiving a last-minute visitor, Pipo Carbonell, the third secretary from the embassy in Belgium. Since they had spent two years living in the same embassy, he had wondered why he had heard nothing from Pipo, who always claimed to be his friend. Carbonell seemed depressed and began by excusing himself for not attending either the wake or the funeral of his mother, whom he had met in Belgium. But he noted something else in Carbonell, a harshness to his manner that was new and that he did not like one bit. He did not know what to make of it, and once Carbonell left he felt strangely relieved.

Carlos Franqui and Harold Gramatges came early to pick him and the girls up, before seven PM, although the plane did not leave until ten o'clock. He said farewell to his grandmother, who told him, "Go with God, my son. Take good care of the girls." Then she spoke about never seeing him again, which after all might well have been true. He said goodbye to his father, who would not go to the airport because he did not like farewells, and who quickly made himself scarce. Perhaps he was crying in the bathroom, where no one could see him.

They departed as they had arrived, in Harold's car. On their way to the airport, the sun set behind them and a purple stillness settled over everything, signaling the end of day and the beginning of night.

They went directly to the VIP lounge. It was still closed, so Franqui went to find an employee, who opened it. He would have liked to take a stroll around the airport and perhaps buy some souvenirs for Miriam. But he decided not to, since he was feeling rather nervous.

< 92 >

Bit by bit, the lounge filled up with travelers and the friends who had come to see them off. He saw Eduardo Corona, who brought him some last-minute instructions for the cultural work. He received them knowing full well they were as meaningless as the instructions he had received three years earlier. Martha Frayde came, accompanied by Beba Sifontes. Martha, with an air of great secrecy yet in view of everyone, gave him several letters to mail in Europe. "Here we can't trust they'll ever get delivered," she said, "as you well know." He took the letters, feeling both amused and taken aback, and put them in his inside jacket pocket. Soon a young black woman who Corona introduced as the daughter of the late Aracelio Iglesias, the Communist leader of the stevedores, arrived and joined the group. She was to be the secretary at the embassy in Paris and was very excited, but in reality she was going to a meeting in Samarra, Iraq, and died soon after in a car accident near the Eiffel Tower.

Their bags were gone and must have already been on the airplane since it was quarter to ten – later on, the time would stand out in his memory. At ten o'clock everyone was to board.

At that moment a telephone call came through. Amidst the partylike hubbub in the lounge Corona answered and came in search of Iglesias's daughter. She went to the phone and almost immediately returned to say that it was him they were calling, that it was Arnold Rodríguez.

He went to the telephone thinking Arnold must have wanted to say goodbye once more.

"Yes?"

"Listen," the voice at the other end said, "this is Arnold."

"Yes?"

"Listen, a bombshell! You can't get on the plane. Dr. Roa wants to see you tomorrow at the ministry."

< 93 >

Right then he did not understand, but once it sank in he had a hard time speaking.

"So what do I do?" was all he managed to say.

"Come back to Havana and be at the ministry tomorrow."

He returned to the group and pulled Carlos Franqui aside, who grew very pale when he heard what had happened.

"What do we do now?" he asked Franqui.

"Didn't he say you couldn't get on the plane? So you can't."

"Fine. Do me the favor of getting my luggage. I'm going to tell Harold."

Later on he could not reconstruct how he managed to break away from the group or get his bags. He knew only that they returned to Havana in Harold's car and that somehow he gave Martha Frayde back her letters.

At home, his brother, Sabá, was more surprised than he was but said nothing. He went to the telephone and called Arnold Rodríguez at home.

"Listen," he said, "I'm back home."

"Ah, good," Arnold said, "come to the ministry in the morning."

He hung up and went back to the living room, where Harold and Franqui were chatting with his father. His brother was on the balcony, enjoying the cool air. He joined him, taking the other rocking chair. Inside, Hildelisa was putting the girls to bed.

Franqui and Harold stayed a while longer. When they were leaving, Franqui asked him to let him know how the interview with Roa went the next morning. He said he would.

Sabá asked how it happened, but he was too confused to tell him and said only that they had taken him off the flight. He was more than confused. The long week of absurdity and strangeness seemed unending. It felt like years ago that José had crashed into the truck in Brussels.

"Well, now what?" Sabá asked.

< 94 >

"I don't know. I'll go to the ministry tomorrow to see what Roa wants."

"So when will you leave?"

"I don't know. I tell you, I don't know anything."

"This is serious. They don't take a diplomat off a flight for nothing."

"It's possible that Roa forgot to tell me something important."

"You're being naïve. If he forgot something, he could communicate by diplomatic pouch."

"But he didn't."

"At least you should have sent the girls to Europe."

"You're nuts! Why? They were going with me and they still will."

"Yes, but when?"

"I don't know. Next Sunday maybe, in a few days for sure."

"I don't like this one bit. You should have put the girls on the plane."

"I tell you, I couldn't. The order was absolutely clear. Besides, under what pretext?"

"Any pretext. You could have said that Miriam was expecting them."

"Now you're the naïve one."

"Okay, okay. So, what are you going to do now?"

"For the moment, I'll go to the ministry tomorrow morning. When are you leaving?"

"I don't know, in a couple of weeks. Tomorrow I'll go to the ministry too."

Sabá was referring to the Ministry of Foreign Trade; he was their envoy in Madrid.

"But I don't have any problems," Sabá added.

"Lucky you."

"Well, the important thing is not to despair. For sure it was some bureaucratic mistake."

< 95 >

"Let's hope so."

"You have to go to the ministry tomorrow and find out why they took you off the flight."

"I don't think there's much to find out. It was by order of the minister."

"Sure. You're going to see Roa tomorrow, right?"

"Yes."

"Ask him directly. A revolutionary shouldn't show that sort of disrespect."

"No, certainly not."

"So they owe you an explanation."

He did not feel like talking anymore. He had not even noticed the departure of Niño and Fina, who had followed them from the airport and gone to chat with his grandmother. Now he realized the house was silent, lit only by a lamp at the back where his father was reading today's newspaper or an old one, or an old magazine. He decided to go to bed, though he knew he would not fall asleep for a long while

AFTER A BREAKFAST of milk mixed with water and sugar and a piece of bread, he went to the ministry. Vice Minister Rodríguez gave him a cheery hello from his sofa.

"I'm here to see Roa," he said.

"I don't think you'll be able to do that today, *chico*," Arnold said.

"Why's that?"

"He's very busy. Even I won't try to see him today. The accident messed everything up."

"But he's all right, isn't he?"

"Sure, but he's been away from ministry business for a week."

< 96 >

He was going to ask how he found time to take him off the flight, but he thought better of it.

"So when do you think I can see him?"

"I don't know. Tomorrow or the next day. Come see him tomorrow."

"Fine. I'll come tomorrow."

He started to walk home up Avenue of the Presidents, taking the sidewalk in the shade. At the corner of 17th, he decided to drop in on Gustavo Arcos.

Gustavo knew what had happened the night before.

"It's that bastard Roa," he said, "throwing his weight around. Why didn't you go see him at his house?"

"I did, twice. Besides, I spoke with Arnold."

"He's another piece of shit. But don't worry, we'll go straight to Italy from here, you'll see," he said, and he smiled.

They talked about other things. With an air of mystery, Gustavo opened a cabinet, pulled out a box of cigars, and offered him one. He accepted and said he would smoke it later, after lunch. He glanced through the louvered shutters – they were in Gustavo's bedroom – and saw the green lawn below and the nearly palatial headquarters of the Writers Union. He considered going there, but decided to leave it for another day.

When he arrived home a novelty was awaiting him: instead of rice and beans on the menu there was rice and potatoes, a diet for an ulcer patient. He could only get it down slowly, which made the meal seem interminable. He cursed his bad fortune, and his grandmother said, "Ay, my son, accept your fate," and added, "though you really shouldn't have come. In the end, you didn't fix anything."

Though he had not stopped thinking about his dead mother for one second, deep inside he realized his grandmother was right. He went out on

< 97 >

the balcony with his binoculars, but in the boiling early afternoon no one was about. He gazed at the buildings across the street, the Chibás and the Palace, one gray and green, the other red and white. Nearly all the windows were open, and each was a dark shadow, a black hole under the sun's vertical rays. On his balcony, however, a fresh breeze came directly from the sea only a kilometer away.

In a short while Anita came to ask for her daily heavenly custard. He went with her to El Carmelo and when he paid he realized he had very little money left. The following day he would go to the ministry to see if he could get some of the pay they owed him.

His daughters wanted to watch a movie on television, but the sun pouring in the wide window made it hard to see the screen. He had them get a blanket, which he hung from the door and the window frame. That worked and he sat down with them to watch the film. Soon, he could not stand the heat.

He went to the bathroom, because he felt a torrid burning in his loins. He pulled down his pants and saw that his groin and penis were covered in fungus. He had had this sort of fungus before, but never so widespread. He decided to take a bath and when he took off his clothes he realized he was still wearing the wool undershirt he had put on in Brussels. He had not bathed in almost ten days. Though in Belgium he bathed nearly every day, he had not noticed. He realized this was an indication of how upset he was. When he came out of the bath he felt better. He hung up the suit and put on the casual pants and sport shirt that Miriam Gómez had packed in his attaché case. Feeling much better now, he passed under the blanket curtain onto the balcony.

A tall, strong, and very dark woman crossed the park and entered his building. He found her attractive, nearly savagely so, and he decided to ask

< 98 >

Teresa, who happened to be taking the cool breeze on the next balcony over, who she was. Teresa said her name, adding that she lived in one of the first floor apartments and was the wife of an architect who was studying in Romania. He made a mental note. Then he saw Leonora Soler come out of the building, very well dressed and made up, and head down Avenue of the Presidents. He watched her until she disappeared from view at the corner. She was one of the few people out walking who did not look like a zombie. The brown-skinned woman who lived on the first floor was another, and he figured the zombies must be passers-by.

That night Walterio Carbonell came to visit. He was pleased to see Walterio, a man he had admired ever since going with him to the battle at the Bay of Pigs and watching him walk through a hail of bullets dressed in a yellow pullover and a pair of black suit trousers from the days when he had been a diplomat.

Walterio congratulated him for his discretion.

"You haven't gone out a single night since you arrived," he said. "That's a wise precaution."

He was going to say he had not felt like going out, but he let it go. For sure Walterio had come to visit after hearing what had happened at the airport. He was like that.

"What happened at Rancho Boyeros?" he asked.

"Nothing, Roa just wanted to see me before I left."

"Have you seen him?"

"No."

"Aha!"

"But I'll see him tomorrow."

"Is everything all right then?"

"Yes. Everything is all right."

< 99 >

"That's good. I thought you might have had a run-in with Security."

It was the first time anyone suggested such a thing. He recalled that Magaly, Walterio's girlfriend, worked as a secretary at the ministry.

"Did Magaly tell you something?"

"Magaly? No, why?"

"No, since she works at Minrex."

"We haven't talked about this at all. But if you want, I can ask."

"No, it's not worth it."

He kept thinking about what Walterio had said, since he was often in the know. He had not forgotten how Walterio was aware that Fidel Castro's favorite prize cow had tuberculosis before Castro himself suspected a thing. Walterio had passed him a note to that effect one day when Fidel Castro was giving an impromptu talk at the university.

The next day, getting out of the taxi at the ministry, he saw Magaly, who said hello and told him, "Listen, I heard you're going back to Belgium as head of mission. Why don't you take me along as your secretary?"

He said he would think it over, then said goodbye and went inside. That morning not only was Roa unavailable, but they told him Arnold was busy with a visitor. He decided to wait in the outer office, chatting with his two secretaries, a man and a woman. But since Arnold was taking a long time, he went over to the payroll office to ask about his wages. The last two payments were already in Belgium. If he wanted, he could set it up to get the next as an advance. He thought for a moment and told them to send that to Belgium too. He went back to Vice Minister Rodríguez's outer office, where he waited a while longer and then left.

This time he walked up to 17th and H and went into the headquarters of the Writers Union. In the bar he recognized Juan Blanco at a table with a man and a girl he did not know. He said hello to the sculptor Tomás Oliva

< 100 >

at the bar and went over to Juan Blanco's table. It was always a pleasure to chat with Juan because he had a great sense of humor. Juan introduced his two companions, but as usual he did not catch their names.

"Would you like anything?"

"No, nothing. Hang on, maybe a cup of coffee."

"Okay, you can have anything except that. Coca-Cola, Orange, Materva, Pepsi-Cola?"

That was a joke: those were the names of the sodas from before. In his youth Juan Blanco was passionate about a time-honored soda named Crema de Hierro. That may be how Juan got the nickname Crema de Hierro back in the days when he was a diving champion.

"No, nothing then."

"When are you going?"

Maybe Juan did not know about the incident at the airport. He acted that way in any case.

"That is the sixty-four-thousand-peso question. I truly do not know. Maybe next week."

"Oh, good. I'd like to ask you to bring me some music paper. You probably don't know but here you can't get a single sheet of ruled paper."

"I didn't know. Sure, I can send it to you here at the UNEAC, in the diplomatic pouch from Belgium."

He said "UNEAC" for the National Union of Writers and Artists; he too had begun speaking in acronyms, it was inevitable. Juan Blanco talked a lot but said little and made no jokes. Soon the table fell silent and he decided it was time to go home.

When he drew near his building, he heard a noise that would soon become familiar: a loudspeaker, no, more like a bullhorn, repeating slogans that were unintelligible at first but soon became clearer. A ringing voice was

< IOI >

shouting slogans for young people and advertising a contest to attend the Youth Festival in Algeria. The racket came from the corner of Avenue of the Presidents and 25th Street, just above his building, where a fancy apartment building had been converted into student housing in 1959. Now it was not so fancy: many of the generous windows were broken and the holes covered with cardboard. In many places the peeling paint was plastered with graffiti, cardboard signs, and banners calling on Cuban youth to go to Algeria.

He entered the apartment engulfed in that noise and figured the campaign must have begun that day, or could it be he was just noticing it? The voice continued screaming, urging idealistic students, young workers, Cuban youth of both sexes: the best and brightest will go to Algeria. For a moment it seemed like Algeria was the Promised Land.

He had lunch, then sat on the balcony, disgusted with the food and bothered by the noise, which seemed to grow louder in the heat of the afternoon. When he went in to lie down he saw his daughters were asleep, but even here the roar of the loudspeakers filtered in. He decided to endure the noise on the balcony. In a little while someone knocked.

It was Leonora Soler. She was a woman no longer young, not very tall, blond, and fleshed out, but once she had been quite beautiful, and she still was.

"Good afternoon," she said.

"Come in."

She settled herself into a chair in the living room.

"I came to ask you to let me give my daughters' dolls to your girls. I've still got them."

Her daughters had gone into exile in Miami more than three years ago, when they were very small and there were rumors the revolutionary

< 102 >

government would abolish parental authority and take Spartan-like charge of all the children in Cuba.

"But of course," he said. "Though you don't need to go to the bother."

"It would be a pleasure to give them my daughters' dolls. I love Anita and Carolita."

"Thank you."

His grandmother came out to say hello to Leonora.

"How are you, Ángela?"

"I'm here, my daughter," his grandmother said, "suffering and afflicted."

"You don't feel well?"

"Well, my girl, it's always the same: this rheumatism is killing me."

His grandmother hobbled back to her room and it was obvious how much pain she lived with. In a little while Hildelisa passed by them on her way to the balcony and, smiling, she said hello to Leonora, who departed a few minutes later, before he had much of a chance to speak with her.

Coming back from the balcony, Hildelisa smiled meaningfully and hummed, "I love you, baby, but I sure ain't gonna be your dog."

It was from a Big Bill Broonzy tune he had quoted in one of his books.

"What?" he asked, with a grin.

She laughed and said, "That one wants something."

"Which one?"

"Leonora, who else? She wants something, from you or your brother. I've seen how she looks at both of you."

"You're imagining things."

"Me? She's the one doing the imagining."

"Doesn't she have a husband?"

"Oh yes, a depart-ner, he won't be back." She laughed.

< 103 >

He liked Hildelisa's sense of humor.

"Did he go by himself?"

"Sure did. He went to the United States and took his daughters with him. She's trying to leave too, though it's taking a while, and in the meantime…"

"Do you know anything about her?"

"Is there anybody we don't know about on this island surrounded on all sides by water, and even above when it rains?"

That was another line of his. He was pleased Hildelisa read his books and quoted them with such confidence. But now he was more interested in learning about Leonora Soler.

"Where does she live?"

"Upstairs. Fourth floor."

"So, what do you think?"

"I think Miriam's going to kill you," she said, laughing. She went back into the kitchen. It really was too bad Hildelisa was such a lousy cook.

That night his brother, Sabá, invited him out to the other El Carmelo on Calzada. That long-standing café/store/restaurant was important to him because it was important in his fiction, and this was the first time he would dine there since returning. It used to be a spot for the upper and middle classes; now it was a favorite of many revolutionaries and not a few from the new privileged class. It had lost much of its charm since a redecoration transformed it from an upscale café into a restaurant with astonishingly bourgeois pretensions. It still had a nice terrace, which against all odds remained intact despite the unappealing bluish décor.

They sat down and a waiter soon came by. He was not one of the old ones. They both decided on a steak with salad and a beer.

They tucked in greedily, devouring the tender meat. Then they ordered dessert and coffee.

< 104 >

At the back of the restaurant he spotted one of the waiters from before, older and fatter, but as petulant as ever. Through the restaurant windows he could see, beyond the terrace, the façade of the Auditorium, now needlessly renamed the Amadeo Roldán Theater – needless because everyone still called it the Auditorium.

They finished their coffee and ordered cigars. He felt happy for the first time since coming back. It did him good to eat meat. They asked for the bill and the tab astonished them: each steak cost six pesos, a price the fancy old café never would have dreamed of charging. His brother paid and they decided to sit on the terrace, away from the air conditioning. He wanted more coffee and ordered it from the waiter, who told him he was very sorry but coffee was only for those having a meal. Explaining that he had just eaten there made no difference, and he had to order a soda, the inevitable clear Coca-Cola.

Later on, Oscar Hurtado joined them and soon, to top all the surprises of that evening, so did Jaime Sarusky, just back from Europe. They chatted until late, mostly about astronomy and certain colorful Martians who came down from the sky and left strange signs all over. Close to one o'clock, they walked home up Avenue of the Presidents. Oscar Hurtado accompanied them as far as 23rd Street, where they stopped to talk some more.

In the morning he was awakened early, not by the bullhorn as he had feared, but by a rooster crowing incessantly in the yard directly below. The bullhorn, or rather bullhorns, started up at a considerate nine o'clock and continued incessantly, indefatigably, until six in the afternoon, urging all to enter the competition to send the best and brightest to Algeria.

That morning he decided against going to the ministry, and in the afternoon, once the loudspeakers fell silent, he went down to the street to read on a bench as he used to do long ago. In a little while a stranger

< 105 >

approached him, asked the time, and went to sit on a bench not far away. He raised his eyes from the page at one point and the stranger was watching him. He looked up another time and the stranger still had his eye on him. When it began getting dark, he headed home, guessing that the man had been spying on him. A few days later another stranger came to ask him the time. It happened on several more occasions. Astonished, he asked his friends at a gathering if something was wrong with all the watches in Cuba, or if Soviet watches did not give the time, because strangers in the street were asking him what time it was all too often. The answer came from Antón Arrufat:

"Those are agents from Social Turpitude," he said.

"What?"

"People from the Interior Ministry. They think you look unusual with your European clothes and unfamiliar haircut, and they want to know if you are homosexual or not."

"Really?"

"It's very simple," Arrufat said. "If you hold your hand like this," and he let his wrist go limp and his hand fall languidly, "to look at your watch, you are a homosexual. If you hold your hand like this," and he held his wrist firmly and his fist clenched, "you are a real man."

He laughed.

"But can that really be true?" he asked.

"What do you mean, can it be?" said Virgilio Piñera. "It's scientifically proven. It never fails."

They all laughed, but an unpleasant feeling hung in the air.

He decided to try the ministry once more. Arnold was busy again and he could not see him. Neither could he see Minister Roa, of course. He went to the passport office and asked for a letter so he could shop at the mythi-

< 106 >

cal Diplomercado, which in the popular imagination was overflowing with exquisite meats and other edibles for diplomats and the regime's privileged. They gave him a coupon he would have to take to the Interior Trade Ministry at the Plaza de Armas in Old Havana, an errand he left for the following day.

His daughters were waiting for him at home with their presents, life-sized dolls that talked (one of them) and drank water (a giant baby) and another that walked. They were truly splendid. He wanted to thank Leonora Soler personally, so he climbed up to the fourth floor, rang the bell, and a maid opened the door. He asked for the lady of the house and was ushered in. Leonora came out shortly, elegant in a blue-and-white embroidered house-coat. The maid went into an interior room and he could see that she was ironing. Leonora greeted him warmly.

"May I offer you something?"

Mostly kidding, he asked what she had.

"I've got rum, whisky, and gin."

He was astonished. She must have read his face.

"I guard it jealously for special occasions."

Perhaps she did not want to tell a civil servant of the Revolution that she shopped on the black market, as he suspected. It was impossible for a bottle of whisky to have lasted four, nearly five years now.

"I could make you a mojito," she said. "Without mint," she added.

"A mojito would be great."

"I'll be right back."

He watched her go into the kitchen and on to the room where the maid was ironing, then back into the kitchen. As he watched, the maid unplugged the iron, folded up the ironing board, and put away the clothes. Leonora returned carrying two glasses, one of which she held out to him.

< 107 >

"Your health," she said.

He repeated the toast, mechanically yet timidly, as always happened with him. He drank and found the mojito to be nearly perfect. The only thing missing was the mint.

"It is very good."

"Really?"

"Yes, truly."

They sipped their drinks. His empty stomach and maybe the lack of protein in his diet or maybe the strength of the rum made him feel tipsy almost immediately. They continued drinking and chatting and in a little while he saw the maid leave the apartment carrying her purse. He had the impression she was not headed out on an errand, rather going farther afield.

"What do you make of Havana?" she asked.

"Same as always."

"You don't find it sadder, sort of tamped down?"

He thought she was stepping over the line, perhaps spurred by the alcohol.

"Not particularly. Remember I only left three years ago."

"Yes, but things here change every day, and not for the better."

"Perhaps," he said. "But it seems the same to me."

It was a lie, but he did not feel like telling her she was right; after all, she was a middle-class woman and it was natural she would feel things were changing.

"How do you feel here?" she asked.

"In Havana? Just fine."

She smiled, then laughed.

< 108 >

"I don't mean in Havana, I mean here," and she indicated the surroundings with a movement of her plump but perfect arm.

"Ah," he understood, "great, just great."

"Really?" she asked innocently.

"Yes, really."

He finished his mojito.

"Would you like another?"

"No, thank you," he said. "I haven't had lunch yet."

"Neither have I."

A sudden impulse he would later regret made him get up from the easy chair and sit beside her on the sofa.

"May I?" he asked.

"Yes, of course," she said.

He put his glass on the table and placed his hand on her shoulder. She did not move, did not even look in his direction. He slid his hand toward her neck and began to caress the exposed part of her shoulder. She had very soft skin. She turned toward him smiling. He came closer. Then he took her arms and brought her closer. She let him. He leaned over and kissed her lightly on the lips. She did not return the kiss, but she let him kiss her. He kissed her again, this time seeking out her lips with his own to part them, which she did right away. They kissed. They kissed again, longer. He slid one hand toward the opening in her housecoat and began to caress her breasts. She allowed him to do that, then to slide his hand to her belly and lower down. When she felt that, she stiffened and stood up. He thought she was going to go, or make him go.

"Come," she said, offering her hand.

< 109 >

He got up and holding hands they went into the bedroom. She pulled back the bedspread and began to take off her clothes. She had a round, white, nearly perfect body. She lay down on the bed and when he saw her lying there he tore off his clothes. He lay on top of her and she felt soft and springy.

Leaving later, he took the elevator, pressing the button for the third floor so that it would look like he had come from the street. But stepping out into the hall he found himself face-to-face with Francisca, the woman who came to wash their clothes, coming out of his apartment. She looked at him, her eyes full of surprise, and then, noting his own surprise, gave him a knowing glance. He went into the apartment without even saying hello to her. He felt embarrassed, since he did not want anyone to know where he had been and especially what he had been doing; he felt guilty for having cheated on Miriam Gómez even if she was thousands of kilometers away.

Later on, after the predictable but late lunch prepared by Hildelisa, he decided to put an end to the penury of life in the apartment and he made the trek to the Interior Trade Ministry, located where the American Embassy used to be many years ago. There, a bad-humored bureaucrat, no doubt resentful of those who could shop at the Diplomercado, issued him a slip that would gain him entry to the fabulously provisioned store.

It was in Miramar, and when he arrived he was surprised to see it was less a supermarket than a small grocery. He went in and soon realized that in a contest with the simplest corner store in Belgium the Diplomercado would come out the loser. There were a few things, like onions and plantains, which could not be had in any Havana shop, but besides that there was not much to choose from. He bought both onions and plantains, and a bottle of rum so he could toast his friends when they came to visit. There was no meat or fish or oil or many other things you used to be able to find everywhere. He

< IIO >

paid and walked up to Fifth Avenue to see if he could find a taxi. They were now as scarce as food.

Hildelisa thanked him for the purchases and asked if there had been any oil. He said no. Then, half deafened by the slogans urging Cuban youth to go to Algeria, he went to take a bath. He was pleased to see something that had worried him that morning: the fungus had disappeared as quickly as it had appeared. He would have been very unhappy had he given it to Leonora Soler.

Early that evening he and Sabá went to Carlos Franqui's house. They were still there when his father turned up.

"I just got pickpocketed," he said by way of greeting. "On the bus they stole 150 pesos from me."

That was the money Sabá had given him that very afternoon to help with the household expenses. Both of them were disgusted, but they said nothing.

Once they left, however, they began to badger their father and continued badgering him in the taxi home. "Guillermo, how could you let yourself get robbed like that?" Sabá said.

"Who knows," his father said. "First I was walking and the bus was very full and when I got off the money was gone."

"But it's inconceivable," he said, "that you could just allow that to happen."

"What kind of a shit are you?" his brother said.

"I can't explain –," his father began.

"You never explain yourself," Sabá said.

" – how they could have pickpocketed me."

"It's truly incredible," he said.

< III >

"No, it's not incredible," said Sabá, "it's all too typical."

Old Guillermo cloaked himself in silence to fend off the insults that kept coming. The taxi driver looked straight ahead and seemed immersed in his task.

"It sounds like a lie," he said, "that you would let yourself get robbed like that."

"No," said Sabá, "that's the way Guillermo is, always. When the fuck are you going to learn?"

By the time they got home he realized the insults, which continued for nearly the entire ride, were due, not to the money stolen, but to the mother lost. Both Sabá and he held their father largely responsible for their mother's death. Even if he had taken her to the hospital sooner and insisted on proper attention, he would still have been guilty, since the only reason their mother returned from Spain, where she had been living with Sabá and the girls in Madrid, were the letters old Guillermo sent to her, complaining that he was lonely and missed her and needed her. The two of them, he and Sabá, were convinced that had she stayed in Europe, in Spain or Belgium, their mother would not have died the death she died.

That night he felt an itching on his thigh and scratched. In the morning it hurt and he noticed a red dot, but gave it no more thought. By afternoon the red dot was tender and he feared it was a boil coming on, as had happened once before he moved to Belgium. That night he was certain of it, since it hurt so much he could not put on his pants. Oscar Hurtado suggested he go to Calixto García Hospital to see his friend Helio Cruz, who was a nurse in the emergency room. The following morning the pain was extreme, so he took Oscar's advice and found Helio Cruz, whom he knew slightly. With great deference, Helio took him to see the physician in charge of Skin and

< 112 >

Syphilis. The doctor diagnosed a boil and prescribed saltwater compresses and as little walking as possible, since the boil was on the main thigh muscle.

He went home limping, put on an old pair of shorts and sat on the balcony with his leg stretched out on a chair. In the afternoon he spoke by telephone with Ingrid González and when she asked him out, he told her about the boil. She thought it was an excuse, but he assured her it was true and said that if she liked she could come see him at home.

Ingrid turned up in the late afternoon with a gift: a pair of slippers that some tourist of communism had given her. He thanked her, since he looked grotesque dressed in shorts and the dress shoes he had brought from Brussels. He had not seen Ingrid except for a brief moment at the wake and he found her prettier than ever and so very young, as if the three years since they had last seen each other had not passed. Ingrid remained with him until night fell.

He ate Hildelisa's food, now slightly less unappetizing thanks to the onion, went to bed early and read until late. Several of his friends had telephoned wanting to drop by, but he said he did not feel well. In reality, the boil hurt and it was a bother to put on warm compresses every fifteen minutes with people there.

The following day the rooster awakened him earlier than usual. The boil was still red and was expanding outward, and at the same time pressing in; he could feel it perforating the thigh muscle. There was no way he could go to the ministry that morning, so he put it off to the following day.

Seated on the balcony, reading and regularly applying the warm salt compresses, he saw Leonora Soler cross the street. It had been days since he last saw her and now watching her peculiar gait (she swung her hips though her behind was small), he thought he would like to go to bed with her once more.

< 113 >

That afternoon Ingrid returned, prettier than the day before despite the fact that she still wore no makeup. Today she had on a low-cut dress which offered more than a glimpse of her large breasts. They chatted about nothing at all for a while and during that time he forgot all about the pain in his leg. He had never been a friend of Ingrid's, despite the fact that she had gone to theater school with Miriam Gómez and had married Rine Leal. Still, there was a current of complicity between them, because in the past she had been the go-between for him to communicate with another classmate with whom he wanted to have a fling. Nothing much came of it, but after that he always looked favorably on Ingrid. That said, he never wanted to sleep with her, perhaps out of respect for Rine or Miriam, who for many reasons never would have forgiven him.

He saw his grandmother's face when Ingrid gave him a goodbye kiss a little too close to his mouth: it was obvious old Ángela did not approve.

"What a girl!" his grandmother said once she had left. "She is a vamp!"

"Why do you say that, Mamá?" he asked, hoping that kidding around would take his mind off the boil.

"You ask why? Am I not looking at her? That girl is an utter vamp. Nobody respects married men anymore."

"That happened in your day too."

"It did, but in my day you didn't see anything like that."

"Oh, Ángela," Hildelisa scolded, coming out of the kitchen, "those were other times. Today people are modern."

"Don't give me any of that modern stuff."

"We live better now," Hildelisa said.

"We used to," his grandmother said meaningfully.

"Well, that's true," Hildelisa said. "We used to."

< 114 >

"Well," he piped in, joking, "stop making the counterrevolution or I'll tell the president of the committee."

Hildelisa let out a laugh and returned to the kitchen. Old Ángela retreated to her bedroom behind the kitchen. He went back to his book. Then he took up his binoculars and saw that the woman walking home from the corner of the Riviera Cinema was indeed Leonora Soler. He tried to stand up, but his leg was asleep and the boil hurt. He wanted to see her and maybe say hello, though he would never commit the indiscretion of going any farther. But she crossed the avenue and entered the building without looking up at the balcony. It occurred to him that Leonora might feel ashamed of their encounter and he returned to his reading.

That night Oscar Hurtado came by and they talked about interplanetary voyages and the possibility of finding intelligent beings on Mars or maybe another planet in the solar system. Sabá joined the conversation when it returned from outer space to earth and Oscar spoke of possible visits from extraterrestrials in millenary times, as described in the Bible and other ancient texts. Oscar left at eleven and by twelve he was in bed, having first spent a few minutes on the balcony chatting with Héctor Pedreira. From his own balcony, Héctor had been listening to their conversation in silence, and when Oscar left they talked about the movies. Héctor, though he was a longtime Communist, was sorry American films were no longer shown in Cuba. They were in the middle of that conversation when his grandmother called from her room that it was midnight and the dew was going to harm his leg.

The boil lasted a week and a half. During that time Carlos Franqui called to say he was heading to the Isle of Pines for a vacation and he should keep him posted on when he was leaving Cuba. After that he felt lonelier, since

< 115 >

Franqui was one of the people he was counting on to get him out of the impasse he was in. (In his overwrought state, by now he had convinced himself that the order not to go to Brussels came, not fifteen minutes before boarding, but after he was already on the plane.) Miriam Gómez also called, and although it did him a lot of good to hear her beloved voice, he felt bad because he had no news about when he could leave for Belgium. Meanwhile, every day or nearly every day, he received a visit from Ingrid, who took better care of his health than his real friends did, though many continued coming over, especially Oscar Hurtado and Arrufat, who never missed an opportunity to visit.

After ten days he returned to the hospital. The doctor squeezed the boil until an ugly pus came out, and though it hurt a lot the deep pain ceased after that. Helio Cruz, the nurse, bandaged it carefully so it would not scab over without healing. He was told to return to the hospital every day.

Although still limping, he felt better, and despite the loudspeakers bellowing so aggressively you could hear them inside the Skin and Syphilis Department, he walked home in the best of spirits. Crossing the park he ran into Horacio, that is, Fernández Vila. Horacio had been his alias during his time underground and everyone still called him by that prestigious moniker instead of his real name. Like everyone in the right wing of the July 26th Movement, Horacio had suffered persecution, but he put his time in the doghouse to excellent use and finished medical school. Now still without a job in the revolutionary government, he said he was thinking of going to Vietnam as a medical volunteer. A few to Africa, others to Vietnam, these disgraced revolutionaries were hoping to become heroes in faraway places or martyrs in strange lands: anything to escape the ostracism they faced in Cuba.

< 116 >

During that week and a half, Alberto Mora came to visit several times. He was another political pariah, not from the right wing of the July 26th Movement but from the leftists around Che Guevara. In the same way that Guevara was mysteriously removed from the Industry Ministry and the country, Alberto, who was too closely associated with Che's politics to survive Che's disgrace, had been fired from the Ministry of Foreign Trade. In his place they named Marcelo Fernández, formerly part of the right wing of the July 26th Movement (along with Fernández Vila and others), who overcame his ostracism by declaring himself to be a Marxist-Leninist and publishing an anti-Che polemic about the monetary policy the Revolution should adopt. Che had argued for an independent policy, while Marcelo Fernández, then president of the National Bank, had sided with the Soviet position. No need to say which of them won the argument, or which lost in the world of politics – which does not always coincide with the world of reality.

He was pleased to see Alberto Mora, not only because they had been friends for years (a friendship cemented by the time Alberto spent hiding in his house when he was underground during Batista's rule) but also because he felt real affection for him. Besides, with Alberto you could talk about four things at once and have more than a simple political conversation. Alberto poked fun at his leg (his jokes always had an edge of hostility, a crustiness that he liked and disliked at the same time) and at the prospect of him taking up his diplomatic post in Brussels on one leg. Toward the end he said reluctantly:

"I've come to say goodbye."

"What do you mean?"

Alberto repeated himself in a louder voice, thinking the bullhorns had drowned him out.

< 117 >

"I've come to say goodbye."

"Where are you going?"

"To Oriente. I'm going to be in charge of a pilot sugar refinery that will be the most modern in Cuba."

"Really? Well, good for you."

He was pleased because it bothered him to see Alberto unemployed.

"We'll see."

"How long will you be out there?"

"I don't know. A week or six months. In truth, I don't know. I'm going to check out the land where the refinery will be built."

"When does construction begin?"

"Apparently right away. I think the plans are complete and the Soviet technicians are already on site."

"Well then, I probably won't see you."

"Probably not," Alberto said, and smiled his lopsided smile. "If that's the case, I'll see you in Europe."

"See you then."

"Okay. Bye-bye, Ángela."

And the old woman responded from her little room:

"Go well, my son."

"Thank you."

A little before lunch Sabá came back from his ministry. He wore a very serious expression.

"Bad news," he said.

"What?"

"Hang on, let me sit down, since the elevator wasn't working I had to take the stairs."

< 118 >

His brother, who had a congenital heart problem, was breathing with difficulty and was pale from the climb. Besides, he was furious.

"I'm not going back to Spain."

"*What?*"

"I'm not going back to Spain. The ministry has decided."

"So…"

"Nothing, I'm trapped here."

On that day, precisely at that moment, he began to see that his obligatory stay in Havana was more than a simple bureaucratic delay. He recalled Walterio Carbonell's question about a run-in with Security.

"Who told you?"

"The vice minister called me in and said that for some time they had been thinking of bringing me back, and now that I was here they would take advantage of the opportunity."

"He told you just like that?"

"More or less in those words; it doesn't matter if it was a little different. The important thing is they're keeping me here."

"You know how it is," he responded with the empty phrase his uncle Niño used whenever something serious or unexpected occurred.

"I don't know what made me come here," Sabá said. "You should have warned me on the phone and not let me. When you had problems with the ministry, I managed to send you a telegram warning you not to come."

Sabá was referring to a minor intrigue sparked by the former chargé d'affaires in Brussels, Suárez, who submitted a report on him in which he claimed to have heard that he had gone to Belgium to write a book. That was enough for the ministry to send for him in June of 1963. He was only able to stay on in Belgium because the ambassador, Arcos, intervened. That

< 119 >

was before Arcos went to the hospital near Prague to seek treatment for the wound he received in the attack on the Moncada Barracks in 1953. The new chargé d'affaires in Arcos's absence, Juan José Díaz del Real, it turned out, knew neither English nor French, and thus had great need of him, something he realized in the first few days they spent together at the embassy. His later work so overshadowed the intrigue that the ministry named him interim chargé d'affaires when Arcos returned to Havana on vacation. But during those difficult days in 1963 he had received a strange telegram from Sabá:

HEARD YOU'RE COMING BACK STOP FOLLOW DOCTOR'S ADVICE AND THINK BEFORE COMING FOR OPERATION.

He understood it was code telling him to think hard before coming because serious things were happening in Cuba. In a few days Minrex ordered him to return to "situate yourself in your new destiny," as the official cable put it.

"But how was I to know," he said, "that you were going to have problems in the ministry?"

"No, I have no problems. This is related to you being taken off the flight, I'm certain of it."

"Oh, how could that be…?"

"I don't know how it could be, but for sure, for sure, the two things are related."

"What connection is there between Minrex and your ministry?"

"That's what I'd like to know," Sabá said.

"Did you have some problem in Madrid?"

"None."

"Are you sure?"

< 120 >

"Well, just small talk by bullshitters."

"Those are the ones they pay the most attention to."

"Well, if that's the case, too bad for them. I only know that I worked like a mule in Madrid and I was good at it."

"Me too, and look at what it got me."

Sabá fell silent for a moment, then exclaimed, "Damn it all! We're trapped."

Curiously, until that moment he had not thought of himself as being trapped, but just before his brother uttered the words, it dawned on him that a conspiracy had been organized against him, possibly affecting Sabá indirectly.

The reason ministries so dissimilar in their operations might agree on keeping the two brothers in Cuba would be the opportunity provided by a single incident: the death of their mother and their return for the funeral. In Sabá's case it was more evidently unjust, he thought, since he had not even arrived in time. He decided to go to the ministry that very afternoon, then thought it better to leave it for the following day. Perhaps, unconsciously, he feared facing the truth.

The next day he saw Arnold, but it was the same as not seeing him; he could not find out when Roa would receive him. Someone in the ministry, or perhaps Gustavo Arcos, suggested he visit the Belgian chargé d'affaires, or maybe he thought of it himself. He called to ask for an appointment, which they gave him for the following day, and he felt better. At least it was something to do and he supposed it fell within his diplomatic duties.

He returned home and to occupy himself he decided to go through his papers. He found old notes, photographs, and a roll of 16mm film he could not recall. He took it to the light of the window and saw a woman with a

< 121 >

splendid body in a bikini running on a beach. It took him a while to realize the woman was Miriam Gómez, and to remember that Orlandito Jiménez had shot the film for the *Lunes* television program. Now he recalled how they went to Santa María del Mar and how enthusiastic he was about that bit of film, which was used in the dramatization of his short story "April Is the Cruelest Month." The idea was for Miriam to run toward the sea, and given how few resources they had – just a camera and a few rolls of film – they would imitate a dolly by having Orlandito hold the camera in his hand and run after her. So he would not ruin his clothes, Orlandito stripped to his underwear. He recalled how he and Raúl Palazuelos grinned while Orlandito ran after Miriam in a scene that must have looked like an imminent rape. He smiled nostalgically now, remembering a past when his only concern was to make good cinema, undoubtedly influenced by Hollywood or Paris, and to use the TV program as a pretext to make movies.

He looked again at the nearly perfect figure of his wife and decided to cut two or three frames from the film to carry with him. He looked for a pair of scissors, cut them out, and stuck them in the pocket of his shirt.

He continued burrowing, now in his mother's bedroom, and found a mysterious pair of sneakers and a box that contained three balls. Then he remembered the sneakers were a present Juan José Díaz del Real (the first secretary in the embassy in Belgium) had sent with his mother to give to a friend. Zoila must have forgotten to deliver them and then her death consigned them here. He decided to make the present his own, since the sneakers would be just right for walking, and all he had were the Belgian dress shoes. He called his daughters over and gave them the balls. They shouted, "Wow, Papi!" and ran off to find their friends.

< 122 >

He was pleased to find an extra needle for Anita's portable record player. He got the player out and inserted the cartridge. Now it should work just fine. Hildelisa said his daughters were at Enriqueta's, a friend of Anita's who lived in the Palace building. He called and told Anita he had a surprise for her and Carolita. Almost in the same moment, he saw them running across the gardens on the avenue under the implacable rays of the noonday sun. They burst in, slamming the door, and when he showed them the surprise, Carolita let out an exclamation that would pain him for a long time. "Oh," she said, "I thought Grandma was back from the hospital." He gave no response and put on a record, but nothing happened. He did not understand, the cartridge was intact, as was the record player. Anita explained:

"Oh, Papi," she said, "it doesn't have any batteries."

He opened the record player and saw that indeed it had no batteries: the new cartridge was useless, since batteries could not be found anywhere in Cuba. His daughters headed back to their friend's house, where apparently they were having more fun than at home.

He sat on the balcony and watched them reenter the Palace under the brutal sun, accompanied by the thundering loudspeakers, endlessly repeating slogans about Algeria. He did not feel like reading and, since there was nothing to look at in the sun-drenched streets, he aimed the binoculars at the ocean horizon. Looking north he located the antennas of the ship that always sat there. Some said it was an American spy vessel plying the coast of Havana. Others swore it was a Soviet ship. No one said it was a Cuban ship for there were no such Cuban ships. He focused on the nearby buildings and saw that nearly all the Venetian blinds were down or the windows closed. He missed Ingrid's daily visits; she had stopped coming once his boil was cured.

< 123 >

To escape the loudspeakers he decided to walk over to the Writers Union, hoping to get confirmation of the rumor that Fidel Castro had publicly insulted Nicolás Guillén at the university. The story was that he had praised Alejo Carpentier's novel *Explosion in a Cathedral* to a group of students, and when someone asked about Guillén, Castro said:

"That guy is a lazy bum! He writes a little poem every fifty years and no one can get him to do any more work."

At the Writers Union, he asked for Guillén and they pointed to the back. From afar he spied his small round figure and the gray ponytail. Guillén greeted him heartily, hugging him.

"Listen," he said, "I'm so sorry about your mother. I was not at the wake because, what a coincidence, I was in Camagüey, at my mother's funeral."

"I'm so sorry."

"She was very old, but your mother was young, much younger than I am."

"Yes," he said, and left it at that.

"Would you like a drink? A coffee maybe? We've got coffee now."

"No, thanks. I just came to see you because I heard what happened at the university."

Guillén made a face.

"Come," he said, and he dragged him out to the garden. He stopped under a mango tree in the middle of the yard and looked all around. Then, pointing at the fruitless tree as if showing it off, he said:

"Imagine. That so-and-so" – he was surprised Guillén would even use that term – "went to harangue a bunch of students to get them riled up against me. It's really serious, tomorrow he might do it to you, or to anybody."

< 124 >

Guillén's tone astonished him, and not only because Guillén was an old and celebrated Communist poet decorated by the Revolution.

"He goes and harangues a bunch of kids who don't know anything from anything and then they turn up under my window practically asking for my head. That guy is worse than Stalin! At least Stalin's dead, but this one's going to live another fifty years and he'll bury us all. Every one of us!"

In his diatribe Guillén forgot all about the pretext of the tree, as he explained to his astounded companion the latest twist in the practices of the Communist religion. It was indeed unbelievable, unless you heard it with your own ears: Here was Nicolás Guillén, who had sung Stalin's praises, who had asked Xangó and Yamayá and all the Afro-Cuban gods to protect him, not only speaking ill of Stalin, but also dumping on Fidel Castro. The rumors of the impromptu meeting at the university were more than true.

Guillén fell silent and looked over his shoulder. He turned less discreetly and caught sight of César Leante crossing the room inside. Guillén, who was president of the Union of Writers and Artists of Cuba, then took him by the arm and guided him deeper into the yard, pretending to give him a tour of the garden, which in another epoch, before the Revolution, had belonged to one of the richest families in Cuba.

When he got home in the late afternoon, feeling good in his new sneakers, he found Ingrid waiting for him.

THE BELGIAN EMBASSY was a mansion beside three vine-covered palm trees in Miramar. The house was spacious and dark, and the conversation with the Belgian chargé d'affaires correct and unambiguous, even if they spoke only in generalities. He had gone hoping to learn something interesting he

< 125 >

could then relate to Arnold Rodríguez and maybe to Rogelio Montenegro, just to feel like he still belonged to the diplomatic corps, and here he was chatting about nothing as if he were at some reception. Once again he felt the same repulsion for the diplomatic service he had felt so often in Belgium. Yet it was his only card to play, his only escape route. He returned to Vedado early, wondering whether to go to the ministry, and in the end decided not to.

When he took Anita to El Carmelo to buy her her ritual heavenly custard, he saw Marcelo Fernández, who was now the minister of foreign trade, coming in. He wondered if he should say hello and ask in passing about Sabá's being retained in Havana, but instead he left by the side door that led to the Riviera Cinema.

For three days he had known his money was nearly gone. Now he decided to go to Carmela's house to ask Miriam Gómez's sister Nena for a loan. Carmela greeted him as happily as ever and he realized three weeks had gone by without him either calling or visiting. She made him coffee, which he savored with nearly voluptuous pleasure. Carmela wanted him to take some ground coffee home, but he refused: it was enough to come asking for money, never mind taking goods that surely must have been hard to obtain. *"Muchacho,* it was a cinch," Carmela said. "Buying on the black market is the easiest thing in the world. What's really impossible now is being a revolutionary." After nearly an hour of beating around the bush, he got to the point. She said she would tell Nena when she got home that night, but in principle she did not think there would be a problem.

Late in the afternoon he received a call from Carlos Franqui, who was back from the Isle of Pines. Who knows why, but he felt better, more supported. Carlos told him he was very tired but that perhaps tomorrow they could see each other.

< 126 >

Early that evening he saw Luis Agüero and they talked literature. Luis was very enthusiastic about an issue of *Gaceta de Cuba* he had just put to bed. It would get him into a lot of trouble, among other reasons because an article introducing several young composers parodied a popular women's radio program from before the Revolution called "The Novel on Air": much too much fun for the Soviet dourness of the Writers Union. When it was time for Luis to go, he walked with him up to the 19th Street bus stop, where he saw a very elegantly dressed young woman. He spoke to her and she answered. The words were inconsequential, but sufficient to initiate a dialogue. Luis moved off to wait in the doorway of a house and he continued chatting with the girl. Though their incipient friendship had barely begun when the bus came, he told her not to get on, and somehow she went along. The moment reminded him a lot of the beginning of a relationship that had been very important in his life almost ten years earlier.

Luis said goodbye and climbed aboard, and he suggested to the girl they take a walk up the avenue. She nodded.

"What's your name?"

"Aurora, Aurora Iniesta," she said. She asked his name and he told her. They walked along the darkened avenue and sat down on one of the benches near 17th Street. After talking about the night and the bus stop he wanted to know what she did.

"I work with puppets."

"With the Camejo Brothers?"

"Yes, do you know them?"

He never could recall when she began to use the familiar *tú*. He had done so right away.

"Yes, of course. For years. What are they doing now?"

< 127 >

"Lots. *Sleeping Beauty*, *Snow White*, and several Soviet shows."

"Aren't they doing *The Love of Don Perlimplín and Belisa in the Garden*?"

"No, not that one."

"Why not?"

"It's got too many dirty parts."

"Lorca's play?"

"Yes, that's the one."

"That's unbelievable! Lorca's play has too many dirty parts!"

"Yes, it's not fit for children."

When they first sat down, he had noticed several people on other benches and assumed they were couples taking advantage of the darkness. Now he could see the figures were moving from one bench to another and all of them were men. One came to stand nearly in front of them and stared at them shamelessly. Even though they were only chatting, he fell silent. Then the man joined them on their bench and continued his stare. He was a black man, quite young, with a rather disagreeable face.

"Why don't we go somewhere else?" she suggested.

"Yes, whenever you're ready."

"Now."

He was about to say something, ask the man what he wanted, but he decided it would be better not to: if it ended in a fight, he would likely lose, since the fellow had a group of friends on another bench.

"Let's go, please."

She got up and he got up with her. When they were a safe distance away, he glanced back and it looked like their visitor was masturbating. He did not say anything to her, but when he recounted the incident to his friends, they explained that that part of the avenue had become known as a place

< 128 >

for homosexuals to meet. But he was certain the man was not a homosexual. The more he searched for an explanation, the stranger the incident seemed.

Now he and the girl were walking up 23rd to 12th Street. Soon he realized they were on the curve of 23rd, near the old quarry known as the Hole. That part of Vedado was not far from where Miriam Gómez lived when he first met her, and the streets around the Hole held a particular charm for him. He put his arm around Aurora and she let him do it. On the corner of 23rd and 22nd, where a ceiba tree marked the end of the street at the edge of the Hole, he stopped and so did she. She turned to look at him and he took advantage of the moment to kiss her. She let herself be kissed, but did not return the kiss. She kissed with her lips closed and there was an intimate resistance that he found intriguing. He kissed her again, and again she did not refuse, but neither did she collaborate. He caressed one breast, his hand on her clothing, and found her body inert; if she was responding at all it was to hold him off. Suddenly it occurred to him that one of Miriam's relatives who lived around there might see him. But then he thought it was pretty late to run into one of them.

He looked into her eyes.

"What are you doing tomorrow?"

"Tomorrow? Nothing in particular. Why?"

"I mean, you aren't working with the puppets?"

"No, not now. They're getting ready for a new production and I'm not part of the shows on now."

"Could I see you tomorrow?"

"Yes, sure."

"Good. Where shall we meet?"

< 129 >

"You tell me."

"Well, look, there's a movie on at the Cinemateca. They're showing *King Kong* and I'd like to see it. Why don't we meet at the entrance, say at eight o'clock?"

"That's fine."

"Will you come?"

"Yes."

"Are you sure?"

"Yes, of course."

He found her responses as cold as her kisses and he did not know what to do. He looked at her. She was not good looking, but there was a certain appeal in her features and she had pretty black hair in a short ponytail.

"Okay, we'll see you tomorrow."

"But aren't you going to walk me to the bus stop?"

"Yes, of course. Let's go to the corner of 26th."

They walked through the empty neighborhood toward 26th Street. The bus – perhaps the last one before the infrequent late night service began – did not take long to arrive. As she got on he got a peek at her long, shapely legs.

In the morning, instead of going to the ministry he went to Carmela's house. The hundred pesos he had asked for were waiting for him. He went straight to the Diplomercado to see if he could buy meat or fish or something else for a good meal, despite Hildelisa.

The store had the same Bulgarian canned goods and the same onions and potatoes; there was neither meat nor fish. He left with more potatoes and onions, feeling rather angry. On the corner he ran into Enrique Rodríguez Loeches and his wife, Teresa, who were headed for the Diplomercado.

"Enrique, how's it going? Teresa."

< 130 >

"Eh, what's up with you?"

"How long have you been here?"

"I got in three days ago. You're still here?"

"So it seems."

"When can we see each other?"

"Whenever you like."

"Give me your number and I'll call you."

He gave him his telephone number. He felt affection for Enrique, whom he had known since the days when Roa was director of culture in the ministry then run by Sánchez-Arango, when Prío Socarrás was president. Enrique worked in the ministry's culture section. His wife, Teresa, he had known since high school. He also sympathized with Teresa's unbridled hypochondria: she saw microbes and illness everywhere she looked. He recalled their brief stay in Belgium, on vacation from Enrique's posting in Morocco, and how much he and Miriam had laughed at Teresa's obsessions; he was especially happy to have found someone more hypochondriac than himself. Now Enrique and Teresa trotted eagerly across First Street on their way to discover that potatoes and onions were the only godsend in the promised land of food.

When he arrived home, the key to the street door went in easily, which made him suppose he would find good news upstairs. He was beginning to let his superstitions take over and this bit about opening the door with the right key was a recent one, positive compared to the negative one about seeing dead birds.

But there was no news other than that Oscar Hurtado had called and wanted him to call back. Oscar and his wife, Miriam Acevedo, invited him to their house for dinner the following midday. An invitation for dinner, not supper: well, that was good news.

< 131 >

In the afternoon he called Carlos Franqui, who urgently wanted to see him that night. What time? Damn it all, it was the same time as he was to meet Aurora at the movies. He told Franqui yes because maybe he had information about his return to Brussels or some other important business. He thought he would stop by the cinema at eight o'clock and tell Aurora to wait for him there, that he would be back by ten thirty, before the film was over.

That's what he did. But at eight he could not see Aurora at the entrance. It had taken him a good half hour to find a taxi (he had left his house at seven thirty for that reason) and now the driver did not want to wait. He looked quickly at all the people going in, but no Aurora. What's more, they were not showing *King Kong* that night, but another film, a Czech one. He went back to the taxi and gave the driver Franqui's address.

When he arrived Franqui had just finished eating. They went up to the second floor, where Franqui kept his books and his record player and records and they put on some music. Franqui had no message to give him, but that only became clear as the night wore on. In his typically evasive style, Franqui wanted to know how things had gone for him, what Roa had told him (if he had seen him: he said he had not), what people in the ministry knew (they knew nothing as far as he could tell), what his opinion was of everything, and that took them to ten o'clock. If Franqui had an opinion about what was happening to him, he kept it to himself. Franqui wanted an overview of the many elements that had led to his being taken off the plane (which is how his friends viewed the incident at the airport) and combine them with what had happened since, which was, as he told him, nothing at all. He spoke of the brief conversations with Arnold, but Franqui did not want to hear anything about Arnold, though Arnold had once been a friend he protected. Franqui explained that Arnold had done something that defined him as an utter shit:

< 132 >

he had baldly asked the presidential secretary Celia Sánchez for permission to visit Enrique Oltuski on the Isle of Pines, where he had been sent for supposed insubordination against Fidel Castro. (Certain pilot farms Fidel Castro was supervising personally had very low yields and Oltuski communicated that fact to Fidel Castro, who, like all tyrants, punished the messenger for the message; thus Oltuski came to spend several months on the Isle of Pines as punishment. In reality Oltuski, who was minister of communications right after Fidel Castro first took power, was considered one of Che Guevara's men and his disgrace came from that association, which hardened after Oltuski was removed from his cabinet position. Only Franqui's protest kept him from spending his sentence working the land alongside other imprisoned counterrevolutionaries.) By asking Celia Sánchez for permission, rather than simply visiting him, Arnold demonstrated so little personal bravery that it was nearly impossible to imagine that in the days of the struggle against Batista he had been a daring saboteur.

Instead of heeding the words Franqui spoke so freely, without his usual concern about microphones in his home, he kept looking at his watch and noticing that the evening was disappearing. At last he was able to leave, and after a long wait at the darkened corner of Fifth Avenue (Havana had once again become a city wrapped in shadows), he found a taxi that left him off at 12th and 23rd, two steps from the cinema. But the lights were out and no one about looked anything like Aurora. He went as far as Fraga and Vázquez, and to the coffee shop across the street, then back to the larger coffeehouse at 12th and 23rd, where he found people he knew at several tables, but none of them was Aurora. He was cursing his luck when Héctor García came over to say hello in his suave way. Héctor, along with Titón, was practically the only person from the Film Institute he was on good terms with.

< 133 >

"What's up?" Héctor said casually.

"Hi, how are you?"

"Very well. *Viejo*, I'm sorry I couldn't make your mother's wake or funeral, but I was sick."

"It doesn't matter."

"How are you?"

"Fine, fine."

"When are you leaving?"

"I don't know yet. Maybe at the end of the month. I don't know."

"I got your message."

He was referring to an invitation from the Belgian Film Center to visit Brussels, transmitted through the Foreign Ministry.

"Okay," he said.

"Yes, but I couldn't go. Thank you in any case."

"What happened to *King Kong*? Wasn't it on the program for tonight?"

"It was, but Alfredo changed his mind." Alfredo Guevara (no possible relation to Che Guevara) was director of the Film Institute, the monopoly that controlled every aspect of cinema in Cuba, from a little roll of film for a box camera to feature screenings. "Imagine this: he told me there were too many American films on the program."

This exchange was brave on Héctor's part, complaining about his boss in public so close to the Film Institute, where he could easily be overheard. He was astonished that the relaxed and mannered Héctor García would show so much more courage than the supposed tough guy Arnold Rodríguez, but such are the contradictions of socialism.

"Well, I'll see you later."

"Aren't you going to stay?"

"No, thanks."

< 134 >

"Come by the Cinemateca some time during the day."

"Sure, I'll see."

He walked one final time by the entrance to the old Atlantic Cinema, now the Cinemateca, and saw no one because the darkness was nearly complete. He continued home.

When he arrived – "Is it you, my son?" his grandmother called from her room – he went to the balcony and sat for a while before going to bed. Héctor Pedreira was on the neighboring balcony taking in the cool air. He told Héctor the story of his evening and Héctor made his diagnosis:

"You never think things through. You went to see Franqui for his usual blah-blah. Why didn't you leave that for another day?"

"I wasn't thinking."

"You've got to think these things through."

"Evidently."

"And you don't have her address or phone number?"

"Nothing. I only know her name and that she works with the Camejos and their puppets."

"You could go there."

"That's a lot of bother."

"But won't it be worth it?"

"Yes, it would be worth it. At least what I saw the other night makes me think so."

"Then go there tomorrow."

"I'll think about it."

"Don't think about it, because you won't do it. Just go there tomorrow. Look," and he glanced back into his house and lowered his voice, "the same thing happened to me a while back and later I regretted it."

"I'll see. Maybe I'll go to the puppet place tomorrow."

< 135 >

Shortly after, he said goodnight to Héctor and went to bed. At five in the morning, the rooster woke him, then it quieted down and he was able to fall back asleep until nine thirty, when the loudspeakers resumed, still urging exemplary youth to head off to Algeria.

He had never been to Oscar Hurtado and Miriam Acevedo's apartment on the eighth floor of the Capi building, with its ocean view. He and Oscar spent some time gazing at the sea through Oscar's binoculars. Oscar told him he had seen an enormous stain on the sea one day: not Martians, but a gigantic floating ray. But today there was no ray or stain, just an infinite number of identical waves.

Lunch was fried hake, the fish that everyone in Cuba used to eat: socialism had wrought equality in food and dress and, as far as he could see, in the way people walked. But it was delicious, well prepared by Miriam and Oscar's cook. She had a surprise for dessert: cheese. It was homemade, a crumbly cottage cheese, but it tasted like the best Cuban cheese "from before," as the cook put it. She made it by collecting cream from her own milk quota, since she had several children under seven. (Oscar and Miriam did not get a milk quota.) Using some gauze and a bit of bicarbonate, he guessed, she had turned the cream into a curd, which they were now eating with a delight that made the cook proud. He wished Hildelisa would apply her genius less to jokes and more to food. Oscar and Miriam laughed when he said so, but it was the truth.

He had had a good time and now was headed home, walking under the young royal poincianas along 13th Street, the sidewalk under his sneakers, the brilliant summer day overhead, and the freshness of the trees all around him. He felt a great peace and also an infinite sadness. He was not thinking about his mother, though the sadness came from knowing she was dead. He

< 136 >

continued toward H Street and then on to the Writers Union. He found no one he knew there, but he saw a very beautiful young woman in a sweater so tight the material was nearly transparent, practically baring her large breasts. He wanted to meet her but saw no one who might introduce them. He went home.

Sitting on the balcony watching the few people crossing the avenue, he wondered where in the world all the people were in this city that used to be so busy. Hardly a car had gone by, the buses heading up and down by the corner of 23rd were infrequent, and pedestrians even more scarce. Reflecting on this he forgot all about the puppet place and instead went for a walk down Avenue of the Presidents to Casa de las Américas, where he had not yet been.

First he went into the library to see Olga Andreu, the chief librarian, and Sara Calvo, his sister-in-law, who was her assistant. He chatted briefly with Sara and Olga and nothing seemed untoward, no hint of what would occur not long after: Sara and Olga would be removed from their posts for including a book of his on the list of recommended readings. For the moment, he was enjoying a honeymoon at the publishing house and he went up to see his favorite person: Marcia Leiseca, who was as beautiful and kind as ever. He liked talking with Marcia because her lovely, cultured voice sweetened everything she said; even the most common banalities sounded angelic. What's more, it was a pleasure to drink in her light, pale pink skin, which so contrasted with her large black eyes and hair, as her voice floated out from between pink, perfectly formed lips.

Soon Retamar came in and greeted him affably. He said he wanted to see him again before he left and he wondered if Roberto meant before he left Cuba or before he left the building, but he said nothing. That is to say,

< 137 >

he said, "Sure." But before going to Roberto's office he asked Marcia if he could see Haydée Santamaría, since he had a question for her from Brussels. Marcia went out and came right back saying that Yeye – that was Haydée's nickname – had a few minutes free right then.

He had an errand from Brussels and Haydée Santamaría was the right person to ask, high enough up the revolutionary hierarchy yet still accessible to him. He should have taken it to Minister Roa, but he doubted Roa would have the courage to bring it to his higher-ups. It had to do with a request from a group of Belgian socialists, delivered by a lawyer friend of the embassy, who wanted information and analysis so they could defend Cuba in debates in parliament. The issue was political prisoners, who, according to circles opposed to the Revolution, numbered more than fifteen thousand. The socialists wanted the exact figure to rebut that argument. He conveyed this to Haydée, who flushed redder and redder – the color of meat, but also of her political sentiments – and then nearly roared her scandalized response:

"Fifteen thousand prisoners? Well, look, chico, tell them there are fifteen thousand or fifty-one thousand, it's all the same. The Revolution does not count its enemies, it eliminates them." And she launched into a rant so piercing it hurt his ears, about the right of the Revolution to put its enemies in prison and the Revolution did not have to report to anyone, friends or enemies, because the Revolution knew what it was doing.

After that virtually Hegelian paragraph, he left the main office as best he could and went to see Retamar, who again smiled at him broadly. Roberto wanted him to write something for *Casa* magazine, of which he was then editor. He promised to send along an excerpt of what he had brought with him from Brussels.

To cleanse himself of the visit with Haydée, he went back to Marcia's office to feast on her skin and eyes and lips that smiled a smile not only

< 138 >

perfect but timeless. Then he went back to the library to see Olga and Sara again and had a soda with them – clear Coca-Cola – in the Recodo Café. He walked them back to the library and continued on his way home. When he passed by the Foreign Ministry, he realized it had been days since he last went. He would go tomorrow.

In the morning he got up early: the rooster had crowed at five, as always, but by nine the bullhorns still had not begun their morning racket, which he found strange. Puzzled, he ate breakfast, and still puzzled he went onto the balcony and saw crowds entering and leaving the building on 25th Street. But the loudspeakers remained stridently silent.

When he reached the corner of 23rd to wait for the taxi or bus that would take him to the ministry, whichever came first, a vendor was spreading *Granma* on the pavement and he read the headline: BEN BELLA OVERTHROWN. He got on the bus and arrived at the ministry to find the employees all strangely atwitter.

In the atrium he nearly tripped over Minister Roa. Roa spotted him, opened the door to a closet and closed it again, then scurried back to his office. Arnold Rodríguez's secretaries were in the outer office and Rogelio Montenegro was reading *Granma*. "No question about it," he said, looking up, "it was a CIA job. That guy Boumediene is an agent of imperialism." It seemed weird that a minor official would automatically echo the theory his higher-ups were then circulating throughout the ministry. The notion that the coup against Ben Bella in Algeria was a CIA operation became semi official a few days later. Bella was considered a friend of Cuba; therefore the new rulers of Algeria were enemies of the Revolution. That explained the silence of the loudspeakers: the festival for Cuban youth in Algeria had been cancelled. This story was the public version. Privately – as he learned days later – Fidel Castro went further, accusing Boumediene of being a traitor. Castro began

< 139 >

to flesh out his theory after Boumediene came to visit Cuba, and Fidel and Raúl Castro took him fishing. After his good morning at dawn, Boumediene did not open his mouth except to say goodnight at the end of the fishing trip late in the afternoon. "The silent ones are the dangerous ones," Fidel Castro concluded, somehow not taking into account that Boumediene did not know a syllable of Spanish. But since Boumediene had already been pigeonholed as an agent of imperialism, any elucidation was unnecessary. There was nothing astonishing about the presumption; what was astonishing was how quickly Rogelio Montenegro had "picked up the vibe," as the revolutionary jargon had it.

He sat down in what by then had become his chair, and listened to Montenegro's comments and to those of Arnold Rodríguez, for which Roa would certainly have been present had he not bumped into him in the hallway. He sat for half an hour and did not ask if Roa would see him today because it was obvious: he had already seen him. To top it off, when he got home and pulled out the key, it was not the key to the street door. The day was turning out as bad for him as it had for Ben Bella and the Youth Festival, whose virtues were no longer blared over loudspeakers. At home Hildelisa's lunch awaited him.

In the afternoon, seated on the terrace, he missed Miriam Gómez so much he went into the bathroom and masturbated while looking at the film frames that showed her running on the beach in a bikini.

Later in the afternoon there was water and he took a shower. Then he sat on the balcony to watch children playing in the park in the median. Among them, riding her bicycle, was his daughter Anita. Closer, sitting on the grass with other girls, he saw his daughter Carolita. He decided to go down to the avenue with a book, and sit and read during the long summer sunset. This time no one came to ask him what time it was.

< 140 >

That night, from his balcony next door, Héctor Pedreira told him that a cousin of his was sick. Her mother had called two days before to say she had difficulty opening her mouth. She was seven months pregnant. Today he had learned she had tetanus, apparently picked up from an injection they gave her at the maternity hospital. Now she was critically ill.

That news seemed to confirm the feeling of disgrace that had washed over him when he tried to open the door at noon, and though he did not know the sick woman, he felt miserable. At the same time he felt afraid for his two daughters: tetanus, in other words, death, could be anywhere. He went to the bedroom and saw his daughters were already asleep. Then he returned to the balcony and told Héctor what had happened with his namesake Héctor García and the suppression of *King Kong*. His neighbor, who had been a member of the Communist Party for more than twenty-five years, thought the pretext that they were American films was no reason to keep the few masterpieces that could still be seen in Cuba off the screen. "They might as well suppress the entire history of cinema," Héctor said, with what he interpreted as a burst of shame.

HE WENT TO VISIT Gustavo Arcos the next day. With an air of great secrecy, Gustavo opened his cabinet, cautiously pulled out a box of cigars, and offered him one, which he accepted with pleasure. He put it away for later, since he never smoked in the morning. Gustavo had called to say he had news and he got right to the point.

"I went to see my friend Ramirito," Gustavo said, referring to Ramiro Valdés, the minister of the interior, "and listen to what I'm going to tell you: our old enemy Aldama is drenched in blood and wrapped in flames. Drenched in blood and wrapped in flames!"

He laughed when he heard that popular expression on Gustavo's lips.

< 141 >

"No, don't laugh, this is serious."

"So, what happened?"

"I had a long chat with Ramirito yesterday afternoon. Then I went out with a few friends; that's why I didn't tell you about this then. Anyway, I was talking, we were talking, because he asked me a few questions about the embassy in Belgium, and I learned Aldama is going down. We had quite a long conversation; he even told me the method he uses to know that sort of thing."

"You mean, 'detect' that sort of thing."

"Okay, detect. *Compadre*, it's not for nothing you're a writer. Aren't you picky when it comes to words!"

The two of them laughed. Gustavo continued:

"Well, Ramiro's method for knowing if someone is guilty or not is to look at his hands when he's interrogating him. He didn't tell me what he sees, but he assured me that he always knows by their hands if they're guilty or innocent."

Gustavo stopped speaking for a moment. He thought about the scientific method employed by the minister of the interior, no less, to detect counter-revolutionaries, which was the name they always pinned on the guilty – and often on the innocent.

"And did he tell you," he asked, "if *your* hands show you're guilty or innocent?"

"I wondered about that and when I asked him, I had to make a great effort not to look at my hands."

"No shit," he said, "it sounds like Professor Carbell!"

Gustavo let out a laugh. Carbell was a famous Cuban astrologist from before the Revolution.

< 142 >

"Well, so what's up with Aldama?"

"Ah!" Gustavo said. "He was asking me about everyone in the embassy and when we got around to Aldama, he made a face and I could see right away the guy is falling, he's falling."

Poor Gustavo: he really was a naïve man caught in the machinery of the Revolution. He felt no desire to tell him what he was about to tell him, but there was no way around it.

"You know something, Gustavo? I think it's just the opposite. Ramiro Valdés was checking *you* out, and when he gave that signal about Aldama it was to trick you: you were the one being investigated."

Gustavo got up from the bed.

"*Compadre*," he said, "aren't you the Machiavellian!"

It must be noted that Gustavo Arcos was detained at the beginning of the following year and imprisoned at La Cabaña Fortress, where the minister of the interior, his "friend Ramirito," would visit him to ask him to confess. Gustavo always said he had nothing to confess and asked him to tell him what he was supposed to confess. The minister would respond, "You know, Gustavo. Just confess." Weeks and months went by like that until Gustavo's bad leg began to get worse and they had to transfer him from the humid dungeons of La Cabaña to another prison.

The story of Gustavo's injury in the assault on the Moncada Barracks in Santiago de Cuba in 1953 is worth telling. He took a bullet in the belly at the beginning of the attack. It came out his back, injuring his spinal column. Having lost consciousness right away, he only came to when the battle was over. A fellow fighter, one of the last to retreat, found him and put him in his car, saving him from possible death at the hands of vengeful soldiers. But the car, full of bullet holes, did not get far and his savior left Gustavo

< 143 >

beside a cottage, where he was given reluctant refuge. There, he was able to call a doctor friend, who came for him and saved his life. One of the ironies of history is that the combatant who rescued Gustavo at the barracks and the minister of the interior twelve years later were one and the same person: Ramiro Valdés.

But another six long months would go by before Gustavo's fortunes turned.

Now Gustavo stroked his bad leg with something between a caress and a massage, and reveled in the future vilification of Aldama, which his companion believed would never occur.

"Bathed in blood and wrapped in flames, yes sirree!"

"Or as Guillén would put it: Why not!"

Gustavo let out a belly laugh. It was obvious his visitor was laughing it all off, so they spoke no more of Aldama or Ramiro Valdés. Now Gustavo, whose lack of imagination (thus his bravery) was matched by a good measure of self-pity, started in on the misadventures of his relationship with a Mexican woman who had turned up in Havana with two children and was threatening to ruin his life. She had managed to win the affection of a few members of the Women of the Revolution (the wives of the commanders) and would not stop bad-mouthing him. What to do? No alternative but to marry the Mexican.

"But I don't love her in the least," he practically whined.

At that moment Doña Rosina, Gustavo's mother, entered the room, walking with the aid of a willowy cane. He felt particular affection for this woman, who one day in the future would visit her imprisoned son at La Cabaña Fortress and insist over and over, "Don't you say a thing, Gustavo! Don't tell those Communists anything!"

< 144 >

"How are you, Doña Rosina?"

"Ah, Señor Cabrera. Here I am, doing my best."

They made small talk and in a little while Doña Rosina went deeper into the house, limping laboriously.

At that point he decided to go home. He walked slowly up Avenue of the Presidents and when he reached his building he pulled out the wrong key. Going up the elevator he had the feeling that bad news was awaiting him once more.

But when he entered the apartment, everything was as it should be: the girls were waiting for lunch, Hildelisa was cooking in the kitchen, his grandmother was hobbling from the living room to her bedroom (arthritis had benumbed and deformed her feet), the washerwoman he had run into the day he visited Leonora Soler was in her cubicle doing the laundry, and his father was at work. He went to shower and, before getting in, he saw that the fungus was still gone, as mysteriously as it had appeared.

By the time he came out of the bathroom and put on his sports clothes, lunch was ready: essentially the same as always, but today there was meat.

"Aha, *carne-val!*" he said to Hildelisa.

"That's right," she answered, "today was our day for the little book," the name everyone called the ration card. Finding himself face-to-face again with what Lisandro Otero would call revolutionary reality, the odd incongruity hit him: he was in his own country, but somehow his country was not his country; an imperceptible mutation had changed people and things into their mirror image; everyone and everything was there, but they weren't themselves, Cuba was not Cuba.

After lunch he lay down, not realizing yet that he had not thought about his mother all day, the first time that had happened since hearing the news

< 145 >

in Schiphol. Taking his siesta next to his daughters, he dreamed he was with Miriam Gómez, and when he awoke the bad humor the food had given him had passed. Hildelisa had taken the meat and turned it into an inedible stew; Miriam would never have done that.

That afternoon he sat on the balcony to watch the few passersby with his binoculars. In a little while Teresa came out onto the balcony next door.

"*Muchacho*," she said, "what a brain! Always watching people with your glasses."

He turned and focused the binoculars on Teresa: she was attractive despite the early gray in her hair.

"Take it easy," she said, "or I'll tell Héctor when he comes."

"For sure he'll kill me," he said.

"Kill you, no, but he'll slap you around."

"For looking?" he said, without lowering the binoculars.

"Not for looking, but for the way you're looking."

"Okay," he said, putting the binoculars aside, "tell Héctor not to leave a luscious woman like you alone so much."

Teresa laughed heartily; like all women, she enjoyed a compliment, even if it was just kidding around.

"Hang on, my love," she said, "it's starting to rain and I've got the clothes on the line."

It was true. In the heat of the afternoon, great dark clouds had gathered over the city. He had been so focused on watching people, he had not noticed. A few huge drops began to fall. He pulled the rocker back toward the living room, but remained on the balcony. He wanted to see a spectacle he had not had the chance to enjoy calmly for three years. The enormous

< 146 >

drops got thicker and a heavy, violent downpour ensued, forming a curtain that virtually blocked the other side of the street from view. Suddenly he thought about his dead mother, alone in the cemetery, all this rain falling on the lid of her tomb, and he felt a great urge to cry, which he held in check because his daughters, awakened by the storm, were running out from the bedroom to watch it rain. But he continued thinking about his mother, about the solitude of death and the abandonment of the dead.

It rained for half an hour and then the downpour abated as abruptly as it had begun. The sun began to shine while it was still drizzling, and rivers of water on either side of the gardens and in the gutters parallel to the curb ran quickly down toward the sea.

He wanted to go out and he invited his daughters to take a stroll.

"And you can buy me a heavenly custard," Anita said.

"I shall. One for you and another for Carolita."

"No, I don't like them," Carolita said.

"Well, I'll buy you what you want."

"I don't want anything."

"Okay, I won't buy you anything. Let's go."

They went out and walked up Avenue of the Presidents to 25th Street, turned and walked to F Street, turned again in the direction of 23rd Street. On F he saw for the first time that plantains had been planted in the gardens next to the clinic. The same was true of other gardens in the neighborhood; people were planting plantains instead of roses, hoping the harvest would supplement the poor diet forced on them by rationing. The discovery bothered him and he did not understand why until he realized it was the implied underdevelopment: Havana was turning into countryside. It was like being back in the miserable hometown he had fled twenty-five years

< 147 >

ago, where people planted trees in their backyards (there were no front yards) hoping for fruit. Now the city, his city, was embarked on a voyage of visible retreat. At the same time he felt sorry for people reduced to planting food in their gardens just to have a little bit more to eat. He did not believe the official justification for rationing, since the US blockade did not cause shortages of the food the country produced; the cause was the bureaucratization of the entire country, which turned farmers into employees of the state and made them utterly indifferent to the harvest. Even in well-functioning cooperatives, the product of their labor was lost through careless picking or lack of transport, and entire harvests sat rotting in rural warehouses or in central supply houses, never reaching the consumer. The excuse of the blockade might explain the absence of cars or radios; it could not explain the widespread shortage of foods the country used to produce in such abundance they were exported. He was aware that this thought, if expressed aloud, would be considered counterrevolutionary in any government office, including the Foreign Ministry, even if it was a commonly held opinion. In this troubled mood he entered El Carmelo on 23rd and bought Anita her heavenly custard, sitting down now at one of the inside tables to wait for her to eat it.

"What's wrong, Papi?" Carolita asked.

"Nothing. Why?"

"You look so..."

He knew she was right and he smiled, stretching it into a cross-eyed, widemouthed grimace. Carolita and Anita laughed at his face and a very pretty girl leaving the restaurant did too. He smiled happily now and thought that if he were alone he would chase after that girl, have a conversation, and maybe find friendship, instead of consoling himself with ogling her gorgeous body through the window and watching her wander under the archways of

< 148 >

the cinema and down the stairs to the street, where she was lost from view. He felt sweetly depressed.

When they got home he received a call from Dulce María Escardó, who said hello as if they were great friends, even though he knew her only superficially and their relationship had never gone beyond the casual. The call caught him by surprise, but he was very polite. Dulce María excused herself for not calling before, but she was doing it now. Besides, she had two tickets for a play that night at the Arlequín. Could he come? He had nothing else to do, but he did not say that, rather he said yes, he would be delighted. Agreed; they would see each other at the theater door at eight.

To cheer himself up, instead of having supper at home he thought he would eat with Dulce María after the show. He changed his clothes, putting on the Belgian suit with one of his father's shirts since his was still in the wash. He shaved carefully, using his electric razor from Brussels, and made sure every hair was in place. In a good mood he walked from his house to the theater and felt happy to be strolling at night down the Rambla, a short urban stretch he loved, for the first time in three years. He reached the theater precisely at eight. Being punctual and speaking French were the two things he had learned from his life as a diplomat. Dulce María turned up about fifteen minutes later and they hugged like old friends. She was older – already over thirty – but still as attractive as ever, her body fleshier but still shapely. They went inside and watched a Cuban play that out of pity will not be named. It was so bad that had he been alone, he would have left at intermission, but Dulce María seemed to be enjoying herself and besides there were people he knew in the audience.

Afterward, they walked to Polinesio, a restaurant in the Habana Libre Hotel which was still open, and instead of eating (apparently she had already

< 149 >

done so) they drank Cuba libres made with clear Coca-Cola, rum, and soda water. They had another and, being a bit tipsy, he suggested they take a stroll. They headed down L Street to 21st, a block he liked to avoid because the Interior Ministry building was there – its presence right downtown somehow threatening constant vigilance – so to reduce his discomfort they crossed to the other side of the street, stepping up onto the sidewalk next to a café in a park that once had been very dear to him. They also passed Delicias de Medina, a café-restaurant that was still open and whose name he liked so much.

They continued all the way down 21st to Victor Hugo Park, where they sat on a bench not far from the Geriatric Institute. By chance, their conversation turned to the Revolution. He did not know why he had thought she was apolitical or slightly counterrevolutionary, but from the moment she opened her mouth she showed herself to be a fierce partisan.

"We've got to clean this country out," she said. "Finish chasing out all the counterrevolutionaries, whether they're undercover or in plain sight. There are lots of people here who only support the Revolution from the mouth out. We've got to flush them out and denounce them for what they are: counter revolutionary scum."

He did not know what to say, so he remained silent. But she went on anyway, perhaps encouraged by the alcohol or by some yearning she had kept hidden all evening.

"Do you see Virgilio Piñera?"

For a minute he thought Virgilio was nearby, and when he realized the question was rhetorical, he felt like deflating it with a joke, saying no, he hadn't noticed Virgilio, but there was such intensity in her tone that he said nothing.

< 150 >

"That guy is a committed counterrevolutionary and here he is putting on his plays and publishing his writing. He's got to be unmasked!"

He thought about poor Virgilio, the target for so many attacks and yet the most inoffensive person imaginable. She continued her hate filled rant.

"...the same with Arrufat and that whole bunch from the Studio Theater. Every one of them is nothing but a counterrevolutionary faggot."

He should have felt aghast at her using the word "faggot," but that surprise was swept aside by his astonishment at her unbidden diatribe against his friends – she *had* to know they were his friends – and the intensity of her hatred. As a costume designer, she must have had contact with actors and playwrights, and some sort of relationship had to exist between her and the people from Studio Theater. That she would hate Virgilio Piñera or even Antón Arrufat, who after all did not do cheap revolutionary theater, did not seem extraordinary, but there had to be others who were her friends, at least he always thought so.

They were alone in the park and the streets were empty, since it was nearly midnight. Although earlier on he had thought they might have an intimate encounter – after all, even if she was no longer young, her white skin and her intense black eyes made her very attractive – now he just wanted to go home. Besides, he was afraid at any moment she would include him among the secret counterrevolutionaries who ought to leave the country. Though he agreed with her that the enemies of the Revolution should depart, the other part of her argument worried him. She kept on talking and for a moment he felt a mixture of attraction – hair mussed and expression vehement, she looked even lovelier than earlier in the evening – and repulsion, which he could not hold in the same thought. She fell silent. He looked at her and she looked at him: she really was rather beautiful. What a shame he had let

< 151 >

the conversation drift to the Revolution, but he had no direct experience of such zealotry and he had nearly forgotten that women can be as fanatical as men, every opinion coming from gut feeling.

He looked into the distance up 21st Street and decided it was late.

"I'll accompany you home," he said.

"No need," she said. "I've got my car at the theater. We can walk back and I'll take you home."

They retraced their steps to the theater. During the entire trajectory he said nothing and she became as silent as she had been at the beginning of the evening.

When she left him at his house, he nearly kissed her. But he discovered he was acting out of fear, to show her he was on her side, so he did not. They promised to see each other the next night, but he knew that was not likely. Although it should have been obvious she did not think like him, she seemed convinced he was a committed revolutionary. If not, she would not have called to invite him to the theater. They said goodnight.

His visit to the ministry the following day obtained the same result as every other time. Arnold was busy, so he visited with the secretaries. Then he decided to go to Casa de las Américas to deliver the excerpt Retamar had requested. Leaving the ministry he ran into the actress Teté Vergara. He had heard that her sister, the comic actress Violeta Vergara, had recently committed suicide: while on guard duty at CMQ Radio she had put her standard issue rifle in her mouth and pulled the trigger. He had always liked Teté, who was a good friend of Miriam Gómez's, and now he felt so sad for her since he knew how much she loved her family. They gave each other condolences.

"How is Miriam?" she asked.

"Just fine. I spoke with her the other day and she's well."

< 152 >

"Good, that's good news."

"It will be a blow when she hears about Violeta."

"Yes, for sure it will."

He would have liked to ask Teté why her sister killed herself, since she was such a popular comedienne, but the conversation was very melancholy and they said a quick goodbye.

Marcia Leiseca was not at Casa and he was sorry not to see her. He went to Retamar's office and found him speaking with a very beautiful woman, or rather a girl, with an enchanting smile and a lot of class. Retamar introduced her, but as always, he did not catch the name. He said he would come back later on, since it was evident the two of them were getting on quite well, but the visitor said she was just leaving and she departed. He was disappointed, but not as much as Retamar.

He delivered the excerpt and Roberto glanced over it.

"Very good," he said, "it will come out in the next issue. And let me warn you that here we pay well."

"That's good news," he said. "How much?"

"At least a hundred pesos."

"Not bad."

"Not at all!"

They talked about trivialities, he avoiding asking who the lovely visitor was and Retamar obviously wishing he had turned up some other time. In a little while, he said goodbye and went to the library to see Sara and Olga; surrounded by inert books and absorbed readers, they were bored to tears.

This time he had the right key in his hand when he opened the door to his building, and in the apartment no disaster awaited him other than Hildelisa's lunch. In the afternoon he sat on the balcony, and watching it rain again, he

< 153 >

again grieved for his mother. Then he called Oscar Hurtado and they made a date to meet at El Carmelo on Calzada that evening.

At the restaurant he was soon joined by Oscar, his wife, Miriam Acevedo, and Ernestina Linares, an actress he greatly admired both as an actress and as a woman. He did an imitation of Laurence Olivier in *Hamlet* that later he would consider pitiful but which everyone at the table applauded. At about nine o'clock, Lido came in and he almost did not recognize her. About three years before, he had introduced himself to her at 12th and 23rd. He had seen her in the building where he was living at the time and where she was sharing with another actress, having just moved out of her parents' home. Back then he had the impression Lido was afraid of men and, despite appearing accessible, was protecting her virginity at all cost. Now, watching her enter the restaurant, he thought she looked more at ease. Her hair was longer, curved bangs in front and straight in the back, and along with her large, somewhat slanted eyes and unusual profile, it gave her the appearance of a tropical Cleopatra.

Obviously looking for someone, she walked across the terrace and on into the indoor dining area. When she came out again, she spied Miriam Acevedo and Ernestina Linares (he guessed Lido had not abandoned her acting aspirations) and stopped by to talk to them. Only then did she notice him; she recognized him and they said hello. Although in the moment he had forgotten her name and perhaps she had never really known his, he invited her to join them and she accepted. Everyone went on chatting, but he could not stop looking at her large eyes and she returned his glances. After a while, she got up to leave and he decided to go with her. He said goodbye to Miriam, Ernestina, and Oscar; Oscar was not pleased to have his audience depart.

< 154 >

She headed down Línea Street and he drew alongside her.

"Where are you going?" he asked.

"Nowhere in particular, home."

"So early?"

"Yes, so early."

He almost asked if she had not found the person she was looking for at El Carmelo, but he held back.

"Why don't we take a stroll?"

"Where?"

"Around, wherever you like."

"Fine," she said, and she slowed down.

They crossed Línea and he turned toward Paseo. He had one thing in mind, to take her to bed, and somehow he was certain he would achieve it. They walked up Paseo, with him leading and she tacitly obeying, never asking where they were headed. Perhaps she knew. He looked up at the sky and on an impulse began to recite: "It is the cause, it is the cause, my soul, – Let me not name it to you, you chaste stars! – It is the cause." Still gazing up at the sky, he repeated the bit about chaste stars several times, until she asked him:

"What is that?"

"That? *Othello*, act 5, scene 2."

"Do you know the whole thing?"

"Only this verse: 'Let me not name it to you, you chaste stars!'"

He was still reciting that lone verse aloud when they reached 23rd. He turned as if heading toward 12th, but in reality he was planning to turn again on 2nd Street to get to 2nd and 31st, where there was a posada, which is what Cubans call a place that rents rooms by the hour. When they made the turn on 2nd, she followed, a good sign, and now he knew she would not put up

< 155 >

any resistance, that whatever was holding her back three years ago had been long overcome. She had to know they were going to that place or someplace like it, so he took her arm to cross Zapata and reach 2nd and 31st. No one was about; it must have been later than he thought. When they neared the posada, the silence was complete and he looked up at the sky one last time and declaimed, "You chaste stars…" She smiled, and smiling still she stepped with him into that establishment built exclusively for making love.

She was quite brown-skinned and her skin color was even across her entire body, which if not perfect was very nice to look at and smell and touch. She was also delightfully warm in the chill of the early morning. He confirmed that indeed she had long ago stopped being a virgin.

THE FOLLOWING DAY THE LOUDSPEAKERS were back to awaken him. This time the same voice urged the best and brightest to go not to Algeria as before, but to "the eastern province," to plant a million eucalyptus trees though the announcer had a hard time pronouncing the word. Again and again the loudspeakers repeated the message:

"The best and brightest will go to the province of Oriente. Let's all plant eucalyptus!" Thus it continued for another week, until the moment for planting a million eucalyptus trees arrived and thousands of buses weighed down with eucalyptus seedlings and filled with boys and girls headed off to Oriente. The irony of this new excursion of the best and brightest became clear while the loudspeakers were still blaring: Alberto Mora returned from Oriente and explained that the campaign to plant a million eucalyptus trees would take the volunteers to the very fields set aside for planting sugarcane for the model refinery he was to administer.

"How could that be?" he asked, almost ingenuously.

< 156 >

"Just the way you're hearing it," Alberto told him. "In a few weeks all the eucalyptus seedlings will be pulled out so we can plant cane."

"What about all the work these boys and girls are going to do?" he asked, and Alberto answered cynically:

"Something's needed to keep them entertained."

In the afternoon, to dissipate the tedium, he hung the blanket over the window so his daughters could watch television, and he sat down to read. At their insistence he also watched a bit, but it was a lousy Mexican drama with Argentine stars, or maybe the other way around. So he took his book to the balcony, since it was too hot and the sun too high to go down to the avenue. Besides, since the balcony faced the sea – offering a view of part of the horizon, interrupted by a few tall buildings – there was always a breeze, no matter how hot the day.

That night he went back to El Carmelo on Calzada and joined Oscar Hurtado not at the lone table at the back where he had sat the night before, but at the one in the middle that Oscar nearly always occupied, facing the corner of D Street and Calzada, which was perhaps the best spot on the terrace. Oscar said he was happy to see him. He knew he was, but he was surprised to hear Oscar express it so seriously.

"I have to tell you," he said, "that little girl Lido is dangerous company."

"Her? Come on! Yummy company is what she is."

"I'm serious."

"Tell me, what's up with her?"

"She's the mistress or at least the lover of a commander."

He was surprised.

"Didn't you see her last night?" Oscar asked.

"Of course I saw her!"

< 157 >

"No, I mean the way she came in looking for someone."

"No, I didn't notice."

"Well, I did. I'm telling you so you can stay out of trouble. The fewer run-ins you have with those people, the better."

"Thank you."

"No, you're welcome."

Seeing that Oscar was not kidding, he felt a little worried. To have a commander of the Rebel Army, which is like a general in a regular army, as a jealous rival was reason for concern. Actually, for great concern, but he only worried a little. He knew himself: if he ran into Lido again that night, he might well take her out again; if not, maybe the next night.

But the following day he woke up with diarrhea. He had no idea when or how he picked it up, all he knew was that in the middle of the night he needed to go to the bathroom. By morning he had lost count of how many times he had had to do something he detested, something he considered humiliating. He felt awful and maybe should have gone to the hospital, the back door of which was diagonally across the avenue, but he could barely walk to the bathroom. And though he could have asked a doctor, Mora Pimienta for example, to make a house call, he did not want to do that for what Cubans considered a simple "bellyache." For three days he remained ill, during which time he did not eat Hildelisa's food, which was no great sacrifice, and subsisted on a brew prepared by his grandmother from herbs brought by Tona the washerwoman. On the fourth day he awoke feeling fine.

In the mirror he saw he had lost a lot of weight, but that did not worry him; on the contrary it made him happy, since in Belgium he had grown fat and had even begun to do exercises on the gym mat Gustavo Arcos had left behind, and to run in the empty lot behind the embassy.

< 158 >

That night he went back to El Carmelo. Seated at the table with Oscar Hurtado – Luis Agüero and his wife, Sara Calvo, came later, and Rine Leal and Lisandro Otero came for a while – he watched Lido and her officer pass by, or rather he saw them leave. He was definitely a commander, he had that unmistakably loutish expression, so he decided to forget all about her, although he did not wish to forget the way she was in bed.

They talked about absurd fanciful things, thanks to Rine Leal, and then about politics, thanks to Lisandro Otero. At one point make-believe and politics came together when Rine brought up the idea of a universal military draft: everyone in Cuba would be in the army; everyone would continue doing his or her work, but would be paid what a draftee is paid, and that way the treasury would not be burdened with high salaries and no one would protest because everyone would be in the army. (When Franqui heard about this idea of Rine's he grew alarmed; only half joking, he asked Rine not to spread it around in case the government caught wind of it and decided to run with it. Rine and Franqui could not know, no one could, that one day not far off a very similar policy would be put in place, whereby everyone would have to do obligatory voluntary labor under a more or less military regime.)

Lisandro Otero brought up the Central Committee of the Communist Party, then being organized, saying he was very curious to know who would sit on it. He even suggested a possible slate.

"I'm fascinated by politics," Lisandro said, "aren't you?"

The question was directed at him.

"No, not me. In fact, politics upsets me. I consider life to be a novel and I believe, along with Stendhal, that politics in a novel is like a gunshot in the middle of Mass."

< 159 >

Everyone laughed and he had trouble explaining that he was not joking. No one, of course, wanted to believe him.

Late that night, along with Antón Arrufat, who had joined them after the theater, they walked down Línea and up Avenue of the Presidents. Near 17th Street he was astonished not to see any mysterious characters in the shadows.

"There's been a roundup," explained Antón, who was up on the activities of Social Turpitude. By mutual consent and in silence, they decided to change the subject. Luis recounted what was happening to his wife, Sara, of late, that she was having hallucinations or visions that she was leaving her body and flying up to the ceiling, and from up there she would look down and see her "other" body lying in bed. With Sara present, everyone took it seriously, that is, except for Lisandro Otero, since he had left earlier. Oscar explained that it was a well-known ESP phenomenon, but Luis was worried and Sara too seemed afraid. Oscar explained how common it was for a person to become divided like Sara, using examples of levitation from books he had read. Sara responded that she was living with it.

By now they were across from his apartment and everyone sat down on a bench facing his building. Their voices echoed in the empty and silent street, while he recounted his strange experience with birds, from the time he was a child and his little sister died to the other day in Brussels soon before his mother passed away. Oscar's response was that he had better watch out for baby birds. By the tone, which was serious in the extreme but whose seriousness was undercut by the word "baby," he could not tell if Oscar was joking, although to joke at that moment would not have been like Oscar; it would have been in very bad taste, since everyone, especially Oscar Hurtado, knew

< 160 >

what his mother's death meant to him. His uncertainty was overtaken by Antón Arrufat telling the tale of his father's death in a train accident, which had been foreseen by his mother, who had also died, but of cancer. "No one foresaw her death," Arrufat said, "but I would have preferred if they had both died in the same accident." He fell silent and for a moment it seemed Antón had wanted his mother to die, until he realized he was talking about avoiding the atrocious death she did have. A long silence descended, all of them deep into the mysteries of life and death. He decided it was time to go to bed, said goodbye, crossed the street, and went into his building, having pulled the correct key from his pocket.

The following day the daughter of his cousin Noelia came to visit. Nersa was beautiful and despite being very young was already divorced, which was why her strict parents, Noelia and Miguel, were keeping a close eye on her. He decided to invite her, along with Anita and Carolita, to the theater that night, to see a presentation of Goldoni's *Harlequin, Servant of Two Masters*, which people were saying was very good.

When it was nearly time to leave, a boy about twenty years old, thin, and on the ugly side, turned up. He was Nersa's boyfriend, but no one at home knew about him. He went with them to the corner where the taxis stopped, and when one came along he got in with them. When it was time to buy the tickets, rather than saying goodbye to Nersa, he showed every intention of coming along, although he made not the least move to purchase his own ticket. So he had to invite him as well. (When they were leaving the apartment, Hildelisa, who never missed a trick, made a face behind the boyfriend's back, as if to say, This one is useless. She remained on the balcony and watched him get into the taxi and the next day, when they talked about the show, she

< 161 >

said, "And for sure you had to buy a ticket for that big dummy." When he admitted he had, Hildelisa said he was a fool, they should have left him on the sidewalk.) Thus, the show was not perfect.

But something interesting did occur. The performance was not bad and what was really good was the young woman, practically a girl, who played the heroine; the program gave her name as Isabel Elsa. Not only was she not bad as an actress, physically she was very attractive. She looked like Miriam Gómez in the days when she was an actress, maybe too much like her. He could not stop gazing at her all evening long and was sorry he had come without his binoculars, since the theater was long and narrow.

After the show, he sent his daughters home with Nersa and he walked to El Carmelo, not far away. Like other nights he saw Ingrid González there, and he invited her to sit at his table. Ingrid was pleased and she smiled as she sat down. Her smile lasted until he asked her if she knew Isabel Elsa, saying he wanted to meet her. Ingrid said she did know her and added, "But she's married." To which he responded, "So what?"

"Oh, just saying so you'll know."

"I know. Now what?" he asked rather brazenly.

"You still want to meet her?"

"Of course I do."

"All right, I'll introduce you. Wait until she's here one night."

That moment would not come for several nights. But right then Ingrid said to him: "Why don't you love me?" And she was not kidding.

"But I do love you," he said, and he caressed her hand. Ingrid let her hand be stroked and looked into his eyes.

"You don't love me," she said.

< 162 >

"Yes, I love you."

"Prove it."

"How?" he said.

"You know how."

"I don't know, I swear I don't know."

She said nothing and he asked her if she was going to leave, since neither Hurtado nor any one else from the group had come. Then he noticed a tall thin girl with a long face and perfect lips, who looked at him for a moment as she left. But it was only for a moment.

"I'll leave whenever you want," Ingrid said.

"Okay, let's go."

"Will you walk me home?" she said.

"No, better you walk me home. Let's go up to 23rd and G."

G was what people in the neighborhood called Avenue of the Presidents, which in sequence with the parallel streets should have been G.

"You're bad," she said.

"I'm not bad. It would be too great a temptation to walk you home."

Strolling along Línea to the avenue, they soon reached 23rd Street. Ingrid was perspiring, which gave an attractive sheen to her sunburned skin. He looked at her for a moment and she noticed he was looking.

"You really won't come home with me?"

"I can't."

"You are bad."

"Really, I can't. I've got to get to bed early."

She looked him in the eyes, then almost turned her back on him and said plaintively:

< 163 >

"Why must I love you like this?"

He said nothing, because he knew she was not just saying it and certainly was not kidding.

"You know I love you, don't you?" she said.

He took a moment to answer.

"No, I didn't know."

"Liar."

"Believe me, I didn't know."

"So, why all this?" she said.

She made a gesture that encompassed the entire night.

"You've caught me by surprise," he said.

"For a while now. I've been this way for a long while."

"I didn't know," he said seriously.

"Well, now you know how it is."

"Yes, I do." And he laughed inside, the phrase reminding him of his uncle Niño.

"What shall we do?" she asked.

"Nothing, what can we do?"

"So, I'll just keep on loving you forever?" She smiled and he knew she was joking now.

"Maybe yes, maybe no. If you behave yourself, you'll get a treat."

"Ha, ha," she said. "I know. Well, my dear. Can I call you 'my dear'?"

"Sure, you can call me 'my love' too, if you like."

"Well, my love, what shall we do?"

"Each of us goes home to our own bed."

It really bothered him to have to reject Ingrid, who was physically very good looking and very affectionate, but he knew that Miriam Gómez would

< 164 >

never forgive him; just as he knew that if he had a fling with Ingrid, Miriam would find out, because he would end up telling her.

"Well, in that case, if you're dumping me, I'm leaving."

"See you tomorrow."

"Goodbye, my love."

He watched her walk down 23rd Street, and when she had gone about fifty steps, he looked both ways and crossed the street carefully to the corner of Castillo de Jagua, then walked the twenty steps to his house. When he went in, he had the right key in his hand and he knew that everything was all right.

The following day, a splendid morning of sun and light and clear skies without the thundering roar of the loudspeakers wounding his eardrums, he decided to go to *Cuba* magazine. He wanted to collect the money they owed him for the interview Antón Arrufat did with him in Brussels and for the extract from his book.

He caught a taxi and as soon as it turned onto Rancho Boyeros, not far from the Plaza Cívica, and continued past the National Library and in between the INRA and the old National Lottery buildings, he felt like he was living in days gone by, back in the time when the newspaper *Revolución* was housed here, in the same building where *Lunes* was. They pulled up at the rear of the INRA, where *Cuba* had its editorial offices.

Lisandro Otero took the time to show him around and introduce him to the editors and other employees, some of whom he did not know. He saw Guerrero, who had worked at *Lunes* years ago, and the photographer Ernesto, with whom he had always got along. They served him coffee – not for nothing was the building the headquarters of the National Agrarian Reform Institute, the highest rung of Cuba's agricultural bureaucracy. He stayed for a while

< 165 >

after they paid him seventy-five pesos for his contribution, then walked home, despite the heat, enjoying the weather he had missed so much in Belgium. But now he was starting to feel like it was not quite home.

After the inane ritual of lunch and the second ritual of buying Anita her heavenly custard (today, since he had money, he bought two and helped her eat the second), he sat down to read on the balcony, where there was a fresh breeze from the sea. He was reading *Laughter in the Dark* by Vladimir Nabokov in a not-too-bad translation, and he reveled in the book's cruel genius. He read other books during those days, though Nabokov and Julio Cortázar's mediocre novel *The Winners* would be the only ones he would remember.

That night (or maybe it was the next) he went to El Carmelo as usual and saw Ingrid, who came over to tell him that Isabel Elsa did not have a performance that night so maybe she would drop by later on.

Indeed, his heart began to pound when he saw the actress step in the door from Calzada Street; in a little while she and Ingrid approached his table. He stood up (something he had not done when Ingrid came to say hello) for the introductions and then invited them to join him. Soon Isabel Elsa went to the ladies' room and Ingrid told him, in an unnecessary whisper, that Isabel and her husband had separated a few weeks ago, though she had only found out that day.

When Isabel Elsa returned, or rather after a conversation about Goldoni and *Harlequín* that was as dumb as it was pretentious, Ingrid got up – very discreetly, it's true – and said she was going to say hello to a few friends whose names he did not catch. So the two of them were left alone at the table. They continued chatting and without them realizing it or understanding how – via a simple allusion, perhaps to Oscar Hurtado at a table not far away – the conversation took a turn and became filled with ghosts. He made a joke or

< 166 >

two and she laughed, weakly, but she laughed. He could see she did not have much of a sense of humor, but what she said next made him think she had something else on her mind.

"I can't sleep at home," she said, and his first thought was that she could sleep somewhere else, although he did not say so.

"No? Why?"

"I'm so afraid."

Now, he thought, she is going to say she is afraid to sleep alone.

"You are? Of what?"

"Of the sounds. The strangest things happen. At midnight a chair begins to rock all on its own, then there's the sound of footsteps, and the apartment is locked and no one could get in."

She looked truly frightened.

"Then I hear sighs or moans and I keep hearing them until I fall asleep."

"How long has it been going on?" He nearly asked if it began when she started living alone, although he did not know for sure if she was living alone or with a relative.

"For a long time. But it's grown louder. I've told several people about it and some say it's witchcraft. Could it be?"

"No, it's something else. A poltergeist."

"What?"

Obviously, not a very well-educated actress.

"Poltergeist," he said slowly.

"What's that?"

"Extrasensorial phenomena, but produced by humans. Maybe by you yourself."

"But how could that be?"

< 167 >

"Unconsciously. Or maybe it's from someone else in the neighborhood."

"I don't think so. They're all really good people."

"It doesn't have to come from enemies. They're phenomena produced by subconscious forces. Often by a child punished by his parents."

"In my house there are no children."

He was about to ask for Oscar Hurtado's help and was looking around for his table.

"Now, they can be got rid of," he said.

"Yes? How?"

"People who know can go to your house and find the origin of the sounds and movements."

He nearly offered himself as the exorcist, but a certain fear of poltergeists, which was likely just another of his superstitions, held him back.

"I'm never at home."

He began to find her more stolid than stupid, and seeing her up close he could see she was not as pretty as she had looked on stage; she had lost all her mystery, despite the mysteries of the house in which she lived.

"You make an arrangement with someone who knows…"

"I don't know anyone."

"For example, Oscar Hurtado."

"Who?"

"Oscar, Miriam Acevedo's husband."

"Oh."

"He knows a lot about these things."

"But I only go home to sleep and it's very late at night when I get these visitations."

"A group could go."

< 168 >

"I don't know."

She had not even smiled at any of his funny remarks. (Although today, recalling them, he does not think there was much humor in what he said.) He began to weary of her. Over the course of the evening he had not seen a single hint that she was interested in him. So when she said she was leaving, that she was tired – apparently she had been all evening – was sure he would not miss her. He stood up to say goodbye and started to extend his hand but she failed to reach out at all. Then he watched her go sit at the actors' table where Ingrid was, and he went to join Oscar Hurtado.

Later on, after Isabel Elsa had left, he managed to get Ingrid's attention. She came over, causing some displeasure on Oscar's part since he did not like having women at his table, except for Miriam Acevedo at first and later on Evorita Tamayo.

"What did she say?" he asked her, and he could see Oscar almost frown.

"Oh, not much. But she says you're very interesting."

"Me or what I said?"

"You, I think."

Ingrid did not feel much like elaborating and he discovered that he really did not care about Isabel's opinion of him. From that point on, she became a figure he would see in the distance at El Carmelo, but whom he never approached.

One day, when he went by the ministry, a curious incident took place; it would have been nearly hilarious if not for his predicament. As always, he went to Arnold's office and this time learned that Arnold was meeting with the Swiss ambassador in the room next door reserved for receiving visitors. Waiting for Arnold to finish, he chatted with his secretaries, one male, one female, and soon the door to the outer office opened and in walked Raúl Roa,

< 169 >

who got to the middle of the room before he realized who was sitting there. Then he tried to leave by the closest door, which led to the reception room. In he stepped, closing the door behind him. Both secretaries laughed out loud, and since he did not understand what was going on, they explained: Arnold was meeting with the Swiss ambassador because Roa had not wanted to see him, and as an excuse they had told him the minister was not in Havana. The secretaries were imagining Roa's and Arnold's expressions now.

The incident made him finally accept that Roa would not see him, that Arnold's call to the airport about an interview with the minister was an excuse as patently false as the one they had given the Swiss ambassador. But if that was the case, why had Roa's name and an interview with him been offered as justification for aborting his trip? Besides, why had they waited until precisely the very last moment to block his return to Brussels? Who, if not Roa, had been behind it? Pondering these unknowables and without waiting for Arnold to finish his interrupted meeting, he left.

That afternoon he told Fidel about it and his brother agreed that the idea was to keep both of them in Cuba. They concluded that a serious accusation must have been lodged against both of them and it likely came from the same source: the Interior Ministry. More concretely, from the intelligence service, then led by someone who was becoming just as notorious as Ramiro Valdés: Commander Manuel Piñeiro, better known by his alias "Barbaroja" ("Redbeard"). That was the moment he realized he was truly in danger. If he had been fired without explanation – effectively what had occurred without him realizing it – the reasons must be a secret, and the only possible secret reasons could be charges against him made by the intelligence service, which, as he later learned, was intervening more and more in every ministry that sent officials overseas. The accusations must have been very recent, since upon his arrival Minister Roa had ratified him as chargé d'affaires in Belgium, and Roa

< 170 >

himself authorized the trip home. What charges could there be against him? Where precisely did the accusations come from? How far would they take their suspicions, and how long before they became formal charges? For the first time since the triumph of the Revolution, he felt afraid and understood what it was to be a victim of totalitarian power.

His first reaction was not to go out at all until he could decipher what was really going on. After three days, he changed his mind and told himself that only by acting with utter normality could he be shrewd enough to save himself. He returned to El Carmelo after a phone invitation from Oscar Hurtado.

That night not only did they speak of space travel, but Oscar suggested the entire group go to the Malecón along the shore to look at the sky. Because few streetlights remained on the Malecón – previously it was much better lit – they found a night filled with stars. Oscar pointed straight up and asked if they could see a moving point of light. "It's a star," someone suggested. "No," Oscar said, "it's an American satellite." He did not ask himself how Oscar knew, rather he told himself that if Oscar said so, it must be true. Gazing at the stars high above, he thought, as he often did, about the ephemeral nature of human passions, the most ephemeral among them being political passions. Even if the feeling was fleeting, he felt comforted by his communion with the cosmos. Sitting there on the wall of the Malecón, a sense of peace he had not experienced for a long time overtook him. He did not say so, but he was thankful Oscar had made him come.

AFTER HIS MOTHER'S DEATH, the neighbors from the first floor of the building next door, who were very religious, wanted to hold a Mass for her. Since only a handful of churches were still open, the Mass was set for the month of September, in other words, three months after her death. When

< 171 >

Soriano, who was a believer in esoteric religions, heard about that, he suggested that his church – the World Church for the Health of the Soul – could also offer a Mass for the eternal rest of her soul. He did not think a Mass of any sort would make a bit of difference, but since Soriano proposed it with his usual quiet passion, he accepted and went to the World Church for the Health of the Soul, which, in perfect incongruity, was a small house on a nearly anonymous street in the neighborhood of El Cerro. The place was packed. He took a seat in the last row, beside his father, brother, and Soriano. The officiant was a character well known on the streets of Havana. Many times he had seen his ratlike face with its close-set eyes; now he was sporting a little beard. The man began the ceremony by calling out several names in a high-pitched voice, among them, he realized with a start, his mother's. Hearing the officiant say, "Zoila Infante," he suddenly felt the entire weight of his mother's death press down on him: here she was being declared deceased among so many strangers, both dead and alive. He felt something close to shame and suddenly he wanted to weep, though in such company he could not. He barely took in the next words of the officiant, who requested light and splendor for the souls of the dead, and who commended them to the Creator in the same screeching tone with which he had recited their names at the outset.

When the Mass – infinitely less spectacular than a Catholic Mass – was over, they went out into the sunshine and the heat and walked down the thoroughfare to catch the bus home. None of them said a word: all seemed to have become a version of Soriano, who hardly ever spoke.

In the afternoon, he went to visit Maritza Alonso at her artists' agency on Calzada. Maritza treated him as well as ever and asked him more than once when he was leaving, since she hoped to see him in Europe on a cultural

< 172 >

tour the government was organizing. Half joking (he still did not admit to himself he would not be returning to Brussels) he told her his trip was still a ways off. When he finished with Maritza, it was still early and for a moment he could not think what do to next. In the end he went home to read Nabokov and watch women pass by on the sidewalk across the avenue.

That night he did not go to El Carmelo, because he felt he was in mourning, a state of grief he had been living with, practically without realizing it, since the day of his mother's funeral. Because he did not want to watch television with his daughters in the living room, he went onto the balcony and studied the sea, where a storm lay on the horizon. He used the binoculars to watch more closely and was fascinated by the number of lighting bolts falling every minute, each sketching a violent streak of luminous white on the blackness of the sea. The lightening sometimes ended in a shining ball that remained for a moment on the surface of the waters before disappearing under the depths. He watched until the storm was over, more than two hours, and barely paid any attention to his daughters when they came to say goodnight. Then he went to the kitchen to drink some cold water from the refrigerator and his grandmother called from her room: "Are you going to bed now, my son?"

"Yes, Mamá," he said, addressing his grandmother as his mother had.

The next day, since he did not plan to go back to the ministry for some time, he had nothing to do. Then an eccentric character he had met days or maybe years before turned up. It was El Chinolope, a professional photographer who eked out a living in a Cuba that had less and less room for any professional who was not a military officer or a politician, or both at once. El Chinolope had a Japanese father and a Cuban mother, a strange mixture most Cubans could barely comprehend, and so he felt obliged to abandon his

< 173 >

Japanese surname and nationality to become Chino López, professionally known as El Chinolope. He had come to take his picture, saying he had been sent by Carlos Barral, the Spanish editor, who needed it for the back cover of the book Seix Barral would soon bring out in Barcelona. He did not really feel like having his picture taken, but faced with the incredible insistence of El Chinolope, possibly the world's worst photographer, whose threadbare clothing contrasted with the shining camera he held in his hand, he gave in to the poor fellow.

He asked for a moment to change and put on the outfit he always wore to the ministry: his Belgian suit, collared shirt, and tie. First El Chinolope took a few indoor shots in the apartment, then they went into the street and all the way down 23rd and Rampa to the Malecón. On the way, El Chinolope had him stop now and again, and he snapped another picture. Then he took one of him sitting on the Malecón wall. They continued the length of the Malecón to Castillo de la Punta, where El Chinolope took several more photos. After that they went down to Old Havana, to the Plaza de la Catedral, for more photographs. Finally, they sat outdoors at El Patio restaurant newly opened by the Revolution and now an obligatory stopping place for politicians, who were the new tourists – and he had a cup of coffee and a glass of water, while El Chinolope took more pictures. They also hiked up to the old palace across from the cathedral, practically in ruins now, and there, amid the decadence of Cuba's long-ago glories, El Chinolope snapped a few more. In the end, tired of walking and posing, he told El Chinolope it was time to stop, and instead of insisting on another pose he agreed and they went back to Vedado. As he got off the bus, El Chinolope, hidden by the crush of people on board, promised to bring him the contact sheets in a day or two so he could review them.

< 174 >

At home he had a message from his old friend Silvano Suárez, now a producer for television and lately of cabaret shows as well. He returned the call and learned that Silvano (whom he always called Antonio, his name in high school) had a show that was ending its run. That night he went to the cabaret at the Habana Libre to see the dance numbers Silvano had choreographed. It wasn't bad, given the shortages of human talent and material for costumes. He really liked the singing of a tall and splendidly built dark-skinned woman named Luz Divina, whom he recognized as someone he had met a long time ago. Back then she sang in a little dance hall called the Saint John, and did not call herself Luz Divina. Now she was a diva.

When the show was over, Silvano came to his table and they were soon joined by Maricusa Cabrera, who was in the show and was Silvano's ex-wife, plus two chorus girls he did not know. There was a funny moment when Maricusa accused Silvano of who knows how many theatrical crimes, which was comical for anyone who knew them. He laughed a lot and Maricusa smiled maliciously, although Silvano did not find it very funny. Then he saw Luz Divina heading out and he said goodbye to Maricusa, thanked Silvano, and followed the singer into the street.

She was walking toward the back of the hotel, down M Street, and he went after her. She stopped to wait for a car to take her home, and he approached. She recognized him, not immediately, but she recognized him. That delay annoyed him, but given the singer's beauty he soon recovered. He recalled a night three years before when they had sat on the wall of the Malecón after her midnight show at the Saint John and she spoke of wanting to leave Cuba, of wanting to go to France, and they had had an intimate moment which she ruined when she touched her hair and told him out of the blue: "I use a wig, you know."

< 175 >

But she was not in the mood to remember that interlude and was more concerned with when the taxi would arrive to take her home. She answered his questions, thanked him for his praise, and maintained an attentive, but cool distance. He did not even try to invite her out that night and they did not speak of the future. Finally, the taxi, which she shared with others also waiting, arrived, and she left. Of course her goodbye was affectionate enough, but he knew better and he walked home along an empty 23rd Street feeling, as he had on other occasions, like a loser.

El Chinolope turned up with several enlargements he liked. One made him look too handsome and he decided that would not do for the publication. But the other photos were good. Following his brother's suggestion he spoke with Rine Leal about publishing something in the literary pages of *Bohemia*, which Rine edited. There could be an interview which Luis Agüero would do, reviews of his previous books, and an excerpt from his forthcoming prizewinning novel. At first Rine was all in favor of the idea, but later on – maybe after he suggested it at *Bohemia* – he seemed a bit reluctant, and he guessed that the magazine, perhaps due to views that curiously overlapped with those of the intelligence service, was not going to publish anything of his. At the same time he felt a bit like Stendhal, seeking reviews and interviews to promote his work, though in this case his goals were higher and more urgent than mere literary praise: the pages of *Bohemia* might be the key that opens the exit door. In the end, *Bohemia* did publish the material, along with a nice photograph by El Chinolope. In the interview he addressed the dilemma of the revolutionary writer, saying that for a truly revolutionary writer the Revolution itself offered solutions. What's more, he promised to devote all his future works to revolutionary literature – not to a literature that was revolutionary but to literature of the Revolution. In answering the

< 176 >

questions, he knew he had no intention of writing such books. He believed politics and literature were locked in a lifelong battle and he had already made his choice, a decision he would not renounce. Sometimes he thought the opinions he expressed in the interview were less a skeleton key than a little push to pry open the escape hatch. In any case, several people came by to congratulate him, but he knew of others – failed writers like the impotent Samuel Feijóo – who picked his interview apart and dumped on the opinions he expressed in *Bohemia*.

One day Ivonne Calvo, his former sister-in-law who worked in the INRA building, told him a co-worker wanted to meet him. (Later on, he learned she had seen his photograph in *Bohemia*, thus he had El Chinolope to thank for the encounter.) He said he would be delighted. The woman, young, quite pretty and shapely, was named Olivia Vals and she came to Luis Agüero and Sara Calvo's apartment, where Ivonne also lived, to meet him. He invited her to go out one night, but she was married so night would not work. They decided she would leave the office early one afternoon and they would meet. He suggested the park across from El Carmelo for several reasons: it was far from where Olivia lived and thus unlikely that anyone from her family would see her and, besides, El Carmelo was just a hundred steps from Rine's apartment, which Rine had offered him.

They met in the park on an auspiciously beautiful afternoon, hot and peaceful. After chatting for a while on a bench, they walked – already tacitly agreed, each knew why the other was there – toward Rine's apartment. They climbed the stairs to the top floor, he with some apprehension about being seen by the family of his former wife, who lived in the building. It always bothered him to meet Marta Calvo's relatives, but now, arriving with another woman, annoyance would turn into embarrassment.

< 177 >

They entered Rine's small apartment and sat side by side on the sofa. He got up to put on a record – after asking her if she liked music and she said yes, very much – and then returned to Olivia's side. Without much preamble, he slipped his arm around her shoulders and she said nothing. Then he came close and kissed her cheek. She let him. He sought her lips and although she did not respond immediately, soon they were kissing and this time she was kissing back. He kissed her with more technique than ardor and she – though she had not said as much, he knew by a single utterance that she felt very lonely – kissed him almost passionately.

He began to take off her clothes without any protest from her, and finally, after she took off her underwear by herself, she stood naked before him. He was still fully dressed and for a moment he contemplated her – that was something he truly enjoyed: to watch a woman undress and end up naked excited him more than anything – before putting his arm around her waist and guiding her to the bedroom.

They made love rather coldly. She, fairly indifferent to his hands and mouth, seemed to be seeking affection in his caresses rather than fully enjoying sex. When they finished, she got dressed right away and went into the living room, as if she were ashamed. When he, still naked, came to find her, what she said stopped him cold.

"You know, this is the first time I've cheated on my husband."

So that was why she had been so passive. But the next time they met, her passivity had practically become a technique and he no longer enjoyed her. Besides, he discovered with disgust that she suffered from hemorrhoids. Thus, there was no third time and, as tacitly as they had come together, they stopped seeing each other. Ivonne told him that Olivia was very much in

< 178 >

love with him and wanted to know when he would go out with her. He did not wish to confess that they had already gone out twice, so he gave Ivonne the impression he was not interested in having an affair with Olivia. His expression of disinterest was such that Ivonne told him, "You're doing the right thing. You shouldn't cheat on Miriam." He never saw Olivia again the entire time he remained in Havana.

A few days later he recalled Olivia Vals because he woke up to a sharp pain in his anus and realized, with a disgust that made him nauseous, that he too had hemorrhoids. He did not want to see the doctor he had made friends with at the Calixto García, because it seemed undignified to get your anus examined. So he remained uncomfortable, practically suffering, for a week, at the end of which he felt better and the hemorrhoid trouble did not return. He figured it must have come from something he ate, but on the other hand Hildelisa's regime – nearly always rice with potatoes, the fault of the ration book – was incapable of giving you indigestion much less piles: that was the word he did not wish to say out loud, but it seemed the perfect one for his affliction.

During those days, Alberto Mora came to the apartment often and they would talk about literature, especially Joyce, since from Belgium he had brought him a copy of *Finnegans Wake* and a book of commentary to unlock the pages of that hermetic tome. One afternoon when Alberto was over, Silvano Suárez (whom he always jokingly called Sssilvano Sssuárez) called to invite him to his new production at the Havana Hilton. He asked if he could bring along Alberto and Luis Agüero, who was also visiting. Silvano said he would have a table ready for the three of them that night – thus three married men went unaccompanied to the cabaret.

< 179 >

An incident occurred that might have had serious consequences. They arrived in time for the show, the only one that night. They watched the chorus girls dancing to a *pacá* tune, which was the rhythm that gave musical shape to the entire show, and listened to the more-or-less popular singers of the day. Everything was going fine when a man at one of the neighboring tables suddenly confronted Luis Agüero. "You bastard, I'm going to kill you for that!" he screamed. Alberto intervened and managed to block the man, while holding back Luis, who was ready to fight, yelling, "Come on! Let him go!" He stood up, not knowing what to do. The only thing he really feared – the police coming – did not happen. But Luis got a bloody finger where the guy had grabbed him trying to haul him toward his table. "Just like a woman, clawing with her nails!" Luis yelled. Right then, Alberto asked the man to explain himself.

"Nothing with you, my friend," he said. "This idiot was passing notes to my wife." The woman was an ideal partner for the angry neighbor: fat, short, and ugly. That Luis Agüero would have wanted anything to do with her was unbelievable. What's more, Luis had been half drunk for some time. Somehow, Alberto managed to calm the neighbor, who sat back down saying, "You come here to have a good time and a jerk like that wants to ruin the party." Luis, meanwhile, mumbled strange challenges. Finally, the three of them sat down. In a low voice, he asked:

"Luis, what were you doing?"

"Nothing, *viejo*, nothing."

"Okay, okay," said Alberto, laughing out of the side of his mouth and clicking his teeth. Luis laughed too.

"What happened?" he asked Luis.

< 180 >

"Nothing, I'm fine."

"But you were sending notes to that woman while Alberto and I were watching the show, weren't you?"

Luis remained silent for a moment, then said, "Okay, yeah. It's true."

"Are you crazy?" he asked.

"Not me, why?"

"Have you taken a good look at that woman?"

While speaking even more quietly than before, he looked beyond Alberto to the next table, where the disputed woman seemed even uglier than before.

"So?" said Luis, unabashed.

"You're crazy," he assured him.

"No," Alberto said, "what happened is he wanted to pick a fight with the husband and couldn't think of a better way than trying to pick up his wife."

The three of them laughed, he trying to hide it because he was facing the couple at the next table.

"You're crazy," he said again. Luis smiled, then brought his bleeding finger to his mouth and sucked on it. The three decided to leave before the show was over: Luis to take care of his bloody finger in the bathroom, Alberto (who was also a bit drunk) to get some air, and he to avoid more trouble with the hotheaded neighbor, who continued making faces at Luis, eyes full of hatred, while Luis returned his stare, not backing down.

They went out into the hallway and looked for the nearest bathroom, where Luis washed off his finger and wrapped it in his handkerchief. He still could not quite believe what had happened.

"On my mother's grave, I swear you're crazy," he said to Luis.

Alberto laughed and then said, "Both of them are crazy."

< 181 >

"No, not at all," said Luis.

"Oh, no," he said. "Absolutely nuts. *Compadre*, imagine trying to pick up such a dog."

Still upset, he had to face the wall so he would not laugh along with Alberto, who was cracking up. Then he broke up too and gave Luis, who had just finished wrapping his finger, a soft slap on the head.

"Crazy," he said. "Utterly bonkers."

They saw people leaving the cabaret and knew the show was over. Fortunately, Luis's furious rival was not among them. The three of them left the building and went to the Salón Caribe and ordered drinks. He did not want any more to drink, but Luis and Alberto insisted they should not bring the night to a close so early. At a certain moment, when he turned to see who was in the bar, he noticed Luz Divina, the singer, at a table in the back in close conversation with a man he could not make out at first. Looking more intently, he thought it was one of Miriam Gómez's brothers. The more he looked, the more the fellow resembled a married brother of Miriam's. The two of them seemed to be having an intimate moment in their corner and, checking them out a third time, he had the same impression. He could not be certain – when you are nearsighted you can never be sure of what you see – but he would have sworn then and even today that it was Miriam's older brother who was enjoying the undivided attentions of Luz Divina. Then he felt jealous, nothing more specific, but jealous nonetheless, and he told himself that Miriam's brother was all too easily winning favors he would have given a lot that night to obtain. The three of them left. Alberto took Luis in his Volkswagen, while he, determined to forget Luz Divina and in order to dissipate the effects of the alcohol, decided to walk home. Alberto and Luis allowed him to go.

< 182 >

The following day he got an invitation to lunch. The elder Carbonell, Pipo's father, asked him out to the seafood bar in Barlovento. He came to pick him up in his car from the Cuban Workers Confederation, where he was an executive, and took him all the way across Vedado, down the Malecón, then through Miramar and beyond to the beaches of Marianao, and then even farther down the Santa Fe highway to Barlovento. They turned off to the right and entered that Batista-era development, whose deserted streets and open avenues were laid out but unpaved and lined with abandoned half-finished buildings. At last, they reached a bar at the edge of a bay filled with calm shining waters that reflected the boiling noontime sun.

They went into the bar, which was cool and dark, and climbed to the much lighter but hotter restaurant on the second floor. They ate rice with seafood, the ubiquitous Cuban paella, and perhaps due to the comparison with Hildelisa's cooking further limited by rationing, he found it delicious. The restaurant even had the liquid that had become so precious in Cuba: beer. He was ready to listen to whatever Carbonell had to say, assuming the father wanted to know about his son's future now that he was divorced. But Carbonell did not speak of his son, although once or twice he seemed on the point of doing so. No, he spoke about Gustavo Arcos, who, he said, had problems now that he was wavering on whether to return to Brussels as soon as possible. He was surprised to learn that Carbonell knew Arcos was in trouble with the government, since he had not told anyone about his conversation with Roa. He guessed that Gustavo's difficulties had reached beyond the ministry itself, but said nothing, only nodding in agreement with Carbonell. (A few days earlier and again a few days later, he bumped into Suárez on the street; it seemed he was to go with Gustavo to Italy and he complained anxiously about how sluggish Gustavo was, doing nothing at

< 183 >

all to clear up his dossier. On both occasions he thought Suárez seemed very nervous, which he attributed to his yearning for an overseas post so he could escape his dreary life sentence in the ministry.) Listening to Carbonell, he realized Gustavo really was in trouble, even if the man himself would deny it thanks to his invincible optimism that was more lack of imagination than anything else.

They returned to Havana, and though the elder Carbonell did not mention Gustavo again, he understood the lunch to be a warning of sorts to be passed along. That very afternoon he went to the Arcos home and found old Rosina hobbling along without her cane. He asked what had happened to it.

"Señor Cabrera, don't ask," Doña Rosina said. "The handle broke on me and Suárez took it three weeks ago to be fixed and it's still not ready. What do you make of this country?"

To lighten Doña Rosina's mood, he answered that she looked as lovely as ever, but ended up agreeing she was right. Gustavo was in his room, as he nearly always was, busy massaging his bad leg.

"What's wrong, Gustavo?"

"Nothing, just since it's been raining my leg hurts more than usual."

"Why don't you go to the doctor?"

"You think anyone here is going to know about damage to the spinal column?"

"I don't know. Maybe."

"Fat chance, *viejo*, since there are only a handful left."

"Well, there's Cubela," he kidded. Rolando Cubela, a commander on the Revolutionary Directorate who had been a student leader, graduated from medical school with unseemly haste after the Revolution.

< 184 >

"Lucky he's a heart specialist," Gustavo said, laughing, "if not, I might fall into his clutches."

Both of them laughed. That was the good thing about Gustavo Arcos, he never lost his sense of humor.

"How are you otherwise?" he asked.

"Not great. Imagine, that Mexican bitch has me at her mercy, threatening me, with the Women of the Revolution backing her up."

Gustavo spoke as if that were a state institution, and in a way it was. The wives of the revolution's leaders were on a crusade to impose the most bourgeois of values regarding the sanctity of marriage, family unity, and the sacrosanct duty of parents to their children. Such "revolutionary" axioms applied to everyone, except of course to Fidel Castro, who could have as many lovers as he liked, as well as a string of apartments and houses to sleep in, a new one every night.

"But, can't you do anything?"

"What could I do, my friend? The only thing left would be to kill her."

Gustavo laughed and went back to rubbing his bad leg. He was about to tell him about the conversation with the elder Carbonell, but instead he said:

"What about Raúl Castro, couldn't he do something?"

"I haven't seen Raúl. Maybe at the July 26th celebration I'll be able to speak with him. I did talk to Faustino Pérez and I already told you about my friend Ramirito. Do you know what he said?"

"No. What did he tell you?"

"People don't have friends anymore."

"Like that, with those words?"

< 185 >

"With those very words and he added a few more I didn't really understand. He told me I shouldn't place more trust in old friends than new ones. What could that mean?"

"I don't know. The commander is an oracle."

Gustavo again laughed heartily. Then he asked, "What brings you here?"

Sometimes Gustavo Arcos had the gift of intuition; he knew there was a reason he had come.

"Nothing. Can't you visit a friend?"

"A new one or an old one?"

"I'd say both…"

Gustavo laughed again. Then they talked about other unimportant things and in the end he left and went to the Writers Union. There he found Walterio Carbonell (no relation to Pipo) drinking a clear Coca-Cola with the sculptor Tomás Oliva. Walterio told him about a speech Faure Chomón had made at the university, in which he advised students not to walk around with a book under their arm, or to dress in the latest fashion, or wear sandals. Those three things, according to Chomón, led to the worst: to homosexuality and therefore counterrevolution. He felt a blind rage welling up inside. He had met Faure Chomón at the beginning of the Revolution, when Alberto Mora praised him as a time-honored hero, and he had observed him up close when he was ambassador to the Soviet Union. He had not thought Faure Chomón capable of giving such a speech, which sounded like the opening salvo to a witch hunt, and he said as much to Walterio, forgetting that they were sitting in the Writers Union, always home to a troublemaker or two from the G2 or stool pigeons in the leadership. Then he was shocked a second time when Tomás Oliva spoke approvingly of the speech and started heaping insults on homosexuals. Tomás Oliva of all people, someone he had met back in high

< 186 >

school and whom he called "strange" then – which in Cuba could mean so many things. What's more, he had always cared for Tomás, not only because of his talent as a sculptor but because of his bad arm from polio.

The three of them left together and walked down 17th to Avenue of the Presidents, then along to 23rd Street. Gustavo Arcos's leg was right: it was going to rain despite the fierce sun. The heat was insufferable. They continued chatting as they walked and when they got to where the pharmacy used to be at 23rd and the avenue, they stopped so he could turn off toward home. At that moment a Skoda pulled over. It was René Álvarez Ríos, now a professor at the university. He said hello to Walterio, an old friend of his from Paris, as well as to Oliva and to him. Then, without budging from his car and seeming to be in a great hurry, he called to him: "I want to speak with you." So he went over.

"Listen," Álvarez Ríos said, "are you a friend of Euclides Vázquez Candela?"

"Yes, why?"

"Could you tell him to get off my back?"

"What's he doing to you?"

"Nothing, just tell him to get off my back."

"But what's going on?"

"He's at me again and again and again."

He nearly thought René had lost his marbles. "But tell me, *viejo*, what has he done to you?"

"He's on my back. Egged on by Euclides, the whole orthodox wing of the July 26th Movement is riding me now."

For a moment he pictured the old Greek mathematician astride René's strong back. But he did not laugh.

< 187 >

"So, what do you want me to do?"

"Nothing, just tell Euclides that I'm not in the old guard of the party."

Here was Álvarez Ríos, who had always felt close to the Cuban Communist Party, even when he was in France, now disowning his old mentors.

"Well, when I see him I'll tell him."

"Make damn sure he pays attention."

He almost thought he said, "Make that boor pay attention."

"We'll see."

"More than anything, tell him to let me teach and stop ganging up on me."

Both René Álvarez Ríos and Euclides Vázquez Candela were university professors, although apparently the latter not only thought he was the better professor, he must have figured he had license to persecute any old Communist, whether an admirer, a fellow traveler, or a Communist-and-a-half. His astonishment at the political and personal convolutions unleashed by the Revolution was boundless.

"Now I have to go, I still haven't had lunch," René said, "but if Euclides you see, don't forget to think of me."

In his agitation, Álvarez Ríos was talking in verse without realizing it.

"Don't worry, I won't forget."

René's last utterance was loud enough that Oliva and Walterio, who had come over to the car, heard it.

"Poor René," Walterio said, after he pulled away, "always in the wrong orthodoxy."

He and Walterio laughed, but Tomás did not.

"Well, if he supports the old party, then fuck him," was what he said.

< 188 >

He deduced that Oliva, perhaps encouraged by his bad arm, had become an utter Jacobin, thirsty for persecution. He said goodbye to them and went home.

In the afternoon, watching the rain, he thought a lot about his dead mother.

JULY 26TH WAS APPROACHING and this year the celebrations would be held in Santa Clara rather than Havana or Santiago. All the members of the diplomatic corps were to be invited, including the Cuban heads of mission who happened to be in the country. He hoped to be invited as head of mission in Belgium, which would confirm his position in the ministry. So when he received a call from the protocol office telling him he had an invitation to pick up, he went there happily. Upon opening the envelope he discovered he had been invited to a reception at the Belgian Embassy. His disappointment was enormous, but larger still was his surprise to learn that the one invited to Santa Clara as head of mission in Belgium was Gustavo Arcos. As Arcos had said, evidently Roa still feared him.

He went to the Belgian reception with Gustavo Arcos and there he saw Ricardo Porro, a man whose politics had always been firmly orthodox. Now he was shoveling shit on the Revolution, so much so he thought it unwise to stand anywhere near him. Soon he felt queasy and wondered if the drink was to blame. Feeling nauseous, he said goodbye early to the chargé d'affaires.

Fortunately he found a taxi at the door, the driver evidently hoping for a good tip. When he got home he had a fever of thirty-nine degrees and after vomiting he went to bed. His grandmother, walking slowly and painfully,

< 189 >

came to him asking, "What's wrong, my son?" She prepared a home remedy, which he drank, and soon he fell asleep. In the early morning he awoke with no fever. It did not occur to him to give credit to the home remedy, rather he assumed it was a forty-eight-hour virus, since he hadn't felt well since the previous day. Not able to fall back asleep, Miriam Gómez flooded his thoughts. It was strange: before, whenever he was ill, he would think about his mother; now that his mother was dead, he wanted Miriam near.

In the morning he learned that his aunt Felisa had come in from the country. He liked her a lot and, what's more, he found her attractive with her long, slender, elegant legs and stylish way of smoking, and her habit of filling a sentence with as many foul words as she possibly could. Her stories always made him laugh and he was grateful she did not mention his dead mother even once. Felisa talked about everything else, especially incidents (practically accidents) involving her large family. She had nine children and who knows how many grandchildren. Unlike his mother, Zoila, Felisa was fated to be happy; her name suited her well.

Later on, he went to the hospital to see his doctor friend. While waiting he took a stroll and was utterly surprised to run into Franqui, there to see a specialist in digestive disorders. Only a few days had passed since their last encounter, but in that time he had grown rather frail. Franqui had a stomach ulcer, which he attributed to a lack of gastric juices and which his friends thought would sooner or later be diagnosed as stomach cancer. Now, in the shade of a tree, Franqui complained about his isolation from official circles; it was as if he wanted to keep him from recounting his own situation at the ministry. But then Franqui himself brought up the subject, and told him his chances of being sent overseas as a diplomat were slim and he had better prepare himself for whatever might be coming. Discretion was Franqui's

< 190 >

mania, he swallowed half his words, which often made conversations with him mysterious. Now, as other times, he did not understand what Franqui was trying to get across, but he caught the tone and went home from the hospital feeling very depressed. So much so that his grandmother asked, "What happened at the hospital, my son?" He had to say nothing had happened, he had not even seen the doctor. Which was true.

Gustavo called because he wanted him to come over and talk. When he got there, he found a very worried man.

"Do you know what happened to me with the Belgian chargé d'affaires?"

"No, what happened?"

"He talked to me about the case of an American citizen married to a Belgian who is being held by the G2, accused of spying. It seems his wife is the daughter of someone very influential in Belgium."

"Do they have a farm in Pinar del Río?"

"Yes, how did you know?"

"I saw his visa application in Brussels, which was being held up. It seems her father has land next to property owned by the king, King Baudouin."

"That's them. Well, the husband, who has the bad luck of being related to John Foster Dulles, has been in G2's jail for about a month and they won't let anyone see him. The Belgian chargé d'affaires asked me to look in to his case, so right away I called my friend…"

"Ramirito," he finished his sentence.

Gustavo smiled. "That's the one. Ramirito asked me to come over to the Interior Ministry so he could show me the evidence against him."

"Did you go?"

"I just got back."

"What was the evidence?"

< 191 >

"The most ridiculous thing you could imagine. A shortwave radio, the kind you or I might have, a few letters written to his aunt that don't say anything important, and two or three things more. Oh, and a pair of binoculars!"

He thought of his own street-watching habit and took note.

"So what did Ramirito tell you?"

"That they caught him in flagrante. Then he asked my opinion about the evidence."

"And what did you say?"

"What could I say? That they didn't seem to have anything conclusive."

"Gustavo, Gustavo," he said half joking.

"What would you have me do? The fact is, it looks like a setup to frame the American."

"A relative of Foster Dulles? A guy like that wants to have a farm in Pinar de Río?"

"You've hit the nail on the head. That's what it's about. They want to confiscate his farm; it's one of the few foreign-owned properties left in Cuba, and they can't think of anything else but accusing the owner of espionage."

"You can't have said that to Ramiro Valdés."

"You're crazy!"

"The two of us are crazy. Like Goerdeler, we should have these chats in a moving car." And he pointed to the walls and roof, which could all be filled with microphones.

"Who's that Gordo guy?"

"Goerdeler, the mayor of Hamburg who conspired against Hitler in the July 20th plot, the anniversary of which, by coincidence, is today."

Now Gustavo laughed.

"You and your funny notions. You're getting like Franqui."

< 192 >

"I just saw him."

"What did I just say? Microphones! Who is going to bother to put microphones on me?"

"Your friend Ramirito. By the way, did you ask him if he looked at the American's hands?"

Gustavo laughed again.

"Are you crazy? I don't make those jokes at the Interior Ministry."

"You're learning."

He went off worried about Gustavo Arcos's utter lack of concern. Many times later on he thought that the problems that befell Gustavo could be traced back to his refusal to say the American was a spy, rather than his lifestyle, as he would claim. One of the apparent accusations against Gustavo was "*dolcevitismo*," which meant he was living a happy, carefree life while the Revolution went on around him; lucky him if he could. The fact is Gustavo had neither the imagination nor the disposition to live a dolce vita.

Those days he barely saw his father, who was busy with his work at *Bohemia* and in the Defense Committee, and who sometimes got home after supper when he had already gone out. His father was the only one in the house who lived a life in tune with the Revolution, more than anything because of his long-standing activism as a Communist. If he was working so hard now it would also be to distract himself from his wife's death, though sometimes he wondered if his father, forever a slay-them-without-a-word womanizer, had another woman somewhere.

The one he himself talked to now and again was Felisa, who like his mother believed in spirits and the power of saints and who gave him advice to get through this bad patch. Sometimes, when the trap he had fallen into was really getting to him, his grandmother would come out of her little room

< 193 >

and tell him: "Don't worry, my son, it will all work out." Then Felisa would make fun of his grandmother, saying nothing works out on its own, and she would tell him to let the spirits guide him. One day she turned up with a leaflet with a horrible prayer to the Holy Spirit, which she insisted he sign and carry with him always for protection and read it every time he was going to encounter the ones his aunt quite correctly called the enemy.

He had promised to spend the July 26th holiday with Lisandro Otero and his wife, Marcia, at the beach house they had at Varadero. But in the end there was a mix-up and Lisandro had to go to Santa Clara, since he was the editor of *Cuba* magazine. Lisandro hesitated, uncomfortable with the idea of him going alone with Marcia. It seemed like jealousy, though he told himself Lisandro could not possibly think that of him. In any case Marcia stayed in Havana, so they went together to a gallery opening along with Oscar Hurtado, Sarusky, and some others. After the event Sarusky proposed they go have a drink somewhere. Recalling the lunch with the elder Carbonell, he suggested Barlovento, where none of them had ever been before, not even Marcia. Hearing his description, she was excited to go.

First, he took her to see the bull ray swimming in a gigantic fish tank behind the bar, explaining they did not last long in captivity and when it died it would be replaced with another. Then they went back to the table where Oscar Hurtado was recounting a long story about hunting fish underwater. (Besides having diving experience, Hurtado knew a lot about fish because his uncle had a fish store on the old Plaza del Polvorín and Oscar spent his youth working there, even though he looked on that chapter of his life with considerable resentment.)

They were drinking and, though it displeased Oscar, he asked Marcia to step outside to look at the water from the small dock. The bay was calm as

< 194 >

could be and reflected the full moon like a mirror. The two of them contemplated the scene in silence and he turned to study her large black eyes as she gazed at the sea. He was very close to her and for a moment he felt tempted to take her by the shoulders and kiss her. All he had to do was lean across and put his lips on her lovely pink mouth, and then he remembered Lisandro's hesitation and the thought crossed his mind that Marcia might be interested in him. (Later on, he frequently told himself that he should have kissed her, and on those occasions he was certain she would have responded with a kiss of her own.) He watched her there in the semidarkness, silhouetted against the terrace lights, a tune from the record player or radio in the bar floating out to them. She looked more beautiful than ever, her black hair shining glamorously, eyes fixed on the sea, not at all indifferent to what he had said about the tranquil beauty of the place, both of them silent. With her aura of a middle-class girl yearning to be a revolutionary at any cost, she was a woman he admired and with whom he knew he could fall in love. Perhaps that was the reason he suggested they go back into the bar.

They returned to the table, where Oscar Hurtado was still talking about fish and the sea.

July 26th came and went and still he heard nothing from the ministry. Miriam Gómez called again, asking what was up, when would he return, and he had to make up an excuse that was not only plausible, but which would sound good to the ears of those who were certainly listening to their long-distance conversation.

One day, following an urge, he went back to Old Havana. Not downtown, rather the stroll along Neptuno and Galiano to Prado and from there back to Galiano by San Rafael. He was astounded at the poverty of the place, which used to be so lively with stores filled with customers. The Miami restaurant

< 195 >

had closed, there had been a fire or something, and now the place was called Caracas. The newspaper and magazine kiosks were shuttered, their dilapidated presence on the sidewalk of Louvre Street another ruin arising. He decided he did not want to see San Rafael Street, one of his favorite places from the days when he lived in poverty at Zulueta 408, a street that in its good times had elegant stores and sidewalks decorated with colored mosaics, and reminded him of the best of Rio.

He returned home and spent the rest of the day reading on the balcony. The only thing memorable about his outing to Old Havana was an encounter with a girl walking ahead of him down Neptune near San Miguel. She was wearing a strapless dress, and her shoulders, back, and of course her upper chest were all bare. Her young flesh was practically edible and for a moment he felt good until he had to pass her since she was heading down Prado. He thought then, as at other times during his stay, that the only thing that redeemed this country of all its historical sins was its natural beauty and its women, another form of natural beauty.

He had begun to write too, composing fragments of a novel in the bedroom where his daughters slept, seated at his old drafting table, using his brother's typewriter and the few sheets of paper in the house. He asked his father to bring him paper from *Bohemia* and he learned paper was in short supply: yet another shortage. But he did not stop writing, yet he told no one about it, scribbling in secret while outwardly cultivating the image of a bachelor diplomat on vacation.

Another day Ramoncito Suárez dropped by. Given that Ramoncito worked at the Film Institute, he had not seen much of him since getting back and the visit seemed to come out of nowhere.

"I have to tell you something," Ramoncito said after the greetings.

< 196 >

"Yes? What?"

"I was at the Foreign Ministry yesterday with César Leante and he talked about you. I don't remember what department I was in, but Leante knew the people there and he asked why they had taken you off the airplane when you were headed back to Belgium. One of them, I don't remember his name, told him it was because of some reports you had sent in about the Congo."

Ramoncito paused and in response he sat there in silence, thinking. He remembered his reports from 1964 about the rebellion in the Congo and what he had said about Gbenye and his people, and about Kasa-Vubu and Tshombe and later Mobutu. He also remembered the day he had to interview a Congolese man and a Belgian who looked like a military officer in civilian clothes, who had come to the embassy to propose a new rebellion if Cuba would sponsor it and cover the cost. He also recalled, with precision, what his reports said about all that business.

"That's a lie," he told Ramoncito.

"It's a lie? But I was there."

"I don't mean what you say, I mean what they said. My reports on the Congo were as orthodox as could be." But he remembered that his reports were not orthodox from the official point of view, in fact they countered Cuba's assumptions about what was going on in that region so far away from Cuba and so close to Belgium.

"Well," Ramoncito replied, "that's what they said. I thought you'd like to know. None of them, not even Leante, knows about our friendship."

He gave Ramoncito his heartfelt thanks. Not only had they been friends for many years, but Ramoncito had married a girl with whom he had gone out long ago.

"What do you think?" Ramoncito asked. "When will you go?"

< 197 >

"I don't know. Truly, I do not know. It might be next week or next month. What I do know is I am going back to Europe."

Up to that moment he had not put this feeling into words, but now, saying Europe instead of Belgium, he realized that he would go back no matter what. From that day on, perhaps encouraged by Ramoncito's revelations, he set himself the unwavering goal of returning at any cost.

Ramoncito stayed a while longer, sitting on the balcony, and they talked about movies, other trivialities. Then, once Ramoncito had left, he called Alberto Mora and told him he wanted to speak with him; Alberto said he would drop by the following day.

When Alberto arrived, he took him into the bedroom at the back, not onto the balcony.

"Come, I want to talk."

He closed the door.

"What's with all the mystery?" Alberto asked.

"Nothing. I just want to speak with you in private."

"Shoot."

"You know what's happened."

"No. What's happened?"

"My situation in the ministry."

"What's the news?"

"Nothing. It's just that every day I feel more certain I won't go back to Belgium as a diplomat."

"How do you know?"

"I don't know anything, that's the impression I get. I'm also convinced that it's State Security that's blocking my return."

"Have you spoken with Roa?"

< 198 >

"No. And that's precisely why I think the decision to keep me here came not from Minrex but from the Interior Ministry."

"That could be. I don't know."

"I called you to tell you one thing: I'm leaving Cuba however I can. If I can't get out legally, I'll seek asylum in an embassy or I'll flee in a boat. But I'm going."

Alberto smiled.

"*Caramba*, aren't you dramatic!" he said. But neither his smile nor his words were in jest.

"No, I'm not dramatic. I'm simply not going to remain here at Barbaroja's mercy."

"The Galician Piñeiro? He's a joke."

"A joke?"

"Of course. That's what he is. Do you now what they call him in the Council of Ministers? James Bond! Know why? All day long he's got his briefcase with him, he even handcuffs it to his wrist, and he takes it everywhere. One day he left it at the Council of Ministers and he came running to look for it. From that day on, no one has taken his mysterious briefcase seriously. They think he's a joke. You should too."

"I don't have that luxury. I called you because I don't know anyone else in the government I can trust. Franqui is totally out of the loop and he's more cut off every day, and Gustavo Arcos has or will have problems."

"Arcos? With whom?"

"With a guy named Aldama, who was an agent from G2 or State Security in Brussels, and things he's brought on himself too."

"Gustavo doesn't have any problems."

"Well, you'll see soon enough."

< 199 >

"So, what do you plan to do?"

"That's why I called you. I want to leave on good terms. I have plenty of pretexts. My novel is coming out in Spain, I've got the money from the prize in a bank in Barcelona, my wife is in Belgium… A lot of reasons, see?"

"One thing. Promise me you won't do anything stupid."

"Fine."

"Another thing. Don't tell anyone about this. I'm going to do all I can for you, but I don't want any surprises like the one at the airport."

"Agreed."

Alberto Mora left and he did not see him for many days.

One afternoon when Luis Agüero was over, Raúl Palazuelos called urgently. That phone call seemed strange, since Palazuelos, who had been practically his brother-in-law and had been his secretary when *Lunes* had a television program four years before, had been avoiding him more or less openly since he got back. Raúl told him they had picked up Oscar Hurtado and something had to be done to get him out. He said he did not know what he could do, and he asked where Hurtado was being held. It seems he was arrested by agents from the DIR, who investigate common crimes. As soon as Raúl hung up, he tried to locate Miriam Acevedo, Oscar's wife, but could not. Later on, Walterio Carbonell and Jaime Sarusky called. They decided to meet at his apartment and go to DIR headquarters together.

By the time they arrived at the station on Egido Street, quite a few of Oscar's friends were there and they chose to go in as a group. Walterio and Sarusky were to find out what was going on. They spoke with the duty officer, and the agent in charge of the investigation was called in. He was a young guy, pale, rather nondescript, whose only notable feature was his olive green

< 200 >

uniform. He was the one who had arrested Oscar. From what he said, Oscar was accused of stealing a handbag. His friends all looked puzzled: it was unimaginable that Oscar Hurtado could have stolen anything. The agent explained that Hurtado denied the charges and insisted he had not stolen the handbag, rather he had found it. That was the crux of the investigation, he said. Whom to believe? Oscar Hurtado, of course, the friends all said. (At that moment no one thought about how funny it was that Hurtado was being accused of *hurto*, robbery.)

Oscar got out late that night, or more accurately very early the next morning. Not until the next day at his house did he offer an explanation.

"It was all a mistake," he said. "I went to have lunch, like I often do, at the cafeteria in the Hotel Capri. They know me there. But by chance the waiter I know wasn't working. That's crucial. Well, I sat down to eat and in a little while I noticed a handbag had been left under the counter at the cash register, which is where they put packages. I thought I would give it to the waiter, but since I didn't know him, I figured I'd better give it to the one I do know, who might be working tomorrow. In other words, the following day. So when I left, I paid, picked up the handbag, and took it with me. When I got home I threw it in a closet, shut the closet door, and forgot all about that blessed bag. But the woman it belonged to did not forget. She went back to the cafeteria to look for it and they told her no one had found a handbag. Then the woman asked if they remembered who was sitting next to her, and the cashier, who also knows me, said it was a customer who comes nearly every day for lunch. The woman left, but it seems she went to the police, and the next time I went to the cafeteria the woman was there with a policeman. They asked me about the handbag and that's when I remembered it. Of course I

< 201 >

went home with the policeman and the woman and I opened the closet and there was the handbag, which I gave to her. Except the policeman had to charge me with robbery. In other words, I was a thief."

"But, Oscar," he said. "How could you possibly have taken the handbag home?"

"Didn't I already explain?"

"Yes, but why didn't you give it to the cafeteria staff?"

"I explained that too."

"I don't get it. Was the handbag old or new?"

"Come on, it was old, ugly."

"You're right, that was a pointless question."

Oscar Hurtado got out of jail right away thanks to the efforts of his friends, among them Lisandro Otero, and he was never brought to trial because the story was so unbelievable he could not have made it up. The DIR investigator went to see Oscar several times, once when he was visiting. He never could tell if it was police work that brought him or he just wanted to get to know a writer.

The next time Alberto came over he brought a story he had written, which he left for him to read. It was the tale of a married man who spent hours in the bathroom without ever bathing. His wife did not understand what her husband could be up to, so one day she decided to find out. She slipped out a window and, risking her life, crept along a narrow ledge three stories above the street to get to the bathroom window. When she peeked in, she was thunderstruck. Inside, her husband was sitting down, fully dressed, with a pistol in his hand. Every so often, the husband would bring the pistol to his mouth and lick the barrel.

< 202 >

He read the story and understood it was autobiographical. When Alberto returned and asked him what he thought of it, he managed to tell him the story was very interesting. He did not confess that what was interesting was the revelation.

He went with Rine Leal one night to the Tropicana. Walking through the verdant gardens and into the cabaret, he felt a strange sensation, a sort of literary déjà vu: during the years since he was last there he had written a story, part of which occurred in the Tropicana, recreating the cabaret in his mind and on paper; and now he looked around and could tell himself, "I have been here before," while still stepping in as if for the very first time.

He thought the show was crummy, but the beauty of the chorus girls was still something to behold. He also liked a duo of black sisters who performed without accompaniment and called themselves Las Capelas. The elder sister, practically a girl last time, had become a woman of rare beauty. In the audience he ran into Raulito Roa, who was with a group of foreign visitors. Raulito said hello with affection and he reciprocated. After the show, he saw Diana Tamayo, who danced in the chorus. He had known her before and whenever they met she always gazed at him with enormous curiosity. He also knew from a story a photographer friend had told that she was a woman of boundless sexuality. So he invited her to his table and later they left together and took a taxi to her house, which was behind the old offices of *Revolución* newspaper.

The building was modest, but her apartment was not bad. She, however, was an indifferent lover and when they finished, she insisted he leave. It was late and he was tired and would have been happy to stay in her bed. Only when she asked him to please not make more trouble for her with the

< 203 >

Defense Committee, since she already had enough, did he get up and go. He did not return to her apartment near Ayestarán Street until one afternoon when he was alone and bored. When he arrived he was surprised to find Pipo Carbonell also there visiting. After fifteen minutes of empty talk, he decided to leave and never return.

His brother, Sabá, came in from the Foreign Trade Ministry one day with a big smile on his face.

"I'm going back to Spain," he said.

"Really? When? How?"

"In two days. They gave me permission to fly over there to collect my things and say goodbye."

"So your time in Spain is over."

"So it seems."

He grew thoughtful.

"Well," his brother said, "tell me what you think."

"No, it's good. What's too bad is that they won't let you stay."

"Well, I'll work that out myself."

"You? How are you going to do that?"

"I'll figure that out when I get to Madrid."

He said no more. Later on, he learned that Marcelo Fernández had told Sabá he would send him back to Spain because he trusted him, and the intelligence service was not going to tell him what to do. Maybe that was true, maybe it was a lie, but that was what he was told.

That afternoon, the two of them went to El Carmelo on 23rd to buy cigars (the good ones they only sell singly), and at the door they ran into Alejo and Lidia Carpentier, who were headed for the Riviera to see a Russian film.

< 204 >

"*Hombre*, how are you?" Carpentier asked. "How's it going?"

"Well, Alejo. Thank you."

"How long will you be here?"

"A while yet."

"Why don't you come see me at National Publishing House?"

"Yes, sure. One of these days I'll drop by."

Alejo turned to Sabá.

"Weren't you in Spain?"

"Yes, and I'm going back day after tomorrow."

"Well, if you see Adrián ask him what happened with my suitcase."

They said goodbye and the Carpentiers went on to the cinema. Then Sabá explained what Alejo had meant. He had left a suitcase with Adrián García Hernández because when he got to Madrid he had too much baggage. Adrián offered to keep the suitcase and take it to the embassy so that it could be sent to him in Cuba. However, Adrián opened it and found it only contained old clothes and a few new shirts bought in Paris. He decided to keep the shirts for himself, and he threw the suitcase out. The two of them laughed.

Sabá wanted to take along the painting that Adrián's mother had entrusted to them, since Adrián was not doing well in Madrid, but he persuaded him not to. On the morning Sabá was to leave, he called from the airport.

"Listen," he said, "I should have brought Adrián's thing. It's quiet as could be here."

He said good, better that way, and he hung up. Then he sat thinking about the phone call and its implications. A few days later he returned the painting to Adrián's mother.

< 205 >

A RUMOR WAS GOING AROUND Havana that Captain Emilio Aragonés, a major figure in the Party who had been the National Organizer of the July 26th Movement, was in serious trouble. People said it was sexual, but no one knew anything for certain. Then Franqui told him Aragonés was accused of organizing orgies and there was photographic evidence, apparently taken by Aragonés himself or with his consent. The orgies were said to have featured everything, even lesbianism and homosexuality. For anyone who knew Aragonés or was familiar with his political ambitions, this was unbelievable. But the photographs left no room for doubt. Did other government personalities take part? No one knew. All anyone knew was that the affair was as bewildering as it was impenetrable.

How the orgies came to light was also complicated. Figures from the new underworld of the Revolution were involved and an important role had been played by a friend of his, Norka, a well-known model and also the former wife of his friend Korda, the photographer. It seems one of the participants showed the pictures to a lover of Norka's, who told her all about it. People said when she found out she immediately tried to locate Ramiro Valdés to tell him. (Norka had relations with high government figures and people said she had been a lover of Fidel Castro, which explains the ease with which she could approach the interior minister in person.) According to the story, Ramiro Valdés went to see her late at night and then threw Norka's lover and his friend in prison. What's more, after Aragonés's arrest, there was an attempt on Norka's life by two unknown assailants. The story grew even more intricate, with people saying that as punishment Aragonés had been sent to fight in a guerrilla war being organized in Congo-Brazzaville against the Republic of the Congo.

< 206 >

Franqui knew no more. He did, however, say that Norka told him Ramiro Valdés had told her that he was going to get serious about cracking down on homosexuals and people involved in other illegal sexual conduct, that now it would be done methodically, with each workplace and the Defense Committee on every block keeping a list of sexual delinquents. That had Franqui worried, and he shared Franqui's concern since he knew how broadly the term "sexual delinquent" could be interpreted in official hands.

Not long after, Franqui was truly ill at a clinic in La Sierra on Mendoza Avenue, whose name he could never remember. Suárez drove him and Gustavo Arcos to see him. When they arrived, Franqui had another visitor, a blue-eyed blonde in a brown tweed skirt and a white silk blouse, with such a youthful air about her she looked like a girl. She did not look Cuban (she had never looked Cuban: not even the day he first met her in 1958, when to strike up a conversation he spoke to her in English as he and Jesse Fernández got out of a taxi on the corner of Infanta and San Lázaro). But when she opened her mouth, she revealed she was more than Cuban, she was a Habanera of humble origins. It was, of course, Norka, who was more beautiful than ever with her hair cut short and her long legs bare below her short skirt. Franqui introduced her to Gustavo, who seemed to know her, which was not surprising since Norka was the most famous model in Cuba after 1959.

They chatted for a while and when Norka got up to leave he said he would accompany her and said goodbye to Franqui, Gustavo, and Suárez. They walked the length of Mendoza Avenue looking for the old Columbia Road and then turned left toward the bridge and 23rd Street. It was late afternoon and the sun was dropping out of sight behind them. They ambled slowly toward Norka's house in Alturas del Bosque. Crossing the bridge,

< 207 >

they saw the sun's orange reflection in the Almendares River. Like nearly all summer afternoons in Cuba, this one was sweet and soft. He felt very good walking beside Norka, breathing in her perfume, listening to her so-very-Cuban speech while the afternoon air ruffled the hair she swept off her forehead with a quick movement of her hand. From the moment they left the clinic, Norka had been telling him the story of her discovery of the high-ranking orgies.

"Listen to me," she said in her strong accent and with the very masculine mannerisms that so contrasted with her profound femininity. "Two guys broke into my house. I got up because I heard the sound, it was about two in the morning, and when I turned on the light in the living room I saw an enormous black guy coming at me and calling to somebody in the kitchen, who turned out to be another black guy with a knife in his hand. When the first guy came at me, the one without a weapon, I caught him with a judo move, picked him up, and threw him at the guy with the knife. The first one, the big guy, fell on the knife and got stabbed. So what do you think the second guy did? He ran like hell out the door and took off, leaving the other guy on the floor bathed in blood."

While she talked, he thought about her voice, her mannish way of speaking, which fit with her judo but was so at odds with her feminine way of walking and the image she projected of a beautiful Nordic model.

"*Viejo*," she continued, "I swear on my blessed mother's grave I am not feeding you a line. As soon as the other guy took off, I grabbed the phone and called the private number Ramirito gave me and in less than five minutes he was parking across the street along with two patrol cars. They took the wounded guy to the hospital and Ramirito was asking me questions and his people were going over the whole place and they figured those two guys that

< 208 >

attacked me had been hiding in my garden for a long time, waiting, one of them even defecated in the roses." He liked that brief incursion into refined speech, even as it surprised him to hear Norka say "defecated" instead of "took a shit."

"What was that about?"

"I guess out of fear, right? What the fuck would I know. The only thing for sure is I was scared out of my wits and the first thing I did was wake my kids and take them with me to my sister's place."

They were nearing Norka's, which was a fancy house in a well-heeled neighborhood filled with elegant homes. He wondered who would have given it to her, Fidel Castro or Ramiro Valdés? She asked him if he would like to come in for a drink. (Apparently, it was also well provisioned.) He said no, he had to go home to eat, they were waiting for him. As she stepped inside, she suggested they go out one night, they could go to a movie, and he said he would call her. In reality he wanted to get away from Norka as fast as he could, since he found everything about the story repugnant, including the new bit Norka supplied.

The following morning Gustavo Arcos called him.

"Listen," he said, "I want to talk to you about that girl yesterday. Don't you know she's in serious trouble?"

He said yes, he knew. That was all Gustavo wanted to talk about, but he did not want to do it over the telephone. They agreed that if he already knew there was no need to talk, but he went to Gustavo's house anyway and discussed all those rumors, which for Gustavo were more than rumors: he had learned that the entire story about Aragonés was true. They laughed about how bizarre it was to hold orgies and leave a trail of photographs. Gustavo received a phone call from Rebellón just then, inviting him to a model farm

< 209 >

that was Fidel Castro's personal favorite. Gustavo told him he was there visiting, so Rebellón invited him along too. They would all go in Rebellón's car the following day. After hanging up, Gustavo related a few stories about the man, who was now close to Fidel Castro. Apparently Fidel Castro used him as a taster for his cooking experiments, and now he was making soups with greens that usually only cattle eat. One recipe was some sort of stew made from digit grass, which Rebellón not only had to try, but had to say was really good, though it was awful. Another anecdote was about the day Rebellón arrived half an hour late for a meeting with Fidel Castro at his farm. Fidel Castro said nothing about his tardiness, but once the meeting was over, he drove Rebellón to an outbuilding at the back of the farm where they stored the tools and made him get out of the car and go in. "Now," Fidel Castro told Rebellón, "you're going to be jailed here for two weeks. For being late." And Rebellón, no joke, spent two weeks imprisoned in the shed at the back of the farm.

He thought the story was horrendous, not only because he had liked Rebellón right from the moment they met in Brussels, but also because of what it revealed about the character of Fidel Castro, a Latin American caudillo who behaved like every other absolute monarch.

The farm proved to be big, though not enormous. There were all sorts of animals, but the cattle got the most attention, especially a cow imported from Holland that was being examined by a veterinarian. He wondered if that cow, like those in Walterio Carbonell's story, also had tuberculosis, though it looked big and strong. They took in the whole of the model farm and when it started getting dark, they headed back toward the main house. He heard a murmur in a cornfield and asked what it was. "Mice," Rebellón said. "That's one of the problems we haven't been able to solve: we can't get

< 210 >

rid of the mice." Then he saw them, coming and going between the cornfield and a ditch Rebellón said was being dug for silos. Thousands of field mice of all sizes, confident, hungry, audacious. They filled the entire field at dusk and even the paths and the farm road. He was fascinated by the kingdom of mice; never had he seen so many in one place, especially in the countryside.

At the main house they ate the same meal everyone else was eating, not good but substantial. "All this is grown here," Rebellón said proudly, as if he were revealing a family secret. There was nothing exotic about the food, nothing that could not have been produced on any old farm. Apparently, Rebellón wanted them to get an exhaustive picture of the place, including the mosquitos, moths, and fireflies, since they did not return to Havana until late. Because there was nothing else to do, they played dominoes to kill time. He had always detested the game and was horrible at it, but he had to play along. They stupidly kept at it until eleven or twelve at night, when Rebellón decided to take them home.

He received a surprise visit from Mariposa, Pipo Carbonell's wife, whose name was not really Mariposa. It was a nickname that turned out to be more lasting than her real one. He had met her in Brussels – just as he had met Carbonell and Suárez and Gustavo Arcos and Aldama and Díaz del Real and Pollo Rivero – and he always found her earthy and very Cuban way of talking comical, and he still remembers his favorite story about her: they were at the table eating fresh cod and she said European fish weren't salty enough (salt cod being a Cuban favorite). Now she told him she was working at the Cuban Workers Confederation, a job she got thanks to the elder Carbonell.

"What about Pipo?" he asked, despite having recently seen him.

"What would I know? We got divorced."

< 211 >

"Oh, I didn't know."

"Oh yes, a while ago."

"So, now what do you do?"

"Now I'm footloose and fancy free," she told him, in a way that was both a statement and a suggestion. He pretended he had not heard or did not understand; though he had always suspected, since Brussels, that she found him attractive, he wanted nothing to do with Mariposa. They made small talk and soon she said goodbye. She returned another day and the conversation was just as meaningless, as empty as before, and after that she did not return. Later on, he often spied her at El Carmelo, always in the company of Germán Puig's sister and never with a male companion.

He went to visit Carmela again, Miriam Gómez's mother, whom he had not seen for a while. He always found his mother-in-law entertaining, since she talked about so many funny things. But that day Richard was there, Miriam Gómez's younger brother, who began to make jokes using phrases he thought he recognized from somewhere, until he finally realized they were things he had written; they were from his letters to Miriam Gómez. The fact that Richard was reading his letters angered him, and he asked Carmela if he could have all the correspondence she was keeping for Miriam. "Take it," Richard told him, "since I've already read all of it, every little bit." The only reason to forgive Richard was his youth. The two of them went to a bakery nearby to buy a loaf of bread Carmela swore was delicious and, unlike so many other things, not rationed. They went to the corner of 23rd and 16th and found the bakery not only closed but surrounded by swarms of bees. He had never liked bees, having been stung many times as a child, and he fled back to the street without even asking if they would be selling bread in the afternoon, while Richard just walked calmly through. He returned

< 212 >

home with no bread and with the shame of Richard's mockery buzzing in his ears.

Franqui was back. Apparently his illness had been a false alarm and it occurred to him that Franqui was not really sick, rather the tension of being a disgraced politician was killing him bit by bit. He went to visit him several times and one day met up with the sister of his wife, Margot, and her family, including a boy about eighteen who was doing his military service. The boy complained that despite having graduated as an artilleryman and doing his service, the people providing political orientation would not leave him alone because he liked to listen to modern music. That was when he learned that "modern" was what young people in Cuba called pop, which was expressly prohibited from Cuban radio. In some mysterious fashion these records were turning up and being passed from hand to hand among the young, and now they wanted to outlaw even listening to such records. Here was a generation, he thought, educated entirely by the Revolution but showing a tiny sign of rebelliousness, and if that seed had not yet flowered in Cuba, at least it had not died. That day he went home feeling strangely satisfied.

His satisfaction grew after a visit to the National Publishing House, though the feeling had nothing to do with that institution. The first person he saw there was Felito Ayón, with whom he had always felt a connection, not just from El Gato Tuerto (the restaurant/club which Felito ran across from El Maine Park) but from before, when Felito was the only truly modern printer in Cuba, and from even further back, long ago, when he first met him at an exhibition of paintings by Carlos Enríquez (one of the first exhibitions he had ever attended) and he had presumed that Felito, given his attire and his ponytail, was a painter. Now they hugged each other. Felito was pleased to see him and he looked happy with his work as lead designer for the publishing

< 213 >

house. Working alongside him, making his visit even more fortuitous, was Cecilia Valdés. He had always found Cecilia Valdés enormously attractive, from the moment they met at a cocktail party at the Bacardí Bar he had gone to with Rine Leal. He could not remember what the occasion was, but he had never forgotten Cecilia and her broken zipper, which revealed an intimate part of her brown flesh. Ever since that first encounter he considered Cecilia to be the epitome of Cuban mestiza beauty. He remembered still her aroma and the pain of her hard, passionate kisses, just as he remembered those breasts first viewed and tasted in the stairwell of her house, as well as the stupid reasons why their relationship never went anywhere. More than anything he remembered one of the last times he had seen Cecilia, on 23rd Street near the corner of N, across from the building where he was living then, telling him: "I heard you're marrying Miriam Gómez," one hand meaningfully on her hip and a foot impatiently tapping the sidewalk. "What taste is that, *muchacho*, marrying that skinny woman."

At the National Publishing House the moment flooded back because it was Cecilia Valdés who was very thin and had cut her hair very short and had lost much of her cachet as a mulatta fatale. He greeted her enthusiastically and she responded coldly: evidently she had not forgiven him for marrying Miriam Gómez. Even so, he was happy to see her. For him, she was the paradigm of the modern Cuban woman, even before the Revolution liberated her, long before her current marriage, which he soon learned was practically in ruins, long before becoming nearly an easy woman, so unlike the difficult girl of other days, of other nights.

Also welcoming him to the publishing house were Edmundo Desnoes (whose real name was Juan Edmundo Pérez Desnoe and whom he always called Juan Pérez) and Ambrosio Fornet. They had become an inseparable duo, thinking and saying the same thing, working in the same place,

< 214 >

and going out to the same spots together. He also saw Sarusky, who he seemed to run into everywhere since that ill-fated day at the Brussels airport, and who he often greeted with: "Sarusky, the one who got away from Hitler." Luis Agüero was also there, he had no idea why, though soon he discovered that, like so many others, he was seeking the favors of Cecilia Valdés, the incarnation of one of Cuba's everlasting myths: that of the indispensable mulatta.

He said hello to other people, none of whom he remembers now, before going into the office of the director, Alejo Carpentier.

"*Hombre*," he exclaimed, "what a pleasure to have you here."

Carpentier in reality said *hombgre* not *hombre*, sticking his French "R" in everywhere, which sounded far too muddy to Cuban ears. But he seemed truly pleased to have him in his office. He went straight on to list all the masterworks of world literature he had published, the innumerable copies he had printed, and the success (not forgetting the political convenience) of his books, with print runs selling out the day of publication, editions in the thousands, something that had never occurred in Cuba before and which not even the most fantasy-ridden mind would have thought possible only three years previous. Carpentier was satisfied with his work, though he did not speak of the books they would not let him publish or the cuts they imposed. For example, in *Moby-Dick*, the central theme – God – had disappeared for new Cuban readers, though not for the old ones who did not fail to note the omission and tell him about it. He, of course, said nothing about that either; he had not come to antagonize Carpentier, rather to say hello. The visit ended with a quick look at the etchings hanging on the wall behind Alejo's desk. One, in particular, was an illustrated map drawn by an English spy, which showed several lovely ephebes lying half naked on a raft, surrounded by ferocious sharks.

< 215 >

"What you see in the background," Carpentier told him in a phrase he would never forget, "is Havana, *chico*."

And sure enough, behind the raft packed with shipwrecked boys, you could make out El Morro Castle and almost see the entrance to Havana Bay.

Since it was the middle of the afternoon by the time he said goodbye to Alejo Carpentier, he went with Sarusky and Luis Agüero and Desnoes and Fornet to a café on Galiano Street to drink clear Coca-Cola. Even though Sarusky knew the location of every kiosk that sold coffee in Havana, there was no coffee to be had. They chatted for a long while and he was surprised that Desnoes and Fornet could spend so much time out of the office; Felito Ayón, who had invited him to his home, was still hard at work, as was Cecilia Valdés, who he recalled he had not even said goodbye to.

"Oh, it's because we're trusted staff," Fornet explained with the pedantic pronunciation he had picked up during his years in Madrid on a scholarship from the Hispanic Cultural Institute.

The insinuation was that trust was political. He was astonished and was nearly tempted to ask, "So, what about Felito Ayón?" But he did not. The conversation drifted toward books and writers and an anthology of short stories that Fornet was preparing for publication in Mexico.

"You've got to be in it," he added, speaking to him.

He did not commit himself, so Fornet insisted:

"I also want you to write an introduction explaining what a short story is for you."

"Something recounted," he said.

"Not like that," Fornet said. "It's got to be a literary explanation."

"Ah," he said.

However, he brightened when Fornet told him he would pay him a

< 216 >

hundred pesos. He said he would get the story and the introduction to him the following week. Then he went on to talk about what he had gleaned at Franqui's house about the new generation. Desnoes was cautious, but Fornet dove right in:

"Wow! The next generation is going to be truly something. They're crazy about modern music, especially American music. And you know what they do? They pool their money to get a shortwave or FM radio, they listen late at night when there's no interference from the authorities, and they record the musical programs on tape recorders. Then somebody gets hold of a few old X-rays, the plates, and they go into a radio station at night and transfer the programs to the plates, which they cut into disks and then they have their records. Those records get handed around and, before you know it, half of young Havana knows all the words by heart. There's no beating them!"

"Right," Desnoes said, "they aren't like us, a generation defeated."

"We," Sarusky said, "are not a generation defeated, we are a generation compromised."

"À la Sartre?" Luis Agüero asked sardonically.

"À la Cuban Revolution," Sarusky said, as if to put an end to the conversation.

"I don't know what we are," he said. "Whether we're defeated or we've defected."

"What do you mean by that?" Fornet asked.

"I mean we should put our cards on the table."

"Didn't we do that at the National Library?"

"Barely," Luis Agüero said.

"We did it before the Library," he said. "When we protested the quashing of *PM* At the Library what we did was arrive at a compromise: let us, please,

< 217 >

continue living our lives and we'll promise to stay in the corner. That was our compromise: a place in the sun, but near the shade."

"Other people did less," said Sarusky, whom he did not remember being very forceful at the Library.

"Agreed," he said, "but we could have done more. We could always do more. For example, Walterio was brilliant at Casa de las Américas when we had the discussion with the people from Studio Theater, but he was not so good at the Library."

"Franqui disappeared too," Fornet said.

"We were all there," he said. "We stayed, too, but we didn't stay to speak, rather to listen to them speak, and the Horse had the last word." (That was Fidel Castro's nickname.)

"He would have had it in any case," Luis Agüero said.

"Maybe not," said Desnoes, "if there had been a real debate."

"Maybe he would have," he said. "Oscar Hurtado was right: when Fidel took off his belt and his pistol and laid them on the table, he was saying, 'Here are my balls.'"

"Well, Hurtado did not exactly stand out for his eloquence," Fornet said.

"All of us," he said, "were pitiful when it comes to eloquence."

"There, the only eloquence," Desnoes said, "was silence."

Everyone agreed with Desnoes, but he added that in his case he was not even allowed silence.

"Sick as I was, I had to go because Rine Leal called me several times, desperate, and I had to speak without preparation. Moreover, as Walterio put it, we tied our own hands when we cut a deal with Franqui at *Revolución* not to call a spade a spade, not to throw the newspaper down the same hole we threw *Lunes.*"

< 218 >

"And in the end," Luis Agüero said, "the newspaper disappeared too. The fact is we were doomed from the start."

"Well," Sarusky said, "that's the past. We have a lot of future ahead of us. We're here and we still have a lot of influence."

"Influence?" asked Luis Agüero increduously.

"Look," Sarusky said, "you can't complain, at least you run *Unión* magazine."

"*Gaceta*," Luis Agüero corrected.

"Okay, the *Gaceta*."

"And Guillén manages it," Luis Agüero added, "the way Carpentier manages the publishing house. You aren't going to tell me that Fornet and Desnoes control things here."

"No," Sarusky admitted, "but they have a lot of influence. In Russia we would all be in Siberia."

"That is true," Fornet said.

"Well," he interjected, "they sent me to the Cuban Siberia, Belgium. I couldn't have been sent farther away."

Everyone laughed, but Sarusky added right away:

"You can't complain. Nothing's more comfortable than a diplomatic posting."

"Or more uncomfortable," he said.

"Well," said Sarusky, "you didn't suffer in Brussels."

"At first I did. Then my instinct to adapt kicked in. But understand me, at first it was an exile like any other."

"I wouldn't mind an exile like that," Sarusky said.

"Padilla got it worse than you," Fornet said. "He got exiled to Moscow. You at least were in the Western world."

< 219 >

"But Padilla likes Europe," he said. "I don't."

"All Padilla wants," Luis Agüero said, "is to feel a coat…"

"An overcoat," Fornet corrected.

"…on his shoulders," Luis Agüero finished.

Everyone laughed: it was true. Padilla was crazy about coats, raincoats, overcoats.

"Well, gentlemen," said Fornet, "time to be getting back to work."

"Yes," Desnoes said, "it's time."

"*To go back*," sang Luis Agüero, in a tango rhythm. "*Our faces withered and snow on our temples. To feel that twenty years is nothing.*"

"That's what Alejo should be singing," he said. Everyone laughed and Sarusky called the waiter, who this time was the café's owner, and paid.

"The Jew is generous," he said.

"*Generous*," Luis Agüero sang, "*you dance so well…*"

He and Luis Agüero got a ride with Sarusky up San Lázaro to L Street. Along San Lázaro parallel to the Malecón, he noticed again, as he had nearly five years before, how the wall of the Malecón, seen down the cross streets, was like an apparition every block. He made a mental note, especially how the level of the wall rose and fell capriciously. The sea remained in view, blue and green.

Norka called and asked him out to the Payret Theater to see a Russian film he forgot the moment the lights came on. It was just to please Norka, whom he found more and more attractive. On the way out they met Rebellón, who gave them a lift to Vedado. On the way, Rebellón must have asked Norka about something personal, because from the backseat he heard Rebellón utter, "Oh, just because he's a friend." So he wasn't surprised when Rebellón dropped him off first. (Anyway, his house was closer coming from

< 220 >

Havana.) He got out, thanked Rebellón, and said goodnight to Norka, who said, "See you later, dear. We'll be seeing each other." "Yes," he said, "we'll be seeing each other." He watched the car head off, not toward Norka's house up 23rd Street, but down Avenue of the Presidents. He went into the building: the key was the right one for the street door.

The following day Gustavo Arcos called. Rebellón had invited them both to lunch at La Roca, still a fashionable restaurant. He was waiting on the balcony to be picked up when Anita asked him what he was waiting for and he told her. "Papi," she said, "aren't you lucky, always getting asked out to eat." He was seized by an uncontrollable fury and he turned and smacked his daughter, who went inside crying. He detested with all his heart the way she had spoken to him, her tone was so vulgar, so Cuban, so low class, but he could not fathom why he had hit her. Neither could he understand his blind rage. At last Rebellón's car came and he went downstairs. Fortunately, Rebellón did not speak of Norka.

At La Roca he had grapefruit, tripe with rice, avocado salad, a beer, and mamey ice cream for dessert. The food was very good and at the restaurant he saw the faces of what must have been the new class; he knew nobody, but nearly everyone knew Rebellón. He asked for a cigar and smoked contentedly. Gustavo Arcos was also happy: there was nothing he liked better than being invited out. Gustavo's friends often laughed about how cheap he was.

When he got home he had a message from Alberto Mora that he would drop by later on. Alberto turned up as it was getting dark. Though a bit antsy because he wanted to go out, he was curious to learn what Alberto had to tell him.

"I have news for you," he said as soon as he arrived.

< 221 >

"Good or bad?"

"Both. I've got things moving. I'm going to speak directly with President Dorticós, but so far I've spoken with Carlos Rafael Rodríguez, and he didn't seem put off by your request. However, I was just at a reception at the Chinese Embassy and Barbaroja was there and we talked about you. Do you know what he said? He said he would cut off his balls before letting you leave Cuba."

"Piñeiro said that?"

"Just like that."

"That's serious."

"No, *hombre*. It's something he's saying for effect. You'll get out, you'll see."

"No, it's serious, really serious."

"Listen, don't be so pessimistic. To stop you from leaving he'd have to go over the heads of Carlos Rafael and Dorticós. That's a big leap."

He fell silent. By chance he had been reading about the Cicero Affair involving the spy in the British Embassy in Ankara who was selling secrets to the Germans. He had reached the part where the spy's German contact, an attaché named Moyzisch, returns to Berlin and is detained there for reasons he does not understand until he discovers the counterintelligence service wants to prevent him from leaving Germany due to internal rivalries. He identified with the attaché, who was the author of the book, and thought he probably would remain trapped in Havana with no possible exit.

Alberto was leaving and he asked if he could take him anywhere. He said no. That night he did not go out, but neither did he spend it reading. He sat on the balcony until late, watching a distant storm at sea, but not through the binoculars.

< 222 >

HE HAD RUN OUT OF MONEY again and did not want to borrow any more from Miriam Gómez's sister. The other person he could tap for a loan was Rine Leal, but he preferred not to do that, either. He decided to sell his jazz records and asked Marta Calvo if she knew anyone who might be interested. Marta thought someone at Casa de las Américas might be. If she found a buyer, could she collect ten percent? That seemed fair. A few days later she reported someone was willing to pay two hundred pesos for the entire collection. It wasn't much but it was something. He sold the records, gave the ten percent to Marta, and paid back the hundred pesos he owed Miriam Gómez's sister, who at first did not want to take the money.

The sale of the records led to an incident that had him worried for several days. Through Marta, the buyer sent him an invitation to his house to listen to music. Guerrero and Luis Agüero would also be there. He decided not to go, partly because he did not know the man. Two days later Luis Agüero turned up at the apartment.

"*Compadre!*" he exclaimed. "You have no idea what I managed to avoid!"

"What happened?"

"Imagine, a guy at Casa de las Américas asked me over to his house to listen to some records, along with Guerrero."

"So?" He was interested.

"So I couldn't go and it turns out the guy and Guerrero got arrested by the DTI."

"What?"

"Just as you're hearing it. It seems they were smoking…"

"Marijuana?"

"What else, a cigar? Of course marijuana. The guy who owned the house was in some sort of snit with his wife and she sicced the DTI on him, and

< 223 >

while he and Guerrero were listening to records two officers turned up. They knocked, walked right in, and grabbed the two of them in flagrante. I was supposed to be there that very night! What a mess I managed to avoid!"

He did not tell Luis Agüero that he too had been invited. He did not even tell him the records were his, since he thought if they had arrested Guerrero and the record buyer, they might well arrest the seller, too. In the end he learned that Guerrero was sentenced to two years and the homeowner got four. Guerrero was released not long after, thanks to Lisandro Otero. He often wondered who might have intervened to help him.

His aunt Felisa departed the way she had arrived, silently and suddenly. She left behind the Prayer Against the Enemy, and she had also put him in contact with someone who lived behind their building, a woman she called the Magus and Hildelisa nicknamed the Witch. The Magus-Witch came one afternoon when he was on the balcony looking at the occasional pedestrian through his binoculars. After speaking with his grandmother, she came out to see him.

"I divined Zoila's trip to Europe," she said, after a few pleasantries. He was not very surprised by her divination but rather to hear such a sophisticated word coming from a woman so evidently unsophisticated. Such contradictions often occur in Cuba and other Spanish-speaking countries.

"I predicted it," she said, "long before it happened." It was also notable how she mixed sophisticated and common terms.

"Yes?" he responded each time.

"Yes," she said. "Your trip is also not far off. You have many enemies, many evil spirits, but you are going to return to where you came from. You don't have to pay any attention to what I say. Read your prayer when you're going to see important people. You should also do a cleansing with an egg and you must trust in the great power of God."

< 224 >

He did not know what a cleansing with an egg could be, but she explained. "You take an egg and one night, preferably a Friday, you go to an intersection with four corners. Make sure you never go back to that place, pick a street you don't usually use. Hold your egg in your hand and on the corner at twelve on a Friday, move the egg all over your body, saying "Cleanse, egg, cleanse." Then toss it over your shoulder. Don't stop to see where it falls, just get out of there as fast as you can. That gets rid of evil spirits."

He expected her to charge him for the consultation, but she did not ask for a cent. "The problem," he said half seriously, "is finding an egg." The Magus did not understand. "With the rationing," he explained.

"There are eggs here," his grandmother called out from her room. The Magus added, "If you don't have one, tell me when you're going to do it and I'll bring you one. I can always get eggs."

Another one like Miriam Gómez's mother, he said to himself, black market mavens. But he said nothing more. In a little while the Magus left and he realized he was thinking of her by his grandmother's name for her, not Hildelisa's. Did that mean he believed in her?

Silvano Suárez's show at the cabaret in the Habana Libre and the performance at the Tropicana confirmed how lousy the popular music of the day was. Both were pale imitations of the shows from before the Revolution and even from the Revolution's first years. Since 1959 not a single new rhythm had been invented, and no new melodies. Nothing but revolutionary hymns, and many of them, like the Hymn for July 26th, were composed long before the Revolution took power.

The absence of new music seemed as symptomatic of the state of society as the transformation of everyone's natural garrulousness into tight-lipped reserve. That said, a new band led by Pello, called Afrokán, was trying to introduce a rhythm strangely called Mozambique. He had not heard Afrokán,

< 225 >

but the state PR organs were trying hard to make it popular; perhaps, like him, they were aware of people's desperate yearning for music, the highest form of Cuban art and the only art form that had been a constant from the earliest days of the colonial period in the sixteenth century. So when Maritza Alonso invited him to hear the dress rehearsal for a show that was going on tour to Europe, he went with real interest.

Although the theater without air conditioning in August was an oven – the Amadeo Roldán, which he still insisted on calling the Auditorium – he stayed to see and hear the entire performance. Most of it was a Cuban ballet by Alberto Alonso, employing the same elements Alonso used to use for commercial television, but perhaps not as good because time had passed and not happily. Then came two or three mediocre singers and a group called Los Zafiros. Though the band would be considered below average in Western Europe, the voices were good and they sang sometimes in unison, other times in counterpoint, all in very good taste. Then it was time for the star of the show, Pello the Afrokán and his band, and they turned out to be mostly a collection of drummers, who made an infernal racket without ever turning it into music. He was surprised at the popularity the band enjoyed in official circles, but said nothing to Maritza Alonso, knowing full well that she was only an agent, though she did have official backing. It all seemed so pitiful that it made him want to cry. He saw it as symbolic of what was happening to the entire country, where the best of intentions wrought nothing but irredeemable flops.

When leaving – or maybe during the intermission, driven outside by the heat – he ran into Humberto Arenal, who told him he was going along on the arts tour (those were Arenal's words), and wondered if there was anything he could do for him over in Europe. He said perhaps he would send a letter

< 226 >

with him to Miriam Gómez. He said no more because Maritza Alonso came over to ask what he thought of the show. He said it was very good, all of it. She was thrilled. Finally, she asked if they would see him in Europe, adding, "We're leaving on Sunday." He said, "Maybe we'll see each other there." But he knew he was lying, and what's worse he knew that Arenal knew he knew he was lying. He said goodbye and asked Arenal to come by his house before leaving.

That very afternoon, walking home along Línea and then up Avenue of the Presidents, he began thinking about the letter he had to write and how to write it so that Arenal could carry it without running into problems, yet have it convey to Miriam everything that was going on while at the same time discouraging her from coming back, telling her not to return, to stay in Europe, that his only salvation was having her on the other side. He spent a long time and a lot of paper writing that letter, until finally he managed to produce a sheet which summed up his situation in a veiled manner, yet still alerted Miriam to the need for her to remain in exile so he could join her as soon as possible.

Arenal came as promised and he gave him the letter in an unsealed envelope. "Read it, please," he said. Arenal said there was no need, that he trusted him, and he sealed it right there. Once Arenal left, he kept thinking about the letter, whether he had betrayed the man's trust, but he was sure he had not, that the letter could be read by the G2 agents who for sure would accompany the artists on the tour, and could even be intercepted by the airport police, and it would read like a love letter, more-or-less desperate but not out of control. The way things really were.

Ivonne Calvo was getting married again. This time his former sister-in-law was marrying over the telephone because her future husband was in

< 227 >

Mexico; it was her way of getting out of Cuba. Even so, the wedding would be celebrated as if it were her first, as if it were a regular wedding in the Cuba of before. All of Ivonne's former brothers-in-law were invited, including Rine Leal (who attended) and Juan Blanco (who did not), plus the friends of Sara Calvo, Luis Agüero, Marta Calvo, and of course Ivonne. The modest party – warmed by a few bottles of rum that were a gift from Alberto Mora and Carlos Figueredo, an extraordinary guest who merits more attention – took place on a Friday afternoon, or rather evening, because the call to Mexico to speak with the groom delayed the wedding until late that night.

It had been a long time since he had last seen Carlos Figueredo, who now worked for the Interior Ministry. He had first met him on the day of the attack on the Presidential Palace, March 13th, 1957. Carlos had turned up at his house at about four in the afternoon along with his cousin Joe Westbrook and Dysis Guira. Carlos was limping, but he did not have far to walk from Dysis's car parked by the curb. They were coming from another attack, on the CMQ radio station, which had also failed. Leaving, they had been spotted by a patrol car and one of their companions, Manzanita Echeverría, had been killed and Carlos wounded. He was surprised to see them, but he understood immediately: they were seeking refuge at his house. Unfortunately, they could not remain there, since the maid was the girlfriend of a soldier and could not be trusted. But they did find a spot in the same building, in Sara's apartment on the fourth floor. Although the second-in-command of the motorized police lived in the building next door, they were able to stay until better refuge was found. When it was, Carlos Figueredo moved to the less secure of two hiding places, while his cousin Joe Westbrook went to the one that was more secure at number 7 Humboldt Street. Days later, someone gave him away and the police killed all the fugitives hiding there,

< 228 >

including Joe Westbrook. The less secure spot, where Carlos Figueredo was hiding, turned out to be the safer place, and Carlos lived to see the end of the Batista dictatorship without any major mishaps. (He had seen him just before the fall of Batista, buying cigarettes at the corner store near his house, but did not see him again until the triumph of the Revolution.) After the Revolution took power, Carlos Figueredo wore a commander's stripes, married a very beautiful girl, and everything was going great until one day, in a fit of jealousy, he set fire to their apartment, where he kept a collection of weapons and munitions. The place exploded, causing a public furor. Carlos went to jail but soon got out and found work at the Interior Ministry.

The party lasted until Ivonne finished her telephone call with her boyfriend, now her husband. When only a dozen people were left, Carlos Figueredo invited them all – except for Rine Leal – to his home. Everyone piled into his car and Alberto Mora's. When they arrived, he was astonished: Carlos Figueredo lived in a mansion. "It used to belong to one of the presidents of Chase Manhattan Bank," Alberto explained. The living room was immense, dominated by a grand piano. They went to the back where Carlos had his music room, a carpeted studio with air conditioning in the middle of which sat a drum set with every sort of drum. There was also an impressive high-fidelity stereo and a glass-fronted cabinet filled with cameras – another of his hobbies. Carlos, always accompanied by two assistants or aides who seemed more like groupies around a champion bullfighter, served drinks and disappeared for a moment into a room at the side, his dressing room. At the party he had worn an Italian suit made of raw silk and now he changed into summer pants and a pullover. (That night he would change clothes twice more, not making a show of it, as if it were normal. It must be said that Carlos acquired this habit during the Revolution, since beforehand he was

< 229 >

only a waiter at Monseñor restaurant, where he always kept a loaded pistol in his locker, under his uniform, hoping some personality from the regime would come in for a meal so he could kill him.)

Carlos stepped out for a moment to the living room with Sara so she could hear the timbre of his grand piano. That was when he slipped into the dressing room and stared agog at the elegant and expensive clothes. When Carlos returned, Alberto asked him to play the drums, which he did and very well. Soon – it was nearly three in the morning – Carlos went into the dressing room again and came out wearing his olive green uniform: the party was over. As they left, he asked Carlos where he was going at that hour and he answered, simply, "I have a job to do." Later on, speaking with Franqui, he learned what sort of job Carlos Figueredo did: he was one of the top interrogators of the Interior Ministry's counterintelligence service. He had his own approach to interrogation: he worked naked from the belt up, usually in a very hot cell, and often he would scratch his underarm or his chest and gather the sweat and dead skin, which he would throw in the face of the person he was interrogating.

One day he received a call from Miriam Gómez: the Foreign Ministry had sent her an airplane ticket back to Cuba, along with a telegram urging her to return. He, speaking with more care than usual because it was an overseas call, told her to pay no attention to the cable or the return ticket and to stay in Belgium until he said otherwise. When he hung up, his anger was irrepressible and he cursed his fate. From the kitchen his grandmother called out: "Oh, my son, don't worry, everything will work out." He did not believe that was true and he called Alberto Mora, who came over that afternoon. He told him everything.

"Leave it to me," Alberto told him. "I'll speak with Dorticós."

"You still haven't talked to him?"

"I haven't had the chance, but I'll do it now. That shit Roa is intimidated by Piñeiro."

"Well, you better not tell him about this. I spoke to Miriam and told her to stay put in Brussels, no matter what."

Alberto seemed to be thinking it over.

"That's fine, I won't say anything about Miriam, but I am going to move now on speaking with Dorticós."

"That sounds good," he said. After Alberto left, he went to see Franqui, who seemed to grow ill when he told him the news, which he had to give him with the record player turned up full volume. Once more he thought about Moyzisch, the German, and the parallel fates of diplomats.

By now his apartment had become a frequent meeting place for artists, intellectuals, and wannabes who came to see him. But he did not trust anyone and he confided his real situation to no one except Franqui and Alberto Mora. Of course the visits did nothing to erase his reputation as a dissident, but so it was. One night Virgilio Piñera, Antón Arrufat, José Triana, José Estorino, and Raúl Martínez, the latter strangely accompanied by Miriam Gómez's brother Richard, came over. Richard had met Raúl at the home of some girls (he did not know who) and they had become friends. There was no relationship between those two, nor could there be, but he worried about it because Richard was very young, inexperienced, and trusting, and Raúl Martínez had been expelled from his teaching post at the Art Schools for corrupting minors, although he also knew the accusation had more to do with Raúl's artistic tendencies than his sexual proclivities, even if the latter were quite real.

That night he and Raúl, who had gone from abstract painter to pop artist virtually overnight, got into an argument. The discussion had its roots in the conversations at the Library and at the First Congress of Writers and

< 231 >

Artists of Cuba, both in 1961, when President Dorticós, among others, practically accused abstract artists of being "bad revolutionaries" and predicted the disappearance of abstract art in Cuba. At that point he and *Lunes de Revolución* began arguing that painters like Raúl Martínez and his group (among whom were Guido Llinás, Tapia, and another who had been exiled for a long time) should be able to express themselves freely. Recently, when he learned that Raúl Martínez had turned away from abstract art to the most obvious representational work, he said that Dorticós had spoken too soon; if he had only waited a couple of years, he would have been rid of all those abstract painters, since they changed on their own to mimic artistic trends overseas, especially in the United States. This comment had reached the ears of Raúl Martínez, who, now a bit drunk, had come in search of an explanation.

"I heard you said I was only waiting for the winds to change overseas to go from being an abstract painter to a representational one."

"I didn't say that," he said. "At least I didn't say it in such a clumsy way." Raúl laughed.

"That's my way of talking, but the idea is the same."

"More or less," he admitted. "What I said is that Dorticós – excuse me, the *compañero presidente* – was wrong; there was no need to wage war on abstract painters, all he had to do was wait."

"That's bullshit," Raúl said. Estorino laughed. He smiled. "Because it's not true."

"It's not? So what would you say you're doing now?"

"The same as always," Raúl said. "Painting."

"Which rhymes with feinting," he said. Everyone laughed, even Raúl.

"Well, so what?"

< 232 >

"Nothing, but I seem to recall before I went away, not even three years ago, you had a problem with a mural commissioned by the Film Institute for the lobby of the Cinemateca, which was rejected because it was a 'demonstration of decadent abstract art.' I also remember that your mural at the office of *Lunes* was destroyed shortly after the magazine was closed."

"Yes, that's true. But that's not what made my art evolve, my art has its own impetus."

"Which happens to coincide with the pop movement overseas, doesn't it?"

"Not necessarily," Raúl said.

"Yes or no?"

"Well, there may be areas where they overlap by chance. But nothing more."

"In other words, you have changed from the inside out and not the other way around."

"Precisely."

"What a coincidence!"

Raúl smiled. The others, including Richard, who had no idea what they were talking about, all laughed.

"Well," said Raúl, "is there nothing to drink in this house?"

"You know we're teetotalers. Besides, you don't need any more," he said.

"You were very different when your mother was still alive."

He said nothing. The rest also remained silent.

The gathering did not end there, but they spoke no more about painting, and the conversation drifted toward neutral, less interesting territory and everyone got bored. But for a moment he felt a real exchange had taken place, that Raúl Martínez showed little of the zombie nature he found in everyone

< 233 >

else. Among his intellectual friends this torpor was perhaps best expressed actively by Edmundo Desnoes and passively by Humberto Arenal (a zombie among zombies).

Another day there was a gathering at his house in the afternoon, but it was smaller, with only Oscar Hurtado, Antón Arrufat, and Virgilio Piñera. Probably they were talking about literature, sitting not on the balcony but in the living room, when the street doorbell rang. He peered down from the balcony, saw it was Martha Frayde and Beba Sifontes, and opened the door to let them in. They said hello to his visitors, then Martha said:

"We were driving by and saw you had visitors and we couldn't resist the temptation."

He always wondered how Martha could see from her car that he was home and had visitors.

"We also came to invite you to lunch, the rest of you please excuse us."

"No bother," Virgilio Piñera said. Oscar Hurtado smiled and so did Antón Arrufat.

"But," continued Martha without a pause, "I'm pleased to find you all here so I can tell you something. Why is it you aren't more active?"

"What are you trying to say, Martha?" asked Virgilio, smiling and continuing to smoke his cigarette.

"More involved. It's up to you intellectuals to carry the flag of activism."

"The revolutionary flag?" he asked sarcastically.

"No," Martha said. "Real activism, which is to question everything and demand explanations from the government when they do something wrong."

"Oh, Martha," Virgilio said.

"Don't give me any 'oh, Martha.' You have to face reality. Listen," she turned to Oscar Hurtado, "why do you spend all your time sitting in El Carmelo eating ice cream and talking about Martians?"

< 234 >

Oscar Hurtado's smile froze on his lips. He said absolutely nothing. In a little while he lit a cigarette.

"Tell me," Martha Frayde insisted.

No one said a thing.

"None of you dares to assume your responsibilities as the intellectuals you are."

"We did that once," he said, "at the National Library and we were noisily defeated by the enemy. Now all we can do is live as quietly as possible."

"Well, you're wrong," Martha said. "We've got to fight. And if the enemy blocks us, then we choose our weapons and fight with whatever we have at hand."

He did not want to say anything that Martha Frayde might find insulting. He had known her for years and had seen how bravely she fought against the Batista dictatorship, and now he saw she was intent on a much more dangerous struggle than the one against Batista. When Martha got up abruptly to indicate the visit was over, he felt truly relieved: her interruption could have undermined his plan to remain astutely silent.

"Whew!" Virgilio exclaimed once Martha and Beba had departed, Beba not having said anything but hello and goodbye.

"So, what's with that woman?" asked Antón Arrufat. "She must be a G2 agent talking about those things."

"No," he said. "She's not an agent of anybody. Martha is just like that."

Which did not explain much. He was the one who knew Martha Frayde best, even if Virgilio spoke to her in the familiar *tú*.

"Well," Arrufat said, "she may not be a government agent, but she is definitely an agent provocateur."

Oscar Hurtado had not said a word since Martha arrived, except maybe to say hello, and yet he knew that Martha was close friends with his wife,

< 235 >

Miriam Acevedo, by way of Miriam's doctor brother Alberto, whom Martha admired greatly and not only as a colleague. The gathering ended nearly as abruptly as Martha Frayde's visit, and he wondered if it was wise for people to come to the apartment. Or maybe he should welcome the malcontents like he did before, when they shut down *Lunes* and he was left without a job and his house became a meeting place for dissidents. He told himself the circumstances were not the same and perhaps hosting gatherings was not what pushed him into exile the first time. Now he decided he would only meet his friends in public places. However, he had to have lunch at Martha and Beba's, and he could not stop visiting Gustavo Arcos or Franqui. These were the only exceptions he made.

THE LUNCH WITH MARTHA AND BEBA was a quiet affair, memorable only for the excellent food. He asked Martha how she managed to put on the table things that in Cuba were considered delicacies – and a delicacy could be something as native as an avocado. "Connections," Martha answered, "connections." He realized she meant not only connections with officials, of which Martha had ever fewer, but the fact that she was a physician for diplomats who every so often gave her edibles to take home. From the shrimp cocktail to the roast beef, he remembers that lunch as a sumptuous occasion. They sat surrounded by Martha's abundant collection of Cuban paintings – in the past she had been a good buyer, friend, and doctor of many local painters. As much as the food, he recalls the atmosphere in that very Cuban home on 19th Street, with its whitewashed walls and floor tiles of various colors. He remembers it just as he remembers Martha asking to be forgiven for "what happened the other day," which she explained as a bad moment made worse by meeting up with Oscar Hurtado, whose frequent talk of Martians and other beings from the great beyond literally made her ill.

< 236 >

Of those August days in 1965 he recalls not only the tedium of the wait, but a few extraordinary occasions. One of them was a garden party – not that it was called that, rather a "meeting of comrade writers and artists" – which took place at the mansion of the Writers Union, whose acronym UNEAC, he liked to say, sounded like magpies or crows. The party was held at six on a splendid summer afternoon.

He went with Alberto Mora and they were directed by the doorman into the garden, where, practically under the mango tree where Guillén had confessed his political-literary doubts, sat a large table covered with a white cloth, a large punchbowl, and many glasses, plus platters with ham-and-cheese hors d'oeuvres. Two waiters were serving punch and handing out the snacks to the crowd, many of whom he knew. As they stood drinking and eating, Ingrid González approached. Alberto knew her, so he did not have to introduce them; Ingrid gave him a kiss on the cheek, very close to his mouth. She smelled nice. They made small talk with her and with Mariano Rodríguez the painter and his wife, Celeste, who also came over. Later on, he spied at the back of the garden the girl he had seen one day wearing a tight sweater over her large breasts. Now she had another close-fitting pullover on, which also accentuated her liberated bra-free breasts.

"Who is that girl?" he asked Ingrid, pointing with his chin.

"Which one?"

"The one at the back, in the sweater."

"Oh. Her name is Oceanía."

"Oceanía?"

"Yes and she's a friend of José Mario's."

He had heard of José Mario: he was the leader of the group El Puente, which had fallen into utter disgrace, even though the writers that made it up were young, all of them educated under the Revolution. UNEAC had

< 237 >

liquidated El Puente as a literary group, it was said, under direct orders from Fidel Castro. Rumor had it that the writer and artist Fayad Jamís had read a book of poetry by someone in the group – perhaps José Mario himself – that contained homosexual poems. Fayad took the book home and waited until Fidel Castro came to visit (he came not to visit him, but his wife, Marta, the widow of the martyr Fructuoso Rodríguez and someone Fidel Castro treated with respect). During the visit, Fayad showed the book to Fidel Castro, pointing out the homosexual poems and calling his attention to the book's having been published under the auspices of the UNEAC. Fidel Castro became enraged – like Zeus, he often flies into monumental rages – and he ordered the entire group suppressed. Thus, El Puente had fallen into disgrace and its members were publicly ostracized; nearly all of them lost their jobs and got by only thanks to their revolutionary guile.

"So, is José Mario here?"

"Yes, I saw him a minute ago. At the back."

Alberto Mora was also interested in the girl.

"Is she part of El Puente too?"

"If she isn't," Ingrid said, "then she's very close to them. She's always with them."

"Introduce me," he said.

"Yes, yes," said Alberto.

"Fine." Very discreetly, Ingrid approached the girl and a few seconds later returned with her.

"Bring 'em back alive!" he and Alberto said in English, laughing.

Ingrid made the introductions. They did not shake hands and the whole time he was staring at those enormous, jutting, liberated breasts under the sweater. They talked and drank and laughed and finally he said to her:

< 238 >

"We are going to have a little private party at Ingrid's house. Would you like to join us?"

Ingrid's expression revealed this was news to her – which was true.

"Okay," Oceanía said, "in principle I'll be there, but I'll let you know for sure in a minute."

And off she went.

"What party am I going to give?" asked Ingrid.

"Oh, a private one. At your house," he said.

"At my house? Nobody will fit, the apartment is too small."

"But we'll fit," Alberto said.

"It's a private party," he said. "Understand?"

"Well," said Ingrid, resigned, "okay, I'll give a private party."

The three of them laughed. Then Oceanía returned.

"I have to speak with you," she said to Ingrid.

"What is it?"

"Come over here."

Ingrid and Oceanía spoke under the mango tree, the tree of revelations. Ingrid returned.

"She says she'll go, but she's got to bring José Mario along."

"What?" he and Alberto said, practically in unison.

"She has to bring José Mario with her."

"With us, in other words," he said.

"Precisely," said Ingrid.

"That won't work," he said. Alberto said nothing.

"I was afraid of that," said Ingrid. "Could you tell me why not? Just so I can tell her."

"I don't like that sort of promiscuity. Neither does Alberto."

< 239 >

Alberto shook his head.

"Well," Ingrid said, "what can you do? I'll tell her it's off."

"Tell her to come alone, with us."

"Okay. I'll go see."

Ingrid had another chat with Oceanía. He saw Oceanía's mouth tighten, but at that distance he could not tell why. He also saw from afar that Mariano was smiling and wagging his finger at him. And he saw Oscar Hurtado join in, wagging his head. He laughed with them.

"No way, José," Ingrid said upon her return.

"Well, what can you do? She's not for me."

"But you're still giving the party," Alberto said to Ingrid.

"Well, all right. I suppose so. Though it's going to be a bit unbalanced: a party for three."

At that point salvation entered the garden in the form of Lido.

He does not recall if Ingrid motioned her over with an imperceptible signal or if she came on her own, but the fact is Lido joined them after Oceanía left. Or was Oceanía still there? He cannot recall. He introduced Lido to Alberto, who smiled his timid lopsided smile. Then he offered her some punch and she accepted. From what he could see, there were no commanders present. Later on, after dark, Lido, Ingrid, Alberto, and he packed themselves into Alberto's VW and drove to Ingrid's.

He knew her small apartment well because it had belonged to Rine Leal before and for a short while Nidia Ríos had lived in it, a model who was a rival and friend of Norka's in the fifties. He entered it not without nostalgia, a feeling soon overtaken by something close to pity: Ingrid did not have a stick of furniture, except for two mattresses that made a bed in the little back room visible from the door.

< 240 >

Soon the conversation became intimate. Without anyone organizing anything, he and Alberto separated the two mattresses, one of which ended up in a corner of the little living room while the other remained in the bedroom. Mercifully, Ingrid turned out the lights. He took off his clothes and asked Lido to remove hers, which she did without much urging. Soon he forgot that Ingrid and Alberto were practically in the same room, as he concentrated on Lido: she still had the same aroma, the same soft flesh, the same emotion in her rhythm.

When they were done, he heard Ingrid and Alberto speaking. Alberto had lit a cigarette or Ingrid had, he wasn't sure because he couldn't see, but he did hear Ingrid saying, "But you don't have any reason to be worried…" He did not want to hear any more, so he said something to Lido, although Ingrid's words echoed in his ears and he wondered then and many times later on what it was Alberto was worried about. In his mind he supplied many answers although he knew there was only one.

"Where have you been hiding?" he asked Lido.

"Oh, here and there. Why?"

"I haven't seen you for a long while."

"I've seen you."

"But you were too busy to see me," he said.

"Precisely. But you were the one who was busy."

"Me?"

"Yes. At least as busy as I was."

"Right. When can I see you again?" he said.

"Aren't you looking at me?"

"I mean meet up with you again."

"I don't know. Tomorrow, the day after, one of these days."

< 241 >

"Right."

He turned over.

"Aren't you happy to see me today?"

"Yes," he said. "Very happy. I haven't had such a good time in a long while."

"I'm glad."

"What about you?"

"What about me?"

"Did you enjoy it?"

"Didn't you feel it?"

"Yes, but I want to hear you say it," he said.

"I enjoyed it."

"Did you really enjoy it?"

"I enjoyed it, really."

He stopped talking because he knew otherwise he would continue with his childish insistence. She did not speak for a while and he decided he had better get dressed. He did so immediately and she followed suit. He would have liked to stay with her longer, but he was worried about Ingrid and Alberto, especially Alberto, and he told himself that was the problem with group love: he wanted to be alone with Lido, at home or someplace else, but it was obvious she had gone with him on impulse and chances were it would not happen again.

The four of them went out to eat. Funny thing: although he remembers that evening very well, he has never been able to recall where they went or what they ate.

Another day Alberto invited him to the beach, to a house in Guanabo that belonged to a friend of his wife's. He never could remember the friend's

< 242 >

name, though he recalled when he first met her she had said she was a friend of Miriam Gómez's from when Miriam first started out in theater. He asked Alberto if he could bring his daughters along and off they went in Alberto's VW, more jam-packed than ever. His daughters went swimming but he – ever vigilant to keep Anita from putting her head under the water – as usual did not.

After lunch he left his daughters playing near the house and lay down in the living room for a siesta. Waking up a short while later, he overheard Alberto and their host talking. He heard her say something like, "If you two are so different, why are you such good friends with him?" Alberto answered, "I don't know, I was always touched by how much he liked my father's name." Years have passed and he still does not know if those fragments of conversation referred to him or to someone else. Since he did like the name of Alberto's father, Menelao Mora, he felt sure they were speaking about him, and it bothered him that Alberto did not evince the sort of friendship he thought they shared. On the other hand, he realized it was very Cuban not to admit deep affection for a male friend, and perhaps that explained Alberto's response or maybe they were not talking about him at all. He cursed his all-too-clever habit of pretending to be asleep when he was not, just as he cursed his friends' habit of talking about him when they thought he was asleep. It wasn't the first time it had happened, and although previous conversations were extraordinarily laudatory, this one worried him for a long time, essentially because he knew his fate lay in Alberto's hands. Depending on someone who might not be an absolute friend rankled.

In the afternoon Alberto's recklessness behind the wheel all the way back to Havana upset him even more, so much so that he mentioned it at home. He had perceived Alberto's suicidal tendency years before, back in the days

< 243 >

of clandestine struggle against Batista, and at times it threatened to cause a hecatomb, the sort of suicide one might call collective homicide. The worst of it was that Alberto had risked his daughters' lives, and it crossed his mind that he was becoming a father in spite of himself.

Another time Franqui invited him to go along with him and Ricardo Porro to see the Art Schools buildings Porro had designed at the old Country Club. They left from Franqui's house in Miramar, which was very close, and arrived about four in the afternoon, when the sun was still high and an endless blue sky hovered over the extensive greenery of the former golf course. The buildings, which they approached on foot, looked like stylized cupolas or miniature minarets in a plastic model rather than an architectural construct. Weeds were beginning to cover the gravel paths, and when they reached a high wall that seemed to be part of an amphitheater, he realized why he sensed a vague air of abandonment: the project had been forsaken, left unfinished. The farther they went into the construction site, the more Porro's displeasure increased, along with Franqui's sympathetic nods. Now he understood why Porro was so bitter the day of the reception at the Belgian Embassy. Evidently they had taken the project, designed but still unfinished, out of his hands. The buildings could still function as schools, but the grand design, which was a source of pride for the architect and reason for admiration on the part of foreign visitors, which had appeared in architecture magazines around the world, would not be completed. The afternoon air, the distant song of a mockingbird, the setting sun, all bestowed a touch of melancholy on their presence amid the ruins of the future. That these ruins were the result of choice was what he found so dispiriting and he told Porro as much. The architect thanked him. They returned to Havana in silence, silence being the first and only possible reaction to all the injustices being committed.

< 244 >

Two days later he met up with Walterio Carbonell at El Carmelo, which he had again begun to frequent. Walterio was alone and he was surprised not to see Magaly with him.

"Listen," Walterio said, "I saw you with someone the other day."

"Yes? Who?"

"It doesn't matter who, what matters is that that person has been fingered."

"By whom?"

Walterio lowered his voice.

"By Turpitude. I don't think it's in your interest."

"That's precisely what I think too. I didn't go out with her, you know."

"Don't do it. That person gets detained by Turpitude regularly. The last time they warned her they would prosecute if she wouldn't collaborate. Do you know what they mean by collaborate?"

"I have no idea "

"Tell them who you go out with and point out the weaknesses of the people you know."

"What do you mean by weaknesses?"

"Sexual habits, for example. They're interested in that, above all."

"Well, if they want I can tell them about mine and even do a few sketches if it helps."

"The important thing is you didn't go out with her. You know, she has nowhere to live and she'll sleep with anyone who offers her a bed."

He did not know. He told Rine Leal about it, who said Havana was full of very young girls from the countryside, nearly all of whom came to attend the Art Schools – and more of whom got expelled than graduated. So they remained in Havana and slept wherever they could. Rine took one to his apartment one night. She got into bed wearing only her underwear and when

< 245 >

Rine touched her she said no, she didn't want any of that, just let her sleep, she hadn't slept in three days because she had nowhere to go. Rine let her sleep. "What happened afterward?" he asked Rine.

"I don't know. She left early in the morning and I never saw her again."

That story made him remember a night when he visited the Hotel National to see how it had stood the passage of time, and he ran into Isabelita, a friend of his daughter Anita's, who was a child when he left for Belgium and was now a short, stocky young woman, though she was no more than thirteen. She and another friend of Anita's, Migdalita he thought her name was (a name he always found funny), were lining up from eleven o'clock at night so they could rent a change room next to the swimming pool when it opened in the morning. He was wondering about their mothers, about why those girls were out so late and prepared to spend the entire night in the street, when a boy came up to them, a young kid, and began to pester Migdalita for five pesos he had given them. It did not take much imagination to see that the two girls were prostitutes or at least prostitutes in the making. His feelings grow darker when Migdalita asked him what Anita was doing, whether she was going with him overseas. "Oh, you don't know what I would give to go with you," she said. "I would do anything." She did not have to tell him what she would do, because he could see it in her face, in her entire tiny body. He had also heard about young prostitutes roaming the hotels looking for foreigners who might have American or English cigarettes or nylon stockings. He had seen them himself the times he went to the Habana Libre and he knew they were around the other hotels all over Havana. He told himself that should be one of the turpitudes Social Turpitude went after. Instead, they spent their time investigating artists, making fabulously long lists of homosexuals, and hunting down dissidents, be they sexual, political, or intellectual. It was obvious the Revolution was preparing to repress the

< 246 >

very corruption it had spawned: Oceanía, Isabelita, Migdalita were children of the regime and they were something rarely seen in Havana beforehand, despite the city's reputation for depravity. He had known many prostitutes, it's true, but none of them did it for Camels, stockings, or sticks of gum. Besides, the phenomenon that Oceanía represented was totally new: the political siren, the charmer, the stool pigeon set up to induce public perdition by the very organisms created to fight that sort of crime. Walterio Carbonell finished with a very poignant revelation: Oceanía told him that so far she had managed to reject the pressure from the agents of Social Turpitude, but she was not sure how long she could hold them off; she doubted her own capacity to resist and told her friends not to go near her.

Harold Gramatges held a gathering at his home, a fiesta, a party. He let it be known that among the guests would be the singer Ela O'Farrill, the musicologist Odilio Urfé, maybe the pianist Frank Emilio, and other musicians. So there would be music. He went because Harold and his wife, Manila, were old friends. Among Havana gossips she was known after the Revolution as Menuditos, because whenever she gave a dinner party, which was often, they claimed she always made the food with *menuditos*, the internal organs of chickens she got through the ration card. But Harold, who had been ambassador in Paris and still had very good connections in Minrex, must have got hold of food through official channels, and, for that night at least, drink as well.

More than forty people were at the party, many of whom he did not know. He went with Alberto and Marian and they got there on the early side. Soon the house filled up and there was a concert of popular music very well sung, numbers from the "feeling" epoch long before the Revolution. The fact was, except for the hymns, not a single revolutionary song was musically worthwhile.

< 247 >

The way he had at diplomatic receptions in Belgium, he began to drink to get into the atmosphere, to be sociable, as they say in Cuba. Halfway through the party he was completely drunk. That was when the new wife of Mayito, Manila's nephew, came over and began talking to him about his mother. He did not know her, but she insisted she knew him and, more importantly, she knew a lot about his mother. They were on the broad front balcony overlooking a park with enormous fig trees, but he cannot recall noticing either the trees or the darkness, only the conversation with that woman, who spoke the sweetest words about his dead mother. Suddenly he began to weep and then the two of them were weeping, sobbing out loud, practically wailing. They went into the living room, which featured a sketch that Picasso had done on the wrapping paper used to protect a painting he had donated to raise funds in Paris after the devastation of Hurricane Flora, a sketch that ended up with Harold. Other embassy employees accused him of stealing it, which was one of the reasons Harold was no longer an ambassador in Paris or anywhere else, but there the drawing sat, on the wall in the middle of the living room, imposing, fundamental: signed by Picasso.

The two of them entered the living room in tears. Despite the alcoholic amnesia, he remembers never having cried so much in his life, and the profound shame of weeping in public made him weep all the more, his sobs mourning his double sorrow: the sorrow in his soul and the sorrow in his mind. They had to be taken to a bedroom at the back of the house, but every time he looked up at that woman, that girl, he just cried more. Finally he had no more tears to shed and he calmed down. Soon he was able to go back into the living room, but now he no longer wanted to be at the party, which had become a small, intimate affair; he wanted to forget all the shame he felt. So he remembers that party as a night of sorrow, since in Cuba the word for sorrow also means shame. It was too bad, because he had been chatting on

< 248 >

the balcony with Marcia, who looked more beautiful than ever that night, and he would have liked to pick up where they left off when they were by themselves in Barlovento. Late that night, Alberto finally took him home. But he could not sleep, thinking about his mother, about death, about the tragedy that his mother's death had made of his life, about his fear that fate would once again knock at his door, and also about the social gaffe he had committed: from that point on he considered that woman, whose name he cannot or will not recall, an agent provocateur.

It was a few days later that Enrique Rodríguez Loeches called and said, "Listen, big news. I'm here at the ministry and they tell me Luis Ricardo just resigned and asked for asylum in England." Luis Ricardo was Luis Ricardo Alonso, the Cuban ambassador in the United Kingdom, whom he knew well and had seen at a meeting of the Western European heads of mission in February in Madrid. He asked, "Anything about Pablo Armando?" Pablo Armando was Pablo Armando Fernández, his close friend and the cultural attaché in London. "No, we don't know anything. I'll call you back when we have more news." Enrique did not call back, but more news soon arrived.

Upstairs in his building, on the fourth or fifth floor, lived Bolaños, a young man who worked at the ministry – he thought in Politics XI or near that department – whom he had met through his parents and who had often relayed news of him to his mother when he was still in Belgium. That afternoon, while he was sitting in the park along the avenue, Bolaños came out of the building. He called him over and asked if he knew about what happened in London. Bolaños did not know, so he told him. Then Bolaños spoke a practically oracular phrase:

"Oh, then they'll recall Pablo Armando."

"Bring him back?" he asked.

"Yes," Bolaños said, "back to Cuba."

< 249 >

"Why?" he insisted. "What does Pablo Armando have to do with Luis Ricardo Alonso?"

"I don't know what he has to do with it," Bolaños said, "but Pablo Armando is facing a very serious accusation."

"Pablo Armando?"

"That's right, Pablo Armando is accused of throwing himself at a courier." That is how he put it; he did not say he had made advances, but the phrase obviously implied something sexual.

"Oh, no! That's ridiculous!" he said.

"Ridiculous or not, the accusation comes from the courier, who had to push him away."

Despite the seriousness of the situation, he could not help being amused at the thought of the courier welcoming sexual advances instead of resisting them, since all the diplomatic couriers were braggarts and bullies, coarse people, astonishingly uncultured. It was predictable, given that they came from the lowest rungs of Havana society. At the beginning of the Revolution, when they needed diplomatic couriers – apparently there were none previously – they asked the ministry, maybe Roa himself, whom they should hire. Communists were thought to be more trustworthy than anyone else, so the Party was consulted. Since couriers have to travel, the Party decided it would be better to send people accustomed to traveling – and put forward as candidates the conductors and drivers of the Havana buses, "who were experts at traveling." All the candidates hired by Minrex, without exception, were real bus drivers: slum life personified. To top it off, he could not recall a single courier who would be good looking enough to justify the charge against Pablo Armando.

"It's absurd," he said.

< 250 >

"Well, *viejo*," Bolaños said, "I'll tell you what I know: Pablo Armando is going to be recalled ipso facto."

On the 1st of September he decided it was time to tell his daughters that his mother, their grandmother, had died. He called them into the living room.

"I have something to tell you," he said.

"What's that, *papito*?" Anita said, but Carolita said nothing.

"You know your grandmother has been very ill." He paused. "Well, I have to let you know that she died."

"Really?" Carolita asked, and said no more.

"She died?" said Anita. "Grandma?"

"Yes, she died and we're going to the cemetery."

Some time before, his father and he had planned a trip to the cemetery for the three-month anniversary of his mother's death. Now he could take his daughters along and no longer be tormented by the fact that he had hidden their grandmother's death from them. After telling them, he felt profoundly relieved and curious about their reaction, which he feared would be so terrible that from the moment he returned to Havana he had tried to protect them from the news. His original plan was to tell them in Brussels, physically removed from the death, now he was doing it far away in time. He could not perceive any reaction at all. Anita, being the elder, must have felt something, but Carolita, who had been very close to her grandmother in recent years, seemed to feel it more deeply. From then on, whenever Carolita would mention her grandmother, it was, "Poor Grandma." But Anita never said a thing. And neither of them ever spoke again about the death of their grandmother, his mother.

The following morning the four of them went to the cemetery. His

< 251 >

mother was still in the tomb of the Mora family – or maybe it was the Bec-
erra family, he wasn't sure if the tomb belonged to the family of Alberto's
father or mother – and they soon found it. He explained to his daughters that
their grandmother was buried here. His father changed the wilted flowers
on the grave for the new ones he had bought beside the cemetery at 12th
and 23rd. The sadness he felt was attenuated by his curiosity about his daughters' thoughts, since their grandmother had been like a mother to them. But
if the girls were thinking anything in particular, they did not know how to
express it. What he remembers most from that visit is the intense smell of
rot emanating from the tomb, which evidently was poorly sealed or maybe
the stone lid was not cut to fit. The unpleasant odor remained in his nose
for many days; it was the only thing left of his mother – except of course the
corrupted body which produced the stench. They left the cemetery without
a word and returned home. When they got off the bus, his daughter Anita
asked him if he would buy her a heavenly custard that day, since he hadn't
in a long time. He said yes.

The Mass in memory of his mother was finally to be celebrated the following day. It would be an early Mass, the only one available, and it would
be at the Church of the Angel, far from the house. Fortunately, the neighbor
women who arranged for it still had a car and they took him and his father
to the church. Before going in, he took a look around a part of Old Havana
he had never visited and which was so famously portrayed in *Cecilia Valdés*,
perhaps the best known Cuban novel of all. The service was about to begin
by the time he went inside and he did not hear his mother's name clearly
when the priest, speaking in Latin, said the Mass. Never having been inside
the Church of the Angel, he was surprised to see it was much like the other
churches in Old Havana; for some reason he had always imagined it to be

< 252 >

different. The service was not long, evidently the priest had more to perform in this church, one of the few still open for worship in Havana – and perhaps in the entire country.

Back outside, more people were in the streets, many of them heading toward the Presidential Palace. Government employees for sure, he told himself. The neighbors took him and his father back home, behaving as they had on the trip over: polite and obliging and Catholic. He was surprised that friendship and neighborly feeling were able to bridge the political divide between these women and his father, who after all was the president of the neighborhood Defense Committee. They said goodbye, with many thanks, in the lobby.

ON THE AFTERNOON OF SEPTEMBER 4TH, Franqui called, saying he wanted to speak with him and with Sarusky, Walterio Carbonell, and Hurtado. He did not say why, only that it was important. He agreed to contact Hurtado and Sarusky and, through the latter, Walterio. The four of them met up at El Carmelo early in the evening. Franqui had said their meeting should happen later on, after ten o'clock. Hurtado arrived, then Sarusky, and Walterio turned up around nine. He saw several beautiful young girls alone and unaccompanied at other tables. One in particular he realized he had seen before, perhaps in that very spot. Thin, dark-skinned, her long face framed by bangs, her hair in a short black ponytail, she had large black eyes that along with her perfect chin gave her face an air of ancient Egypt. She was with another girl, shorter and heftier, with a nearly round white face and long wavy hair, and they were seated at the table by the door that led out to the sidewalk patio along D Street. By chance, that was where Sarusky had parked his car, so they all left by that door to go to Franqui's. The dark-

< 253 >

skinned girl was playing with her wooden bracelet, pulling it on and off her wrist. Sarusky, or maybe Walterio, said something to her and she answered. That set off a little contest – he never knew who suggested it – that consisted of seeing whose finger she could toss her bracelet onto. Sarusky and then Walterio offered their respective index fingers, and on both occasions she missed. Hurtado then declined his turn. So he held up his index finger. The bracelet came flying, landed around his erect index finger, and remained there, hooked.

"Okay!" the dark-skinned girl said.

"I won, didn't I?" he said.

"So it seems," she said. Her friend laughed.

"What's the prize?" he asked.

"Oh, the prize," the girl said. "You'll find out later."

"It had better be now," he said, and he glanced out at Oscar Hurtado, who was waiting impatiently on the sidewalk, while Sarusky was swinging the keys to his car on his finger, and Walterio was saying something to the dark-skinned girl's companion that he did not hear.

"Not now," she said. "Later on."

"Let's get going, gentlemen," Hurtado said, coming over.

"Well," he said, "we have to go. Too bad."

"Yes, too bad," the girl said.

"See you later," he said.

"See you later," she said, and added, "good luck."

"Thank you."

They got into the car and when they pulled away he looked back at the restaurant and could see her beside the sidewalk patio, playing with her bracelet again.

< 254 >

They arrived at Franqui's house and rang the bell. No one answered. They rang again and still no one came. They tried a third time. Nobody. He stepped away and looked the house over from top to bottom. Not a light was on.

"It looks like nobody's home," Sarusky said.

"That Franqui," said Walterio.

Neither he nor Hurtado said a thing. They rang the bell again. Nothing. They waited a while, tried once more, and still no one came.

"What should we do?" he asked.

"Leave," Oscar Hurtado said.

"Try ringing the bell again," Sarusky suggested.

He rang it and no one came.

"Let's call him on the telephone. He told me he would be home after ten o'clock."

"It's nearly eleven," Sarusky said.

"Let's call," said Hurtado.

"From where?" asked Sarusky.

"Let's go back to El Carmelo," he proposed. "We can call from there and if he's home, we'll come back. If he isn't, we can stay there for a while."

"Nothing else we can do," Walterio said, and he wondered if he and Walterio were thinking the same thing.

"Okay, let's go," said Sarusky.

They drove back to El Carmelo, went inside, and sat down.

"I'm going to call," he said, and he went out to the telephones on the sidewalk patio and dialed Franqui's home number. No answer. He let the phone continue ringing. Finally someone picked up.

"Hello?"

< 255 >

It was Franqui's voice. "Carlos, what happened?"

"What do you mean, what happened?"

"We were there and we rang and rang and nobody ever came."

"Well, I was here the whole time. I didn't hear a thing."

"Okay, fine. Then we're on our way over."

"Fine."

He was hanging up when he spied the dark-skinned girl and her companion heading for the exit to Calzada. He left the telephone corner and intercepted them practically at the door.

"Hi," he said, "you're leaving already?"

"Yes," the companion said, "we're leaving."

"Would you like to come?" the dark-skinned girl asked.

"Where?" he asked.

"That's something you don't ask," the girl said.

"No," her companion said. "We're going to have a cup of coffee at the stand next to Las Vegas."

It had been a long time since he had heard the name of that nightclub, and even longer since he had been there, although at one point the place was very important to him. But he was not thinking about that right then. He said:

"Sure."

"Come on," the companion said, "my car is parked over there."

They walked to the car. It was not a beat-up old Ford like Sarusky's, rather a Buick, though just as old, four or five years at least. The companion got into the driver's seat and then opened the front passenger door. He thought of opening the back door, but the dark-skinned girl got there first and made

< 256 >

space so he could sit beside her. He got in and before the car started moving the dark-skinned girl said:

"My name is Silvia, Silvia Rodríguez, and this is my sister Elsa."

"Pleased to meet you," he said, and he gave his name and also said hello to Elsa. They pulled out and did not stop until Infanta and Hospital, where they left the car parked. They walked over to the coffee stand, which was crowded at that time of night. Among the coffee drinkers was Eric Romay, a black actor he knew who said hello. He also said hello to Silvia and Elsa. He gave Silvia a special hello, he thought.

They waited their turn to get coffee. It was hot and tasty and the three of them were pleased. Every so often he stole a glance at Silvia and once he looked at Eric, who winked at him in a particularly complicit manner: Eric knew he was married to Miriam Gómez. They finished and said goodbye to Eric. When they reached the car Elsa said, "Well, we'll give you a lift back to El Carmelo." They turned around and all too quickly they were back at the Calzada entrance.

"Thank you very much," he said.

"You're welcome," said Elsa.

"When can I see you again?"

Silvia gave him her home number.

"Why don't you call me?"

"When?"

"Tomorrow or the next day. Whenever you want. I'm almost always home in the afternoon."

"Fine. See you later."

"Please do call me."

< 257 >

"I will," he said, and he went into El Carmelo and spoke with his trio of companions as if he had just come from the telephone.

"Franqui's home. He's waiting for us."

"What took you so long?" Oscar Hurtado asked, or maybe it was Walterio Carbonell.

"Oh, I have a good reason. Do you remember the girl with the bracelet and her companion, who turns out to be her sister? They took me for a cup of coffee at the stand next to Las Vegas."

"Why didn't you tell me?" Sarusky said. "I would have gone with you."

He could not tell if Sarusky was saying he was interested in Elsa or in the coffee, since he had to drink coffee frequently to raise his very low blood pressure.

"It didn't occur to me," he said, since it really had not occurred to him.

"Ah, *viejo*," Sarusky said, "you should have thought of it."

In the car on the way to Franqui's, Sarusky continued muttering. He poked him at Sarusky, but the man was serious. Apparently, he had taken it to heart

"You should have told me, *compadre*," Sarusky said, still in a huff.

"I should also have told Walterio and Oscar," he said. "We should have all gone with them, as a committee."

At last, after the Miramar tunnel, Sarusky laughed.

"Next time don't leave me out," he said.

"I promise."

At Franqui's house the downstairs lights were on. They rang the bell and Franqui let them in right away and took them to the second floor.

"Well, what's up?" he said.

< 258 >

"Nothing," Franqui responded, and indeed there was no news, and he did not know whether to be angry or grateful. In truth he ought to have felt grateful, since, had Franqui not called the meeting, he would not have gone to El Carmelo that night and would not have gone out the door to D Street at the moment he did, and therefore would never have met Silvia. Not that in the moment he gave it much importance, but in retrospect he now sees that is precisely how the devil works.

Franqui wanted them all to share their impressions. He felt isolated at home without any contacts in government, except for the few times Celia Sánchez would call, and if she felt like it talk to him about Fidel Castro. But none of the four knew much about what was going on. Perhaps the one best placed to know anything was Sarusky, since he hung around the Writers Union, the National Publishing House, and sometimes the Cultural Council. But Sarusky kept his mouth shut, because whenever he said anything about the government he had to mention Lisandro Otero, and he knew Franqui had had a fight with Lisandro and hated to hear his name spoken in his home. So in the hour or two they spent with Franqui, they just gossiped about things that were more or less known. Astutely, he made no mention of Alberto Mora's efforts on his behalf; he does not think he would have even if he were alone with Franqui: he shared Franqui's belief that the house was carpeted in microphones that transmitted every conversation directly to the Interior Ministry, either to the offices of Ramiro Valdés or to Barbaroja Piñeiro's lair. Arriving home very late that night, he remembered that he had forgotten to tell Franqui what Bolaños had said about Pablo Armando being recalled; he would tell him on another occasion.

< 259 >

His grandmother woke him early in the morning, shortly after six, to say he had a telephone call. He asked who it could be, but his grandmother said the caller had not identified himself.

"Listen, I'm here already," he heard, and immediately he recognized Pablo Armando's voice.

"That's great! When did you get in?"

"I just arrived."

"When can I see you?"

"Pretty soon, I'll head over."

"Come right away."

"No, first I have to get my hair cut. It's really long and I don't want to walk around like this, I could have problems."

He realized Pablo Armando was right, better to get his hair cut and then come over. He told him so.

Pablo Armando arrived a little after nine, gave him a big hug, and hugged and kissed his grandmother, who nearly started crying, and then he kissed the girls.

"We have a lot to talk about," Pablo Armando said, and it was true. He told the story of Luis Ricardo Alonso, someone they both called, not Ambassador or by his full name, but simply Luis Ricardo. Despite how close they were, Luis Ricardo had not said anything to Pablo about planning to resign, much less asking for asylum in England. He had waited until Pablo was out at a cultural event, then he called in Maruja, gave her all the keys to the embassy, and told her he was resigning. By the time Pablo Armando returned, Luis Ricardo was nowhere to be found, and Pablo had to inform the consul and the Cuban trade office in London that the ambassador had fled. That very night someone who had no diplomatic status was designated to take charge

< 260 >

of the embassy, a post that by rights and ranking should have gone to Pablo Armando. That was the first irregularity. The second was when the new chargé d'affaires sent a flurry of cables to Havana. According to Pablo Armando, everyone suspected him of knowing about Luis Ricardo's intentions, but Pablo Armando swore – and he believed him – that he was completely in the dark. Of course the dogmatists at the trade office and especially the chargé d'affaires thought he was lying. The usurping chargé must have been the one who sent the cable to Havana that got Pablo Armando in trouble. Naturally, he did not want to tell Pablo Armando what he had heard from Bolaños or even hint at the real reason he had been recalled. Pablo Armando said he had been brought back for consultations, but he must have known there was more to it.

With a voice full of emotion, Pablo Armando said he was going right away to the cemetery to put flowers on Zoila's tomb. But he was not so eager and said he would only accompany him as far as the gate, old Guillermo could take him to the grave. They bought flowers at 12th and 23rd and staring at the rickety flower stands Pablo Armando said, "My God! This looks like Alabama. What poverty, my God!" Pablo Armando must have been referring to the poorer parts of Alabama, perhaps the black neighborhoods he had visited many years before. He could only respond, "Really?" while also gazing at the misery that had descended on 12th and 23rd in only five years. After the cemetery he wanted Pablo Armando to come home for breakfast, but Pablo claimed he had already eaten, adding that they had enough milk at home. It was obvious he did not want to abuse his hospitality by drinking the tiny bit of milk in the house. When they were on the way back to the apartment, he noticed that Pablo's hair was very short, the way he had worn it before.

< 261 >

"Who cut your hair?" he asked. "Pepe Pintado?"

"That's the one."

"I've got to get a haircut too," he said, realizing he had not been to the barber in three months; it was not a good idea to walk around in newly bureaucratic Havana with hair too long or pants too tight, and indeed the pants from his Italian-cut suit were pushing it. (He wore them less and less, partly so they would last since he had noticed the seat was wearing thin.)

They spent the morning together, then when it was nearing lunchtime Pablo left, saying he had to visit Marcia and Lisandro, and also try to see Yeye, Haydée Santamaría. He understood Pablo did not want to stay for lunch, and mildful of Hildelisa's culinary talents and the meager food supply, he did not take offense. Pablo Armando also wanted to meet up with Virgilio Piñera and Antón Arrufat, maybe at Pepe Rodríguez Feo's house, since Virgilio lived next door, but he told him he had better leave that for later. Without his having to say anything else, Pablo Armando understood and agreed to visit them later on.

On Sunday, he and Pablo spent the afternoon at Franqui's house. He accepted the shots of rum Franqui served and, since he had not eaten much, by midafternoon was fairly tipsy. Pablo and Franqui were no longer talking about problems at the embassy or at Minrex, rather about the hurricane heading toward Havana if the National Observatory could be believed, now that Corvette Captain Millás, who had gone into exile, was no longer in charge. He left them on the patio next to the garage (Franqui's favorite spot for meetings, being outside and away from possible microphones) and went into the living room to call Silvia. He had not written the number down and he prayed to God he remembered it right. He did and she answered the

< 262 >

phone. After trading a few half-jesting compliments, since she had a lovely voice on the telephone, he asked if he could see her that day. She said no, she was very sorry but she had a commitment: she was going with the Ghanean cultural attaché to an art exhibit and then home early. They agreed to meet the following evening at El Carmelo. Her goodbye was very sweet, even if all she said was see you later.

He remembers he arrived at El Carmelo early that Monday night and sat on the sidewalk patio that extended all the way to the corner, taking a table facing the windows of the restaurant, so he could keep an eye on both entrances. He saw her coming from Calzada, walking toward him across the patio, her hips swaying. She was alone and she greeted him with a pleasant smile. He stood and said good evening. She nodded in answer and sat down.

"How is it going?" he said.

"Just fine. What about you?"

"Fine, very well. What are you going to have?"

"What can you have?" she asked sarcastically.

He smiled. "They've got Coca-Cola and Coca-Cola."

"I'll take the first," she said. They fell silent for a moment, then she said, "I told my sister…"

Nervous, he interrupted her. "How is she?"

"She's fine. She'll be by later to pick me up. I told her," she insisted, "that you were very nice."

"Oh, thank you."

"But what I really told her was that you were lovable, somebody you could love."

This declaration caught him totally by surprise, so much so that for a few seconds he said nothing. He could not think of a thing to say.

< 263 >

"Say something, please."

He thought he ought to respond, but nothing came to him.

"Franks, I mean, thanks," he said.

She laughed, although he was not trying to make a joke; his tongue really had mixed up the words. After she stopped laughing, she lowered her head and moved it from side to side in a gesture he soon would learn was typical of her.

"Okay," she said, "the girl's a little forward."

She was speaking of herself, declaring herself to be what in Cuba people call pushy. He still had no idea what to say. He felt that all eyes in the restaurant and patio were on them, and he also felt something he had not felt chatting with Isabel the actress or when he picked up Lido in that very spot.

"Are we going to stay here all night?" he asked.

"No, why?"

"No reason, but why don't we take a stroll?"

"Good idea," she said. He called over the waiter, paid, and they left.

They walked down Calzada to Avenue of the Presidents and turned left, crossing the street and heading toward the Malecón. On the other side of that broad avenue once filled with cars, he saw five black boys playing on the wall, pushing one another and laughing, their shrieks reaching them across the street.

"You see?" she said. "Can you imagine what this country would be like without black people? It would be simply intolerable!"

He liked her saying that, because he held the same opinion. He had often given thanks to Father Las Casas for having encouraged the importation of Africans, turning Cuba into what it was, instead of the insufferable island

< 264 >

it would have been without their influence. He did not reply, but he smiled. She went on, saying she liked Havana a lot, she liked Cuba. He thought of asking her if she had been to other countries, but he was certain she had never been outside Cuba. In any case, he must have been no different before ever traveling. He let her go on talking because he liked her voice, he liked the very Cuban way she spoke, slightly mannish, not in its timbre, but in the words she chose to express herself and the cadence. In a way she reminded him of Norka, although she was not as vulgar. They walked for a long while side by side, then she said her sister must already be at El Carmelo, so they made their way slowly back to the restaurant.

It was true, Elsa was there waiting for them, sitting by herself.

"Hi," he said.

"What's up?" Elsa said pleasantly.

They sat down.

"Have you been waiting long?" asked Silvia.

"A little while."

"We were taking a stroll," he said, though no one had asked. Elsa smiled in response.

"Would you like anything?"

"No, thanks. I already had a Coke."

"What about you?" he asked Silvia.

"No, nothing. I think we'll be going. At least my sister wants to go, right?"

"I've got to get up early tomorrow to go to work."

"My sister not only wants to go," said Silvia, "she wants to make me feel bad because I don't have to get up tomorrow, since I don't work."

Elsa gave her sister an unfriendly smile, then went right back to looking serious.

< 265 >

"My sister is so cute," Silvia said, "isn't she?"

"Incredibly cute," Elsa said. "Can we go?"

"Let's go."

The two of them stood. He did too.

"Can we see each other tomorrow?" he asked.

"Yes, of course," Silvia said. "Right here, same time."

He said goodbye and nothing more, because it was clear Elsa did not like being her sister's chaperone. The two of them walked toward Calzada and he remained on the patio for a few minutes. Since he saw no one he wanted to talk to, he too decamped and walked home. He felt like calling Silvia right away, but realized how late it was and left it for another time.

The next day he saw Rine Leal. He wanted to ask him for a loan and also for the keys to his apartment, certain that Rine would not refuse. He asked for a hundred pesos and Rine made a face, though nearly imperceptibly.

"Well, I can give it to you tomorrow after I go to the bank. When do you want the keys?"

"Today."

"For how long?"

"I don't know. A week or so. Is that a problem? I'll only use it when you aren't there."

"No, it's not a problem, but I want to know."

He could tell that Rine, despite being his obliging friend, was not happy to lend him his apartment for more than a day, but he had no other solution. He could not take Silvia to a hotel as he had Lido. He decided not to worry about any possible conflicts with Rine and there weren't any.

That night he went back to El Carmelo and found Silvia already waiting for him at a table.

< 266 >

"Hi, how are you?"

"Hi, lovable."

He pretended not to hear, though it really pleased him that she called him that. It reminded him of the time he picked up his grandmother to take her to the doctor, before he moved to Belgium, and she said he was lovable. Aunt Felisa, who was visiting then, started to call him Lovable. He liked hearing the adjective converted into an affectionately familiar name. Now Silvia added a light erotic touch, and though it had put him off balance the night before, now he accepted it as a friendly greeting.

"Where's Elsa?"

"She'll be here later on. If she comes. My sister has romantic problems."

"She does?"

"Yes, like me."

"I don't believe it."

"Just the way you're hearing it."

He did not ask about her romantic problems because he was certain they had to do with him, but soon, once they were out walking, he said:

"I have to tell you something."

"What?"

"Yes. I think I'd better tell you once and for all so there'll be no misunderstanding. I'm married. My wife is in Europe and I'm going back there to join her very soon."

"Oh, golly!" she said. "What luck I have."

"Why?"

"No, no reason. I have to tell you I have a boyfriend. He's Hungarian and he's in Hungary now. He's married, but he's going to get a divorce so he can marry me. Are we – ?"

< 267 >

"Even-steven," he said, and he smiled. She had smiled only when she mentioned her luck. Now they walked on in silence. He did not know if he had done the right thing in telling her, and he realized he had said nothing to Lido or Leonora Soler. Why did he have to tell Silvia? Maybe because she was different or he wanted to be different with her. In any case, she was not very happy. Suddenly she turned to him:

"I said 'what luck I have' because the men that interest me always seem to be married. I'm telling you because I'm very frank."

"I am too."

"I can see that."

They continued walking toward the Malecón. They could not hear the waves but they could smell the sea.

"How old are you?"

He thought she would say you're never supposed to ask a woman that, but she said:

"Eighteen."

"You know you could be my daughter."

"Really?"

"Yes, I'm thirty-six."

"Sandor, that's his name, is also older, but not as old as you."

"I'm practically an old man."

"No, not at all, but you are a mature person."

"Thank you," he said, smiling.

"You're welcome," she said, and she smiled too.

They walked along the Malecón, then turned down C Street. They were going to go by Rine's house and he touched the key in his pocket with his fingertips. They were across from number 69, the digits illuminated by a lightbulb.

< 268 >

"A friend of mine lives here. Would you like to visit him?"

It was a subterfuge, since he knew Rine was not at home.

"No, I don't feel like visiting," she said. "Let's talk instead."

"All right, as you wish."

They crossed the street to the park and sat on a bench where they had a view of the patios of El Carmelo, the Auditorium, and the building where Rine lived. They could also look at the park bandstand and the dry fountain with its statue of Neptune. It seemed to him that a Neptune on dry land was a bad omen.

"Do you know how I met him?"

"Who?" he asked, thinking of Neptune.

"Sandor, who else?"

"Oh. How did you meet him?"

"At the Habana Libre Hotel. I was a telephone operator and he was staying there. Somehow whenever he asked for a call, it went through me, and I loved his voice and his accent."

"Okay." Hearing her speak about the other fellow bored him.

"When I saw him, he looked even better than his voice."

It was a night of confessions. Would this be as far as he would get with her?

"But, you know what?" she said, and fell silent.

"What?" he said at last.

"Because of him, the hotel kicked me out. I mean from my job. Rule number one: stay away from the guests, and they caught me coming out of his room."

"Bad luck."

"Or good luck. That was what made him decide to marry me. In any case the job at the hotel was really boring. All day long with the phone in your face

< 269 >

connecting stupid people with dumb ones. Sandor went back to Budapest on vacation, but actually he's going to divorce his wife to marry me."

"When is he coming back?" he asked, calculating his possibilities.

"In a few days."

"Did he write to you?"

"No, he didn't write, but I know he'll be back soon."

Probably before I go to Belgium, he thought. I'd better get a move on.

"What shall we do?" he asked.

"When?"

"Now."

"Let's go. My sister must be waiting already."

They got up and forded the dry fountain, heading toward El Carmelo. From afar he saw Elsa seated at a table with Walterio. She saw them too.

"Too bad for your friend," Silvia said. "What's his name?"

"Who? Walterio?"

"Is that his name?"

"Yes."

"Well, poor him. He thinks he's going to get somewhere with my sister, but she hates blacks. My sister's stupid. Besides, she's in love with Captain –"

She stopped in the middle of her sentence.

"Well," she said, "I might as well tell you. With Captain Juan Nuiry, despite the fact he's married too. It's a family thing, you know."

"What is?"

"Falling in love with married men."

She said falling in love very clearly and he heard it, but he chose to say nothing. In any case, they were already at the restaurant.

"Hi, how are you?" she said very affectionately to Walterio, who stood up. Walterio had been a diplomat and he still maintained the traits of a good

< 270 >

upbringing that were becoming ever rarer in Cuba. So he was not surprised when people at the surrounding tables looked at him and laughed. He urged everyone to sit down. But they did not stay long.

"Well," said Elsa, "we have to go, don't we?"

"Why so early?" asked Walterio.

"I have to work tomorrow," Elsa said while Silvia moved her lips, mimicking the words in time with her sister. Then she leaned close to whisper in his ear: "I know it by heart." Elsa did not hear, but she looked disapprovingly in her sister's direction.

"Let's go," Silvia said out loud.

"Well," he said, "see you tomorrow."

"No, not tomorrow," said Elsa.

"You heard her, so I don't need to repeat it," Silvia said.

"Tomorrow I can't come," Elsa said.

"Can't you come by yourself?" he asked.

"Ha, ha," Silvia said, imitating an ironic laugh, "and you'll marry me? Because at my house they won't let me in if I come back alone. No, seriously, they still don't let me go out alone at night."

"Well," he said, resigned – and remembering it now he thinks Cubans, or at least those from Havana, must start every declarative sentence with 'well' – "then, the day after tomorrow."

"Fine," said Silvia, biting her lip in another typical gesture, "the day after tomorrow, same time, same place."

"Well," Elsa said to Walterio, "it's been a pleasure."

"The pleasure is all mine," Walterio said.

"Aren't we proper," Silvia said, and he laughed, but Elsa did not even smile. He thought the sisters were not the kind to get along. They departed at last. Once they were some distance away, Walterio asked him:

< 271 >

"So, any progress?"

"It seems," he said.

"Congratulations, *compañero*," Walterio said. "The sister is a tough nut to crack."

"It's because she's in love," he said. "Guess who with."

"Who?" Walterio asked.

"Juan Nuiry."

"Oh, our friend Nuiry. What a couple: two sisters who like married men."

"So it seems," he said. In reality he had told Walterio that Elsa was in love with Juan Nuiry because he wanted to see Walterio hang his head. But now, after Walterio's remark, he wished he hadn't. Then he told himself he was being too sensitive.

"Are you going to stick around?" Walterio asked.

"Why? Are you leaving already?"

"Yup."

"Well, then let's go. Let's walk up to 23rd Street," he said, and insisted on paying the tab; he knew Walterio had been unemployed for years and had no money. They walked along Calzada to Avenue of the Presidents and then up to 23rd Street, where they said goodbye. He did not know it at the time, but this would be their last opportunity to talk, just the two of them, before a political firestorm hit Walterio.

He received a letter from his brother, Sabá, in which he said he was moving up his return to Cuba and asked when he would be back in Europe. The letter had come in the diplomatic pouch of the Ministry of Foreign Trade, but no one had opened it. When his sister-in-law Regla brought it over, she told him that Ceferino Atocha, a Spanish trade official who had become friends with Sabá in Madrid and had visited with his mother, Zoila, several times, would drop by. Atocha was in Havana on business.

He received him at home and sat with him on the balcony one afternoon when the summer weather was softer and more charming than ever. Atocha extended his condolences, and it felt as if no time at all had passed since his mother died. Then they talked about Sabá. Atocha told him Sabá was not at all well in Madrid. They would not give him any work to do and he seemed like a ghost at the trade office. In his opinion, Sabá ought to return to Cuba as soon as he could and he had told him as much. He voiced his agreement, although that was just for show, and the Spaniard left believing that he was sensible and thought as he did, precisely the impression he wanted to leave, since you never know who Atocha might speak to. He did not think this conversation would reach very high in the ministry, but he knew from experience that when it comes to political gossip, small voices are the ones that travel farthest. It was no coincidence that the agents of G2 or the intelligence service were always third or fourth secretaries, if not lower down the diplomatic ladder.

The next time he went out with Silvia, he told her about Rine's apartment. He said of course that it was not his own, but that a very discreet friend had lent it to him. He did not say what they would use the apartment for, but it was obvious she knew. She said flatly no. He did not ask why, figuring that would lead to an argument. Silvia belonged to a generation that, as far as sex goes, was much more spontaneous and free than his own. What's more, she was not one of those Cuban women he had known so well in the past, who hypocritically refuse right up to the last minute, saying no with their heads as they shed their clothes and pull their partner on top. He also knew she had other reasons not to have a sexual relationship with him. Not yet, he hoped. That night she decided to tell him about her personal life.

"Do you know I'm one of the ones that got expelled from the Art Schools?"

< 273 >

"No, I did not know."

"Well, that's the case. My expulsion was funny," laughing her sarcastic laugh, "and the best part is there was no reason to expel me."

"No?"

"Absolutely none."

"Was that before meeting Sandro?" He got the name wrong on purpose.

"Sandor."

"Forgive me. Yes, Sandor."

"A long time before. Didn't I tell you I met him when I was a telephone operator at the Habana Libre?"

"Yes, sorry, I forgot."

She looked at him as if she knew he had not forgotten and had asked just to put her off balance and maybe get her to reveal something unexpected.

They were in the park again, walking around the fountain. She talked while he listened and looked now and again at the waterless fountain or maybe at the patios of El Carmelo.

"There was a girl who was accused of lesbianism. That's a serious charge at the Art Schools, but it could be leveled at anyone. This girl was or is a lesbian and I knew that, but I also knew they were going to expel her and once she was expelled she wouldn't have anywhere to study. And she was very talented. She still is, although I don't know where she is now. So, at a meeting they decided to expel her and I stood up and said I did not agree, that they had not proven any of the charges. Why did I do that! Then other students called for my expulsion and so I got the boot along with that girl. What's really ironic is I didn't care. At home that went over like a lead balloon, but I didn't care. What bothered me more was what happened to that girl, because she really had talent and I didn't have any. The only bad thing

< 274 >

is now I can't study anywhere, and after they fired me from my job at the Habana Libre, I can't do the work I'm interested in, which is anything to do with foreign visitors. I speak English, did you know that?"

"I did not."

"*Yes*, my darling. I studied it by myself and there aren't many now who speak English here. I could work at the People's Friendship Institute or some place like that, since there are lots of people who speak Russian or Czech, but few who speak English. I mean few who are young women, which is what they mostly use as guides. So, here I am," she said, and she turned to face him, hands on her hips, "a real parasite. I live with my family, although that can't really be called living. Oh, why don't you marry me? No, you can't, you're already married. Besides, you made me forget I'm going to marry Sandor."

He smiled what felt like a timid smile. He had nothing to say except that he was really sorry they had expelled her from the Art Schools.

"No, my dear," she said, "don't be sorry. I'm not, not at all. I deserved it. That's what happens when you're a – what's it called? – a good Samaritan. I've even forgotten my Christian religion."

Immediately, the conversation shifted, as if she were afraid of feeling sorry for herself.

"Do you know I have an incredible neighbor? She lives next door. Well, at the back of the building, in a little room – she's a mulatta who says the most sensational things. I should repeat them to you every day before I forget, because there are so many I can't remember them all. Today she told me she has cancer of the waydownthere, and you know what she said?" He shook his head briefly. "I've got cancer of the cuntle! Isn't that marvelous?"

She laughed uproariously and he laughed more in sympathy with her amusement than because he liked the coinage itself.

< 275 >

"Yes," he said, "that is a new word, at least I've never heard it before. It reminds me of two little girls I met once on 23rd Street, around 23rd and B I think. It was a while ago. One wanted to cross the street before the light turned green and the other said: 'Girl, aren't you hurritive!' Get it? Hurritive!"

She laughed loudly.

"Were they black?" she asked between guffaws.

"No. Sort of dark skinned."

"That's marvelous! Marvelous!"

The next time they went out, he put together an excursion with Sarusky in his car: Sarusky with Elsa, and he with Silvia. They went to one of the few nightclubs still open and had a few drinks. At about midnight, he came up with the idea of visiting Rine Leal. Sarusky agreed, but Elsa asked:

"Wait, who is that?"

"An inventor friend of ours," he said, and laughed. Silvia and Sarusky laughed too, and they nearly lost their chance of going to Rine's house, because Elsa thought they were making fun of her. Then Silvia said, "You've got to be careful because my sister can be really bitchy." And it was true. He convinced her by saying that Rine invented impossible inventions and she agreed to go along, just as she had agreed to go out with Sarusky: in part to make Captain Nuiry jealous, and in part because she was feeling very jealous herself, since Nuiry paid her barely any attention. Like all women in love, she believed her beloved should do nothing but fret about her, and so she wanted the captain to find out about her date with Sarusky.

Fortunately, Rine goes to bed late and was not asleep when they arrived. He was reading, so he said, and he came out to greet them with his best smile (he always envied Rine's perfect teeth). Since it was hot, they went up to the rooftop that Rine had transformed into a terrace with two or three

< 276 >

beach chairs and a folding chaise lounge. The two of them – that is, he and Silvia – occupied the chaise lounge at one end of the rooftop, facing the park. The others sat down to chat. In the darkness he gave Silvia what he recalls as their first kiss, which she more than returned.

They were there for a long while, he and Silvia kissing and occasionally talking and sometimes listening to the conversation among Elsa, Rine, and Sarusky. From Elsa's laughter it seemed she liked Rine, and he took advantage of her having momentarily forgotten about the two of them.

It was quite late when a sudden cloudburst sent the other three running to take refuge in the apartment. He and Silvia stayed where they were, the driving rain in their faces and on their bodies and clothes. This time he was not thinking about his dead mother.

In a little while they went in, totally drenched.

"Jesus, look at you!" shrieked Elsa. "You're going to catch cold."

Sarusky smiled, laughed, and Rine wisely suggested they go into the bedroom to dry off. As soon as they did, he very silently turned the key, and they went back to kissing, more ardently than on the rooftop, almost frenetically. Then he tried to take off Silvia's wet clothing, but she would not let him. He was really excited and he tried every which way to strip her naked, but she resisted just as tenaciously, until he backed off.

"You want to vent your passion?" she asked, and he recalled that the expression surprised him. "Well, I say no, and fuck you."

It was the first time he heard her say a bad word, and did profanities ever sound good coming from her perfect mouth. Over the following days, he would hear her swear quite often, but never did it surprise him like that first time. He was so surprised he thought she really meant what she said. But then she went back to kissing him hard on the mouth, and he returned her

< 277 >

kiss and kissed her neck and continued lower until his mouth was between the tawny breasts bursting from her neckline. At last she made a gesture of desperation and began to unbutton her blouse and in a rush she peeled off her bra and panties and was completely naked and shivering in his arms. He took off his shirt (he had already left his coat on the bed) and pants and briefs, and he pushed her toward the bed, where he lay on top of her. She stopped shivering and began moving under his body and in a moment he was surprised at how easily he penetrated her.

Now they could hear the conversation among Elsa, Sarusky, and Rine in the living room (which in that small apartment was practically right outside) and he was pleased that she responded to his caresses without cries or moans. He had a question on the tip of his tongue, and even though he had asked it on other occasions, now he wondered whether he should. Then it slipped out almost without him realizing – he had repeated it mentally so many times he thought he had not said it aloud, and what he said was not exactly what he had in mind:

"Were you a virgin the first time?"

He expected her to react like other women, with near violence or anger, but he saw her smile and say, "Of course," and that was when he realized he had not formulated the question properly.

"What I mean is with Sandro."

Now he had really put his foot in his mouth, he was nervous.

"Sandor," she said.

"Yes, with Sandor."

"Yes."

He tried to make a joke of it.

"Ah, the gypsy bastard!"

< 278 >

But she was the only one who laughed. They had not turned out the light and he liked how her large breasts quivered when she laughed. She did not really have large breasts, but since she was very thin they looked large by contrast. She was all a tawny chestnut, except for the marks left by a bikini on her breasts and pubis.

"Do you go to the beach a lot?"

"I went to the pool at the Habana Libre every day until they fired me."

He felt the urge to talk, the opposite of what he had felt with Leonora Soler, with the woman he will not name, or even with Lido, whose skin was the same color as Silvia's.

"Your skin color looks really good on you."

"Sure," she said, indicating she knew as much.

From outside they heard laughter and he looked at his watch: it was three in the morning.

"Do you want to go out now?"

"Are you asking for me?"

"Well, yes."

"You don't have to. I'm not as much of a hypocrite as my sister. She knows I love you."

Since he could not say the same – not yet – he fell silent for a moment.

"We'd better go out," he said.

"Fine."

When they did, Elsa was chatting animatedly with Sarusky and Rine and did not look at them. He was feeling a bit sheepish, not knowing what to say, but Silvia, smiling her usual smile, her lips closed, was practically defiant: she had done what she wanted without any ostentation, but also without hypocrisy. He realized he was thirsty and he went into the little kitchen for

< 279 >

a glass of water. When he came back, he saw Silvia was part of the group, chatting too.

In a while Elsa looked at her watch and said, "Yikes, it's late!" and Sarusky got ready to take her and Silvia home. He went with them and they left Rine reveling in Elsa's exclamations of what a good time she had had. Before going, Elsa looked at him and smiled. When they reached the second floor, he asked them to wait because he had to tell Rine something. He went back up and found Rine about to get into bed.

"I have to ask you something."

"What?"

"The key, could I keep it for a few more days?"

"Yes, just remember I don't always go out at night."

"What about the afternoons?"

"I'm at *Bohemia*."

"Then I'll fix it to come in the afternoon. It's better that way."

"Well then, fine."

"Another thing. Are you in shape to lend me the hundred pesos?"

Rine said nothing for a moment. He did not like to let go of money, even as a loan.

"When do you need it?"

"Tomorrow. The day after at the latest."

"Well, let me see. I could go to the bank tomorrow... Okay."

"A million thanks, *viejo*," he said, and he left.

Elsa and Sarusky were in the front seat, chatting, and he and Silvia were in the back. Every so often, they kissed.

"We're here," Elsa said.

"Can we see each other tomorrow?" he asked.

"Not tomorrow, Silvia," Elsa said.

< 280 >

But he waited for Silvia to decide.

"The day after?" she asked. "Remember my father. I can't go out so much at night."

"Why don't we get together tomorrow afternoon?"

Silvia thought for a moment.

"Fine. Where?"

"At El Carmelo," he said.

"Tomorrow what time?"

"How does three o'clock sound?"

"Fine. Tomorrow at three."

Neither Sarusky nor Elsa said a thing. All of them said goodbye. When they were driving away, Sarusky said:

"*Compadre*, you don't waste any time."

He smiled.

"Tonight he outdid himself," Sarusky said, and he was pleased to hear Sarusky, who was probably not born in Cuba but in Russia, being Cuban enough to speak in the third person in that popular way. He smiled again.

"Come on," Sarusky said, "say something."

"What can I tell you? Hey, can't we leave something for tomorrow…? Better let's get a cup of coffee."

"I'm on my way," Sarusky said happily, and he turned toward the far side of Vedado, toward 12th and 23rd, where there was a coffee kiosk that was open all night.

THE FOLLOWING DAY LISANDRO OTERO invited Pablo Armando and him out to lunch. They went to La Roca, but stopped first for a drink at Club 21. Like the Tropicana and the area around Las Vegas and La Rampa, Club 21 figured prominently in his novel. So did the Saint Michel, which

< 281 >

was sort of a hangout for homosexuals that opened in 1958 and the Revolution was quick to close. In September of 1965, Club 21 was still operating, although like all bars and cabarets it would not remain that way for long. They sat on stools at the bar and asked for daiquiris, which were still done well there, as they were at the Floridita. Like many things in Cuba, the club was a ghost of its former self: the tables and chairs and the bar were set out as they always had been, but somehow the club was not the same. Underscoring the decay were several holes in the burlap padding of the leather bar top, so you had to be very careful to put your glass down far from the soft edge.

"What do you make of this?" Lisandro said in the same tone his wife, Marcia, had used when she asked him what he thought of Havana. The question was virtually an answer, given the sorrow at its core.

"It's falling apart," Pablo Armando said.

"Everything is like this," Lisandro said.

They kept their voices low, but spoke freely, taking advantage of the fact that the bartender was mixing the drinks and the club was empty at that time of day.

"Isn't there some way to fix this?" he asked.

"What for?" Lisandro said. "Before you've finished fixing it here, it'll break over there," pointing to the end of the bar. "Everything is like this."

Pablo Armando laughed his mirthless laugh, air whistling between lips edged by his beard and moustache.

"Truly," Lisandro said, "everything is going to pieces."

"Let's talk about something else," he said cautiously.

After lunch he took the taxi he found by some miracle to Rine's house. He asked Rine, who had the hundred pesos for him, if he would be home later

< 282 >

that afternoon. No, he would be at *Bohemia*. He told him he was going to use the bedroom (just like that). From Rine's house he went to the Diplomercado (he chuckled at the contrast between its name and its appearance) and bought a bottle of rum, then returned to Rine's, put the bottle in the kitchen, and walked over to El Carmelo. Silvia arrived punctually and he was happy she did not make him wait. Without asking if she wanted anything, he stood and took her to 69 C Street. With her clothes off, she looked more lovely than the day before. No, "lovely" is not the word; she was not a big woman, or tall, rather average height for a Cuban and very thin. She had good-looking thighs, but her legs were a bit crooked without being knock-kneed, and her behind hung down a bit while her back curved up. No, she was not lovely, but he found her very attractive – even more than her body he liked her sensuality and her intelligence; he could say, like Mephistopheles, that he wanted not her body but her soul.

They left the window open to the pleasant steady breeze. He had plugged in the record player in the living room and put on one of Rine's records, Dave Brubeck and his quartet, which he would always associate with making love in that borrowed apartment. They were there all afternoon and when night fell he invited her to supper at El Carmelo, something he could not have done before, since he had had no money. But she was not interested in eating and only asked for a pork appetizer. He ate and ate well. They decided to stay on at the restaurant, and though she had said the day before she could not go out at night, she remained at his side until ten o'clock, when she went home by herself, having promised to see him the next day at the same time and place.

The following day he had to have lunch with his Czech translator, Libuse Prokopová, and with Antón Arrufat. Libuse was now director of the

< 283 >

Czech-Cuban Friendship Center and she wanted to see them both. They went to El Jardín, which he had frequented a lot during one period in his life and which was now fixed up and redecorated. It was a pleasant spot, although the food was not as good as at El Carmelo or La Roca. After eating they chatted, and Libuse revealed her alarm at the Stalinism looming over Cuba. Those were her words and they stuck with him, because he considered Czechoslovakia to be a Stalinist country and now here was a Czech telling him how worried she was that Cuba was going the same way. After lunch he and Antón went to a park nearby to talk over Libuse Prokopová's well-intentioned comments. Arrufat said I told you so, meaning that from the moment they first talked at his house soon after he returned, he had been right: Cuba was heading for dark days and they had better protest before everything fell under a ferocious tyranny. Thinking about his travel plans, he acknowledged that Antón had been right, but said he did not believe anything could be done, that the future had to be accepted as an inexorable fate. Those were not his exact words, of course, but that was the gist of it.

Antón left after a while and he remained, because it was nearly three o'clock. From the park he could see both El Carmelo and Rine's building easily, even the rooftop terrace above his small apartment, and he thought about the triangle formed by the park and his two immediate destinations, though when he met up with Silvia he forgot everything, even the conversation he had had with Arrufat a few minutes before – he very nearly forgot his travel plans.

Waiting for Silvia he had lost patience and had left El Carmelo to stand on the corner where the bus stopped. When she still did not arrive, he thought maybe she had come along Calzada and he returned to El Carmelo to see if she was there. But no, so he went back to the bus stop and waited again.

< 284 >

The buses were few and she was not on any of them. He continued to walk back and forth between El Carmelo and the bus stop. Seeing it was already half past three, he began to wonder if she would come at all. Then it crossed his mind that he was in love with Silvia and in thinking it he also thought it impossible, because he loved Miriam Gómez far away in Belgium. But, he wondered, suppose it is true? If he were in love with Silvia, what would happen? Could he love two women at the same time? He told himself that when Silvia came, he would tell her he was going back to Europe, he would tell her before they went into Rine's house. However, when she finally arrived unexpectedly on a different bus, when he saw her get off with her curvaceous body, when he saw her smile, he forgot everything and thought only about getting to Rine's apartment as quickly as possible, into the bedroom, out of their clothes, and into bed.

Afterward, sitting on the edge of the bed to put on his socks, he noticed his belly and tried to pull it in by holding his breath, and he heard her say:

"Even if you hold it in, it still shows."

She laughed, but he did not. He was disgusted by his little middle-aged belly against which nothing could be done. But she was the one who repaired the hurt she had inflicted.

"You know," she said, "Sandor goes waterskiing and he's got the body of an athlete, but I like you more."

"Thank you," he said, half joking.

"No, seriously," she said. "I've practically forgotten him."

"You haven't forgotten much," he said, "since you just mentioned him."

"That was a comparison, you idiot. I wanted to say that I don't care about your belly. It's more: I like your little belly. You look more like my dad."

"A fault confessed is half incest," he said. She laughed.

< 285 >

"No, it's no Electra complex or anything like that. Do you know what my mother spends her whole life saying?"

"No, what does she say?"

"Well, in reality she's jealous of how much I love my father, who's pretty short and he's dark and he smokes cigars. She tells me, 'You're going to end up marrying a short, dark man who smokes cigars.' That's what she says."

"The one who brought you into the world guessed right, because I do smoke cigars."

"I know, that's why I'm telling you. Isn't that marvelous? 'You're going to end up marrying a short, dark man who smokes cigars.'"

She shook her head, as she often did, and laughed.

"I swear on my mother that my mother is nuts. Today my father said he wouldn't let me go out because I came home late last night, then she was the first to suggest I go out."

"She wanted her prophecy to come true."

"You're going to end up marrying a short, dark man who smokes cigars," the two of them said in unison, and they laughed heartily. She fell back on the bed and he looked at her face of an Egyptian gypsy – thinking about it now he likes the redundancy – and her color of mature tobacco, of chestnuts, of a tanned hide, and he threw himself at her. They began again.

Afterward, they showered together, and by the time they left it was dark. They headed for El Carmelo, where they found Walterio Carbonell and Sarusky – the pair he jokingly called "the black and the Polack." They chatted about nothing until Oscar Hurtado arrived, whom he had not seen for several nights and who began to speak of Martians and agents from outer space. His choice of topic might not please Martha Frayde, but at least it was innocent enough not to attract the obsessive attention of the G2 or whatever

< 286 >

they called the agency from inner space set up to detect counterrevolutionaries, real or invented.

To Oscar Hurtado he had simply said, "You know Silvia," half statement and half question, and Oscar Hurtado responded, "Pleased to meet you," and sat down. In truth he was not pleased. He could not stand to be in women's company. When he wanted to discourse on Martians and Venusians and all, he did not even want his lover, Evorita, around. (Remembering this now, he recalls how a commissary once boasted about uncovering a nest of infiltrators in a sawmill where the names of the owners were posted, each followed by "Cia," short for "company." The boaster said, "The sign made it clear as could be that they were from the CIA." He wonders where all those unfortunate people might be, if they were imprisoned or are free.)

At one point that evening, taking advantage of a pause between Saturn's rings, he asked Sarusky to take Silvia home. To his surprise Sarusky agreed, on condition they stop first at San Lázaro near the corner of Infante, where there was a coffee kiosk, so he could have the coffee he could not get at El Carmelo. They took Silvia home and said goodbye. Then they returned via 12th and 23rd, where Sarusky stopped for another cup of coffee. His chin started to tremble, as if he were about to cry: after four coffees in a row, he was finally feeling his blood pressure return to normal. He wondered what Sarusky would do the day – which ironically would arrive soon after that – when no coffee could be had in Cuba. Maybe he would emigrate and become the only Cuban exiled for lack of coffee. He thought Sarusky's true home must be Brazil, or maybe Costa Rica or Colombia, or pre-revolutionary Cuba, where coffee was the people's food.

Instead of returning to El Carmelo, he asked Sarusky to leave him near his building. As soon as he got home, he went to the telephone and called

< 287 >

Silvia. He thought Elsa might answer, but Silvia did, and he soon learned it was not by chance because she said, "What a coincidence! I was hoping you would call." They had not agreed to a phone call, but he had followed a very familiar urge. So as not to awaken anyone in the apartment, he spoke in a low voice and Silvia said, "Ooh, *mi vida*, keep talking like that, you've set my insides all atremble!" They talked about innocuous things that she considered important, and in a few days so would he. After they said, "See you tomorrow," knowing they would go to Rine's together, he heard his grandmother call from her room: "My son, Hildelisa made a sweet for the girls. They left you a piece." "Okay, Mamá," he said, and she answered, "Rest well, my son." He went to the refrigerator and found the pastry produced by Hildelisa. It wasn't bad and he decided that, as far as desserts were concerned, Hildelisa had potential. A sudden spasm of fear gripped him. Was he beginning to think of staying? No, that could not be, he told himself, and he went to bed persuaded that his determination to go into exile was stronger than any possible attraction.

In the morning he decided to finally get his hair cut, since he wanted to be as unnoticeable as possible. He went to the Habana Libre, to Pepe Pintado, the barber he liked, though whether for his skill or his name he could not say. While working on his hair, Pepe Pintado complained in an undertone about the situation, about his stomach ulcer for which he could find no milk, about the barbershop having been nationalized so he had gone from owner to lead employee. He liked the way Pepe Pintado talked with affected precision, like any barber expecting no replies, just wanting to keep the conversation going, and dwelling at length on the iniquities wrought by the Revolution. He wondered why Pepe Pintado risked speaking like this, and figured the

< 288 >

barber saw him as a fellow unfortunate, or at least a fellow traveler: a fellow traveler on the counterrevolutionary voyage.

When he looked at himself in the mirror, he saw that the chatty Pepe Pintado had cut more than he wished, but that was all right, since a short haircut makes you look younger and now he did not want to be old enough to be Silvia's father. Unlike one of his favorite authors (Hemingway), he hated having to call the woman with whom he was having an affair "daughter."

Before lunch, the Magus appeared (he had decided to call her that) and told him she had consulted regarding his problem, she did not say with whom. "Everything is ready," she said. "You will go just as you wish. No one can stop you." Then she asked, "Did you do the egg?" He did not know what to answer, so he made an ambiguous gesture. But the Magus understood. "You have to do it," she said. "At least you must have prayed the prayer." He was going to say he had read it, but not prayed it, but said instead, "Yes." "That's good, it will protect you." The Magus half closed her big, round, yellow eyes, and he thought, She has eyes of an owl. "You have to do the egg as soon as you can," she insisted. "Don't forget: the crossroads least traveled." He said he would not forget.

Once the Magus had left, he obeyed a sudden urge and went to see Carmela, Miriam Gómez's mother. He asked to look at pictures of Miriam and other things of hers that Carmela still had in her possession. She gave him a metal candy box filled with Miriam's papers and notes. In it were her ID card from the old actors association, unidentifiable receipts, a blue belt, and at the bottom, photographs, some of them of Miriam as a child, others of her when she was older. Among the family photographs, he found two ID-sized pictures of her. They must have been taken when she was seventeen or

< 289 >

eighteen: she looked really young and her hair was cut very short. He was certain they were passport pictures. Once he had them in hand he was convinced he would indeed go.

That very afternoon he went with his daughters to the shop at 12th and 23rd, the only place in all Vedado that did pictures, and they had passport pictures taken; they would be ready in five days. Coming out of the photographer's they ran into Toto, who used to be the doorman at the Atlantic Cinema and now was a doorman at the 12th and 23rd movie house. They chatted with him for a while and he was surprised that Toto's former good humor had given way to a new resentment, a bitterness. Toto told him his brother had been sentenced to thirty years for being a counterrevolutionary and that he himself would leave Cuba the first chance he got, that is how he put it. When Toto asked him, "What about you?" he did not dare confess that he too was leaving. He believed in the superstition that to declare your intentions makes it difficult, if not impossible, to carry them out.

As soon as he dropped his daughters off at home (not before buying Anita her hundredth heavenly custard), he took the bus from the corner to El Carmelo. Silvia was already waiting. She made an appreciative gesture when she saw his haircut. "We got younger," was her comment, but her voice showed no ill will, rather love. That was when he decided to speak with her.

He waited until they finished making love. Dave Brubeck was playing for the third or fourth time, and they were lying naked faceup on the bed. Without looking at her, he said:

"I've got to tell you something."

She answered immediately:

"What's that?"

< 290 >

He waited a few seconds before saying, "I'm leaving."

"When?" Her voice was guarded.

"I don't know. It could be next week, next month, but I know I'm leaving."

She was silent. Then she spoke up:

"I knew it. I swear by my mother, I knew it."

There was no bitterness or pain in her voice, but he knew she was hurting.

"We had spoken about it, hadn't we?"

"But not like that," she said, and then, "Do you have to go?"

"Yes."

"Do you want to go?"

"I ought to."

"You know what? I thought if Sandor came back I'd have to choose between you two. Now I don't, because you've made the choice for me."

There was no pathos in her voice; she was only stating facts, but she added:

"However, I would have liked it to be different."

He turned to her and saw she was not crying, just staring at the ceiling.

"Let's forget about that, all right?" she said, and turned toward him.

"Let's do that."

He kissed her, first on the lips, then on her neck, on her breasts, on her belly, practically all over her body.

It was dark when they got to El Carmelo.

As was almost always the case, Sarusky, Walterio Carbonell, and Oscar Hurtado were there. They greeted them and, feigning a happiness he did not really feel, he delivered his usual line to Sarusky:

< 291 >

"*Caramba!* The only Jew who got away from Hitler!"

Walterio and Hurtado and Sarusky himself all laughed. Then Walterio noticed his hair and asked what had happened to make him look so good. Silvia answered for him, smiling with her perfect lips:

"It's love."

WHEN PEPE PINTADO WAS SHAVING the back of his neck, he had scraped a mole. In fact he had several moles there, one of them particularly dark. One morning he decided to go see his doctor friend at the Calixto García. He was worried about the moles that grew and changed shape, and he even came to think that one of them, the one that always bothered him when he put on a shirt and tie, must be cancerous.

"They're polyps," his doctor friend said after examining him. "Let's go over to Skin and Syphilis so they can cut them out." It sounded like two goddesses, almost like Scylla and Charybdis. Many people were waiting, but they went directly into the back where several young doctors or advanced students were examining patients, cleansing wounds, and doing surgical removals with electric pincers. The doctor friend said to a young colleague who was finishing up, "Here take a look at this fellow who has moles on his neck. They're polyps, right?"

The colleague examined the moles, and giving them no importance said, "Polyps." Then he brought his electric pincers close and after a buzz and a pinch he asked him to rub his neck. He did so: the ugliest and most protuberant mole was entirely gone. Afterward, he did the same to the other moles on his neck and all of them disappeared as if by magic.

"You see?" his doctor friend said, "a magic potion! Let's go."

< 292 >

"Hang on a minute," said the young colleague who had removed the moles. "This fellow can go," he said, pointing at him, "but not you." And he went over to his doctor friend and stared intently at his face, touching a small gray mark near his nose with his index finger. "What's this, eh?"

The colleague stood back, looked at his friend, who had grown pale, and said: "It's nothing, we'll just have to give you a little pinch there, or some radiation."

"Why?"

"It looks like an epithelial sarcoma." He saw his friend grow even paler, so much so that he thought he might faint. It never occurred to him that a physician could be so afraid of disease. But the man recovered and said:

"Really?"

"Really." On the spot they made an appointment for either an operation or a radiation session. On their way out, he thought about the unexpected irony: the healer being healed.

Once again, afternoon at El Carmelo; it was practically a ritual. He knew that for now he could not live without it, because it would lead to the later rendezvous at Rine's apartment and love, love, love. He was still not in love, he thought, although having to say he wasn't implied a time when he might be in the future – if his exit from Cuba did not come sooner. For the moment, he knew how excited he was to see her arrive and sit by his side and drink in his kisses.

Late that afternoon, they decided not to return to El Carmelo, but to walk up to Avenue of the Presidents and 23rd Street and wait for the bus there. When they emerged from Rine's it was already dark, though it was earlier than usual. After walking up the avenue a distance, he glanced up and saw

< 293 >

black clouds gathering. At that very moment the skies opened. At first they ran, then realized that running was the same as walking, there was no possible refuge, so they let all the waters of heaven, so it seemed, descend upon them. They got absolutely drenched, their feet submerged at times as they made their way through a river of rainwater that swept past them on its way to the sea – and at no time did he think of his dead mother in the cemetery facing all that water alone. He felt cured of the sentiment that had so tortured him before. Now he walked with Silvia on his arm (or rather his arm around her fragile shoulders, perhaps protecting her from the nasty weather, which was in reality a delightful joy) toward his apartment, suddenly aware he would take her home, even though the thought had never before crossed his mind.

They arrived soaked through, although it had stopped raining by the time they reached 23rd Street. His father was not home and that was a relief. His daughters greeted him with astonishment, first at his appearance, like a wet chicken, and then with (he thought) a slight questioning when they laid eyes on Silvia.

"Silvia," he said, "this is Anita and this is Carolita." And to the girls: "Quick, bring a dry towel."

He helped dry off her arms and face and head before Hildelisa came out of the kitchen for a moment, as if by chance, to see what was going on in the living room, only to turn back with a twisted smile on her lips. His grandmother came out of her room and he introduced her: "Mamá, this is Silvia." He barely heard his grandmother's imperceptible, "Pleased to meet you," but he saw Silvia, standing in the living room, her friendly smile wavering between timid and thankful. (Later on, he thought she had no reason to be thankful for anything: he had taken her home on impulse, it could have happened any other day, and she had no reason to thank him for introducing

< 294 >

her to his family; after all, in Cuba no one is that formal, although informality itself creates strange forms of social behavior.)

He headed to his bedroom to change and on the way went into the kitchen and said to Hildelisa, offhandedly, "Do you think there is a dress around that Silvia could put on while her clothes dry?" With the first part of the sentence, he meant to imply one of his mother's dresses that might have ended up in the apartment after her things were divvied up. He thanked Hildelisa when she went to look and found one, and he called out to tell Silvia to change in the other room.

He was pleased he had not dressed up that day, wearing only the sports pants and short-sleeved shirt he had brought from Brussels, instead of his only suit. But he remembers now that he felt even more pleased when he came out of the bedroom in his suit pants and a shirt of his father's, and saw Silvia wearing an old dress of his mother's which fit her perfectly, and he found confirmation of what he had already imagined: the living Silvia and his dead mother had the same body.

They stayed a good hour and he offered her the food Hildelisa had put on the table, but she barely touched it. Though as usual it was not tasty enough to want to wolf down, he ate with gusto after the cloudburst and the running. Then they sat in the living room, without talking, looking at each other while the girls watched television – and he believes that was the moment he knew for certain he had fallen in love with her in a way he had thought impossible, the way he had fallen for Miriam Gómez, the way he should not have fallen for Silvia. And immediately he thought this would be another obstacle to his departure.

He accompanied her to the corner and waited with her for the bus home, remembering the sweetness with which she had said goodbye to everyone

< 295 >

(including Hildelisa), especially to his grandmother and his daughter Carolita, whom she seemed to really like. Then, when he was sure she had made it home, he called her on the telephone and they talked for about two hours, he listening sometimes to her pleasant voice, other times speaking in a whisper that moved her so much she nearly melted at the other end of the line. When they said goodbye, it was nearly midnight.

The following day he saw Alberto, who had not yet had a word with President Dorticós, but he had spoken again to Carlos Rafael Rodríguez and got across how essential it was for him to leave Cuba for a time, due to the publication of his book in Spain – the pretext they had agreed on. He had also asked his brother, Sabá, to request a letter from his Catalan editor indicating his need to be in Spain for the same reason. And indeed he received a letter from Carlos Barral which put it in the clearest possible terms, adding that he had to be there to go over the proofs, though that was obviously a lesser need, since the proofs could be corrected anywhere – even in a Cuban prison.

Alberto was optimistic; he mentioned no encounter with Piñeiro or any other evident roadblock. The news made him happy enough on the outside, but something inside him told him the trip would be postponed; maybe it was simply his desire to spend more time near Silvia. A letter from his brother yanked him out of that sweet reverie.

Sabá wrote via the Ministry of Foreign Trade's diplomatic pouch and his sister-in-law Regla brought him the letter on her way home from work. Sabá reported that the ministry had given him a final deadline of October 3rd to leave for Cuba, and so he was getting ready to return. He would bring with him, he said, all his film equipment (16mm and 35mm cameras, tape recorders, boom, etc.) to hand over to the Film Institute. The letter continued

< 296 >

with hyperbolic praise for the Revolution and the ministry, and reiterated that they should expect him at the airport on October 4th.

He only had to skim the letter to realize it was a signal and meant the very opposite of what it said: Sabá would not return to Cuba on October 3rd and most likely he would ask for political asylum in Spain. (He ended up asking for asylum in the United States.) The more he reread the letter the more convinced he became of his brother's intentions. Alarmed, he called Carlos Franqui and Pablo Armando Fernández, both of whom came over to the apartment that afternoon. He remembers well the moment he handed the letter to Franqui in the living room. After reading it, Franqui made a face:

"What does it mean?"

"It means I'd better get out before October 3rd, which is the deadline they gave him for leaving Spain. It's obvious the letter means the opposite of what it says."

"But that can't be!" Pablo Armando jumped in. "If he stays in Spain he'll have to ask for political asylum, and if Sabá asks for asylum, you'll never leave Cuba."

"That's what I'm saying," he said.

Franqui shook his head and started pacing about the room.

"What Sabá's doing is bullshit," he said. "He's always been selfish."

He did not agree, but said nothing.

"If he does it, if he does what you say he's going to do, he'll bring us all down. Neither you nor Pablo nor I will ever be able to leave."

"Why you and Pablo?" he asked. "I don't get it. I understand they wouldn't let me out because of family ties or out of vengeance. But you have nothing to do with him."

< 297 >

"But we do, *chico*," Pablo Armando said. "Don't you see we're all in this together, linked by the same damn thing?"

"Why the shame damn thing?"

"Argh!" said Pablo Armando.

"Cut the jokes," said Franqui.

"I wasn't joking. I meant to say why the same thing. I can't see anyone linking you to Sabá. It was Alberto Mora, when he was minister, who sent Sabá to Spain as commercial attaché, not you, Franqui. And it's Marcelo Fernández, the current minister, who told him to return, not you, Pablo Armando."

"Yes, my love, yes," Pablo Armando said, "but don't you realize they're going to associate him with you, and you with us?"

"That's it," Franqui said. "We've got to keep Sabá from seeking asylum."

"I don't know how we'll do that since he's halfway around the world. What we have to do, what I have to do, is accelerate my departure."

He spoke again with Alberto Mora, explaining to him, as he had to Franqui and Pablo Armando, what Sabá was planning to do. Alberto promised he would approach Carlos Rafael again and try to speak once more with President Dorticós. After Alberto's reassurance, he felt calmer but still foresaw that he would have to remain in Cuba, perhaps forever. He was despondent thinking about Miriam Gómez alone in Brussels; he would not allow her to return to Cuba, no matter what happened to him. The only thing that consoled him now, or at least allowed him to put his plight out of mind, was his relationship with Silvia, the bed they shared, which was truly becoming a land of lotus eaters.

That afternoon he did not see her, but he phoned her that night and they spoke until very late, talking in whispers. They saw each other the following

< 298 >

day and he remembers how, after some time in bed, he went to put on the Dave Brubeck record, and as he slid it onto the turntable and pushed the play button, he turned his head toward the bedroom and saw Silvia at the door, leaning against the frame, completely naked, one leg half hidden by the other, one arm raised over her head, the other reaching down the length of her body in an imitation of a cheap pinup pose, on her mouth a mocking smile that showed her stance was a parody to make him laugh – and laugh he did. Or rather he did not quite laugh: he only smiled, because emanating from her was a sexual attraction so strong he soon forgot all about comedy and concentrated on love, on the most complete possession of that girl, a true nymph – in the sense we Cubans use the word, but also in the mythological sense. He remembers he returned to the bedroom and loved her, possessed her as he had never possessed her before, completely and totally.

Afterward, the two of them showered, him washing his head with the little stub of soap that was left and making a mental note to go to the Diplomercado the next day to get Rine a new bar. Then they went to El Carmelo. He ate – a pork appetizer and a beer – but Silvia did not want to, she only had some of his coffee. That was when it occurred to him that she never ate with him, and he began to worry about how thin she was and how little she ate, since he was certain there would not be much food for her at home; as no home had enough food now, anyone not around at mealtime would likely not find any leftovers. Not everyone had a grandmother like his, ever watchful, and not everyone could depend on the culinary arts of Hildelisa, who always made sure there were leftovers.

He knew he was waging a battle against time, trying to put some distance between himself and the reality of his immediate future, but he also felt that love – yes, he was certain now it was love – introduced a new dimension

< 299 >

into whatever time he had left, as he raced to gain on the visible or invisible enemies set on holding him (imprisoned to expiate an imaginary crime) forever on an island that should have felt like home, but that he no longer recognized as his: the place where he came into the world was as dead as the woman who had brought him to life. He thought about the possible efficacy of all the charms – the ones dreamed up by the Magus and the ones planned by the few friends of his who had some modicum of power – and he realized that his enemies were powerful, not so much because they were usually invisible, but because they could materialize at any moment. He knew he had been vigilant, that he had worked assiduously and astutely, cautiously, that not for a moment had he failed to apply himself to his mission, which, as he had realized soon after his return, was to leave Cuba. At the same time he could not ignore the fact that his internal vigilance was matched by a parallel external vigilance, carried out by others well versed in their role of keeping him from doing what was ever more clearly the only thing he could do: to be like Francesco Guicciardini, the contemporary of Machiavelli's, and flee as far away as possible from the tyrant as quickly as one flees the plague. During those days, two things happened, both of which would affect his immediate situation.

One was the authorization "for all Cubans who wished to do so," as the informal decree put it, to leave for the United States. The resolution to allow mass emigration was adopted only after the government took measures to counter an exodus already underway. They spread propaganda about the "horrible life" awaiting emigrants in the United States, and even published in multiple printings a book by a woman who had returned to Cuba from exile. She painted the city of Miami as a version of hell, in which

< 300 >

prestigious physicians, well-known lawyers, public celebrities, were all working as waiters or gardeners, in the worst occupations. But none of the regime's attempts at propaganda – deployed most rigorously against blacks – could stem the growing number of Cubans who against wind and tide had decided to leave their country for good. At first the exodus resembled Dunkirk, since relatives already living in the United States who had some form of marine transport were allowed to pick up their family members. Soon, the naval traffic between the port of Camarioca near Havana and the different ports of southern Florida grew intense. The flow back and forth was such that the government prohibited departure by sea and instead allowed American planes to pick up the emigrants-cum-perpetual-émigrés at the resort town of Varadero, 130 kilometers from Havana, in what were soon nicknamed "freedom flights."

A few days after the announcement allowing Cubans to emigrate, he was watching pedestrians with his binoculars when Héctor Pedreira came out on his balcony and said:

"What a phenomenon! Remedios" – the town where Héctor was from – "was supposed to be a bastion of the Revolution, and so many people applied for emigration they ran out of stamps."

"Is that so?" was all he managed to say, being cautious since they were out in the open and Héctor broadcast everything he said.

"Yes, mass exile is what it is. If it goes on like this, the country is going to be left without a labor force."

Those were Héctor's words. He always used Communist terminology instead of saying the country would be left without people, as any other Cuban would have. Héctor was honestly concerned about the possible

< 301 >

consequences of the exodus for the country, but at the same time underneath his words ran a current of enthusiasm. Héctor's elderly mother – who was his adoptive mother, but whom he idolized – had gone into exile. The poor woman, forced to choose between some of her children and others, was brokenhearted at having divided the family. Being a longtime Communist, Héctor must have known that he would never choose exile and would never see his mother again, but deep inside him the massive exodus seemed to give him vicarious pleasure.

Héctor recounted individual cases of people he knew well in Remedios who were taking off in yachts, in speedboats, in anything that floated. He also told him a recent counterrevolutionary joke about a hypothetical conversation between Interior Minister Ramiro Valdés and Fidel Castro. The joke had the two of them obsessing about what to do about homosexuals, whether they should be locked up in work camps – which in the end is what happened – or leave them doing their faggotry out in the open. Commander Ramiro Valdés suggested the best solution for any convicted or confessed homosexuals would be to deport them. To which Fidel Castro responded: "Ramiro, that's crazy, so they can sodomize half of Cuba?!" Only Fidel Castro had not said "sodomize," he'd used a dirtier expression.

Héctor and he laughed heartily. Then Héctor asked for the binoculars so he could ogle a particularly attractive woman on the sidewalk across the street. He handed them over, but Teresa came out immediately, as if she had been watching, and caught her husband red-handed. "Aha!" she said. "So this is what you do when you come out for a little air!" He laughed harder at the matrimonial discord than he had at the joke. Teresa kidded him about having corrupted her husband, and he answered, half in jest, that she should leave her man in peace, that voyeurism is the most inoffensive of sexual practices

< 302 >

– of course he did not put it like that, rather he used normal Cuban language: "Let your husband fortify himself by ogling, it won't harm anybody."

The second thing that happened began with a call from Carlos Franqui, followed by another from Pablo Armando. Franqui wanted him and Pablo to meet him urgently at his house. Pablo Armando wondered what Franqui knew, and the two of them concluded that maybe Franqui, who was truly isolated from those in power, felt lonely. They decided to go together.

When they arrived at his house, Franqui was in the yard, where he had cut a tall sugarcane and was entertaining himself eating the sticks with a campesino's delight. Walking with his slow-moving, almost swaying stride, he led them into the garage, which with no car looked like an empty hangar. Franqui asked Castellanos, his driver and bodyguard, who happened to be a close relative, to leave. He finished his last bit of sugarcane in silence, then with a shake of his head he said:

"Something very serious has occurred."

The two of them waited. Franqui went to the garage door, looked in all directions, then returned.

"Arcocha just gave the government an ultimatum." Arcocha was Juan Arcocha, the press officer of the Cuban Embassy in Paris and a close friend of all three of them.

"What!" he and Pablo Armando said, almost in unison.

"Arcocha just wrote a letter to Fidel, and he says things that have to do with you. I mean, with us."

"Juan did what?" Pablo Armando, who was Arcocha's oldest friend among them, was incredulous.

"Well, not exactly. He put your problem to Carrillo" – Carrillo was the ambassador in Paris – "and asked what was up. Then he insisted Carrillo

< 303 >

write a report, not to Roa, but to Fidel Castro, saying that he, Arcocha, was prepared to come here whenever was convenient, but at the same time announcing that he was considering resigning and staying on in Paris."

"He did that?" asked Pablo.

"Franqui, you know how it is!" he said, copying his uncle's favorite expression, which out of context meant nothing, but in the moment said it all.

"He also said," Franqui continued, "that American agents had approached him encouraging him to seek asylum. Of course, Carrillo sent all that in a hurry to Cuba, right to Celia, who's the one who told me."

Celia was Celia Sánchez, the secretary, adviser, muse, housewife, and lover of Fidel Castro. She was, at that moment, the only contact Franqui had in government, since it had been a long time since he had last managed to see Fidel Castro.

"Did you read the report?" he asked.

"No," Franqui said, "apparently Fidel had it, but Celia went on at some length. Fidel apparently considers Arcocha's attitude to be quite honest, at the same time he's worried about the implications of anything Juan might do."

"Franqui, this is fire," he said.

"Blazing, blazing, blazing," said Pablo Armando.

"Well," he said, "what do you think is going on, Franqui?"

"I don't know. But now your case has been put to Fidel, and I don't think he knew about it before."

"You don't think so?" he asked.

"No, yours is something more on Piñeiro's level."

"Well," he said, "but Roa was certainly up to speed."

< 304 >

"What, you think Roa would put your case to the council of ministers?" asked Franqui in response.

"No, I never thought that," he said, "but I bet Roa must have said something to Dorticós. In any case, he's the one who looked bad when they took me off the plane after he named me minister in Belgium."

"That's something else," Franqui said. "Roa was angry about that business with you, but all he did was go around repeating, 'And I sent flowers and my son to his mother's funeral!'"

"He's impotent," he said.

"Careful, careful," said Pablo Armando, pointing around at the walls as if to say they had ears.

"Well," he asked, "what are we going to do now?"

"I think," Franqui said, "you are going to be able to leave and you are going to be able to stay in Europe. Of course, exile…"

"*Exile?*" he asked.

"Well," said Franqui, "it's a manner of speaking. To live in Europe on your own is no piece of cake, believe me."

"For me, living in Cuba would be a lot harder," he said.

"I know," Franqui said, "but you want to go without breaking with the Revolution. That's not an easy position to hold, though I encourage you to maintain it. Look at Ehrenburg, the way he stayed on in Paris until everything became clear in Russia. He's a good example for you to follow."

He was about to say he considered Ehrenburg, the Soviet writer, a repugnant role model, but he held his tongue.

"The important thing," Franqui said, "is that Fidel knows about the issue."

"Dorticós already knew about it," he said.

< 305 >

"But that's not the same," said Franqui.

"It's not the same, it's not the same." Pablo Armando had the habit of repeating himself.

"Now we've got to be very cautious," Franqui said. "Have you heard any more from Sabá?"

"No, which for me is confirmation he's going to take the plunge around the third."

"Shit!" said Franqui.

There was silence, then Franqui said:

"In any case, what Arcocha did is really good. He called attention to your problem yet managed to stay loyal to everyone."

"That's right, that's right," said Pablo Armando.

Events followed in a chain reaction. Alberto Mora came to see him the following day.

"I spoke with Carlos Rafael and things are going well. I also spoke with Dorticós, but by phone. He told me Carlos Rafael had already spoken to him and the issue would be decided very soon. Now, there is a little problem," he said, and he paused. He waited to hear about the little problem that would probably turn out to be huge. But Alberto remained silent.

"What is it?"

"Well," said Alberto, and he scratched his shadow of a beard, "what I'm going to tell you is confidential. I have it on good authority that the Galician" – referring to Commander Piñeiro – "is fucking around with your case. He's got it in his thick skull that you have to stay here."

"I figured."

"But hang on. It's a question of knowing if he's going to have more clout than Dorticós."

"I don't doubt he will."

< 306 >

"Well, start doubting it. On top of having the president on our side, we have Carlos Rafael. We could go all the way to Fidel if we need to. I hope it doesn't go that high, because that always brings trouble, but I believe, I'm convinced, we're going to win this one. But there is another problem…"

"What's the other one?"

"Well, you've got to be very careful until you go."

"Careful in what sense?"

"What you say, what you tell people, who you meet up with. All that. You know as well as I do."

"No, I don't know."

"You ought to know by now," Alberto said, and he smiled for the first time, although it was the lopsided smile he saved for when things were not going well.

"What do I have to do?"

"It's more what you shouldn't do. Like I told you: be careful who you go out with…"

"Or you'll kiss me goodbye," he said, smiling.

"No, no, it's no joke."

"I've never been more serious."

"You've got to be. Exaggerate it. Turn into a model intellectual."

"So leaving is a reward. I thought it was more like a golden bridge."

"You aren't an important enemy. You aren't even an unimportant enemy."

After that, the conversation turned to what behavior was acceptable in the Communist world, but he was no longer listening to Alberto. He was going over in his mind the areas where some hidden problem might lie. He recalled seeing Pipo Carbonell twice at El Carmelo while waiting for Silvia – and he remembered it once more that afternoon when he again saw Pipo

< 307 >

sitting at a table with an army lieutenant. Pipo might just be an agent of the G2, he thought, and he tried not to look toward his table. He did answer his greeting and responded to Pipo's mischievous smile with one of his own that he hoped conveyed that it was true he was waiting for a woman, but it was no frivolous adventure. He knew that Pipo knew that he knew, and all that was expressed in his smile. Then Silvia came and off they went to number 69.

Afterward, lying in bed, she said:

"You know what, love, I have to tell you something."

He thought it would be something trivial and he said go ahead. But she hesitated.

"I don't know how to tell you. I should have told you right from the beginning."

"Does it have to do with the Hungarian?"

That's what Sandor had become.

She looked at him astonished.

"No, I swear it's not that."

"So what is it?"

"It's something very important. I mean, you'll probably think it's important." And she fell silent.

"But, what is it?"

"Well, I told you a lie."

"A lie?"

"Yes, a big lie. About who I am."

Suddenly Alberto Mora's warning flooded his thoughts and a column of ice descended from the pit of his stomach to his scrotum.

"About who you are? Who are you?"

< 308 >

He recalled Rolando Escardó's innocent, virginal, practically ethereal girlfriend, who would come by the *Lunes* office after Escardó died, and he remembered the day she showed him a little wristwatch she had in her handbag that was a microphone and tape recorder, and what she told him: "Ramiro gave it to me," meaning that none other than the minister of the interior had given it to her. And in another flash of memory he saw her one afternoon walking up La Rampa accompanied by a girl she was always with and two foreigners, who were obviously South Americans, and he went near to catch what she was saying: "Now we work" – she was referring to herself and her girlfriend – "for the Institute of Friendship Among Peoples." So that afternoon, when Silvia wanted to tell him a secret, he thought she too was an agent, probably assigned to keep an eye on him, maybe to record his conversations – and in a rush he thought of all the people they had met and all the possible conversations and secrets revealed and moments recorded. All that must have been reflected in his face, because she said with real fear in her voice and her expression:

"What's wrong?"

"Nothing. I'm waiting. Who are you?"

"Well, I'm not your daughter. I couldn't be your daughter, because I'm not eighteen, I'm twenty-one. Now you know how it is. Jesus."

"And that's your secret?" he asked incredulously.

"Yes, that was my secret. It pisses me off, not being your daughter."

He then let loose a rumbling and joyful guffaw, laughing like he had not laughed since before his mother's death. Happy, relieved, his confidence in the human species restored, in particular his trust in women – and even more, even closer, his trust in this girl, or better put, this woman.

"What's up with you now?" she asked. "Why are you laughing like that?"

< 309 >

"I'm happy."

"Go ahead, be happy, but it pisses me off."

"I'm happy, what do you want?"

And he kissed her like he had never kissed her before, all over her body beginning with the well-drawn mouth that had revealed her secret and ending with the dark, small, practically childish pubis. He laughed all over again.

"So you're twenty-one," he said.

"Yes, I know. It was wrong to tell you I was something else. I should have told you the whole truth, I made a mistake. Will you forgive me?"

"Of course I forgive you that you could not be my daughter."

"Do you feel younger?"

"I don't only feel it. I am."

"And I'm older. Shit!"

He, who hated women who swore, found it charming when she did, and now more than ever. He was nearly tempted to ask her to swear more, to repeat the small obscenities she had uttered in the days they had been together, to say them all at once. But that would have been a waste of time and now it was a question of gaining time. Back on top of her, he kissed her again from tip to toe.

That she was not an agent he viewed as a triumph over Piñeiro, over the G2, over the regime's entire repressive apparatus: a triumph of the flesh over the Revolution – and he considered it to be a good omen. More than the calculations of Franqui, more than the maneuvers of Alberto Mora, the victory that afternoon persuaded him that he would indeed be leaving, that he would escape the enemy – and it filled him with a special sadness, for he would have to leave Silvia behind. At the same time it pleased him, since he had always believed a truncated love to be much greater than a fulfilled

< 310 >

love, its lack of realization conferring another dimension: the memory of the love alongside the love itself. Although he felt adult enough now not to consider the memory of things better than the things themselves, he knew that he would treasure the memory of Silvia beyond the time his love for her would last, something which writing about this very love and romance has demonstrated.

VIRGILIO PIÑERA'S BLIND and very elderly father finally passed away. The family and above all Virgilio had been anxious for him to die, so they could get some relief from a burden that had grown heavier by the day. Of course Virgilio did not say that and never would have admitted it, since Virgilio Piñera, a man devoid of hate, hated death more than anything. But at the wake the relief wrought by the old man's demise was obvious. It was a much smaller gathering than for his own mother, Zoila Infante, but everyone at the modest funeral home had also been present the day he returned to Cuba. In place of the heavy weight of sorrow, this gathering had much of the spirit he remembered from legendary Cuban wakes of the past. Even though the coffee and chocolate and cookies were all lacking, conversation was had in abundance.

He spent a moment in the chapel, then went downstairs with Virgilio to sit among friends and hold a literary soirée reminiscent of the good old days at *Lunes*. Pablo Armando, who certainly would have been crying at his mother's wake, was recounting stories about London that were funnier and more engaging than if he were telling jokes. Franqui looked happy (later on, he learned why). Antón Arrufat discussed literature with his usual skill. Calvert Casey lost his stutter and shared in the laughter and conversation. It was a good wake.

< 311 >

He went to see Carmela. He felt somewhat guilty about her and very guilty indeed about Miriam Gómez: there he was speaking with her mother in the morning and in the afternoon he would be in bed with Silvia. However, the feeling was minor compared to the guilt he had felt other times; now he knew his relationship with Silvia was fated to end, and even if Miriam Gómez found out – most likely he would tell her everything when he returned to Belgium, and indeed he did – it would not be so serious because the romance was confined to a moment that was over. No way could he explain that to Carmela, however, since Miriam's mother was too simple and forthright to understand. Chatting with her, he had the impression she knew, perhaps another manifestation of his feeling of guilt.

During the visit, Carmela kept insisting Miriam had to come back, she wanted to see her, she needed to have her youngest daughter nearby. He tried to erase the notion from Carmela's mind, explaining that Miriam could not return, even if he wanted her to, that to make her come back would kill her. Miriam Gómez could not tolerate a day, an hour, a single minute of Cuba as it was. Carmela did not seem to realize this and continued asking for her, pleading with him to make her return. The conversation lasted nearly the entire morning, and when he left he sensed that Miriam's mother was not well, that in some fashion she had lost touch with reality, that her absurd insistence was not absurd to her because she had gone a little crazy. This realization made him sad: mental illness always saddened him as it saddens anyone's life.

Alberto Mora was waiting for him with a piece of news.

"I spoke with Dorticós," he said.

"And?"

"It's all set. To avoid problems I went to see Ramirito. I spoke with him about your exit permit, and he told me they would give it to you right away.

< 312 >

Varona from Immigration is going to call you to get your basic information. How do you like that?"

"I like it just fine. As long as Piñeiro doesn't get in the way."

"He won't. You know, I asked Ramirito if he wanted your telephone number and he told me: 'No need. We have it. Do you think we're the Interior Ministry just for fun?' That was what he said."

Alberto smiled his lopsided smile. He too smiled, but Moyzisch, the German attaché, came back to mind.

He called Carlos Franqui right away to tell him about his conversation with Alberto Mora. Franqui advised him to go to the Foreign Ministry immediately to press them to issue passports for him and his daughters. He said he would and since he had forgotten to ask Alberto about the passports he called him at home. Alberto said Dorticós himself was going to have a word with Roa. So he decided to postpone his visit to the ministry to the following day. First, he had to do something urgent: speak with Silvia.

He waited until they were in bed that afternoon. With the only record playing one more time, he turned to her and said:

"I'm leaving."

"What?"

"I'm leaving. I'm going back to Europe."

For a moment she tried to make a joke of it:

"Fuck, I thought you were leaving here!"

"Not here. Cuba."

"Silvia," and she was addressing herself, "don't marry a short, dark man who smokes cigars."

"Seriously, I'm leaving."

She was silent. She did not even chew on her lower lip. Then she asked, "When are you going?"

< 313 >

"I still don't know. It could be next week. Or the week after. Or maybe sooner. I don't know."

"Well, don't talk to me about this anymore," she said, and she kissed him.

But soon, to reach her orgasm, she started pleading:

"Please, tell me I'm your daughter! Tell me I'm your daughter! Adopt me! Take me with you! Please!"

It was the first time he felt sorry for her. The second time was when they went to the movies. She wanted to see *Some Like It Hot*, since she never had. She especially wanted to get a look at Marilyn Monroe. So they left Rine's apartment early and walked up Avenue of the Presidents to the Riviera Cinema. But in the end they could not watch the movie: looking at Marilyn Monroe alive on the screen but dead in reality made her so sad that she started to cry, first silently, then in loud, disconsolate sobs. They left the movie house, wiping away tears from her reddened eyes, while behind them the audience chortled along with Jack Lemmon and Tony Curtis. She asked him to forgive her, she didn't know what had come over her. But he knew why she was crying.

They went to El Carmelo, partly because he wanted to eat something, partly because he wanted to see his friends and make his travel plans known. He should have waited, but some impulse he could not pin down urged him to pass on the news. (A few days later, he realized that a part of him did not want to leave.)

Virgilio Piñera was there on his first outing after his father's death. He introduced Silvia, and a smiling Virgilio said in English:

"Who is Silvia? What is she?"

And Silvia answered in English:

< 314 >

"*Silvia is she and she is in love.*"

Virgilio's smile grew wider as he puffed on his cigarette and made as if he were applauding.

"Wonderful, my dear," he said.

She was accepted.

Afterward, the usual suspects gathered: Sarusky, Walterio Carbonell, Arrufat, and Oscar Hurtado. When he said he was going back to Europe, that he might settle in Spain until his book came out, and maybe stay on there for a year or two, Hurtado said, "That sounds great, make sure you go live in Salamanca." He was moved by Hurtado's ingenuousness, not only because he had named Salamanca as his destination, thinking like a contemporary of Unamuno, but also because he felt that he had fooled them all – he knew he would never return to Cuba – all, that is, except for Silvia. She knew, and maybe that was why he felt happier than ever. He decided he would keep her by his side as long as he could.

The following day he took her to Franqui's house, only to learn Franqui was at the home of the painter Mariano Rodríguez a few blocks away. They walked over and from the moment they stepped inside he could see that the painter's wife, Celeste, was annoyed with him for bringing Silvia. It was curious that the wife of a bohemian and revolutionary reacted just like a bourgeois woman. Silvia could tell because Celeste immediately started talking about painting and at one point she mentioned Picasso and turned to Silvia saying, "You know, Picasso," practically spelling out his name. That night Silvia recalled the incident and said, "I nearly felt like telling her, Don't fuck with me!"

He had gone to the ministry that morning. Arnold knew about the order from above to issue passports and tickets to Belgium for him and his two

< 315 >

daughters, the same as last June. Arnold pointed out, however, "You know they aren't going to be diplomatic passports." He nearly answered that nothing would make him happier. The following day he went back to the ministry with the photographs of himself and his daughters, plus the two small photographs of Miriam Gómez when she was seventeen, which he held in his hand like a talisman.

He learned something new about Silvia, actually two things. The second, especially, left him thinking about how life ironically imitates art, if you can call a story art. In any case, about how life copies literature.

They were at El Carmelo, standing at the D Street door and about to leave for Rine's apartment, when a boy or rather a very young man walked by and Silvia stopped him with an affectionate hello. Then she turned to him, "This is my cousin." He said hello and the young man walked on. The boy was obviously mulatto, practically black, and he said to himself: "So, she has black blood." It wasn't apparent. Yes, she was very tan, nearly brown, and her lips were dark and her eyes black, but her sister was very white and it was not until she introduced her cousin that he realized she must be a mulatta – although nothing like Cecilia Valdés. He wasn't troubled in the least, but it was like knowing she was twenty-one and not eighteen: a revelation.

The second revelation occurred two days later, or maybe three, when she exploded in loud guffaws and he noticed her teeth for the first time. She had, like him, a long upper lip and tended to smile rather than laugh, or if she laughed, she'd cover her teeth with her lip. But this time he saw them and saw that she was missing molars, maybe two, and that her upper teeth were stained a sickly yellow, not from nicotine, but as if they had lost their enamel. He committed the indescribably thoughtless folly of mentioning it and telling her she should go to the dentist, that it could be fixed. She did

< 316 >

not seem pleased, not only that he was sending her to the dentist, but that he had noticed her teeth did not correspond to her shapely lips, that her mouth was not perfect.

But those revelations had no affect on their relationship.

Alberto came to look for him to go visit Enrique Oltuski, who had just been released from the Isle of Pines – the revolutionaries called it punishment, but it was a punishment that seemed too much like a sentence without a trial. He had spent four or six months doing forced labor, at first alongside the other prisoners. They went in Alberto's VW (not his, but the Sugar Ministry's) to a house in Nuevo Vedado. It looked as if Oltuski had just moved in, but in reality he had been living there before being detained. The near total lack of furniture was striking. Wooden boxes were scattered here and there. They must have contained his belongings or kitchen utensils but they looked empty. What's more, the house had no glass in many of the windows. They weren't broken, rather it looked as if the glass had never been installed.

Oltuski was in a room that he explained – at least he believed that is what he heard him say – would be his study. It too lacked panes in the windows and if memory serves him the windows were boarded up. But that was not the important thing. The important thing was that Oltuski greeted them with his usual smile, not seeming to show the least resentment for having been imprisoned without being guilty of anything beyond telling Fidel Castro that the farming project Oltuski ran was going to be a disaster. (In truth, Oltuski – like Alberto Mora, like the sugar minister himself, Borrego, who each were relegated to low-level posts – was in trouble for having belonged to Che Guevara's circle.) Oltuski displayed the same optimism, generosity, and humility he had when he was named minister of communications in 1959 at the age of twenty-four. He adapted so well to the shifting revolutionary

< 317 >

winds, it was as if he had gone native, become Cubanized, despite having been born in Poland or Russia, and being Jewish.

They continued chatting in his room without any reference to his recent punishment. Alberto did most of the talking, while he remained silent and Oltuski kept smiling. Alberto revealed that he too was going to Europe, after saying that this one here would be going first, in just a few days. Alberto said he would follow very shortly, since he was going to Paris to study economics, sent by direct order of President Dorticós. It was the first he had heard about this and he nearly voiced his surprise, but Oltuski's reaction so intrigued him that he made no comment.

"So you're leaving? I mean, the two of you?"

"Well," he said, speaking for the first time, "I have to return to Europe. My wife is there, Miriam Gómez."

Oltuski failed to see the logic and seemed about to say that Miriam Gómez could return to Cuba more easily than he could go to Europe. But it was Alberto who responded, more or less correcting him:

"He's also going because his book is coming out in Spain."

"Ah, yes," Oltuski said, more out of courtesy than interest.

"Yes," he said, "it's coming out in Barcelona in a few days."

"I'm very happy for you," Oltuski said.

"Well," said Alberto, "the important thing is that he be there when it comes out."

"Yes, of course," Oltuski said, and he said no more.

"So, what do you think of my trip?" asked Alberto, who seemed either not very determined to go or just playing with a new idea.

"I think it's fine, although in my opinion you're more needed here."

< 318 >

"Needed? What am I doing now? Nothing! Better to go away for a while."

There followed a silence that was nearly embarrassing, which Alberto soon broke.

"Why don't you go too?" he asked Oltuski.

"Me? No, no way," Oltuski said, smiling. "I'm rooted here."

He was surprised how quickly Oltuski had picked up not only rural expressions, but even a peasant's intonation. Then he recalled that Oltuski grew up in Las Villas. The punishment must have brought out the country in him.

"So, what are you going to do now?" Alberto asked.

"I don't know," Oltuski said. "Maybe I'll go work with Faustino." (Faustino was Faustino Pérez, the minister of hydraulic resources, and like Oltuski a member of the original July 26th Movement; both had been accused, along with the new minister of foreign trade, Marcelo Fernández, and the minister of education, Armando Hart, of being members of the movement's right wing. But while Faustino Pérez and Marcelo Fernández were back in government, their former sins forgiven, the other members of the July 26th Movement or the Revolutionary Directorate who belonged to Che Guevara's group, like Alberto Mora and Enrique Oltuski, were still in disgrace.) "They need people at hydraulic resources," Oltuski continued, and then he remembered Oltuski was an engineer. "But I'm still not sure," he finished, smiling his good-hearted smile, his curious eyes gazing at them through the thick lenses of his glasses.

"Well, I'm going off to school," said Alberto.

"He who goes far from Cuba, goes far from the Revolution," Oltuski said, unaware that he had just coined an aphorism.

< 319 >

"That's not true," Alberto responded right away. "Look, this fellow here is leaving soon and that doesn't make him a counterrevolutionary, and Adrián García Hernández has been living in Madrid for two years and he isn't a counterrevolutionary."

"I didn't say he who leaves is a counterrevolutionary," Oltuski replied, and he understood the clarification was for his benefit. "What I said is, he who leaves here goes far from the Revolution, and that's true."

"Not necessarily, not necessarily," Alberto said, smiling. He realized repeating a phrase was not the exclusive habit of Pablo Armando Fernández, rather something very Cuban.

"Unless you're going as a diplomat," Oltuski said. "Even so," he added, then failed to finish his sentence.

"Diplomats live extraterritorially," he said, just to join in the conversation and not seem to be accepting the accusation with his silence. "I mean, even living overseas they are on Cuban territory."

"Another point in my favor," Oltuski said, and that phrase revealed the essentially childish nature of the disagreement between Oltuski and Alberto. What's more, he thought, we Cubans are all pretty childish. A cultural flaw?

"At least, that's what I think," Oltuski added finally, almost excusing himself, as if believing in his aphorism did not mean he was insulting those present.

"Well, I disagree," said Alberto, always pugnacious. "I don't believe it at all."

"Neither do I," he said, and he felt that Oltuski's nearsighted eyes could see right through him, see that he was lying, since even without leaving Cuba he felt like a counterrevolutionary.

< 320 >

"Well, maybe in your cases," Oltuski said, striking a conciliatory tone, "but I couldn't leave even for five minutes. I wouldn't leave for all the gold in the world. Right now, I've been away from Havana for a while" – this was his first reference to his time in prison – "and I feel like I've lost touch a bit with what's going on. But going away brought me closer to other revolutionary issues, the countryside and farming. No, all in all, I couldn't go away from here because I would lose my grounding."

Alberto nodded and smiled. It seemed that Alberto, who had fought so long and hard for change, was now not so sure of himself. Evidently, he did not respond sharply to Oltuski's words because it was Oltuski who spoke them.

"Well, gentlemen," said Oltuski, changing the topic, "I'm not offering you coffee because there isn't any. But if you'd like a glass of water." And he smiled. Obviously water was the only thing in abundance at Oltuski's house.

You're lucky, he was going to interject. Plenty of homes in Havana are also short on water. But he said nothing.

He went to see Gustavo Arcos to tell him it seemed he was finally about to leave. He did not want to spread the word around certain places, while in others he thought it wise to do so. He had to tell Gustavo before he heard some other way.

"Great! I'm pleased! So, Caoba, you're leaving."

Gustavo called him Caoba when he was in a really good mood. He picked the name up from an American novel from the last century about Cuba's wars of independence, *Caoba, the Guerrilla Chief*. A first edition had ended up in Gustavo's hands in Belgium, sent by a friend of the embassy. Eventually, Gustavo donated it to the National Library, but he retained the title as a friendly nickname for him.

< 321 >

"I am," he said, understanding Gustavo's words as a question.

"As a matter of fact, I was about to call you. On Sunday we're invited to a pig roast in Santa María del Mar. Universo Sánchez" – a well-known commander of the July 26th Movement – "is doing the roasting and there'll be other friends." Gustavo always said friends and not *compañeros*. "Would you like to come along?"

Instead of thinking about it, he said:

"No, I'm sorry, I can't. On Sunday I've got to visit some relatives." He invented this lie on the spot because he had no wish to go to the feast: he thought such gatherings put Gustavo at risk, although he did not dare tell him that and chance a misunderstanding. And in effect so it turned out: as noted before, among the accusations against Gustavo Arcos months later was that of *dolcevitismo*, which meant that the accused had indulged in a dolce vita despite the Revolution's difficulties.

"Too bad," said Gustavo. "You would have had a great time."

"As good as at the farm with Rebellón?"

Gustavo laughed, understanding what he was getting at.

"No, of course. That was awful."

"And this time you'll be all-full."

Gustavo laughed heartily, as always enjoying his jokes without taking offense.

"No, seriously, I can't go."

"Well," said Gustavo, "you're the one who's going to lose out."

"Do you want to send anything to Belgium?"

"Well, I suppose we'll see each other again before you go."

"Sure, of course we will."

< 322 >

HE DID NOT DETECT ANY CHANGE in Silvia's attitude, except for the sobbing in the movies – and that might have been about her love for Marilyn Monroe or maybe her hatred of death. She continued showing up for their encounters. One or twice she was late, and he paced nervously back and forth between El Carmelo and the bus stop. As she explained, the reason was always the bus, which took so long to come.

But now she looked worried.

"I have to tell you something," she said when she arrived.

"What, another disclosure?"

"The one who's been making disclosures lately is you, not me."

"True, you're right. What's up?"

They were still walking through the park on the way to Rine's building.

"Nothing."

"No, tell me, what's up?"

"It's not important."

"Yes it is. I can see it in your face."

She walked on without saying anything.

"Well," she said at last, "my period hasn't come. I'm three days late."

He felt the gravity of her confession. If she was pregnant, that would be a serious complication. Not overly so, like at the beginning of the Revolution when they persecuted doctors who did abortions, but nevertheless serious because getting an abortion was still difficult. He knew that if everything went well, he would not have time to see her through it as he should. Besides, it was his nature to run away from such things.

"Are you sure?"

"Of course I'm sure," she said, and added, "but don't worry."

"How am I not supposed to worry?"

< 323 >

"No, don't worry, I'll fix everything myself."

"Have you been pregnant before?"

"No, never, and I don't even know if I am now. I'm just late."

"Great, what a coincidence."

"Why a coincidence?"

"No, no reason."

"It's not a coincidence, it's a consequence," she said.

"Well put." And he kissed her.

Two days later it turned out to be a false alarm and he wanted to celebrate in his own way: by bathing himself, literally, in her blood. With her blood dripping from his mouth, smeared across his lips, he smiled at her and she exclaimed:

"That's horrible!"

To which he responded:

"I am Count Dracula and you are my Transilvia."

She laughed but he didn't think she got the reference to Transylvania. He was going to explain when he remembered that Transylvania was as Hungarian as Sandor.

She told him something else revealing after having showered at the end of the afternoon, while he was getting dressed and she was making up her eyes. (When they made love, he had observed her eyes changing as the black liner got smudged and her eyes lost their houri quality, as she went from being a nymph to being a child. Maybe that was why the only makeup she wore was on her eyes. Another time, when she was putting on her eyeliner, he asked where she managed to get cosmetics now, and she flashed a smile. It was because of the smile that he did not believe her explanation: "They give it to my sister. People at the ministry who travel." He thought it more

< 324 >

likely she got it through some embassy where she had friends, so he did not press her.) Now, as she carefully attended to her eyelids, he went behind her to the shower – to wash his hands maybe, or to wet his hair, he does not remember – sliding between her and the bidet and toilet on the other side. Since she was facing the mirror, leaning with her head poking forward and her body back, perhaps to keep her clothes from touching the sink, he had to squeeze up against her to get by, holding her by the waist and rubbing his fly along her behind. She turned to him and said: "You know, my father rubbed up against me the other day just like that. What do you make of it?"

He could not refrain from kidding her:

"That incestuous old man," he said.

"No, he's not an old man," she said.

"It's a manner of speaking, a manner of speaking," he said, remembering Pablo Armando and Alberto Mora. But he did not say more, since he was pondering her words and wondering who the incestuous one was – the father or the daughter.

Days later, a rumor made the rounds of the city: Walterio Carbonell was in trouble. "To be in trouble" meant to have political problems and that meant problems with the police; not with the law or the justice system, neither of which existed anymore, but with the police, and there was only one kind of police. Walterio Carbonell was in trouble with the political police.

It turned out that the People's Friendship Institute (or perhaps a similar organism) had invited a group of French businessmen – businessmen, not intellectuals – to visit Cuba. On the program were trips to collective farms, education centers, scientific organizations, and maybe one or another excursion to potential industrial parks, which were few but could be found. Also – and it caused no surprise or barely any – a visit to Casa de las Américas.

< 325 >

Nobody knew what French businessmen were doing at Casa de las Américas and certainly not how Walterio Carbonell found out about the event. What people knew was that Walterio was in the audience and he asked to speak – apparently the event was set up theater-style and became an assembly of sorts, or maybe that was the intention. Walterio proceeded to explain to the French businessmen that not everything in Cuba smelled of roses, as the preceding speakers evidently had painted it. There were problems, he said, and one of them, perhaps the most serious, was freedom of expression. At that moment, when Walterio pronounced the phrase "freedom of expression," the Cuban interpreter refused to continue translating. But Walterio – who had not spent his anti-Batista exile in Paris for nothing and was neither laconic nor lazy – went right on in French, saying the same things he had said in Spanish, or better put, picking up where he left off. He started with suppression of Sabá Cabrera's short film *PM* four years earlier, and went on to the closure of *Lunes de Revolución*, the stifling of El Puente group, and other reefs the Revolution chose to roll over rather than navigate around as could easily have been done. As Walterio gathered momentum and became more eloquent, Harold Gramatges, who was presiding over the event (not as one might think because he was a musician, but because he was the former ambassador to France) called for order, and Roberto Retamar shouted threats (apparently both in Spanish) that must have made it clear to Walterio that consequences were inevitable. The proceedings came to a close somehow and Harold and Roberto took their song-and-dance straight to the directorate of Casa de las Américas, to Ada Santamaría, sister of Haydée. (All of Haydée Santamaría's siblings have names starting with A – Aldo, Abel, etc.; she herself escaped only because her parents thought that Haydée was written Aidé, of course.) No one knew for sure what Ada Santamaría said, but everyone knew she

< 326 >

threatened to take the G2 to Walterio's house or Walterio to the G2; either could happen. Walterio Carbonell was in trouble.

It was several days before he saw Walterio one night at El Carmelo. They walked a few blocks down Línea Street, then turned onto Avenue of the Presidents, accompanied by Antón Arrufat, Oscar Hurtado, and Jaime Soriano. (He is not certain Hurtado and Soriano were there, but Antón Arrufat was for sure.) He remembers they sat down to talk – not across from his apartment, but farther up the avenue on the pedestrian walkway that begins at 25th Street across from the Palace building and the student dormitory. He thinks there was no express intent in sitting some distance from his building, they could have done it much farther away, but he remembers how the distance facilitated the conversation he had with Walterio Carbonell.

During the stroll Walterio had told him what he already knew: his strange adventure at Casa de las Américas and the possible consequences, at that point still unknown. (Walterio Carbonell would not go to jail on this occasion, but he would three years later when he was accused of trying to organize a version of Black Power in Cuba.) He said that although he agreed with Walterio, he did not agree with his methods; in Cuba you had to remain quiet and calm, noiseless if possible, keeping the lowest of low profiles, and if you could not bear it, then you had to leave. Walterio said he was more or less in agreement, but he had nowhere to go.

"Why not Paris?" he asked.

To which Walterio responded: "What am I going to do in Paris?" Meaning how would he support himself, how would he live, how long would he stay?

He answered that he did not know, but if he had lived in Paris before, why couldn't he do it again? The circumstances were different, Walterio answered.

< 327 >

He urged extreme caution, because he sensed terrible days were coming for everyone, and he suggested what Francesco Guicciardini had recommended four hundred years ago. He can't swear that he mentioned Guicciardini then. Perhaps he learned of him later on. But he remembers having said something like it. In any case he spoke of not confronting the repressive apparatus of the Revolution, of remaining quiet instead, and fleeing at the first opportunity. He remembers that Antón Arrufat seemed to differ, but Soriano's silence showed his utter agreement.

They spoke in guarded voices, so the echo bouncing off the tall buildings on that part of the avenue would not amplify their words, but not so low as to make themselves suspect. He recalls the sad tone of the conversation, Arrufat's despondency, and the stoicism that at that moment made a hero of Walterio Carbonell.

(Here is the place to relate the odyssey that began some days later, after he had already left Cuba or was in the traveling headspace that starts before departure and extends beyond the trip itself. Walterio Carbonell was summoned to the Writers Union to be tried, apparently by his peers, but in reality by a tribunal which had agreed on the sentence before rendering the verdict. What saved him, for the moment, was the ironic fact that José Lezama Lima, the Union's vice president, was on the tribunal, though he was in the minority compared to people, like Lisandro Otero, who had gone from being Walterio's friends to being his relentless accusers. Moments before the sentence was read, Lezama announced they had not come there to cut off Walterio Carbonell's head, rather to hear what he had to say regarding what he had done. "You cannot simply ignore," Lezama said, "the fact that Carbonell spent years in Paris, where he became accustomed to a more

< 328 >

lively literary debate in plazas and cafés, on street corners and avenues. This is certainly what Walterio Carbonell wanted to continue at Casa de las Américas." This honorable intervention by Lezama, who had never been a friend of Walterio's, spared him immediate expulsion – and maybe prison. The tribunal decreed that Walterio Carbonell had to write a retraction, which would be published in the *Gaceta de Cuba*. Walterio wrote something as they asked him, but in place of a retraction he produced a document affirming all that he had said at the *petite* assembly at Casa de las Américas. The Writers Union then decreed his expulsion, a notice of which was published in the *Gaceta de Cuba* – such are the ironies of communism – when that magazine was being run by Jaime Sarusky!)

He remembers that the last time he saw Walterio it was a poignant scene. He was with Oscar Hurtado and Antón Arrufat at the El Carmelo on 23rd late one night, when Walterio arrived. Hurtado, Arrufat, and he were inside the restaurant. (At the El Carmelo on Calzada they preferred the sidewalk patio, but at the one on 23rd Street they always sat inside.) He had an ice cream, a frozen custard that tasted more like an emetic than the delicious ice creams of the past, while Arrufat had tea with lemon. He does not remember what Hurtado had, but he does recall that the usual glasses of cold water and the familiar sugar bowl were on the table, and that Arrufat had not used more than half his lemon. While they talked, Walterio took a glass of water, added sugar, and asking Arrufat if he wanted his slice of lemon and being told no, squeezed it into the glass, making his own lemonade on the spot. In that act of Walterio's there was an intimation of the nasty fact that the Revolution had made life nearly impossible for him, like for the former members of the El Puente group; Walterio had not even the money for a lemonade. It also

< 329 >

showed he retained sufficient pride from his days as a diplomat (when his life under the Revolution seemed to reach its climax) not to ask any of his three friends to buy him a soda or an ice cream. That was one of the last times, if not the last time, he saw Walterio Carbonell.

He met Pablo Armando at Casa de las Américas late one morning, to have lunch with Marcia Leiseca, who had invited them. They ran into no one and that was a relief: he did not want to see Retamar after the incident with Walterio. The three of them headed to Old Havana, not to the part he had visited before (and had sworn never to visit again, that Old Havana he wandered through as one wonders through a ghost town filled with ruins and the dust of memory), rather to the area abutting the train station. They were going to eat at the Spanish tavern behind the terminal. Entering the place was a disappointment in itself: instead of chorizos, hams, *butifarras*, blood sausages, and mortadellas hanging from the ceiling in front of shelves lined with bottles of wine, the tavern was entirely bare, and of the former splendor not even a hint remained. They ate what was on hand: lentil stew the color of chocolate and bread. There were no desserts, no beer, and the water they drank was room temperature because the tavern's refrigerator was broken.

They were sick at heart when they left and Marcia was the one who took it the hardest. To dispel their sadness, he suggested they walk the streets of that hot and dusty part of the city over to the Prado across from the Capitolio, a view that always cheered him up. Marcia was walking between the other two, her arms linked in theirs, and she cast her sadness off into the streets they left behind. They walked alongside the Saratoga Hotel and suddenly emerged in front of the Martí Theater, one of the few places in Old Havana that was not falling apart. In fact, it had recently been renovated, the cinema turned back into a theater, and the façade and interior restored to what they had been

< 330 >

in the previous century. The two men insisted on going in. The building was open and they stood for a while inside, admiring the restoration up close, with its imitation gaslights, its open seating reminiscent of a Mississippi steamboat. It was the proudest (and only) achievement of the new director of culture, Carlo Lechuga, who people said was so enamored of the restoration that he had moved his office into the theater. As they stepped outside, Marcia exclaimed, "I feel so good being with you! You always make me feel like a tourist." And her declaration filled him with love for this girl who wanted so badly to be a revolutionary and for whom Cuba's reality was so horrific that she was happiest when she felt like a visitor. He does not recall if he really gripped her warm, white arm more tightly in his own, but he does remember that he did so metaphorically. Using Silvia's vocabulary, he thought Marcia Leiseca was also lovable.

Alberto Mora organized a luncheon at the restaurant in Barlovento; about fourteen people went. He took his two daughters and Silvia, and during the meal he had to keep an eye on them as if all three were his daughters, since Silvia, just like the girls, refused to eat. He was not angry, but he was annoyed that he had to plead with her to eat. One thing that may have contributed to his mood was the fact that she was not eighteen, but twenty-one, and was behaving as if she were twelve, and he felt old and tired. Truth be told, the food was excellent – the usual rice with seafood, the Cuban paella – and he enjoyed it, except for the time he spent keeping an eye on Anita's table manners and begging Carolita to eat, while nearly ordering Silvia to at least taste the food. He did not know why she refused; she said she had no appetite, that she never ate much, that she had already eaten a lot. It also bothered him that Alberto and Marian were so amused by his fretting that at one point Alberto exclaimed, "The plebs, the plebs!" and smiled his lopsided

< 331 >

smile. After lunch they walked on the broad pier beside the restaurant and once more he saw Havana in the distance, shimmering like a mirage.

Silvia stayed all day, and after bringing the girls home (where Alberto in his battered car dropped them off), they took a bus to Rine's apartment. He realized her lack of appetite at the table was balanced by her voracity in bed and he thought of saying so, but in the end said nothing.

Anita's birthday came and her mother, Marta Calvo, organized a little party at her apartment in Retiro Médico. He went with Silvia and Carolita and Anita. Beforehand, they listened to records at home, or better put, they listened to the same record many times, the only one that had not been sold: Billie Holiday's *Lady in Satin*. The recording had surprised and pleased him from the day he bought it in 1958, and he liked the fact that Silvia – who had a very good ear for music and an excellent voice – could appreciate the suffering art of Billie Holiday. Then they walked down 23rd Street as far as La Rampa, which they followed all the way to Retiro Médico. When they drew near the building – he had not come by way of La Rampa in a long time – he had the sensation of approaching his old home, and since the September day was cool and cloudless, with a high blue sky unlike the white sky of summer, he felt good, because to return is always good.

The party was a simple gathering of children without a cake – birthday cakes were no longer made in Cuba – and clear Coca-Cola. They went down to the playground on a sixth floor terrace, where all the children cavorted about until one of them invented a new game: throwing fistfuls of gravel from the flowerless garden down to the street. The party ended more or less then and there, but the girls stayed on with their mother, while he and Silvia went to Rine's apartment. Before leaving, Marta's husband, Ramón, who as the current husband of his former wife had a relationship with him that

< 332 >

was if not ambiguous at least unusual, took him aside and told him he had wanted to speak with him for some time, but only now had he found the opportunity: he wanted him to know that he could rely on him, that if he had to leave the girls in Cuba, he could leave them with their mother and he would raise them as if they were his own. He replied that there was no need, that the girls were going with him, both of them, but in any case he thanked him very much. During the entire party, he could see that Marta felt jealous – what would you call it, future jealousy? it wasn't current or retrospective – of Silvia, which he found perversely entertaining: in some manner Marta Calvo was taking on the role of Miriam Gómez.

Someone who cannot be named called to invite him to a party at her house, saying he could bring anyone he liked and asking him to please invite Pablo Armando. The two of them decided to go, and he asked Silvia and her sister Elsa to accompany them. Pablo came over that day and they went together to El Carmelo on 23rd to wait for Silvia and Elsa. There they began drinking; when the sisters arrived he was having a rum and Pablo a Scotch made in Cuba (which he said tasted like disinfectant, while the rum had the distinctive tang of bright light, which is what Cubans call kerosene). The girls should be named in that order, because that is how they arrived, or at least how he saw them. Elsa was very elegant in a dress that was pink (the color in his memory) like nearly all of her attire, but Silvia, who usually did not dress particularly well (no one dressed particularly well in Cuba anymore) was even more elegant. She wore a dress he had never seen before: gray with large black flowers, that draped her thin body stupendously, and she had combed and cut her hair and put on makeup (much more than her usual eyeliner). She looked truly beautiful. He was pleased to see her, pleased that she came, pleased that he was with her.

< 333 >

They arrived at the party neither late nor early, which also made him happy. He introduced Silvia and Elsa to the host, who then introduced her mother when she joined them at the door. The living room of the house (it was in the old part of Vedado) was roomy with a high ceiling, painted white, and furniture half hidden by the guests but which he believed was something colonial. He knew most of the people (among whom were the architect Porro and his wife and this time he was not complaining like at the Belgian Embassy; later on he would find out why) and anyone he did not know he was introduced to, among them a French woman named Yvonne Berthier who worked for the Cultural Council. This time he did manage to hear her name during the introductions.

He and Pablo Armando continued drinking, since there was plenty to be had, which did not surprise him given that the woman who cannot be named was militantly orthodox. Even Silvia had a drink, though she was begging him to slow down. He could not say what was driving him, but it was not nervousness about a social occasion like in Brussels. He had got drunk other times in Havana, like at Harold Gramatges's party, but he had not felt the need at the Belgian reception. At this party maybe it was because he felt good, not happy but at least good enough to warrant a celebration.

At the midpoint, by which time he was fairly soused, someone called to him from the sofa where Yvonne Berthier was sitting, and when he went over, that person, whom he realized he did not know, got up so he could sit next to the Frenchwoman. She turned toward him and, smiling, asked in Spanish, "I want you to tell me about *Lunes*." Drunk though he was, he still perceived she was speaking to him in the informal *tú*, which she had not done when they were introduced. So he answered, "It's a day of the week."

< 334 >

She laughed a false laugh – or maybe it was her real laugh and her teeth were false. "I mean *Lunes de Revolución*," she said. Of course he knew what she meant, just as he knew he should not tell her a thing; it was obvious she was taking advantage of his inebriation to get, not information (the case of *Lunes* had long been more or less public) but his opinions. "I'm sorry," he said, "but I do not wish to speak about that." And he stood up without another word. He did not look back and thus did not see the Frenchwoman's reaction.

Later on, late that night, he found himself next to Silvia in the middle of the room and felt an irrepressible urge to kiss her. "Come," he said, and he took her to another room which was in darkness and was separated from the living room by a wrought-iron door. They sat on a sort of sofa (it was harder than a sofa) and began to kiss. He remembers that her kisses had the liberated passion they always had at Rine's apartment, but he cannot recall how long they were there. He does remember that suddenly the lights came on and he saw, standing next to the wrought-iron door, the mother of the hostess, who glared at them but said nothing. He does not recall having got up immediately, but since the lights were on and stayed on, they finally returned to the living room. At one end of the room the mother was speaking rudely to her daughter, it was almost a fight, and every so often the two of them glanced over at them. He has no memory of anything else, not even how they left the party. But at three in the morning he was at Las Playitas, on the beach at Marianao, at an open-air pizzeria eating pizza that was more like a cracker with ham and cheese. Then Pablo Armando told him Rivero Arocha was sitting at a nearby table, "El Pollo" Rivero, whom he had not seen since returning, whom he did not wish to see, whom he did not even turn his

< 335 >

head to glance at. Rivero, who was a pathologist, had been the commercial attaché in Belgium and they had had a fight due to problems in the embassy that had nothing to do with either of them. It was an irony of fate or history that he was the one Alberto Mora got to do the autopsy on his mother, so he had a hand in his mother's destruction, a woman he knew when she was alive and well in Brussels. He could not finish his pizza and of course could not make Silvia eat her own.

NOW TIME WAS GROWING SHORT, squeezed by goodbye parties and obligatory bureaucratic procedures, and with every goodbye came a new complication, making it seem he never would leave. Convoluted paperwork filled his days, consecutive goodbyes his nights.

The passports were ready, Arnold told him, but then he realized he needed visas. He would send the passports himself to the Spanish Embassy, since they ignored all requests from the ministry, but that would take a day, maybe two, and now all that separated him from his departure – the window his brother, Sabá, in Spain had given him – seemed to be only hours and minutes.

Good news: from afar he saw Franqui go by at the corner of Avenue of the Presidents and 23rd, traveling in a large automobile that must have been a Chevrolet less than three years old, an official car no doubt. A phone call confirmed it: Franqui was again in the good graces of the powerful. He now had a car and a driver and a strange appointment in charge of the Revolution's historical documents. Evidently Juan Arcocha's ultimatum got Franqui an interview with Fidel Castro – though that was all. While he never thought it would achieve anything other than Arcocha's definitive return (which would

< 336 >

occur six months later), now suddenly Franqui was in a position, if not to advance at least to ensure his departure took place on time. He does not know, he never knew, what Franqui did on his behalf during those final days, except tell him to go to the ministry and "go above Arnold's head," something he would have done in any case. There was, however, one concrete result: the plane tickets were in his hands; and he knew, at least, that he had three seats on the plane leaving on Sunday the third.

Out of the blue he received a call from Immigration, which was part of the Interior Ministry. Varona was on the other end of the line. He knew this man Varona was a nephew or cousin of his father's and an unequivocal revolutionary, which is to say a fanatic. The call began in a strangely vague tone: Varona did not call him the usual *compañero*, but neither did he call him *ciudadano* (citizen), which is what *compañeros* become when they leave paradise. He simply asked him to give his name, then asked if he had requested an official permit. He laughs remembering this, since what permit in Cuba would not be official? But he did not laugh, rather he answered:

"Yes."

"For how long?"

He hesitated a moment. "Well, for a year or two."

Down the line came what in Cuba is known as the precision question:

"Well," Varona said, "one year or two? How many?"

"Well," he replied, "two years."

"Good, very good," the voice said, "it will be ready for you when you depart."

At no moment did either of them acknowledge that they were related. Among the many things the Revolution destroyed were family ties.

< 337 >

He decided to sell his record player, the only relic left from the good days of 1961, when Miriam Gómez came to live with him. He could get five hundred pesos for it now, despite its age and the fact that no needles could be had. He let his father sell it to a friend of his, who gave him two hundred pesos up front and would pay the remainder over the coming months. With that money he settled his debt to Rine, who, strangely, did not want to be paid back "now." He was on the point of telling him if not now he never would, but he did not say that. Not even to his most intimate friends did he reveal his intention never to return to Cuba. Maybe deep inside, he still did not admit it to himself. In the end, Rine took the hundred pesos.

There was an incident with Rine that put an end to his idyll at the apartment. He does not remember if it was the last time he and Silvia were making love there, but he recollects it like the very end, even if the real end occurred later on. That day maybe they had stayed too long at the apartment or had arrived late (often they arrived late now and it was his fault) or maybe it was, as usual, too many orgasms. He remembers the light was dusky and he was on top of Silvia, lost, not hearing, not seeing, just feeling and smelling, when Silvia jumped and cried out, "Rine's here!" He was startled to hear her say something so precise. Such was his surprise that at first he did not understand and thought it was one of the tiny obscenities she liked to mutter during their trysts. But she repeated it, and this time he heard it loud and clear. He sharpened his ear and indeed someone was in the kitchen, then puttering around the apartment, which was extremely small, and it sounded like he was right there beside them. Of course it was Rine and he had to admit, with something close to anger, that they were not making love by themselves. Right then, privacy meant a lot to him. It would not have mattered so much with another

< 338 >

woman, for example with Lido the night they went with Alberto Mora to Ingrid González's apartment. But now it did and he remembers his climax was a fiasco, or better put, practically an anticlimax, but still a moment too important to share with somebody else, even your closest friend. Afterward, while Silvia changed in the bathroom (they saw no one about after they had finished), he went out wearing only his pants and found Rine at the back of the rooftop terrace, one foot on the wall and looking down at the street. He said nothing, they said nothing: they just shook hands and Rine kept looking down, wearing the shadow of a smile, like someone who had pulled a fast one. Rine said nothing about his mischief, and they did not exchange smiles, because he believed Rine had no right to interrupt them in their intimacy: for the time the apartment was loaned, it belonged to them. Now he had no choice but to return the key, which he did. Thus, sexually, there was no goodbye between him and Silvia. Curiously, however, there was a romantic goodbye. But that happened a few nights later.

One of the goodbye parties took place at the painter Raúl Martínez's house, where he had never been before. Raúl lived in Old Vedado, way up 25th Street on 7/th, in a house that was not new but had several rooms and an enormous kitchen adorned with arty ceramic pots. The living room was large and featured many of Raúl's paintings, although there was no trace of Pepe Estorino, Raúl's partner, who was as nondescript at home as he was anywhere else. The gathering was of Raúl's friends who were also his: Virgilio Piñera, Antón Arrufat, Calvert Casey, Jaime Soriano, and later on Luis Agüero (his sister-in-law Sara Calvo's husband).

He did not want to see Luis Agüero that night, since he knew Luis had let it slip (perhaps at Felito Ayón's house) that in his opinion Silvia was a

< 339 >

loose woman (maybe he said loose girl) and that as soon as he was out of the way, he, Luis Agüero (tall as a jockey, he adds now in anger) would win her over just like that – at which point he presumably snapped his fingers. He heard about it, of course, right away, and the communication was so quick he cannot recall the messenger, only the message. As soon as Luis arrived, he took him to one end of the room and out the door to a terrace, and there, the two of them leaning on the railing that separated the terrace from the void, he told Luis Agüero he knew what he had said about Silvia and he was a shit for having said it. He spoke in a very low voice and thus obliged Luis Agüero to respond similarly. Luis did not defend himself, other than to say he had been drunk and it was something he should not have said. "But do you believe it?" he insisted, and Luis remained silent. He did not wait for an answer, because Alberto Mora and Marian had just arrived and Silvia came out to find him.

Of that night he recalls the incident with Luis Agüero and the records they listened to, especially one by Miriam Makeba that Raúl Martínez had (or maybe Alberto had brought it, in which case the record had been his, and he had sent it to Alberto from Brussels). They were listening silently to Makeba's voice and her African songs, which owed so much to Cuban music (there was even one in Spanish), and the only thing that interrupted the musical moment was a comment Marian made about Miriam Makeba, saying that the melody reminded her of an open prairie. The following day Silvia said she could have killed her for breaking the spell, especially to say something so corny, so tacky. And it was true: it was enough to make you want to kill her, but no one did, and Alberto, who had the most at stake, did not even notice the gaffe.

< 340 >

He and Silvia drove to Varadero with Lisandro and Marcia, Sara Calvo and Luis Agüero, in Lisandro and Marcia's car. It had been years since he had last seen Varadero and he liked the idea of saying goodbye to Cuba from a beach that had always filled him with a sense of adventure. The feeling was special and it came from much more than having to travel 150 kilometers to get there. Along the way, the things one would expect to occur did: pleading with everyone not to tell the same tired joke when they passed the sulfur plant right before Matanzas and someone inevitably would use the palest of euphemisms to ask, "Who farted?" Then leaving Matanzas behind, they had a lovely view of the bay and a few sailboats. The white of the sails vibrating against the indigo waters moved him, and he pointed them out to Silvia, who was singing a Paul Anka song, in perfect English and impeccably in tune, for Luis Agüero. (She felt no resentment toward Luis, and the night before he had decided to forgive him: Luis was too young to understand the love he felt for Silvia.) She ignored him and continued singing, which disappointed him and made him a bit sad. Afterward, while the car was still making its way around the bay and he remained wrapped in his own contemplation of both the view and her rejection, Silvia brought her mouth to his ear. After kissing it, she said, "Yes, my love, I saw them," and added, "but why would I say anything?" which taught him a lesson.

They reached Varadero in time for lunch at a restaurant near Lisandro's house (in fact, the house belonged to Lisandro's aunts, who had left it to him when they emigrated), and then they went to the beach. No one went in the water: it was nearly October and in October no Cuban swims in the sea. They walked on the beach instead. He took the green gauze kerchief Silvia liked to wear around her neck and wore it himself, as a sort of scarf. Marcia and

< 341 >

Sara made fun of him, saying he looked like he was disguised as an exiled movie director – though they did not know his exile was closer than anyone thought. When the sun started going down, he and Silvia walked the empty beach again. As the sun set off to one side, out on the horizon, amid the purple waves, a solitary dolphin leapt out of the waters again and again. Neither of them could articulate the symbolism of what they were seeing, but each felt the sadness and solitude of that apparition of the dusk.

Early in the evening they returned to Havana. Lisandro and Marcia wanted to stay until the following day, but Silvia could not spend the night away from home and Sara had to get back to her children. The return, as always, was sad and no one sang. Upon entering Havana, in order to put an end to an argument Sara had provoked about the tiny bit of milk people were allowed to buy, he made a hypocritical speech (how infinitely hypocritical only he knew) that Sara should stop whining about milk, he was fed up with Cubans' preoccupation with food; he wanted to talk about the deeper reasons for being unhappy. And when he found his words turning into something quotable, he was not surprised, since it was precisely what his small audience wanted to hear, as well as the explanation he needed of why this time he would depart once and for all. That same night, later on, he felt bad about scolding Sara, since after all she was the only honest one in the car when she started crying about milk the way one cries about a mother lost.

With Silvia's kerchief still around his neck, he managed to make a joke as they turned from 25th Street onto B, heading for 23rd to drop Luis and Sara off at home. He pointed at a man crossing the street and exclaimed, "That man is still here!" And Lisandro asked, "Who? Who is it?" paving the way for his response: "I don't know who he is, but evidently he's still here."

< 342 >

He made the quip up on the spot and it was sufficiently counterrevolutionary to hold their attention and just innocuous enough not to hurt anyone, not even those listening – and certainly not the joker.

One night – perhaps the night Rine turned up while they were making love, or maybe a different night, but in any case one of the last nights he remembers – he was walking with Silvia through Neptune Park (no, that is not the name of the park, but he never knew for sure what the name was) and they stopped suddenly because she was in tears. He thought it was because he was leaving, but no, it was Fidel Castro's speech coming from the loudspeakers at El Carmelo (like all public places in Cuba, the restaurant broadcast propaganda assiduously). It was the speech in which Fidel Castro pulled back the veils on the impenetrable mystery of Che Guevara's disappearance, and read out his farewell letter/testament that said goodbye to Cuba, hello to world revolution. He heard Silvia utter unbelievable words, murmured yet distinctly audible: "Fucking great, what that man says!" She was awed by the speech's revolutionary fervor – it was empathy, absolute agreement – and now he can not help remembering his tears that she would reveal herself to be an agent of the secret police. He saw she was crying, crying at the words left behind by Che Guevara and read out by Fidel Castro. He wondered how it could be that this girl, who had received from the regime nothing but shoves and doors slammed in her face, could feel any attachment at all, much less fervor, for a cause that for him (who, compared to her, had received nothing but kindness) had shown itself even in that speech, especially in that speech, to be an abomination. He still can't comprehend it, but he does understand the fellow who once said women tend to be more fanatical than men. And he thinks Silvia's near tears or real tears were the visible manifestation of

< 343 >

her fanaticism, and not, as his paranoia would have it, a sign that she might have been an agent after all.

He went to the ministry to pick up the passports and got the fright of his life.

"Listen," Arnold said, with the same intonation he had used on the fatal night which seemed like years ago, "there is a problem with your Belgian visa."

He waited for Arnold to go on.

"Here are your passports with the Spanish visa, but the Belgians don't want to give you one."

He could have said he would arrange his entry into Belgium from Spain, but that might reveal an urgency to leave Cuba that could give away his plans. So he said, "Leave it, I'll try to get Gustavo to fix it."

"Well," Arnold said, "if you can get it fixed, do it. Here are your passports. Have you already got the tickets?"

He said he had and thanked him.

"Well, have a good trip and good luck."

He found Gustavo at home, which was a good sign. He explained what was up and Gustavo laughed: "Consider it done!" And he called the Belgian ambassador. He set up an interview, not for that day, unfortunately, but for the next, on Saturday morning.

"Gustavo," he said, "there isn't much time left. You should have tried to seem him today."

"Ah, don't you worry. Everything will get straightened out tomorrow morning. You're leaving on Sunday, right? There's plenty of time."

He felt encouraged by Gustavo's limitless enthusiasm, but it did not diminish his anxiety about the little time left to obtain the Belgian visa. If

< 344 >

he could not get it, he would have to travel on the Spanish visa alone and try to go rescue (he had to smile when he used the word, but he was thinking in those dramatic terms) Miriam Gómez in Brussels – or in any case Miriam could meet him in Madrid. The essential thing was to leave Cuba as soon as possible.

He would have liked to say goodbye to Silvia in bed, but after the last time he felt some trepidation about 69 C Street. Besides, he had returned the key to Rine that very day in a gesture he considered a silent rebuke, but Rine had accepted it quite naturally. In reality Rine was a Cuban Candide: everything was always great, in the best of all possible worlds. He was convinced that Rine's capacity for adapting to anything would ensure he never had any problems in Cuba. Had not Rine told him in a memorable conversation that whatever Cuba's future might be, he would embrace it as good, since after Stalin came Khrushchev, since even Hitler improved over time? Of course their friendship did not end with the handing over of the key, which had been, in truth and for a good while, the key to happiness inside misery. But on some level he could not forgive Rine for his lack of tact, no matter that it was his own home he had entered (at his best Rine was careless). More than anything, Rine's behavior showed an utter lack of refinement, and after the incident lack of refinement was what the apartment on C Street seemed to represent to him. That said, he knew himself well enough to know that what he would remember would be the caresses, the sex, the first time he went to bed with Silvia, the successive times they made love in that tiny, hot room miraculously cooled by the only window above the bed, where they had bathed so many times together – for him a form of communion – and where they had listened to music he wanted to hear over and over, music he wanted Silvia to keep but did not dare ask Rine for, not even to suggest trading it

< 345 >

for one of his own records (which of course he had already sold). In the end the apartment was for him a sort of lasting monument to the love that was receding, a monument that would endure in his memory, if not in any other form.

After all, he thought, it was better for his sexual liaison with Silvia to be cut short, as indeed it was, rather than come to an end on its own; this way it remained inconclusive, not yet over, incapable of ending – in other words, endless.

Still, he continued meeting up with Silvia as he had every afternoon since the first time in September. Now, October already, she came to his apartment and they sat in the living room listening to Billie Holiday. This would be one of their last times together, since soon the buyer would come for the record player and he was leaving on Sunday. (For him there was no doubt he would make it out this time, all the omens pointed to success. Even the Magus had come to tell him he was leaving, she had consulted with the saints and all of them agreed: he would travel, he would travel.) The girls came into the living room and chatted with Silvia. Carolita took her green kerchief and started dancing, fluttering the kerchief in the air, waving her arms, moving to the rhythm of music that she alone could hear (they had stopped listening to Billie Holiday the moment the girls came in, so Silvia could talk with them), and intoning: "I am an enchanted princess." This, in turn, enchanted (yes, that is the word) Silvia, who could not stop herself from getting up and going over to the dancing Carolita – or perhaps she waited until her improvised routine ended – taking her in her arms and giving her a hug and a kiss.

"Okay, I'll give you my kerchief." It was an act of great generosity, for giving away a piece of clothing that has meaning (and no doubt it did for Silvia: she always held it in her hands, wore it on her forehead, around her

< 346 >

hair; perhaps it was – love's ironies – a gift from the Hungarian) was not at all common in Cuba those days, when there was nothing in the stores and the only chance to buy a dress came, if it came, twice a year when you had to take whatever fabric was on offer, nearly always the most unappealing, nothing like the kerchief, which was unquestionably fine, certainly scarce.

Silvia stayed for a while that afternoon and then went home to change and return so they could go together to Lisandro and Marcia's house, for the final – and the best – goodbye party his friends would give him. She got back just after dusk. She was wearing the same dress she had worn to the party given a few days before by the woman who cannot be named. He felt a sweet sadness for Silvia and went to the closet where the few things left from his mother were stored. There were, he recalled, a few pieces of fabric that no one had taken, though he did not know why. They would be for Silvia, but he thought he had better give them to her another day. When they went out, he took along the Billie Holiday record to listen to at Lisandro's house; he did not know what impelled him to do so and later he regretted it. After waiting a long time they managed to get a taxi that would take them to the neighborhood of La Puntilla, on the other side of the Almendares River in Miramar, where Lisandro and Marcia lived. At the entrance to the neighborhood stood a guardhouse that had been there since the beginning of the Revolution, where all cars were stopped, since there was an anti-aircraft emplacement where La Puntilla juts out into the sea. He had to give the name of the house where they were going and they got through. He was happy not to have to walk the remaining blocks in the darkness, where he might have been stopped by a watchman or maybe shot at without warning; these things happened and he would not have been the first to get shot by a zealous or fearful guard. Fortunately, they arrived without incident.

< 347 >

Lisandro and Marcia lived in the same house he had known so well before he moved to Europe, with its one large room broken up into a sitting area, a library, and a dining room, and at the back the enormous enclosed balcony with large windows overlooking the mouth of the Almendares River, as if it were in Venice. He showed Silvia around, and when Marcia joined them (the maid had shown them in) and he saw Silvia's empty hands reaching out to greet Marcia, he remembered: "The record!"

"We left it in the car," Silvia said, after a moment's thought.

He had paid the driver and he remembered handing the record to Silvia without a word, meaning to convey that she should hold on to it. He answered Marcia's queries with only, "Too late now." And looking at Silvia, he saw she understood that the loss of the record would leave a deep scar. The evening, the occasion, their very relationship would not be the same.

Lisandro's appeared and his praise of Silvia's beauty helped to dissipate their feeling of loss. Then the others began to arrive. Fornet even brought a check, which he handed over in his usual furtive manner. He was puzzled. "It's for your collaboration in the anthology," Fornet said. He looked at it and saw it was for a hundred pesos; he had not expected so much for his story, he had not in fact expected to receive anything, and he thanked Fornet. Still implying some mystery, the man said, "You're welcome, *viejito*, you're welcome."

The party was much like the one Lisandro and Marcia gave him when he first left for Belgium, all that was missing was Miriam Gómez and the food. This time there was only a tiny bit to drink in the Otero household and no one said anything about eating. At one point he went into the kitchen to ask the maid/cook/driver for some water and when she opened the refrigerator he saw there was nothing inside except bottles of water. The party seemed

< 348 >

sad for all these reasons, but also because he knew what they did not know: he might never in his life see these friends again, including Silvia, above all Silvia. But he did not let on and the night went by quickly amid stories and jokes and everyone's plans to visit him in Europe soon – everyone, that is, except Silvia. Of all of them not one would carry through on those plans, not even Lisandro, who was best positioned from a bureaucratic point of view to make an overseas trip. There was, yes, the mercy of time. Time goes fast, and the party was over a bit after midnight, at which point he left, accompanied by Sarusky, who as on other occasions gave Silvia a ride home. But this time was the last, he hoped and he despaired.

ON SATURDAY MORNING, after reading the prayer his aunt Felisa had found for him, he went to Gustavo's house so they could go together to the Belgian Embassy. Suárez was not available to drive them, so they took a shared taxi on the corner of Avenue of the Presidents and 17th Street and headed for Miramar.

Not allowed into the embassy portion as on the previous occasion, they entered the consulate. After making them wait a few minutes, the Belgian ambassador came in. His greeting was rather cold: he must have known that neither he nor Gustavo had any connection with the Cuban Embassy in Brussels anymore, or maybe he had other reasons. Gustavo explained what was up, more or less, that he was going back to Europe, this time with a regular passport, and he needed a visa for Belgium. With no hesitation, the Belgian functionary said it would be impossible since he had no power to automatically grant visas; he would have to make an application to the Ministry of Foreign Affairs in Brussels and await their response, which would take about two weeks. His tone of voice implied that the visa would not be granted.

< 349 >

Instantly, he felt everything fall apart. Even though he had an alternative, he had been counting on the Belgian visa to get out of the country. He might be able to leave with only the Spanish one, but suppose the ministry found out before he got on the plane?

A desperate solution occurred to him and he spoke up: "Isn't there another type of visa?"

Reluctantly, the ambassador admitted, "Well, a transit visa allows the holder to remain a minimum time in Belgium, but…"

"That'll do for me!"

Gustavo stepped in: "My friend is not going to be in Brussels for long, just enough time to collect his things and go to Spain."

The official reluctantly agreed to give him a transit visa. Everything was fixed. The only obstacle remaining was the airport security police – and what an obstacle!

In the afternoon Pablo Armando called to make sure he remembered the event that night at the Writers Union, and Alberto Mora called to remind him they were going to see Carlos Rafael Rodríguez that night to thank him for his efforts and to say goodbye. He explained to Alberto that he had a cocktail party to attend at UNEAC. Alberto insisted he had to thank Carlos Rafael and say goodbye. They reached an agreement: Alberto would pick him up at the Writers Union halfway through the party, a good compromise because, on the one hand, the party might turn out to be as boring as other UNEAC events (unlike the last time, Lido would not be there to help him get through the evening) and, on the other, government functionaries were in the habit of receiving visitors late at night. Alberto would pick him up at the Writers Union at ten o'clock.

< 350 >

The reception, celebrating the annual UNEAC literary contest, was precisely as boring as he had feared. The only surprise was that Pablo Armando had too much to drink and began to talk about the status of poetry "in the current situation" (those were his words), a monologue that soon went from friendly chat to cruel invective. Pablo Armando spoke ill of Guillén's poetry with Guillén standing only a few imbibing bodies away. He was behaving like Harold Gramatges, who in his heyday (long over) was capable of chatting with one person and trashing the friend next to him. But Pablo Armando was no master of this art, and he worried he would go too far. (Once or twice he alluded to Minrex, giving the word a derisive pronunciation.) So he spent practically the entire evening running herd on Pablo Armando, to prevent him from going inside the mansion where his monologue might have turned into a dangerous dialogue with any of the UNEAC staff (and there were many) or the inevitable agents from Security (doubtlessly no fewer) rubbing elbows on that apparently innocuous occasion.

That is why he could not really focus on Captain Juan Nuiry, whom Juan Arcocha used to speak so well of and about whom he was curious after the suffering he apparently caused Elsa and the mirth her distress brought out in Silvia. When they were introduced, he could tell Nuiry was also interested in speaking with him.

Alberto finally arrived to pick him up, and he left Pablo Armando to his own devices, although he asked Miriam Acevedo not to let him drink any more and to make sure he watched what he was saying – or was about to say, which could be worse. Because he was busy with Miriam he missed the exchange between Alberto Mora and Juan Nuiry, both of whom were astonished to find themselves, two evidently reluctant militants of the regime,

< 351 >

hanging around with the writers of Revolutionary Cuba in the literary halls of the Writers Union. Despite any misgivings about the regime, he could see these two still shared the belief deep in the heart of all patriots that this writing stuff only amounted to frivolous faggotry, which is how a police captain in the time of President Carlos Prío Socarrás had characterized such activities and the label stuck. Just because the Revolution took writers in (and over) did not mean that literature wasn't a dangerous frivolity. Thus the smile that Alberto and Nuiry exchanged when they found themselves face-to-face. He would have to ask Alberto about him, but he would not learn much.

And, of course, he did not learn much. As Alberto's Volkswagen sped toward the old *Diario de la Marina* building, now the mysterious ministry run by Carlos Rafael Rodríguez, there was not much opportunity for conversation, since Alberto was truly worried about the impression that he, his passenger, would make on the man they were about to meet.

The building was virtually impenetrable. They had to cross several checkpoints (some of them bureaucratic, with tables or desks) until they reached the waiting room outside the sancta sanctorum. Carlos Rafael received them right away. He was pleased to meet the traveler whom he had met on so many different occasions, going back to 1957 in the underground against Batista, on up to the present when Carlos Rafael was an *éminence rose* (obviously gray was not his color) of the revolutionary government.

"So you're leaving us?" Carlos Rafael began, and he used the short form of his name, which he usually did not care for, though in this case he didn't really mind.

"But not for long, Carlos."

He too used the short form of his name, which not everybody did; after all, he was following suit, and in any case Carlos Rafael had known

< 352 >

his father for many years at the old newspaper *Hoy*, where both of them were writers.

"So, where are you going?"

"First to Brussels to pick up my wife, then to Spain, where my book is coming out soon."

"Ah, yes, your novel that won the prize."

"What's it about?" Alberto jumped in, trying to soften a conversation that from the start seemed to veer toward dangerous waters for reasons he could not say.

"I'm sure it's very interesting," Carlos Rafael said, "and besides it will be very useful for the country. At least the title is promising." And Carlos Rafael repeated the title, which in fact he had been planning for a while to switch for an earlier one (or perhaps another like it). He thought about that and at the same time tried not to let it show on his face, all the while knowing his thoughts always showed through.

"That's good," Alberto said.

"Well," said Carlos Rafael, "are you writing anything now?"

"No," he lied, "I haven't had time. That is, any free time I've spent reading."

"And making love," Alberto said, laughing, hoping Carlos Rafael would be amused at the mention of such a typically Cuban activity. But Carlos Rafael did not laugh, since love was the Cuban pastime of another era. Now it required an adjective and had to be dedicated either to the Fatherland or to the Revolution, each with a capital letter. Wasn't the daily life of the Revolution filled with examples of good revolutionaries who put their duty to the Revolution and the Fatherland far ahead of conjugal and even filial love?

< 353 >

Carlos Rafael had sufficient tact to say:

"I'm sure you'll find more time now. In Europe, I mean. Where are you going to live, Paris?"

"No, first I have to go to Barcelona, where my book is coming out. Then I have to find a place where I can live cheaply."

"Well," said Carlos Rafael, "it doesn't matter where, what counts is that you not forget your roots."

He ought to have said, "Never," but he just smiled his acquiescence.

"What do you make of the national panorama?" Carlos Rafael asked.

"Very interesting," was all he said.

"The work of the Revolution," began Alberto, but Carlos Rafael interrupted him:

"No, not that. We talk about that every day. I mean the cultural panorama. After so many years away…"

"Three," he filled in.

"Has it been three years already? Time flies! It seems like the Cultural Congress was just yesterday."

"That was four years ago," he said.

"So what do you think of the Union?"

"Good, very good. I've just come from there."

"I know."

"I had to pull him away from a reception," Alberto said.

"They keep inviting me, but I have no time for that sort of thing," Carlos Rafael said. "I don't have time for anything. Even so, I try to stay on top of what's being written. Have you read anything new that's worthwhile? Cuban, I mean."

< 354 >

"Not really. Although it seems Carpentier is having great success, even officially."

"Yes, his *Explosion in a Cathedral* is now required reading for the Rebel Army."

He was going to add: To the eternal sorrow of Guillén, who gets compared to him. And not favorably, it seems. But he remembered the old and close friendship between Guillén and Carlos Rafael, and said nothing.

"I gather Raúl liked it a lot," Alberto said.

"Yes, that's true. Although, just among us, I'm worried about the book he's writing now."

"*El año '59?*" he asked.

"Yes, don't quote me, but the first few chapters they published took me aback. More than that, I found them really worrying. I don't think Carpentier really understands the struggle against Batista and the first days of the Revolution."

"Well," said Alberto, "he wasn't here during the underground."

"No," said Carlos Rafael, "and he doesn't seem to know much about the first period after the Revolution took power. I don't want to jump the gun, but there may be problems with the book as a whole. Of course we don't want a *Doctor Zhivago*, and we have to ensure the book doesn't become one, without of course censoring in advance. In any case, that's just my impression."

He thought: If Carpentier finds out, he'll die of fright. A silence fell when no one spoke. It lasted longer than half a minute. He looked at his watch and said:

"Well, Carlos, we don't want to steal any more of your time. I only came to thank you for what you have done for me."

< 355 >

"No need to. Now we've got to see what you can do for yourself."

He did not understand what Carlos Rafael meant, then Alberto intervened:

"Don't worry, I'll keep an eye on him."

"Ah, that's true, you're going to Europe too. When?"

"Well," said Alberto, "I hope soon. That's in Dorticós's hands now."

"I'm going to give him a little nudge."

"That would help. Thank you."

The two of them stood up. Carlos Rafael offered his hand and he took it.

"See you later. Have a good trip."

"See you later. Thank you."

They departed down hallways made of plywood partitions. He felt very relieved. They said nothing until they were in the street, but Alberto was smiling.

They returned to the Union, more than anything because Alberto wanted a drink. When they arrived, however, only a few people remained – Pablo Armando and Miriam Acevedo and Arrufat and Virgilio had all disappeared – and there was nothing left to drink. After a few minutes, Alberto took him home. That night he barely slept, thinking about what the following day would bring – his last day in Cuba, if all went well.

In the morning he went early to say goodbye to Carmela, who was still insisting Miriam should spend some time in Cuba so she could see her. This time he did not contradict her, saying that maybe they would come together soon, leaving her with that hope. Miriam's brother Richard behaved like an adult this time, maybe because he was thinking they would not see each other again – or maybe because his growth spurt was internal as well as in height.

< 356 >

He returned home to pack his bags well in advance, and more than anything to ask Hildelisa to take care of the girls' things. He was unable to stop her from putting the pieces of fabric he had planned to give to Silvia into the big suitcase. Later on, he took them out when no one was looking, but upon opening the suitcase in Brussels he found two of the pieces inside: for sure Hildelisa had packed them up again. Or maybe it had been his grandmother, who always kept a vigilant eye on everything that occurred in the apartment.

Mamá spent the entire day in her tiny room, without saying a word, and it pained him to know she had shut herself away because her feelings were overwhelming. He was certain she knew she would never see the girls again.

Close to noon, he heard an insistent car horn and peered over the balcony. Gustavo Arcos was calling to him, leaning his head out a car window. He went down and saw that someone he knew, but could not identify, was behind the wheel.

"I came to say goodbye," Gustavo said. "I'm headed for the beach now."

"I was going to drop over to bid you and Doña Rosina farewell."

"I'll tell her for you." Then turning toward his driver, he said, "You know Paco Chabarry, right?"

It was Francisco Chabarry, once very influential at Minrex and an intimate longtime friend of Gustavo's. He had never liked him at all, not before and not now.

"Yes, how are you?"

"What's up, *chico*."

"How's everything going?" Gustavo asked.

"Just fine. The thing's tonight at ten. Now it seems we really are going."

"Well, have a good trip and take care."

"Thank you. We'll see you in Europe."

< 357 >

"Ha, ha. I hope so," Gustavo said, transforming his laugh into a smile.

He would have liked to speak with Gustavo alone, to insist once more he had to leave Cuba, to make him see sense, but in that moment it was impossible. He wished the other times he had spoken to him had had more effect.

In the afternoon, the apartment filled up. His uncle Niño and Fina came early, as did Silvia, and Héctor and Teresa from next door. Many of his friends did not show up: some did not know today was the day, others may have forgotten, and he was relieved not to have a very large crew accompanying him to the airport like the last time. Franqui would pick him up; he did not know whether Harold would come. He had not seen much of him lately, and given his treatment of Walterio at the Casa de las Américas event, it was just as well.

The girls ate their last meal prepared by Hildelisa. He could not eat and was glad to have his nerves as an excuse. Toward dusk the canary began to sing and that reminded him. He brought Silvia over to the cage and told her it was hers, that it had belonged to his mother, but now he was giving it to her to remember him by. She said she would come for it later, although he never found out if she did. There, in the canary's corner, he handed her the check Fornet had given him, duly endorsed. He had put it in a white envelope.

"What the hell is this?" Silvia said, pulling it out of its envelope.

He wished she had waited to get home before taking it out, when no one was present and there was no chance she would refuse it.

She looked at the check, front and back.

"It's for you," he said.

"Is this an advance payment? No, more like a late one."

He smiled.

< 358 >

"I want you to buy something you like."

"What the hell could I buy? Don't you know the stores are empty?"

"Well, use it as best you can."

"I don't want it."

"Do me the favor of accepting it. As you can see, it's not payment for anything. It's very little for all I owe you. Even in the worst sense it's lousy payment. I'm not going to spend it. Who better than you to have it?"

"A hundred pesos and a canary, when I wanted a short, dark man who smokes cigars."

She made a joke of it and he was pleased: she had accepted it.

Franqui arrived with his driver. Elsa came too in her own car. He had decided – also on Franqui's advice – not to commit the mistake of turning up early at the airport like last time. According to Franqui that gave Security extra time to act. But he knew that if Security (or whoever it was) wished to keep him from leaving Cuba, they would stop him even if he turned up five minutes before departure. In the end, they decided to go neither very early nor very late.

Like on the other occasion, his father disappeared when it was time to say goodbye: he hated goodbyes. Mamá, his grandmother, came out of her room to kiss her great-grandchildren and her grandchild.

"Oh! My son, I'm so happy you can go at last! I know I won't ever see you again but it's better for you this way, and what's good for you is better for me."

Hildelisa hugged him, crying silently. Finally, they departed, but not without him first giving Héctor Pedreira a firm handshake. Downstairs there was some confusion at the cars, and he decided to go with Silvia and Elsa. His daughters went with Niño and Fina; Franqui and Margot went in their

< 359 >

own car with their driver. At the last moment Pablo Armando, whom he had not laid eyes on since his drunken scene at the Writers Union, turned up. He got into Franqui's car.

They arrived at the airport and he went alone into the room for all passengers who were not officials – the one called, with a mixed metaphor, "the fishbowl for worms," meaning it was the glassed-in room for passengers leaving as exiles. Since he was going as a secret exile, he would later make his way to the protocol lounge used by the Foreign Ministry for its diplomats and by the other state bodies for guests in Cuba.

More than anything in the world, he feared the moment when he would have to present his exit permit to the official on duty, who this time (nothing new) had the face and mannerisms of a bulldog. The policeman took his documents and examined them suspiciously, as if he figured they must be false. He studied them, studied them again, and yet again.

"Where are the other passengers?"

Like the other functionaries, this one had not honored him with the title of *compañero* or its opposite, *cludadanu*.

"They're those two girls outside," he said, and he pointed to the hallway where Anita and Carolita stood with Niño and Fina.

"Ah, okay."

The policeman scrutinized the exit permits once more, and finally stamped and returned them. He thanked him, but the man did not respond: it was obvious he hated people who left Cuba, no matter under what circumstances. He collected his documents and returned to get his attaché case and traveling bag where he had left them. He did not notice then, but a box of cigars was missing; a packet of margaritas Felito Ayón had given him after searching for it across half of Havana. By the time he discovered the theft

< 360 >

upon arriving in Madrid, he was too overwhelmed, practically stupefied, to worry about it. He never knew who stole them.

Now, instead of going to the protocol lounge, he went into the bar and sat next to Silvia. Earlier, before getting out of Elsa's car, he had noticed almost against his will that Silvia's eyes had a telltale shine; now she was near tears. At that moment he first became aware that they were blasting a speech by Fidel Castro over the loudspeakers. It was not a repeat of the other day, rather a new one, as interminable as the previous, to mark yet another anniversary of the creation of the Committees for the Defense of the Revolution. Without understanding a word, he listened to the speech as music, an appropriate soundtrack for his departure. He asked for a rum and began to drink. He knew he had to, so as to avoid thinking about the policeman who would certainly arrest him as he stepped out, one sent expressly by Barbaroja Piñeiro. Nor did he want to think about Silvia, who he could see was now crying silently.

Franqui was talking about something he paid no attention to, although he nodded as he sipped his rum with clear Coca-Cola. Not even the goodbye took away the rum's taste of gasoline, undiminished by the insipid mixer. Across from him, Silvia was also having a rum cocktail with clear Coca-Cola and now he looked at her face. The timeless smile formed by her perfectly Egyptian lips was gone, as was the last of her restraint, and tears were smearing the eyeliner she had painted on her lower lids. He picked up and held her hand, but there was nothing he could do to keep her from weeping. Everything had already been said, and although in her posture there was the same pleading she had been directing at him for several nights – "Don't go, please!" – for once she had nothing to say, and he had nothing to add. All they could do was wait.

< 361 >

Time took its time: on the one hand he wanted it to accelerate so he could finally head out to the tarmac, and on the other hand he wanted to delay the moment when he would have to say goodbye to Silvia forever. As always, fate knocked and the moment arrived: it was time for the protocol lounge – he had the vague sense he owed that privilege to Franqui, though maybe it was for anyone leaving Cuba as a friend – and he got ready to depart. He did not kiss Silvia and she did not lean over for him to kiss her, rather she sobbed, only once, a loud, strangled sob. He shook Elsa's hand and said goodbye to Niño and Fina; he hugged Pablo Armando and was careful to make it appear casual. His papers said he would return and there was no reason to show the enemy that would not be the case. He heard once more the thin, spineless, monotonous voice of Fidel Castro during the pauses between goodbyes, and he and his daughters entered the protocol lounge at last, accompanied by Franqui. Inside, there was no one he knew and again he was pleased: nothing like last time's agglomeration of friends. A few moments more, and the flight was announced with a shout, since all the loudspeakers were occupied by Fidel Castro's speech. He shook Franqui's hand, passed his traveling bag to Anita, and with his free hand took Carolita by the hand.

Leaving the air-conditioned lounge for the tarmac, a warm haze enveloped him, too warm for an October night. The weather was perfect and he could see the stars above. He walked quickly to the airplane, and once inside, the stewardess showed him where he had to sit, across from a very elderly couple who by their threadbare clothing and yearning expressions he could see were on their way not to a foreign airport but into exile. "Like me," he dared to hope, though he had sworn to himself he would not even think about his destiny, would not allow himself the least taste of it until the plane was far from Cuba.

< 362 >

It seemed they had been on the runway for hours waiting to take off, although in reality it was only a few minutes. All the while he expected his enemies to come for him. He knew of cases where travelers – that is, exiles – had been taken off the plane and their seats given to functionaries making a last-minute voyage. But the only thing that happened was the stewardess going up and down the aisle, making sure everyone's seat belt was fastened. Then the plane began to move, rolling slowly, then stopping, racing its engines, and finally accelerating faster and faster. They took off.

He kept track of the time on his watch. He knew that four hours into the flight they would reach the point of no return, when no one could make the plane go back to Cuba. He waited patiently, looking at his daughters sleeping beside him, feeling the effect of the alcohol as it wore off bit by bit. He did not think about either Silvia or Miriam Gómez or the relatives he was leaving behind or the friends inside or outside: he simply waited. When the moment arrived, that point of no return he knew about from the movies, he opened his attaché case and looked underneath the handful of photographs and blank sheets of paper for his handwritten notes; he unfolded them and began to read what he had written. "Cabrera Infante usually sat next to the driver out of some shallow democratic sentiment. But that afternoon, on the 1st of June 1965, Jacqueline Lewy, the secretary, had asked him to drop her near her house and he decided to sit in the back with her. That saved his life."

< 363 >

PERSONALITIES MENTIONED IN THE TEXT

ACEVEDO, MIRIAM (1928-2013)
Actress once married to Oscar Hurtado who left Cuba in 1968 for Italy under a work permit and did not return. She died in exile in Rome.

AGÜERO, LUIS (1937)
Writer and film critic, husband of Guillermo Cabrera Infante's sister-in-law Sara Calvo. He lives in Miami.

ALONSO, ALBERTO (1917-2007)
Dancer and choreographer. He died in exile.

ALONSO, LUIS RICARDO (1929-2015)
Writer and Cuba's ambassador in London in the 1960s. Born in Asturias of a Spanish father and a Cuban mother. In 1965 he went into exile in the United States.

ALONSO, MARITZA
Spaniard resident in Cuba. Artists' agent and organizer of cultural events, she represented Sara Montiel, among others. She invited Guillermo Cabrera Infante to give a series of lectures at the Fine Arts Palace, which were published as *Arcadia todas las noches*.

ÁLVAREZ RÍOS, RENÉ
University professor.

ANDREU, OLGA (1930-1988)
Old friend of Guillermo Cabrera Infante and first wife of Tomás Gutiérrez Alea. She committed suicide.

< 364 >

ARCOCHA, JUAN (1927-2010)
Writer, journalist, and friend of Guillermo Cabrera Infante. Fluent in French and Russian, he served as interpreter for Fidel Castro on many occasions. In 1971 he went into exile, and in 2010 he died in Paris.

ARCOS, GUSTAVO (1926-2006)
Cuba's ambassador in Brussels and veteran of the attack on the Moncada Barracks. He was jailed in 1966 and died in Cuba.

ARENAL, HUMBERTO (1926-2012)
Writer and theater director who since 1948 lived in New York and visited Cuba regularly. After the Revolution, he returned to Cuba at Guillermo Cabrera Infante's urging and remained there for the rest of his life.

ARRUFAT, ANTÓN (1935)
Writer and dramaturge long sidelined for being a homosexual. He lives in Cuba.

AYÓN, FELITO
Cultural activist and owner of the club El Gato Tuerto. Friend of intellectuals and artists.

BARRAL, CARLOS (1928-1989)
Spanish poet and editor at the Barcelona publishing house Seix Barral when Guillermo Cabrera Infante won the Biblioteca Breve prize.

BATISTA, FULGENCIO (1901-1973)
Cuban dictator. He was president of Cuba 1940-1944 and 1952-1959.

< 365 >

BLANCO, JUAN (1919-2008)

Composer of classical music, lawyer, and former brother-in-law of Guillermo Cabrera Infante (married to Ivonne Calvo, the sister of Cabrera Infante's first wife). Blanco got the writer out of jail when he was detained on obscenity charges.

BOLA DE NIEVE (see Villa, Ignacio)

BORREGO, ORLANDO (1936)

Writer who participated in the guerrilla struggle with Che Guevara. During the period of the book he was sugar minister.

BOUMEDIENE, HOUARI (1932-1978)

President of Algeria 1965-1978.

CABRERA, MARICUSA (1937-?)

Dancer of popular music, married to Silvano Suárez, a friend of Guillermo Cabrera Infante. She died in Cuba.

CABRERA INFANTE, ALBERTO (SABÁ) (1933-2002)

Younger brother of Guillermo Cabrera Infante. Cineaste, co-creator with Orlando Jiménez Leal of the short film *PM*. In 1965 he sought political asylum in Rome and in 1966 he moved to New York. He died in the United States a few years before Guillermo Cabrera Infante.

CALVO, MARTA

First wife of Guillermo Cabrera Infante, mother of his daughters, Anita and Carolita, and sister of Sara and Ivonne.

< 366 >

CAMEJO, CARUCHA AND PEPE (brothers)
Celebrated puppeteers who founded the puppeteer movement in Cuba.

CARBONELL, "EL VIEJO"
Father of Pipo Carbonell. Union activist before and after the Revolution.

CARBONELL, LUIS (1923)
Reciter of what he called "Antillean Poetry."

CARBONELL, PIPO
Cuban diplomat, third secretary of the Cuban Embassy in Belgium, a post
he obtained through the efforts of Gustavo Arcos. Married to Mariposa.

CARBONELL, WALTERIO (1920-2008)
Journalist and intellectual author of a controversial work on the African com-
ponent of Cuban culture, who founded a "black power" movement in Cuba.
Friend and colleague of Guillermo Cabrera Infante. He attended university
with Fidel Castro and was expelled from the Communist Party for congrat-
ulating Fidel Castro on the day of the assault on the Moncada Barracks. Not
allowed to publish, he died in poverty in Cuba.

CARPENTIER, ALEJO (1904-1980)
One of the greatest of Cuban novelists, author of *Explosion in a Cathedral*,
The Kingdom of this World, and many other works. He left Cuba in 1966 and
settled in Paris, where he died.

CASEY, CALVERT (1924-1969)
Writer who worked at *Lunes de Revolución*. He died in exile in Rome.

< 367 >

CASTRO, FIDEL (1926-2016)

Maximum leader of the Cuban Revolution. He was prime minister 1959-1976 and president 1976-2008.

CHINOLOPE, EL (GUILLERMO FERNÁNDEZ LÓPEZ JUNQUÉ) (1932)

Photographer who worked at *Carteles*, where he met Guillermo Cabrera Infante. He was close friends with the writer José Lezama Lima, whom he photographed many times.

CHOMÓN, FAURE (1929, death year unknown)

Former leader of the Revolutionary Student Directorate. With Carlos Gutiérrez Menoyo, he led the attack on the Presidential Palace of Cuba in 1957. The goal of this attack was to murder Fulgencio Batista, but ultimately, the dictator escaped.

CUBELA, ROLANDO (1932)

Member of the Revolutionary Student Directorate. After the triumph of the Revolution he was promoted to the rank of Commander of the Rebel Army. In 1966 he was linked to a plot to assassinate Fidel Castro and received a thirty-year sentence. Freed in 1979, he now lives in Spain.

DESNOES, EDMUNDO (1930)

Writer who authored the novel *Memorias del subdesarrollo* (published in English as *Inconsolable Memories*), which gave rise to the film of the same name by Tomás Gutiérrez Alea. Once married to Maria Rosa Almendros, sister of Néstor Almendros, he moved to New York in 1979.

< 368 >

DÍAZ DEL REAL, JUAN JOSÉ
Diplomat. Aide to Ambassador Gustavo Arcos in Belgium.

DORTICÓS, OSVALDO (1919-1983)
President of Cuba 1959-1976, he is said to have killed himself after reading the article in which Guillermo Cabrera Infante said that decent people in Cuba commit suicide.

ECHEVERRÍA, JOSÉ ANTONIO "MANZANITA" (1932-1957)
Student leader and member of the Revolutionary Student Directorate who took a very active role in the struggle against the Batista dictatorship. He participated in the seizing of Radio Reloj and was killed immediately after, as he walked toward the University of Havana.

EHRENBURG, ILYA GRIGORYEVICH (1891-1967)
Soviet writer, journalist, translator, and cultural figure.

EMILIO, FRANK (1921 2001)
Blind composer and pianist, one of the greats of Afro-Cuban jazz.

ENRÍQUEZ, CARLOS (1900-1957)
Painter who was one of the artists of the Primera Vanguardia Cubana.

ERNESTO (ERNESTO FERNÁNDEZ NOGUERAS) (1930)
Celebrated Cuban photographer who began his career at *Carteles*.

ESCARDÓ, ROLANDO (1925-1960)
Cuban poet who was given the rank of lieutenant in the Rebel Army. He died in an automobile accident.

< 369 >

ESTORINO, PEPE (1925)
Cuban theater director and dramaturge.

FEIJÓO, SAMUEL (1914-1992)
Cuban writer and self-taught artist.

FERNÁNDEZ, MARCELO (1932-2005)
Minister of Foreign Trade 1965-1980.

FERNÁNDEZ, PABLO ARMANDO (1929)
Poet and storyteller. An old friend of Guillermo Cabrera Infante, he was assistant editor of *Lunes de Revolución* and chief editor at Casa de las Américas. In 1965 he was the cultural attaché at the Cuban Embassy in London. They grew apart after Guillermo Cabrera Infante's statements published in the Argentine weekly *Primera Plana* in 1968. He remained in Cuba and still works at Casa de las Américas publishing house.

FERNÁNDEZ RETAMAR, ROBERTO (1930)
Poet, essayist, and literary critic. Part of the nomenklatura, he held many posts in the regime's cultural institutions. In 1965 he was editor of the magazine *Casa de las Américas*. He received the National Prize for Literature in 1989, and now runs Casa de la Américas publishing house.

FERNÁNDEZ VILA, ÁNGEL "HORACIO"
Physician and writer.

FIGUEREDO, CARLOS "EL CHINO" (1927-2009)
Member of the Revolutionary Student Directorate. During the Batista dictatorship he participated in the attacks on Radio Reloj and the Presidential

< 370 >

Palace, and managed to escape. After the triumph of the Revolution he was involved in the creation of the organisms of state security. He committed suicide.

FORNET, AMBROSIO (1930)
Literary critic, essayist, editor, and screenwriter, he worked as an editor at the Ministry of Education, the National Publishing House, and the Cuban Book Institute.

FRANQUI, CARLOS (1921-2010)
Writer, poet, journalist, critic, and political activist, he was one of the most influential people in Guillermo Cabrera Infante's life, though in exile they had many disagreements. He went into exile in 1968, and died in Puerto Rico.

FRAYDE, MARTHA (1920-2013)
Physician who took part in the struggle against Batista, participated actively in the early days of the Revolution, and was a diplomat at UNESCO. A critic and dissident, she denounced the abuses of the system and in 1976 was imprisoned and given a twenty-nine-year sentence. In 1979 she was pardoned and went into exile in Madrid.

GARCÍA, HÉCTOR
Member of the Cuban Film Institute (ICAIC).

GARCÍA BUCHACA, EDITH (1916-2015)
Historic Communist leader whose first husband was Carlos Rafael Rodrí-guez. She was tried for her role in the Batista-era massacre at 7 Humboldt Street.

< 371 >

GARCÍA HERNÁNDEZ MONTORO, ADRIÁN

Descendent of a family of educators and member of the Communist Party, he was a close friend of Guillermo Cabrera Infante. He went into exile in Madrid and then became a professor in the United States.

GONZÁLEZ, INGRID

Actress married to Rine Leal.

GRAMATGES, HAROLD (1918-2008)

Composer, member of the Communist Party, and activist of the regime.

GUEVARA, ALFREDO (1925-2013)

Founder of the Cuban Film Institute (ICAIC), he exercised rigid control over cultural policy. He was a declared enemy of Guillermo Cabrera Infante and of *Lunes de Revolución*.

GUEVARA, ERNESTO "CHE" (1928-1967)

Argentine-Cuban politician, guerrilla fighter, writer, and physician, he was one of the historic leaders of the Revolution.

GUILLÉN, NICOLÁS (1902-1989)

Poet, named president of the National Union of Writers and Artists of Cuba (UNEAC) in 1961. Because of his important cultural and political posts and his prestige throughout the Americas and Europe, he represented Cuban intellectuals at innumerable events.

GUTIÉRREZ ALEA, TOMÁS "TITÓN" (1928-1996)

Filmmaker who studied at the Centro Sperimentale di Cinematografia in Rome, he was a childhood friend of Guillermo Cabrera Infante. He was

< 372 >

married to Olga Andreu, and was one of the founders of the Cuban Film Institute (ICAIC).

HART, ARMANDO (1930)
Leader of the July 26th Movement, he was minister of education 1959-1965, and minister of culture 1976-1997.

HURTADO, OSCAR (1919-1977)
Poet and authority on science fiction, he was married to the actress Miriam Acevedo and, later on, to Evorita Tamayo. He collaborated wth *Lunes de Revolución* and died in Cuba after suffering from Alzheimer's.

IGLESIAS, ARACELIO (1901-1948)
Communist leader of the port workers.

JAMÍS, FAYAD (1930-1988)
Writer and artist.

JIMÉNEZ LEAL, ORLANDO (1941)
Filmmaker, co-director with Sabá Cabrera Infante of the short film *PM*.

LEAL, RINE (1930-1996)
High school friend of Guillermo Cabrera Infante, theater critic, and professor of theater, he was also a journalist. He was a member of the staff of *Lunes de Revolución* and had previously worked at *Carteles*. He died in Venezuela, after moving there in 1994.

LEANTE, CÉSAR (1928)
Writer, Socialist Youth activist, and student leader, he was public relations

< 373 >

secretary of the National Union of Writers and Artists of Cuba (UNEAC). In 1981 he sought political asylum in Spain.

LEISECA, MARCIA
Member of Cuban high society who participated actively in the Revolution. She was married to Lisandro Otero and then Osmani Cienfuegos, and is vice president of Casa de las Américas publishing house.

LEWY, JACQUELINE
Secretary at the Cuban Embassy in Belgium. Her family, of Jewish origin, had fled to Argentina.

LEZAMA LIMA, JOSÉ (1910-1976)
Writer and poet, author of *Paradiso* and other works, one of the greatest figures in Spanish-language literature. Though his works were suppressed for many years, he remained in Cuba.

LINARES, ERNESTINA (1928-1973)
One of Cuba's leading actresses, she was a member of the Prometeo Group and a founder of Studio Theater.

MARIO, JOSÉ (1940-2002)
Poet of the El Puente group who died in exile in Madrid.

MARTÍNEZ, NORMA
Actress, married to the producer Faustino Canel.

MARTÍNEZ, RAÚL (1927-1995)
Painter and illustrator for *Lunes de Revolución*, where he was also the designer.

< 374 >

MAYITO (MARIO GARCÍA-JOYA) (1939)
Photographer.

MILLÁS HERNÁNDEZ, JOSÉ CARLOS (1889-1965)
Corvette captain who was director of the national meteorological station
and the country's official weatherman.

MONTENEGRO, ROGELIO (1933-2001)
Underground combatant of the July 26th Movement and Cuban diplomat.

MORA, ALBERTO (1929-1972)
Revolutionary and son of another revolutionary, Menelao Mora, he fought
in the Escambray Mountains and achieved the rank of commander. While
underground, he hid for a time in Guillermo Cabrera Infante's home. He fell
into disgrace due to his close relationship to Che Guevara. He remained on
the island and ended up committing suicide.

MOYZISCH, LUDWIG CARL (1905-)
Diplomatic attaché of the German Embassy in Ankara, Turkey, during World
War II, where he led the work of the Nazi secret services in Turkey. Author
of the book *Operation Cicero*.

NORKA (NATALIA MENÉNDEZ) (1938)
One of Cuba's most famous models, she was married to the photographer
Alberto Korda.

NUIRY, JUAN (1932-2013)
Captain of the Rebel Army.

< 375 >

O'FARRILL, ELA (1930-2014)
Cuban singer and composer.

OLIVA, TOMÁS (1930-1996)
Cuban painter and sculptor.

OLTUSKI, ENRIQUE (1930-2012)
Communications minister in the first cabinet under Manuel Urrutia after
the triumph of the Revolution. Later on, under Che Guevara he was vice
president of the Central Planning Board. After a period relegated to lower
posts, he remained in the upper echelons of government until his death.

OTERO, LISANDRO (1932-2008)
Writer, journalist, and diplomat, he was a close friend of Guillermo Cabrera
Infante since journalism school and was married to Marcia Leiseca. Because
of "the Padilla Affair," which counterposed Cabrera Infante's works to
Otero's, the two became enemies; Lisandro Otero then deployed the regime's
political machinery to criticize Cabrera Infante. He was director of the Cuban
Academy of Language.

PADILLA, HEBERTO (1932-2000)
Poet and writer, friend of Guillermo Cabrera Infante, and collaborator of
Lunes de Revolución. After the closure of the magazine he became *Prensa
Latina*'s correspondent in Moscow. In 1968 his book *Fuera del juego* (*Out
of the Game*) was declared "ideologically contrary" to the Revolution. His
defense of Guillermo Cabrera Infante's work and his critical stance led to
his arrest in 1971 and his subsequent "retraction," which became known as
"the Padilla Affair." He managed to go into exile in 1980 and died in the
United States.

< 376 >

PALAZUELOS, RAÚL
Married to Ivonne Calvo (sister of Sara and Marta), he was an assistant at *Lunes en televisión* and later director of *Bohemia*. He died in exile.

PEDREIRA, HÉCTOR
Member of the Communist Party and friend and neighbor of the Cabrera Infante family. A great movie buff, he worked as a waiter in large hotels and liked to discuss films with Guillermo Cabrera Infante.

PÉREZ, FAUSTINO (1920-1992)
Minister for the recuperation of embezzled property and president of the National Institute of Hydraulic Resources.

PÉREZ FARFANTE, ALFONSO (1921-2005)
Pediatrician.

PIÑEIRO, MANUEL "BARBAROJA" (1933-1998)
A founder of the July 26th Movement and one of the creators of the Castro regime's intelligence and security organisms. In 1965 he was vice minister of the interior under Ramiro Valdés. He was married to the Chilean Marxist Marta Harnecker. His death in an automobile accident evoked speculation as to whether it was murder or suicide.

PIÑEIRO, VIRGILIO (1912-1979)
Author, playwright, and member of the "Origenes" literary group. He later co-founded the literary journal Ciclón. He was known to be friends with writers like Jorge Luis Borges and Witold Gombrowicz, both of whom influenced his work. He was jailed in 1961. After his release, he won the literary award, the Casa de las Américas Prize, for his play Dos viejos pánicos.

< 377 >

PORRO, RICARDO (1925-2014)

Architect who undertook graduate studies at the Sorbonne and returned to Cuba after the triumph of the Revolution. Fidel Castro commissioned him to design the National Art Schools. He soured on the regime and in 1966 went into exile in France, where he died.

PRÍO SOCARRÁS, CARLOS (1903-1977)

The last democratically elected president of Cuba. He ruled from 1948 to 1952, when he was overthrown in a military coup led by Fulgencio Batista.

RAMÍREZ CORRÍA, CARLOS (1903-1977)

Father of Cuban neurosurgery.

REBELLÓN, JOSÉ

Captain and president of the Engineering Students Association, he founded the Cuban scholarship system known as "Aid Program for Training University Technicians."

REVUELTA, VICENTE (1929-2012)

Theater director and teacher who was a founder of Studio Theater and an old friend of Guillermo Cabrera Infante.

RÍOS, NIDIA

Actress and model, one of the photographer Korda's favorites.

RIVERO AROCHA, "EL POLLO"

Cuban commercial attaché in Brussels, forensic physician, married for a time to the singer Elena Burke, and a big fan of jazz.

< 378 >

ROA, RAÚL (1907-1982)
Intellectual, politician, and diplomat, he was minister of foreign relations and later ambassador to the United Nations. He wrote many literary and journalistic works.

RODRÍGUEZ, ARNOLD (1931-2011)
Vice minister of foreign relations, he was known for his participation in the 1958 kidnapping of Argentine racing car driver Juan Manuel Fangio by the July 26th Movement.

RODRÍGUEZ, CARLOS RAFAEL (1913-1997)
Member of the Communist Party since his early youth, economist, and intellectual, he and Guillermo Cabrera Infante knew each other since childhood. A close friend of Fidel Castro's, he occupied important posts in the hierarchy. He was married to Edith García Buchaca and died after contracting Parkinson's disease.

RODRÍGUEZ, FRUCTUOSO (1933-1957)
A leader of the Revolutionary Student Directorate, he took part in the 1957 assault on the Presidential Palace and was one of those murdered in the Humboldt Street massacre.

RODRÍGUEZ, MARIANO (1912-1990)
Painter known for his surrealist and Fauvist paintings of fighting cocks. After the triumph of the Revolution he served as cultural attaché at the Cuban Embassy in India. Upon his return he led the plastic arts section of the National Union of Writers and Artists of Cuba (UNEAC).

< 379 >

RODRÍGUEZ FEO, JOSÉ (1920-1993)

Patron of the arts and personal friend of José Lezama Lima, he founded *Orígenes* magazine and, later on, with Virgilio Piñera, the magazine *Ciclón*.

RODRÍGUEZ LOECHES, ENRIQUE (1924-1978)

Revolutionary who dedicated his life to the struggle against the dictator Batista. After the triumph of the Revolution he became Cuban ambassador in Washington and a cabinet minister, ending his career at the Institute of Social Sciences of the Academy of Sciences.

ROMAY, ERIC (1941-1980)

A celebrated television actor, he acted in the all-black adaptation of the classic Cuban novel *Cecilia Valdés*, as well as in several films of the new Cuban cinema.

SÁNCHEZ, CELIA (1920-1980)

An active participant in the Cuban Revolution, she fought in the mountains with Fidel Castro. In 1965 she was secretary to the president.

SÁNCHEZ, RENÉ

An actor, he went into exile in the United States.

SÁNCHEZ, UNIVERSO (1919-2012)

Commander of the July 26th Movement and comrade of Fidel Castro.

SÁNCHEZ-ARANGO, AURELIANO (1907-1976)

Lawyer, politician, and university professor, he was minister of education and of foreign relations.

< 380 >

SANTAMARÍA, HAYDÉE (1923-1980)
One of two women who participated in the assault on the Moncada Barracks (in which her brother died), she was married to Armando Hart. She ran Casa de las Américas publishing house and was very influential in politics. She committed suicide in 1980.

SANTOS, ELOY
Member of the Communist Party, close friend of the Cabrera Infante family.

SARUSKY, JAIME (1931-2013)
Writer and journalist, he collaborated at *Lunes de Revolución* and received the National Prize for Literature in 2004.

SIFONTES, BEBA
Companion of Martha Frayde.

SORIANO, JAIME
Movie critic and screenwriter. He met Guillermo Cabrera Infante at the Cinemateca and worked with him at *Carteles* and at *Lunes de Revolución*. He went into exile in Puerto Rico.

SUÁREZ, RAMÓN "RAMONCITO" (1930-2016)
Cineaste, friend of Guillermo Cabrera Infante from a young age, he died in exile in Paris.

SUÁREZ, SILVANO (1930-2013)
Playwright and television director, he was a friend of Guillermo Cabrera Infante from his years at the Cuban Film Institute (ICAIC) and became a

< 381 >

regular character in all his books. He was married for a time to Maricusa Cabrera and died in Havana.

TAMAYO, EVORITA
Second wife of Oscar Hurtado.

TEIXIDOR, JOAQUÍN
Art critic.

TITÓN (see Gutiérrez Alea, Tomás)

TRIANA, PEPE (1931)
Playwright who published in *Lunes de Revolución* and lives in exile in Paris.

UNAMUNO, MIGUEL DE (1864–1936)
Spanish essayist, novelist, poet, playwright, philosopher, professor, and later rector of the University of Salamanca.

URFÉ, ODILIO (1921–1988)
Pianist and musicologist.

VALDÉS, CECILIA
The title and main character from the 1839 novel by Cirilo Villaverde. The novel is based in Havana, Cuba and follows the mulatta daughter of a wealthy slave owner named Cándido de Gamboa. It's regarded as one of the most important Cuban novels of the 19th century for its illumination of fraught race relations in Cuba.

< 382 >

VALDÉS, RAMIRO (1932)
Military officer and politician. At the time of the book he was minister of the interior.

VÁZQUEZ CANDELA, EUCLIDES
Journalist who was assistant director of *Lunes de Revolución*, he appears in several of Guillermo Cabrera Infante's books.

VERGARA, TETÉ (1914-1981)
Actress.

VERGARA, VIOLETA
Actress, sister of Teté, she committed suicide in 1965.

VILLA, IGNACIO "BOLA DE NIEVE" (1911-1971)
Renowned musician, singer, and composer, whom Guillermo Cabrera Infante wrote about on numerous occasions.

< 383 >

TRANSLATOR'S AFTERWORD

Guillermo Cabrera Infante was no stranger to run-ins with Cuba's official-dom, even before the events narrated in *Map Drawn by a Spy*. A movie-lover who first came to prominence as a film critic, he did a stint in prison under the dictator Batista for his pointedly political reviews and was barred from publishing under his own name. After the 1959 Revolution, he provoked the ire of his higher-ups by fostering a critical discussion of arts and letters as head of the Film Institute and especially as editor of *Lunes de Revolución*, an influential weekly arts magazine and supplement to the national newspaper run by Carlos Franqui. Official leniency toward culture was short-lived: the supplement was shut down in 1962, the artists and intellectuals around Cabrera Infante sidelined, and he was sent as cultural attaché to Brussels, far from where he might inconvenience the authorities.

His return in 1965, related in this memoir, confirmed his worst fears about Havana's decline and prompted his evolution from frustrated supporter to covert opponent of the regime. His public rupture with the Cuban government, however, did not occur until three years later, when his friend, the poet Heberto Padilla, was publicly slandered and his poetry declared "ideologically contrary" to the Revolution. Cabrera Infante then abandoned pretense and became one of the Cuban government's most implacable foes. The show trial and imprisonment of Padilla in 1971 prompted writers around the world to follow Cabrera Infante's lead and denounce Fidel Castro.

Written shortly after the events it narrates, *Map Drawn by a Spy* remained unpublished for decades, although portions of the story were recounted in the author's essay collection *Mea Cuba*. He apparently considered the book unfinished, and may have wished to keep the personal details it discloses from his family. Cabrera Infante's widow Miriam Gómez, dreading such

< 384 >

revelations, did not read the manuscript until some years after his death in 2005, and only consented to publication of the Spanish original in 2013.

The author's notes indicate he toyed with calling the book *Return Visit to Ithaca*, alluding to Odysseus' fateful homecoming. The actual title refers to an illustrated eighteenth-century map of Havana Bay that fellow novelist Alejo Carpentier shows Cabrera Infante midway through the book, claiming it was drawn by an English spy. And indeed this memoir offers a telling portrait of the damped-down and disrupted city, sketched by a man who was treated like a spy and came to think of himself as a foreigner in his own country: an agent not of a distant power but of a previous epoch.

—Mark Fried

< 385 >